Meghan March

D0145469

the
BOOKWORM
box

Helping the community, one book at a time

DEAL
WITH THE
Devil

FORGE TRILOGY BOOK ONE

MEGHAN

NEW YORK TIMES BESTSELLING AUTHOR

MARCH

CONTENTS

DEAL WITH THE DEVIL

Book One of the Forge Trilogy

Meghan March

"You can put that man in a suit, but he'll never be tame."
One look at Jericho Forge, and I knew the rumors were
true. He was a predator, and he had set his sights on me.
I knew better than to bet more than I could afford to lose
that night. I knew better than to bet myself. But despera-
tion leads to bad decisions, and I thought there was no way
I could lose.
I was wrong.
Now I have no choice but to make a deal with the devil.

Deal with the Devil is the first book in the Forge Trilogy.

FORGE

When a billionaire walks into a room, you feel it. Especially if you're the billionaire.

I didn't intend to be here tonight, but heads turn as I stride across the casino floor and try to block out the scent of tropical-perfumed air Jean Phillippe pumps into his jewel, La Reina de Ibiza.

They know my name. Know my profile. They think they know everything about me, but they don't.

No one does.

They don't know I'd rather be on the deck of one of my ships, at the mercy of the open ocean, instead of surrounded by flashing lights and grating chimes indicating someone just won or lost a fortune.

They're here to gamble, and I'm here . . . I don't know why the fuck I'm here. Call it curiosity. Call it a sixth sense. It doesn't matter. All I know is that I don't like it when someone tries to hide something from me.

Like this high-stakes game tonight.

Regardless of whether I'm in residence on my island,

less than a mile away from Ibiza, Jean Phillippe sends me an invite to the private games. *Always*. He never misses an opportunity to bring more money into the casino's bank. So why, of all the games played at these tables, would my old acquaintance neglect to invite me to this particular one?

Because somebody doesn't want me here.

It won't be the first time I've shown up where I wasn't wanted. Luckily, I don't give a fuck what people want.

Jean Phillippe isn't stupid, and he knows he's risking more than my money at his casino if he's deliberately hiding something from me. My displeasure has made more than one man wish he were dead.

Ahead of me, the door to the private poker room closes an inch at a time. Once it's closed, no more players can join the game.

I pick up my pace and the crowd parts, making way for me. I walk without seeing any of them. They're merely a blur of dark suit jackets and snowy-white shirts, interspersed with splashes of color from the women and more daring men.

The slice of light spilling from the doorway narrows, and I clock the exact moment Jean Phillippe sees me. His grip tightens on the knob as his dark eyebrows shoot up toward his silvering hairline.

In a moment, he recovers his composure, pulling his shoulders back and stepping around the door. It continues inching closed behind him as he pastes a smile on his face like he's happy to see the biggest whale ever to step foot in this casino.

The smile's a lie, and we both know it.

"My friend! I didn't think you were in town tonight. I would've—"

"Bullshit. You don't want me here, and that tells me I need to be here. Don't even think about closing that door."

Jean Phillippe's movements still, but he can't control the emotions playing out across his features. His brown eyes widen as he drops the French accent he intensifies around new marks. "It's not like that, Forge. You know I wouldn't—"

"I'm playing tonight whether you want me here or not."

Jean Phillippe inhales sharply, and then exhales like a terminal patient accepting his fate. "This game isn't one you—"

"Move, or I'll move you myself."

His chin drops toward his chest. "It wasn't personal, *mon ami*," he says as he steps away from the opening.

I walk through the doorway and stop dead.

What the fuck is he doing here?

Bastien de Vere. The entitled trust-fund prick who got away with murder. Literally.

The hot burn of rage blazes from the pit of my gut until I shut it down. Stone cold. That's the only way I can keep myself from killing him with my bare hands.

Death by a thousand cuts. That's how I've made him suffer for fifteen years, and I'll do it until the day I finally end him. *That day is coming*, I promise myself. The de Veres' money and influence won't last forever. I'm draining it away one penny at a time.

When de Vere catches sight of me at the door, his

shoulders brace and his mouth flattens into a hard line. "Invitation-only game, Forge. And you weren't invited."

The blonde next to him stiffens as de Vere says my name. Even with her head down and no glimpse of her face, she's stunning. Honey-gold curls lay over her bare, tanned shoulders, leading a man right to her generous tits.

Fuck. Me.

She can't be one of de Vere's regulars, or I would have already stolen her from him. Unless . . . *no,* he couldn't have managed to hide a piece that fine. He'd be showing her off right and left. That means she has to be a new conquest. Maybe someone he's trying to impress at the table . . .

Which gives me one more reason to stay and take every penny of his trust fund he's willing to wager tonight.

"I don't need an invitation." I look to Jean Phillippe. "Do I?"

"No. No, sir. Of course not. You're always welcome at La Reina's tables."

"That's what I thought."

De Vere glares at me, and I look away from him to scan the rest of the players standing in the room, giving them each a nod. What I see tells me my gut instinct was 100 percent right.

Something big is going down here.

Sheikh Ahmed Al Jabal, the oil billionaire whose superyacht I've docked next to in Monte Carlo before, nods back at me. He's a decent enough player, but one with more money than skill, which makes him my favorite kind.

"Mr. Forge, I hope you brought the money of mine you took in Monaco."

"All that and more, sir."

"Very good."

I shift my attention to the next man—Alejandro Cruz, the American tech billionaire who fancies himself a poker player of the highest order, but mostly just bluffs because he knows more about coding than he does about cards.

Cruz sits straighter in his chair. "It's been a while, Forge. Thought you'd decided never to come back to land."

"The company is better out to sea."

Cruz guffaws. "I wouldn't doubt that. Good to see you, and it'll be even better to win some of your money."

"Jericho Forge. My old . . . what to call you? Not a friend," says Dmitri Belevich, a Russian whose ties to the Bratva keep the police from asking too many questions about his luxe playboy lifestyle on Ibiza.

"Always a pleasure, Belevich."

The net worth of these men would add up to more than the GDP of a few small countries combined, which means that my failure to get an invitation to this game is entirely by design. De Vere's design.

That fuck.

I'm happy to ruin his plans for the night.

"I trust there are no objections to me joining the game, gentlemen." It's a statement, not a question.

"I have no problem taking your money, Forge." This comes from Belevich.

Cruz and the sheikh both shake their heads, which

brings my attention back to de Vere and the woman. He moves in front of her as if trying to shield her from me.

And he should. Because when it comes to Bastien de Vere, I have no qualms about taking everything he cares about. But who the hell is she? If she were just arm candy, she wouldn't be allowed a seat at the table, and the stack of chips in front of her says she's here to play.

She could be a party favor he planned to use to distract the other men to give himself an advantage. He wouldn't be the first to employ such a basic tactic.

"I ob—" de Vere tries to speak, but I cut him off.

"No one gives a shit what you want, de Vere, especially me." I step around him to get a better look at the woman.

I stop beside Cruz, who stands behind the seat next to her. Finally, she looks up, and her vivid purple-blue eyes deliver a punch to my gut—along with a tidal wave of recognition.

India Baptiste. The former darling of the poker circuit, and the woman who is almost as famous for her *royal flush over full house* win as she is for telling Bastien de Vere to go fuck himself in front of a roomful of poker royalty.

When I heard the story, I was amused and intrigued, but not enough to care beyond the entertainment value of de Vere being humiliated. After seeing her in the flesh? Intrigued is only the beginning.

I nod at the chair in front of Cruz. "You don't mind sitting on the other side of the table, do you?"

The dark-haired man smirks. "You want to sit next to Queen Midas? Go right ahead. I'll probably play better if I don't."

Queen Midas. An apt nickname for a woman who turns her seemingly shitty poker hands to gold with almost legendary regularity.

A ruthless smile tugs at my lips, but I quash it in favor of studying her the way I would anything else I plan to acquire—like it's already mine.

Her gold dress wraps around curves that make a man want to revert to the days when pirates pillaged enemy ships and took what and who they wanted. Because I would definitely fucking take her. Lock her in my cabin. Eradicate every single thought of Bastien de Vere from her brain. She'll be another trophy I will take from him. Just like I've taken everything else that matters to him, one piece at a time.

"Unless you have an objection, Ms. Baptiste, I'm joining the game."

Her indigo eyes flash with heat at my dare, and the fire behind her sharp stare intensifies.

As a rule, women don't challenge me. Ever. My billion-dollar portfolio wipes away all pretense of playing hard to get. India Baptiste's refusal to look away while she considers how to respond will be her downfall.

Tonight just got a hell of a lot more interesting, and I know exactly how it's going to end. With the woman Bastien de Vere wants in my bed.

2

INDIA

*N*o. *No. No. This can't be happening. He can't be here.*

As I stare into Forge's endless dark gaze, I want to squeeze my eyes shut or at least look away, but I can't. Instead, I plaster a bored smile on my face as I take a measured breath that's supposed to be steadying, pretending to consider whether I want him in the game, let alone sitting beside me.

Instead of calming me, the cloying sweet-scented air of La Reina casino nauseates me. Or maybe that's because it's taking everything I have to keep my composure, and I'm already on the verge of losing my shit. I can't let anyone see how much effort it takes for me to keep myself together, especially Forge.

I'm the professional here. The *only* professional here.

With that reminder, I take another slow breath as I study the man who could ruin all my carefully orchestrated plans.

"I don't believe we've been introduced, Mr. . . . ." I

trail off, pretending I don't know his name. Total bull-shit, and a ploy to take him down a peg. It probably won't work, but at least it buys me a few moments of time.

Unless he knows I'm already bluffing. There can't be many people in Ibiza who don't know exactly who Jericho Forge is, which is exactly why I didn't want him here.

I've watched him play before. Actually, I'm pretty sure everyone on the poker circuit has, because although he's not a professional card player, he's a professional victor. I've seen him strip every chip from the stacks in front of men at the table with him like a vulture picking clean the bones of a carcass alongside the road.

Not tonight, though. That's *my job.*

"Jericho Forge," he says as he holds out a hand. Next to me, I feel Bastien stiffen with fury as I reach to take it. "It's a pleasure."

Bastien's animosity escalates to rage as Forge lifts my hand to his lips. But he doesn't kiss it. Instead, he turns my hand over to glance at my palm.

Shivers emanate from every shred of contact, to the point where my arm threatens to tremble in his hold. My lungs burn with the breath I'm holding, waiting for him to release me.

"I don't see any magic here. How do you manage to turn everything to gold?"

I tug my fingers out of his grip, desperate to escape his charged touch, and retract my arm. Discreetly, I exhale and roll my eyes.

"I see my reputation precedes me." I keep my tone even.

One of his dark eyebrows quirks up. "And I don't believe mine doesn't."

A cold knot tightens into my gut, but I don't let a single flicker of emotion cross my face.

He's already calling me on a bluff, and we haven't even started playing the game.

This is why I didn't want him here. People have claimed Forge has an uncanny ability for sensing the truth, an ability that borders on eerie. I didn't believe them until now.

Doesn't matter. I have to play. Have to win.

I promised myself I'd never gamble out of desperation again. Which means I lied to myself. *Again.* Never before has a poker game been more important. Never before have I had more on the line.

Ten million dollars in ten days.

That's the ultimatum I was given three days ago, and if I don't meet the terms . . . That knot in my stomach twists at the horrific consequences.

I will win. I have to. I don't have a choice.

Normally, I steer clear of Bastien in the same way I steer clear of every entitled British douchebag on this island, but I needed him to use his connections to assemble the players I personally handpicked. Men with deep pockets. Men who won't think twice about throwing down the cash I need. Men whose playing I've studied for hours, learning their tells and exactly how to beat them.

And then Jericho Forge shows up like a goddamned wild card, blowing up all my perfectly laid plans.

Because of Bastien.

"Sorry to disappoint you, Mr. Forge. Apparently, your reputation isn't as pervasive as you thought."

"No disappointment, Ms. Baptiste. If anything, it makes you even more intriguing."

Great. Just what I don't want to hear.

"I have no problem with you joining the game, sir, but I am ready to start. Take your seat if you're playing." As I sit, I nod at the chair Cruz vacated for him, in an attempt to kill the conversation.

To my right, Bastien's hand grazes my knee, and I brush him off. The last thing I need is for these two sworn enemies to be tugging at me like well-dressed junkyard dogs fighting over a bone.

No one in Ibiza could possibly be unaware of their bad blood, although the cause of it is only whispered about in hushed tones and the story constantly changes. It's become something of an urban legend on this island. Because I've done my best to avoid Bastien and everything related to him after the first time he made a fool of me, I didn't listen very closely.

From the way Jericho Forge stares at me as he decides how to reply, I wish I had.

I'm used to the looks I get from men, especially when I put on a dress like this—formfitting, shiny, and 100 percent designed to distract them from their cards and wagers. But that's not the kind of look I get from Forge. It's like he doesn't even see the gold dress. His ruthless stare strips me bare. Like he knows all my secrets and everything I have on the line tonight, which is impossible. *No one can know how desperate I am.*

Confidence is my most valuable asset, and I won't let

him take that from me. I won't let anyone take that from me.

"Indeed, let's get started. I'm more than ready."

The rumble of his voice ripples through me like an aftershock of an earthquake.

I can't let him affect me like this. I can't let him affect me at all.

But still, I can't help but think of the stories I've heard about how ruthless he is at the negotiating table, and even more so on the deck of one of his legion of cargo ships. *More pirate than CEO.* That's how people describe him, and he looks the part. His shiny black hair brushes his white collar, and a thick gold hoop pierces one of his ears.

I turn my attention away from Forge, but I still feel the intensity of his examination as he pulls out the chair and lowers his broad-shouldered form into it. Heat radiates through the fabric of his perfectly-tailored suit jacket, like he's more beast than man.

I swing my hair over my left shoulder as if it's going to create some kind of buffer. A girl can hope. Maybe looking away from a predator isn't the smartest thing I could do, but right now, I have no choice. I have to center myself and prepare for the game ahead.

I'm not here to play. I'm here to win.

"Million-dollar buy-in, Forge. But that's pocket change to you, right?" Bastien's drawl has a mocking edge to it as he reaches out to rest his arm along the back of my chair.

I keep my shoulders straight, trying not to make it obvious that I'm avoiding his touch, but Forge misses nothing.

"Mummy and Daddy give you a big enough allowance

to cover yours, de Vere?" Forge asks, his deep voice turning into a growl.

The other men at the table chuckle at the jab, no doubt sending Bastien's temper into dangerous territory.

"Excellent! We shall begin." Jean Phillippe, who I'm pretty sure has been holding his breath this whole time, claps and waves the dealer over to the table.

Before she can sit, Forge waves her off. "Fernando or Armand. Your choice, but the game doesn't happen without one of them dealing."

"Not your call, Forge," Bastien snaps.

I lean back in my chair, wishing I could move to any other seat at the table, because I feel like a stupid fish caught between the snapping jaws of two sharks.

Forge looks around the table. "Any objections, gentlemen?" His flinty gaze finally lands on me. "Ms. Baptiste?" The edge in his voice challenges someone to contradict him, but no one, not even the sheikh, dares.

Anka was my choice for dealer, because she's one of the few I can be assured won't get flustered by the men in the room and somehow screw up the cards.

Pick your battles, Indy. Just focus on taking his money.

Jean Phillippe motions for Anka to leave the room. "Get Armand. He's at table twelve."

Forge leans back into the chair beside me, his broad shoulders covering every inch of it. At first, I thought it was a show of dominance to have Cruz move, but now I think it's because he wanted a clear view of the door rather than having his back to it.

Habit? Afraid someone's going to slide a stiletto between his shoulder blades? Probably a viable threat, although I can't imagine anyone having the audacity to try.

Armand enters the room moments later with sealed decks of cards and holds them out for inspection. Everyone at the table nods, but Armand's attention is solely on the pirate of a man beside me.

Forge doesn't have to say a single thing to own the room. He's already taken control of it, and every man within these walls looks to him for direction.

My confident mask threatens to slip in the face of his commanding presence, but I force it back into place.

I give all of them a dazzling smile. A smile that has come before relieving plenty of other men of their fortunes.

Which is exactly what I'm going to do tonight. Including Jericho Forge's.

I have no other choice.

Except, I should have known this game wouldn't be like any other I've ever played.

3

FORGE

*I*ndia Baptiste can wrap that decadent body in gold, but she's not as good at hiding her desperation as she wants to be. Or maybe she can from every other man in the room, but not from me—and not from Bastien de Vere.

He senses it, and that's why he's finally gotten up the balls to go in for the kill. She doesn't realize it, though. She thinks she's playing him just like she's playing all the men at this table who can't stop staring at her tits.

De Vere's downfall? As always—*me.*

If he wants her, I'm taking her. That's the way we operate. That's the only reason he didn't want me here tonight. He knew I'd see through him and revel in ripping her straight from his clutches.

One mystery solved. One more way to make him suffer.

He may never fully know the intense pain of loss like he inflicted on me, but I won't stop until I've exhausted every possible avenue for making his life miserable.

And now he's introduced a new variable to the table. It's unfortunate for India Baptiste, but she should have known better than to keep company with a murderer.

I shut down my thoughts about de Vere as Jean Phillippe sets a tray of chips in front of me. It takes me only a few seconds to count them and nod at him.

Cruz claps his hands. "Let's do this."

"Blinds, please."

The sheikh and Cruz ante up as Armand shuffles and deals the cards. I watch his movements carefully, even though he's one of the two dealers I trust in this place. Then again, no one is completely trustworthy.

He slides each of us two cards across the green baize, and the atmosphere of the room charges as everyone surveys their hand. "Bets please."

Cruz glances at me, but I keep my head lowered. From the way his gaze darts around the table, he's already nervous. *Perfect*.

One by one, we all throw our chips in. The woman beside me plays smart, and everything I've heard about her skills tells me that she's not using even a quarter of them yet, despite her single-minded intensity.

Did de Vere organize the game for her? It would make sense. I don't believe for a moment that she didn't know who I am. Which makes me wonder if she was the one who didn't want me here.

As if on my command, India looks up, taking stock of the rest of the table, but her blue eyes don't make it all the way to me. She cuts back to her cards like I don't exist.

I watch her through the flop, the turn, and the river.

She's not easy to read, but then again, I wouldn't

expect a pro to have tells you can spot from the minute play begins.

We all show our cards, and I win the first hand. Only then does she meet my gaze.

"Congratulations, Mr. Forge." Her tone is cool and even, and you'd think she was the dealer and had no skin in the game.

What an excellent little actress. I file the information away as we venture into the next few rounds.

De Vere rakes a small pot on the second hand, and India takes the third and fourth, winning just enough to lead the other men into deeper play out of sheer competitive natures. She loses the fifth to de Vere and leans forward on her elbows, finally using that dress and her tits to distract.

Cruz and the sheikh are fucked. It's like they haven't seen a woman in a decade. The Russian isn't immune either. His pale blue eyes keep shifting to her when he should be paying attention to the other men.

Two hours pass like minutes, and she's flexing her wings, playing the men at the table like the well-skilled competitor she is.

She doesn't look at me anymore, purposely staying out of the hands I play. She also doesn't direct my way any of her flirty banter that she wields like a weapon. If she's purposely trying to ignore me, she's doing an excellent job.

It won't last long.

Her disinterest only piques my curiosity further. She should know better, but then again, she doesn't know me.

No one knows me. No one ever will.

That's how I like it.

"You're on quite the streak, aren't you, Ms. Baptiste?"

Her chin tilts in my direction as de Vere glares at me for daring to address her.

Did you really think she'd stay yours after you brought her here tonight, de Vere? I don't voice the question aloud, because I already know the answer.

He planned out exactly how he thought this night would go, but he didn't plan on me. You'd think he'd learn. But then again, it makes my mission easier when he continues to underestimate me due to my lack of blue-blooded pedigree.

"I'm enjoying the game, Mr. Forge. Just like everyone else at the table," India replies with an emotionless smile.

"I'm not sure everyone's enjoying it quite so much as you." I nod to the stack of chips growing in front of her, trying to unsettle her again. I've been looking for her tell since the first hand, but I've yet to spot it.

She leans back in her chair, a confident mask settling over her features. She's managed to blunt the desperation from earlier, and I can only assume it's because she's gaining ground.

She has to have a tell. Digging into my memories, I vaguely recall someone saying she almost won the World Series of Poker, but someone outbluffed her. That someone had to have figured her out.

The play turns even deeper. Piles of chips rise and fall around the green baize table, most of them finding a home in front of either me or her. Cruz salivates over India, even as she takes his chips from him, stack by stack. She has to be up a few million by now.

She leans back in her chair again, and this time, her lips purse as she watches the sheikh place his bet. As soon as he does, her mouth firms into a thin line.

"Two million," de Vere says, pushing his stacks of chips into the middle of the table, and once again, Indy's pursed lips flatten.

Belevich drags his gaze from her tits to his cards and she stills, schooling her expression.

"I'm out," he says with a shake of his head, and her pout relaxes.

It can't be that easy.

The sheikh and Cruz follow suit, tossing in their cards as I keep my posture rigid, not letting on what I've just discovered about our resident cardsharp.

The sheikh rises from his seat. "I've lost enough tonight. I'll leave you to finish your game." He nods to Jean Phillippe. "Thank you for your hospitality. I think it's time I return to tables that don't drain my resources so effectively."

India watches him leave, and a brief flash of panic skates across her expression. She needed his money. *But why?* It's a mystery I'll solve sooner rather than later.

De Vere isn't watching me as I eye my chips. He's not watching anyone but India. He wants her with almost as much desperation as she wants to win. It's going to make taking her from him all the sweeter.

"I'm calling your bluff, Bastien," she says as she pushes her stacks of chips into the center of the table.

Bastien's gaze narrows on his cards and his fingers flex.

Idiot.

India's right. He's bluffing.

And I know exactly how this game is going to end.

4

INDIA

I'm almost there. The chips are on the table in front of me, and with this last pot, I'll have a solid portion of what I need.

Only two men stand in my way, and Bastien is full of shit. Which leaves Forge, the only one I can't read.

He has the power to destroy everything, and I'm praying to anyone who will listen that he doesn't. It's a naive thought at best, and a stupid one at worst. But right now, all I have are hopes and prayers to help me bring this home.

I purposely slow my breathing, trying to keep myself focused and calm. *I'm so close.*

"Action is to you, Mr. Forge," Armand says, and I keep those prayers rolling.

I need this money more than any of them. It's the only way I can save her. Please, please don't let me fail.

I should have known better than to think any divine power would listen.

Forge looks at the chips in front of me, and I swear I

see the glimmer of victory reflected in his gaze before he goes in for the kill, pushing every stack of chips in front of him to the center of the table.

"Raise."

No. No. No.

My heart tumbles in my chest as my stomach drops to the floor.

"Ms. Baptiste, back to you."

I flatten my cards out on the table and look to the corner where Jean Phillippe sits.

"Jean Phillippe, a word?"

He rises and comes toward me. "Yes, Ms. Baptiste?"

"I seem to need a line of credit this evening," I say, my voice low.

"We're only playing what's on the table tonight, Indy," Bastien says, leaning back in his chair and crossing his arms over his chest. "You made the rule."

Goddamn you, Bastien, I curse silently. *You're going to cost me everything, all because I refuse to sleep with you.*

My chin dips. I do another mental tally of my chips, but it's pointless. I don't have enough, and the side pot won't even come close to what I need to win.

"Then I guess that means . . ." My heart clogs my throat, and I can barely get out the words I need to speak. The words of defeat.

"You're not done yet," Forge says.

After an entire night of purposely avoiding the man, I turn to face him. "What do you mean?"

"We're not playing by casino rules . . . only our own, correct?"

I have no idea what the hell Forge is getting at, but I can't imagine it's going to help me.

"Correct," I reply, caution underlying my tone.

His gaze drops to the space in front of me. "Then you can play whatever's on the table."

I look down to see the condensation dripping from my untouched champagne flute . . . and the keycard beside it. The keycard for the suite Jean Phillippe comped me for tonight.

Oh, fuck no. Just *no.*

Silently, I meet Forge's dark gaze without blinking. He doesn't even bother to try to hide the hunger in it. There's no question what he wants.

Me.

"You can't be serious," I say, but we both know it's a waste of breath. Forge has probably never joked in his entire life. *And now he wants to put a monetary value on my room key and have me toss it in the pot?*

"You fucking bastard," Bastien says with hatred practically incinerating his words.

Forge's attention cuts to Bastien, and the triumph in his gaze tells me exactly what his goal has been all night. Destroy Bastien through any means necessary, including taking away the one thing he wants more in this room than money—me.

"I'm not a whore." I force out the words from between clenched teeth.

Forge's gaze shifts to me. "Whores don't get millions for a night with me."

Chills shoot down my spine, and they have nothing to do with the air-conditioning being on full blast. No, they have everything to do with my all-too-vivid imagination conjuring images of a night with the untamable Jericho Forge. Him slipping this dress off my body. Gripping my hair. Taking my lips. Sliding between my legs. Moving over me as I dig my nails into his shoulders.

My nipples peak, and I slam my eyes shut. It doesn't help. The scene plays like a movie in my head.

I knew when he walked in the room that he was dangerous on every level, and I wasn't wrong. *Everything* about Jericho Forge screams to me to run in the other direction.

I shouldn't be affected by him. But there's no arguing the truth.

I open my eyes and stare the man down before making the only real choice I have left. I lift my hand from the edge of the table, and like I'm moving through quicksand, my fingers hover over the keycard.

There's no going back if I do this.

I have to win.

I don't have to look down at my cards to see the full house I'm holding. I haven't been bluffing.

I will win.

FORGE

*A*s soon as her pink-tipped finger touches the keycard, a surge of something primal charges through my veins.

Victory. Need. Possession.

I'm an unapologetically acquisitive man. If India Baptiste had stayed off my radar, I never would have known I wanted her. But she didn't, and now she's going to be mine.

I can already feel her smooth skin under my fingertips. Taste the salt from the sea air as my tongue traces the thundering pulse at her neck. Hear her voice break as she begs me for more . . .

With every bit of self-control I have, I push those thoughts from my mind.

I watch for the tell as she pushes the card into the center of the table.

"Fine. I call."

Nothing.

She's not bluffing.

The three of us turn over our cards.

De Vere chokes as he leans forward, his jaw practically hitting the space in front of him.

"No fucking way," Cruz says softly.

The Russian chuckles.

But I don't give a single fuck about any of them. I'm waiting for her response. That's the only thing that matters right now.

A shocked exhalation escapes India's lips. "No. No. That can't be possible."

I rise from the table where my straight flush crushes India's full house.

I won.

She's mine.

"Jean Phillippe, collect my chips. I have more important things to worry about for the rest of the evening."

I retrieve the keycard from the center of the table and step toward the door, then hold out my arm.

"Ms. Baptiste. After you."

6

INDIA

I lost.

      I lost.

I lost.

The realization hammers through me as I stare at Jericho Forge's jacket sleeve and tanned hand. My mouth goes as dry as the Sahara, and my knees shake as I rise from my seat.

I bet myself and I lost.

I've done a million reckless things in my life. BASE jumping in Italy. Skydiving in Dubai. Sneaking into a royal wedding, just to prove that I could.

But never something so reckless as this.

Above all, I know my self-worth. And now I've whored myself out to a man who only pushed me to bet myself because he knows that Bastien wants me.

I shake my head. *As soon as Forge walked into the room, I went from a player to a pawn at the poker table.* All over bad blood that has nothing to do with me.

I want to tell them both to fuck off and run out the door. *But I can't.*

I lost, and I never renege on a bet. Not paying my losses to Jericho Forge would mean kissing my entire career good-bye. No one would ever let me sit a game again.

One night. It's only one night, I remind myself. *Surely, I can survive it.*

But my reputation may not. If this gets out . . .

Who would ever take playing poker seriously with the girl who bet herself and lost?

I'm damned either way.

I look at Bastien, the person I desperately want to blame for all of this, but I can't. I asked for his help. That was my choice. I brought this on myself.

I meet the gazes of every man in the room but Forge. "Gentlemen, I trust that none of you will speak a word about what happened in this room tonight."

Cruz nods solemnly.

"Of course. You insult me to think otherwise," Belevich says.

Bastien's scowl darkens before his expression turns mocking. "You'd like to think that, wouldn't you?"

I open my mouth, but before I can speak, heat hits my back in the form of a body.

"You won't say a fucking word." Forge's commanding tone raises goose bumps along my bare shoulders and arms.

"Is that right?" Bastien asks, and I want to slap him for trying to taunt Forge.

"Try me, de Vere. I dare you."

New chills ripple down my limbs at the threat Forge delivers so easily—and yet there's no question of its gravity. I wouldn't put anything past someone rumored to be as ruthless as Forge.

And now I have to spend the night with him.

Bastien's lips curl up into a sardonic grin. "Enjoy your toy for the night, Forge. Try not to break her. I'll be ready to remind her what a real man is like as soon as you're done."

That fucking asshole. He sits with his ankle crossed over a knee, talking shit while someone's life hangs in the balance. Not that he knows what hangs in the balance. Because I would never trust him enough.

I should have known better than to ask Bastien for help.

I shouldn't have been so cocky at the table.

I should have called off the game as soon as Forge showed up and upset my carefully constructed plan.

But I didn't. Now I have to live with the consequences.

Ten million in seven days or else . . .

Forge's massive hand curves around my hip and splays across my belly, cutting off any semblance I have of rational thought. With a single move, he pulls me back against his chest, and it feels like every inch of his body has been carved from granite.

"There won't be anything left for you when I'm done, de Vere."

My brain is a scattered mess as Forge guides me out of the room. Shock. Disbelief. Overwhelming despair. They all rip through me as his hand slides from my belly to my hip as he walks me toward the elevator.

The elevator.

That will take us up to my room.

The room that opens with the key that he won.

I freeze a dozen feet away from the double doors, and he immediately stops beside me.

For the first time since we left the card room, Forge looks down, those stormy eyes scanning my face as if he's trying to see inside my head.

From all the rumors floating around about this man, one might almost be convinced that he can read minds.

My mind goes blank as my body absorbs his presence. His intoxicating scent. It's too much.

"Second thoughts?" Forge asks, the bass-toned pitch of his voice cutting through the din of the crowded casino.

Second thoughts? That comment disproves the mind-reading rumor. I passed second thoughts before we stepped out of the card room.

I knew what I was doing. I was so damn sure I would win tonight. I considered all the angles.

Except him.

I fucked up. Big time. And it might cost my sister her life.

"I don't think *second thoughts* quite describes what I'm thinking," I tell him, keeping my tone calm, even as my brain spirals downward to the potential consequences of my actions.

"Stop thinking then." His order is simple, but effective, and he takes another step to direct me toward the elevator.

Stop thinking?

No. I can't. I've lived the last fourteen years with only

my wits, and not thinking is the last thing I need to do. But I can stop *overthinking.*

Pause. Rewind.

He won my room key. That's it.

Not me. Not my body. Not my mind.

Just my fucking room key.

I go stiff and he waits, his gaze narrowing on my face. Forge says nothing, presumably waiting for me to say something. Well, he won't have to wait long because I've no shortage of things to say to him right now, starting with . . .

"You overplayed your hand. You didn't win *me,* Forge. You won a *hotel-room key.*" I nod toward the jacket pocket where he slipped it. "Enjoy the room with my compliments. I have other things to do this evening."

With my chin high and my shoulders straight, I step away from him, congratulating myself on outplaying the player and immediately thinking about how quickly I can put together another game.

I make it exactly one step before his hand wraps around my wrist.

"I don't think so, *Indy.*"

His use of my nickname pisses me off. "Only my friends call me that. You are not a friend."

Something flits across his harsh features. The dark stubble of his five o'clock shadow adds to the piratical look with his severe jawline and rough-hewn cheekbones. I don't know the man well enough to know what it is, and I don't want to know.

"But de Vere is?"

"That's what all this is about, isn't it? The pissing match between you two?"

His expression goes blank and, beneath the stubble, his jaw shifts.

"You needed to win tonight. I don't need to know why to see how desperate you were in there. I'm guessing you need another game now. You're probably already trying to figure out how to put one together and where you're going to come up with your stake. But no one, and I mean *no one*, is going to let you sit a game when I let it be known that you didn't honor your debt to me."

I already know he's right, but it doesn't stop me from swallowing the saliva pooling in my mouth, and wishing the heat of his touch and his stare weren't causing equally heated reactions in other areas of my body.

I cannot be turned on by this high-handed, dictatorial behavior. I can't.

Another lie to myself.

"What exactly do you want from me, Mr. Forge?" For the first time all night, I get a reaction out of him that's something beyond his stony-faced stare.

One corner of his mouth curls up, and it's like the hand-painted ceilings of the casino cracked open and light shined down from the heavens. Well, maybe not exactly, but close.

A half smile from Jericho Forge does more than unleash heat. My nipples peak against the bodice of my dress, and without a bra, there's nothing I can do to hide my body's traitorous reaction to him.

"You're not ready for an answer to that question, Ms. Baptiste."

Something about the timbre of his voice and the absolute certainty in every word releases another wave of concerning reactions. It's like he's already playing my body, almost better than he played me at the table, and he hasn't so much as moved his hand.

I have to make a stand. Say something rational. Demand answers. Even if it's only to prove I can.

"Why? Why me? Why tonight?"

Forge's hooded gaze drops to my cleavage, and I feel more exposed than ever in this dress.

"Because de Vere wants you, and I enjoy taking things away from him."

My bottom lip drops. "That's it? It's really, truly only about *Bastien*?"

I don't know why, but that pisses me off even more. Maybe because some part of me—a stupid part—wanted him to want me for *me*. Not because of some ridiculous grudge.

"You should be more careful about the company you keep."

A loud burst of harsh laughter from beyond our bubble tears Forge's attention off my face.

Bastien.

He's twenty yards away and pretending to laugh with Jean Phillippe while he glares daggers at Forge.

"We'll finish this discussion in your room. I'm not having it here."

My gaze snaps back to Forge's rock-hard features. "And if I say no?"

"I'll throw you over my shoulder and try every room in this fucking hotel until the keycard opens one."

33

I can imagine him throwing me over his shoulder like the pirate I thought he resembled earlier. Especially because I know not a single soul in this entire building will be able to protect me from him.

An inappropriate curl of lust has me shifting in my Prada pumps. *Do I really want to be protected from him? Would I run into Bastien or Jean Phillippe's arms to escape him?*

No.

My gut says I can't trust either of them any more than I can trust Forge. And wasting time acting like a terrified virgin isn't going to help me win the money I need any faster. I need tonight over and done with. I have to come up with a new plan.

I level a stare on Forge. "I'll go with you, but I won't hesitate to call every law enforcement agency and media outlet in the entire damn world if you touch me without my consent ever again."

This time, both corners of his mouth turn up in a smirk.

"That's not a concession you needed to ask for, but I'll give it to you anyway. Let's go."

7
FORGE

I have to give her credit. She's a bold woman, hanging on to the tatters of her pride with a scrappy strength that helps me form an opinion of her character.

She's also reckless as hell, which for some reason piques my interest in her even more. A woman willing to take these kinds of risks should have few inhibitions when it comes to everything I want from her.

From the blue fire in her gaze to the incensed set of her lips, I can tell she'd rather be anywhere but near me, but her body tells a different story.

She shifts in her fuck-me heels, and her nipples are hard enough to cut glass. I know when a woman is interested, even despite herself, and India Baptiste is fighting a losing battle.

Drop your guard, and I can show you a whole new world.

The stubborn set of her shoulders says she won't, at least not without encouragement. Or manipulation.

Women aren't as complicated as the world makes them out to be. Watch them. Listen to them. Learn them. Use your knowledge to get what you want. Every human is capable of being manipulated, and India Baptiste will be no different.

Inside the elevator, the floral aroma isn't as strong, and I finally get a hint of the spicy perfume she wears. Audacious, just like her. The urge to rinse her clean to get to the true scent of India's skin takes me by surprise.

She's not special. She's just a pawn in a game to fuck with de Vere. Don't forget it.

I remind myself of what matters, but somehow it doesn't eradicate the desire to strip her bare and find out what really drew de Vere to this woman. I see the surface appeal. Thick blond hair, indigo eyes, a body that has enough curves to stop traffic. But that's not the whole picture, because there are dozens, if not hundreds, of women who fit that description, passing through Ibiza.

She humiliated de Vere years ago when she shot him down publicly, but for some reason, he hasn't given up wanting her, and he hid it well enough to escape my notice. Which means one of two things—either he can't resist the challenge of her, like any other man. Or she's the kind of woman who makes a man think long and hard about what he wouldn't do to possess her.

Either way, it doesn't make a damn bit of difference. Clearly, de Vere still wants her, and that's enough reason for me to take her and break her so that he'll never have her.

Perverse? Fuck yes.

Do I give a damn? Hell no.

"Floor?" I ask, swiping the key across the card reader that will allow the elevator to move.

She glares at me, and I resist the urge to smile at her contrary nature. It shouldn't turn me on, but nothing about this woman is following my normal rules.

"Eight."

I'm content to stay silent in the elevator after I press the appropriate button, but India speaks as soon as the car moves.

"How did you know about the game tonight? Who told you?"

"Does it matter?" I ask, avoiding the question. It's a lifelong tactic that continues to work no matter how often I've employed it. Most people are happier to answer questions than ask them, and most are too nonconfrontational to call me out on it.

"I wouldn't ask if it didn't matter." India's short reply and straight-ahead stare clue me in to the fact that she's not going to be as easy to outmaneuver one-on-one as she was at the poker table.

Luckily, I get off on the challenge.

"People tell me things, especially when it's a high-stakes game happening in my own backyard."

"I bet they do. You probably have paid informants across the damn globe. Are they friends with the women you keep in every port?"

My lips quirk into a partial smile, which has to be a record for tonight. I'm so rarely amused that I'm thrown off by the oddity of the feeling, but I shut it down.

"So you were lying when you said you hadn't heard of me. Good to confirm my assumption."

She flicks a glance my way. "Could you be more arrogant?"

"Probably."

"I assume that goes with being *infamous*."

She's right, but she doesn't understand the reality of the situation. Infamy brings with it another set of problems that average humans can't possibly comprehend. Then again, my gut says there's nothing average about India Baptiste. I wouldn't be standing in this elevator with her if she were.

I don't need ordinary in my life.

I only want the extraordinary, and I work my ass off to attain it.

With a quick move of my hand, I hit the emergency button of the elevator and crowd her against the mirrored wall of the car. India's eyes widen with shock, and her pulse throbs against the side of her throat.

"You can assume whatever you want about me, Ms. Baptiste. But let me tell you what I expect from you."

I step forward, ignoring the buzz of the elevator alarm, planting my foot between the heels of her fuck-me shoes. I'm playing on a hunch here, one that I need to confirm before things take another leap forward into territory where they can't be undone.

Her throat works as she swallows, but she doesn't attempt to evade. No, her pupils dilate, and that's either due to fear or arousal.

From the state of her nipples before we entered the elevator, I'm going with the latter.

She blinks, hauling in a deep breath that causes her tits

to lift and brush against my suit jacket. *Fuck, I want to feel them on my skin.* What the hell is it about this woman?

My dick, which is always under ironclad control, fills with blood.

"I don't care what you expect, Mr. Forge." Her voice shakes, even as she attempts to imbue it with confidence. She can try to deny it until the sun rises, but she wants me.

"You will, Ms. Baptiste. I have absolutely no doubt about that."

8

INDIA

I don't know what his game is, but Jericho Forge's proximity is more potent than any drug I've ever taken. And that's saying something, given my prior lives.

When I pegged him as being dangerous, I was right. But I didn't realize the extent of the threat. It's not just the fact that he's strong enough to literally break me in half in this elevator. No, it's because I want to get even closer to him.

His scent—sandalwood mixed with salt and something fresh and clean—is addictive, dragging me even closer to him to get another whiff. I've avoided men for almost a decade because they can't be trusted. Every experience I've had has shown me that they bring nothing but trouble into your life. But after only minutes alone with Jericho Forge, I know that I've never come up against a man like him. He makes those hard-on popping party boys seem exactly like what they were—*boys*. Not men.

I swallow, trying to think of something to say or do to

break this spell settling over us, but my head is buzzing like I've downed two bottles of my favorite red.

He dips his head and inhales—like he's breathing me in the same way—and instead of it being creepy and weird, it's sexy as hell.

Stop it, Indy. This is bad. Back away.

When he steps back and punches the button to silence the alarm and allow the elevator to keep rising, I tell myself we had some kind of skirmish I didn't know was happening. Regardless, I'm going to say I won.

Another lie.

Every inch of my skin is humming with anticipation, begging silently for the brush of his skin on mine.

I shouldn't want him to touch me. He's a stranger. A threat. I've clearly identified him as a danger, which means I should scuttle to the other side of the elevator and put as much distance between us as possible, but that would put me at even more of a disadvantage.

I face my problems head-on. I don't run from them. *But I've never faced anyone like him before.*

He's already proven that he's a wild card when it comes to my life, an uncontrollable variable, and now slick heat coats my thighs because this dress wasn't exactly panty-friendly.

I take what I hope is an imperceptible step away from him, not that it helps shield me from the effect of our close proximity.

When the door opens, and the ornate white plaster molding and gold-leaf accents of the casino's hotel appear in front of us, I'm finally knocked loose from his spell.

Get your shit together, girl. And don't get trapped in

any other small spaces with him. Clearly, you can't handle it.

Even I'm not going to try to lie to myself about that. I can't handle Jericho Forge. I know that like I know my own name.

Which means I need to think, and quickly.

He holds out an arm to block the doors from closing again, and waits like a gentleman for me to step out of the car ahead of him. But we both know that there's nothing gentle under that suit. I felt the hard planes of his body against my curves.

He felt absolutely fucking delicious.

No. Stop. Don't think like that.

But it's hard to stop thinking about it when I've been on a self-imposed hiatus from men for what seems like forever. If I'd been getting laid regularly, I wouldn't be reacting like this. *Right? Right.*

I step into the hallway, and I don't wait for his hand to hit the small of my back. Instead, I turn in the direction of the room I used to get ready for this ill-fated night and stride toward the door. At least the room is bigger than the mirrored elevator car, and I'll be able to put some distance between us.

Forge catches up to me in seconds with his long-legged stride. I almost expect him to make some remark about me being in a hurry, but he stays absolutely silent as he falls into step beside me.

Any other man of my acquaintance would fill the void with meaningless words, throwaway compliments, or teasing quips. Not Forge.

Then again, why would I expect him to be like anyone else?

He's clearly in a class all his own.

We reach the door at the end of the hall much too quickly, thanks to the pace I set. My heart hammers like I sprinted in my pumps instead of walking as calmly as possible. The thought immediately reminds me of the last time I did have to sprint in heels . . . because of Summer.

Summer.

How could I have forgotten about my sister for even the few minutes it took to get up here? I blame Forge for that too.

I straighten my shoulders and shore up my posture with every bit of courage I have remaining. I will survive this encounter with my wits intact because I have no choice. Tomorrow, I have to start putting together another game. That $10 million I need isn't going to appear overnight in my bank account, and the men who are holding my sister hostage aren't going to take Monopoly money for her ransom.

And if she's lucky, after I pay her ransom, I *might not* kill her myself for getting us both into this horrific situation. Why did she—

I cut off the question I've asked myself dozens of times because it doesn't matter. Little sisters are put on this planet to complicate the lives of their older siblings. Or maybe that's only in my case because I've probably enabled her behavior to the point of being unhealthy, trying to make up for her shitty childhood. Clearly, I've done neither of us any favors.

I will save you, Summer. I promise.

Forge's hand flashes out with the keycard, and the indicator light on the brass plate lights up green.

Rather than shy away from what's coming next, I let my newfound determination drive my actions. My fingers beat his to the handle and I push it open, slipping between his body and the entrance to the room. The door swings on silent hinges, and I smirk this time, because in no way, shape, or form did I have any plans for a seduction scene to be happening in this room. In fact, I would have put money on that *not* happening.

If Forge was expecting a scene set for a romantic interlude, he'd be dead wrong.

My makeup is strewn all over the vanity next to my straightener and curling iron. My hair dryer is tossed on the massive bed, where I left it so I wouldn't forget it like I did at the last place I stayed. The hotel robe is spread over the chair with my jean shorts and the tank I wore here.

The door clicks shut behind me, and I tear my gaze off the state of the room and swing around to face him.

Like I just did, Forge takes in every detail of the room, and I don't mean the expensive wall-coverings and rococo furnishings. When his attention returns to me, his dark eyebrows edge toward his hairline.

I cock a hip, sliding into my confident persona once more.

"What? Did you think this"—I wave a hand up and down my body and face—"happened by accident? I didn't exactly wake up this way."

Kill the fantasy. Show him the reality. That's my game. No man wants to truly see behind the curtain.

Instead of being put off by my confession, Forge lifts

his lips into that mocking smirk again. "You think that changes anything?"

And there it is. Cards on the table, so to speak.

"It should. No man wants a woman who's obviously this high-maintenance, right?"

For the first time, the smile extends to his eyes as some kind of new light shines in them. He surveys me from head to toe with a long, lingering stare that sends a thrilling charge across every inch of my skin.

My heart beats faster. My lungs fight for more air. My lips press tighter together.

"I don't think you have the first clue what a man like *me* wants, Ms. Baptiste."

I prop my hand on my hip, trying to shut out the feeling of my body going haywire.

"That's where you're wrong, Mr. Forge. I'm sure you'd like nothing more than for me to strip off this dress, climb on that bed, and spread my legs for you so you can mount me like the conquering villain you obviously think you are."

A dark chuckle rumbles from his lungs as he shakes his head slowly. "Not a single fucking clue."

He takes a step toward me, and my instinctive reaction is to step back. My generous ass hits the vanity, and I curse myself for showing such obvious fear.

"Liar," I say, trying to cover up my mistake with bravado. It won't be the first time I've brazened out a situation, and it won't be the last.

"You think a man like me wants anything that comes easy? I like the hunt. The chase. The challenge. That's what drives a man like me."

"Then you picked the wrong girl, Forge," I lie as I formulate a new plan to escape this room with my wits intact. "I'm as easy as they come. No chase. No challenge."

I reach under my right arm and pull down the hidden zipper of the dress. My heart rate kicks up another million beats per second as the bodice falls away from my unrestrained breasts, and I wiggle enough to shove the dress to my feet. I don't care that the action makes me feel like a slut. I'm all about bluffing to get myself out of this situation.

"I'm ripe for the taking. No effort required."

His stormy gray eyes never leave my face, not even a single dip to look down at everything I've uncovered. The air around us turns electric. My nipples harden further, and I tell myself it's from the air-conditioning in the room and not because I'm dying for him to give them attention.

But Jericho Forge does nothing of the kind. He steps around me.

What the hell?

I whip around, one arm covering my breasts and my right hand automatically going to cover my other lady parts.

Forge grabs the robe off the chair and tosses it at me. "Cover yourself up. You're not a whore. Don't pretend you know how to play one, or I won't think twice about taking what you offer next time."

FORGE

J have to give her credit; she's trying to manage me with every bit of skill and cunning she has.

The problem with that? India Baptiste doesn't realize her own appeal when she tries such a ballsy stunt. The confidence it took to do something like that just makes her more fascinating, in a way I didn't expect.

I come to a snap decision of my own that takes even me by surprise. Before, all I cared about was taking her from Bastien and breaking her, but now . . . things are more complicated.

First, she won't go to Bastien willingly. That's clear from the words exchanged in the card room. Second, I doubt it's possible to break her easily. Every instinct of mine says she's too damn resilient for that. All she wants to do is survive me and move on with her life, preferably never seeing me again. Which is too bad, because I want the fire and sass and intellect she wields like blades. *I want her*—and that changes everything.

India clutches the robe to her chest and stares at me

like I've lost my goddamned mind, and maybe I have. She holds up the terrycloth like a shield, which is ironic considering she just shamelessly bared herself. But the red flags of color rising on her cheeks tell me that move cost her.

I catalog the knowledge, filling in the gaps of the picture of her that's already formed in my mind.

She's not just desperate, bold, and impulsive. She's wary and on edge, and I'd bet a cool million that it's been a long time since she last let her guard down around a man.

That's a challenge I can handle, because her body doesn't lie.

If she truly didn't want me or react to me, I would have let her go . . . after sufficient time to torture de Vere.

But not now. She blew it with her stunt. I can't turn away from the hunger in her gaze that she's too inexperienced to hide, regardless of the masterful poker face she had at the table.

Of the hundred things I plan to teach her and show her, that's one I'll never school her on.

"What the hell is your game, Forge? Are you into some weird—"

I cut her off as I step toward her. I drop my gaze to her chest, covered by the robe securely belted around her waist, and once again meet her gaze.

"If I want you to strip, I'll tell you. You don't make the rules here, Ms. Baptiste."

I bend over to pick up the crumpled gold fabric of her dress and bring it to my nose, breathing deep. "How long has it been since you had a good, hard fuck to keep you in line and out of trouble?"

Her blue eyes widen again, those pupils telling me everything I need to know in the dim light of the room. It's been a long fucking time. It shouldn't make my dick jerk, but it does.

"Wh-what?"

"Listen very carefully to me, Ms. Baptiste. If you pull another stunt like that, I'll spank your tight little pussy until you scream. I don't care where we are. You and I are just getting started."

INDIA

I bite down hard on my lip to keep my mouth from dropping open.

He did not just say that.

But he did.

Jericho Forge isn't going to play by the rules as I know them. Thinking he would was just one more mistake in the long line of them I've made tonight. Now he's staring at me like he has the right to do what he just said.

Heat pulses between my thighs, and I hate that my body is on board with his plan—a fact I will lie about until the world comes to its final end.

Forge drops into the one empty chair and clutches my dress in his lap like it's his possession. His heavy stare rakes over me, and he jerks his chin toward the bed, reinforcing that he thinks I'm his possession now too.

"Sit. We have things to discuss, and I'm not a patient man."

"I don't take orders from you or anyone else," I tell him,

trying to retain some kind of authority in this situation. I won't offer myself up to him on a silver platter again. Not when my brilliant reverse-psychology ploy backfired completely.

"I don't give a fuck about anyone else. You take orders from no one but me."

That shouldn't turn me on. It really, really shouldn't.

"Sit, India." His final order helps me regain my grip on my anger.

"I'm not a dog, Forge. Don't treat me like one."

He leans back in the chair. "But you play the bitch, don't you?"

My temper flares, and there's no question that I'd shoot him right now if I were holding a gun. "I'm not playing the bitch. This is me. If you think you've got some sweet, innocent idiot who's going to bow to your orders, you've misjudged me completely. I promise I'm not nearly as interesting as you've no doubt convinced yourself I am. Plus, I'm not even a good lay."

Again with his freaking smirk. "That's easily fixable. You might even thank me when we're done."

Fucking smug bastard.

"Hell will freeze over first." I kick off my heels and march to the bed and sit, my arms crossed over my chest. "And just so we're clear, don't even think about touching me. In fact, if you put your dick anywhere near my mouth, I'll bite it off. Swear to Christ."

For some reason, my brash declaration makes him laugh, and his deep chuckle conjures visions of a dark prince designing new ways to torture his victim.

But I'm not a victim.

"You won't get the privilege of my dick anywhere near your mouth until you earn it."

"Go fuck yourself, Forge."

His sardonic grin evaporates like it never existed. "Respect. That's the other thing you've clearly never learned. I'll add that to your list of lessons, along with being a good fuck."

"Over my dead body." Anger scorches through me like someone released a torrent of napalm. There is nothing this man could do or say that could make me want him now.

Even if I'm still wet thinking about him.

He leans back in the chair and crosses one ankle over the other. Every movement seems lazy and inconsequential, but there's no way anything he does is anything less than supremely calculated.

"Your body is exactly why we're here. Not only are you desperate enough to gamble yourself, I'm guessing that desperation just tripled after you lost to me. You need a lot of fucking money, and you need it very, very badly. Why?"

I shove my hair over my shoulder and try to affect the same disinterest that he radiates. "You think you deserve some kind of reward for figuring out that I need money? Sorry, I'm fresh out."

"Your pussy coming on my face will be the best reward," he replies, his nonchalant tone belying the erotic picture his words paint.

Now I can't stop picturing myself riding that scruff around his mouth until my body ignites. *Stop it, Indy. You need to focus on getting the hell out of here and never seeing this man again.*

Dropping all attempts at pretense, I ask him a question point-blank. "If you're not looking for a quick fuck, then tell me what you want from me so we can both get the hell out of here."

The lazy grin that stretches over his face sends shivers rippling down my spine.

"Everything."

Forge stares at me with those dark eyes, practically drowning me with his all-consuming attention. I'm trying to figure out exactly what he's going to say next when the sound of someone knocking on the door has both of us turning our heads toward the noise.

Oh my God. Bastien. He's coming to the rescue like he's not a complete fucking asshole.

Forge rises from the chair and strides across the room to yank the door open, pissed that we've been interrupted.

I crane my neck, expecting to see Bastien's golden hair, but it's not. It's a massive man with black dreads who looks like he stepped out of a movie where he played the part of the villain's henchman.

He says something in a language I don't understand, and Forge's posture stiffens before he swings around to face me. Every trace of the emotions he's shown since he entered this room is completely absent.

"Get out." His expression is hard and blank. It's like he's been swapped for the evil-twin version of himself.

My mouth drops open. "What?"

"We're done. I don't have time for this. Get the fuck out."

Done? The word echoes in my brain, and as soon as I

process them, part of me wants to argue, but that's the stupid part.

I bolt to my feet, reaching for my dress and my clutch. "But my stuff—"

Forge waves his arm at the open doorway as the giant steps inside.

"Go. Now."

*W*alking down the hall in my bare feet, wearing only a hotel robe and my dress and clutch in my arms, is sobering.

This is how far I've fallen.

Curls of anger lick up from my belly with each step I take toward the elevator like a zombie.

He threw me out.

He really threw me out.

The man who stared at me like I was going to be his last meal on this planet *threw me out of my own room like I was nothing.*

What in the ever-loving fuck?

I should be skipping down the hall with joy because somehow, some way, I was spared from having to face final judgment from Jericho Forge, and now I can go back to figuring out how to raise the money to save my sister.

Then why am I so fucking pissed?

Because part of me wanted him just as much . . . and he

made it clear exactly where my importance stands in the grand scheme of things.

Nowhere at all.

Sobering, indeed.

Which means I'll be doing the barefoot walk of shame back to my flat, dodging the crowds, wearing a rumpled cocktail dress. Because there's no way in hell I'm going to go ask Jean Phillippe for another room. He proved where his loyalty stood when he crumpled under pressure as soon as Forge appeared at the card room door like one of the four horsemen of the apocalypse.

Laughter comes from the elevator bank as I creep around the corner. Four people spill out from between the doors, and the two women in the lead pause when they see me, causing the third woman and a blond man to run into them. A man I recognize all too well. A man who is partially responsible for exactly what's happening right now.

Fucking Bastien.

All I want to do is run and hide under a rock, but that's not possible. I'm caught out in the open, and there's nothing I can do to pretend otherwise.

Every trace of mirth disappears from his expression the second he sees me. He pushes past the women, scanning every inch of me. "What the fuck happened?"

"Don't act like you actually give a fuck, Bastien."

His features tighten, and I wonder if it's some indication that Bastien actually does give a fuck. Either way, it doesn't matter at the moment. Right now, I have to figure out what the hell I'm going to do to get $10 million in seven days.

"Did he hurt you?" A vein ticks in Bastien's forehead that I've never seen before. Actually, in the decade that I've known him, I've never seen him look remotely this angry.

Doesn't matter.

I sidestep him to try to reach the elevator doors, but Bastien reaches out and catches the sleeve of my robe.

"Indy. Stop." He pushes the women away with his other hand. "Go wait by the room."

The women, each wearing sky-high heels and a dress that barely covers their tits and ass, and neither at the same time, glare at me as they whine at him.

"But, Bastien—"

"Go," he orders, and they scurry away.

I tug my sleeve from his grip and punch the elevator call button.

"If he fucking hurt you, I'm going to kill him."

I'm surprised to hear what could pass for genuine concern in Bastien's voice. But that doesn't mean I'm about to share anything with him about what happened between Forge and me.

"None of your goddamned business."

"Indy . . . I might be a fucking bastard, but at least I don't hurt women. Unless they ask for it. What the hell happened?"

"Nothing. Nothing happened. Now I'm going home."

His concerned tone disappears. "He got a look at you naked and tossed you out? You have a third nipple I don't remember? I mean, I was drunk at the time."

I whip around to face him, and as soon as I see

Bastien's face, I realize that's exactly what he was trying to accomplish with his insulting words.

"What do you want from me, Bastien?"

His gaze shutters. "What I've wanted for ten fucking years—another chance with you."

"Never going to happen."

"Maybe. Maybe not. From where I'm standing, you look like you're running out of options. I know you need a fuck-ton of money, Indy."

"What's your point?"

He purses his lips, and I can see the gears turning in his head. Bastien's always playing an angle, and I practically see him choosing it now.

"What if I could help you?"

"How?" I keep my response short because I'm not going to fall into his trap. Not again. This game was supposed to help me save Summer, and all it did was throw me to the shark named Jericho Forge.

"Tell me how much money you need and why."

The men who have my sister expressly told me not to tell *anyone* what was going on. Not the police, Interpol, *anyone*. If I do . . .

My stomach twists at the memory of what they said they'd do to her.

"I can't tell you."

Bastien's jaw tenses. "Then what if I knew there was another game you could sit, and this one you could win easily?"

The temptation is strong. Too strong to resist. Or maybe it's my desperation pushing me. "Where?"

"Where do you think? Monte Carlo."

Of course it would be Monaco. Bastien's other favorite place to play with his family's money.

But I just lost every cent I had. I could charge the flight, but I don't have enough funds left to tap for a buy-in. I liquidated everything I had for tonight.

But if I could get the money . . .

Now I sound like a gambling addict, and I already know what happens when I go to the table desperate. I make stupid decisions that end up with me standing in a hallway of a hotel wearing nothing but a robe.

"I can't."

Bastien's gaze drops to my bare feet and drags up my body, like he's inspecting the merchandise for sale. "I'll front you the stake."

Oh, wait, he does think I'm merchandise for sale.

"In exchange for what?"

"My family wants me to settle down. Start producing the next generation of de Veres to carry on the family name. My sister's brats can't inherit the title, and the earl doesn't want to lose it to another branch of the family tree. Wouldn't you like to be a countess someday, Indy? You already act like a queen. You'd fit the role perfectly. You fit me perfectly."

I blink twice, trying to wrap my head around what he just said. "You want me to . . ."

"Marry me."

My stomach flips.

"No way in hell," I whisper.

Bastien's expression doesn't shift, even though I just threw his proposal back in his face. "You were willing to sell yourself to Forge. Why not me?"

"We both know you're the one who fucked me at the table."

"Not so well as I'd like to fuck you as my wife." He moves closer and trails a finger down the lapel of the robe. "Do you have another plan? What about the luxury of time to come up with one?"

I take a step back, out of his reach. He knows damn well that I don't have another plan, and I can't let my sister be sold as a sex slave, no matter how badly she fucked up. I'm still mulling over my lack of options when Bastien's expression loses its intensity and morphs back into the easygoing guy I recognize.

With a shrug, he backs away toward the end of the hallway where the women wait for him.

"I'm leaving the island Monday at five. My proposal stands. Think about it, Indy. At least I'm the devil you know."

12

INDIA

Climbing out of the back of a cab in my gold dress and the white spa flip-flops I traded the robe for at the gift shop feels worse than any walk of shame the partiers on this island will be doing in the morning. And to make it even worse, when I push open the door to my flat just before midnight, Alanna is sitting on my sofa with an espresso cup and saucer clutched in her petite hands. I told her to stay home tonight and I'd call her in the morning, but it doesn't surprise me she didn't listen.

"Did you win? Did you get the money?" she asks as she bolts up. The ceramic clatters as dark brown espresso spills over the sides of the mini cup.

I don't know how much coffee she's drank to stay awake this late, but from how her hands are shaking, I'm guessing she used every last Nespresso capsule I have in the flat.

The crushing defeat from earlier comes back with a vengeance now that I have to admit to my adoptive mother just how badly I've failed.

I give her a quick shake of my head, and her lily-white skin, the product of dedicated avoidance of the sun's rays, turns ashen.

"What does that mean? You didn't win *all* the money we need?"

I force the words I don't want to speak from my throat. "I lost it all."

"Oh, sweet Jesus." Her knees give way and she drops onto the sofa just as quickly as she rose. "How? You . . . you're—"

"Jericho Forge showed up. Bastien backed me into a bad bet, and Forge swooped in for the kill. I . . ." My words trail off because I don't want to tell her the rest of it. I can't bear to see the disappointment on her face.

I've come a long way from being the wary and rude sixteen-year-old that Alanna Clark plucked off the street after she caught me stealing her groceries. That was six months after our mom bailed on us in Ibiza after dragging our asses all over Europe while she stripped and used every spare dollar for booze and drugs.

Apparently, I wasn't as stealthy as I'd thought, because Alanna had been watching us for weeks. She first spotted me on the street, using Summer as a distraction to hustle tourists with three-card monte. We made just enough to pay for a shithole room and a bathroom shared with junkies, but food was never a guarantee.

Why a woman would want to adopt a sixteen-year-old and her eight-year-old sister, I didn't understand. But she smothered us both with love and home cooking, and even though I watched for any indication she was waiting to take advantage, I never saw it. She was simply a good person wanting to help us.

The adoption was final just before I turned eighteen, and even now, I know there's no other human on the planet I would have allowed to adopt me. Alanna is everything kind and sweet and wonderful in the world.

Which makes it even more devastating that I failed her.

"What, Indy? Tell me all of it. No secrets." That's her one rule. The rule that Summer broke when she lied to both of us about her fabulous new fashion marketing job that was letting her travel and make bank.

My sister didn't have a damn fashion marketing job. She was playing underground poker, and not only did she lose, but she *cheated and got caught.* A $5 million pot. The men in charge of the underground games didn't take kindly to her actions, and by didn't take kindly, I mean they kept the money and threatened to kill her unless she paid them back double. When she told them she didn't have the cash, they came to me with the ultimatum that's now ruling my life—$10 million or my sister goes up for auction to sex slavers.

Given the situation we find ourselves in, it's impossible that anything I tell Alanna will be more shocking.

"I ran out of money at the table. Forge pushed me to bet my room key . . ."

Alanna's eyes widen. "Your room key? *Jericho Forge?* But—" She cuts off her question because she's a smart woman. "Oh. Oh no. Did he— Are you—" She abandons the cup and saucer on the table and darts toward me, her gaze scanning from top to bottom for any sign of injury.

"I'm okay. I promise. He didn't touch me."

She reaches out and squeezes my hand. "I don't understand. Why would he do that?"

"I don't know. His business associate interrupted. I guess it was my lucky day." The words sound hollow as they come out of my mouth, because there was nothing lucky about tonight.

With her fingers threaded through mine, Alanna presses her lips together. "What are we going to do now?"

I let my eyes close for a moment. "I don't know." I swallow, remembering Bastien's proposal. It sits in my brain like a grenade with the pin slipping free.

I can't marry him.

It's not that I think marriage is sacred or anything, because I've never had any shining examples of it in my life. Alanna always talks about her beloved husband, Hal, and how they sailed around the world before breaking a mast near Ibiza, then decided to settle here permanently instead of going back to America. But Hal passed away five years before she found us, and Alanna never fully recovered from his loss.

Regardless, it's not like I expected to have a relationship like Alanna and Hal's. My experience with married men is mostly limited to the ones here on stag weekends where even the groom-to-be fucks every young, nubile girl in sight who will sit on his dick.

And then there's the night Bastien and I met. Or more accurately, the morning ten years ago when I woke up in a hotel room to a woman screaming that I stole her fiancé. Little did I know he made me the pawn in an elaborate scheme to get his bride to call off the wedding, because his family wouldn't let him back out.

Fuck you, Bastien. What makes you think I'd ever marry you?

Oh, wait, that's right. The $10 million I need. Except he doesn't have a clue how much I need or how quickly. I know his family has nearly more money than the queen of England, but that doesn't mean he could get his hands on a sum that large.

Am I considering his offer? No. No, I am not. *But Summer . . .*

"You can get invited to another game, right? Or set one up, this time somewhere else? Farther from home, maybe?"

Alanna's guarded optimism is enough to almost bring me to my knees. Her faded blue eyes plead with me to come up with a solution, but I don't have one.

"If I had anything left to buy in, maybe. But I don't. I took everything I had to the table tonight." It shames me to admit it, but she asked for the truth.

"I'll sell my flat. We should be able to get at least a half million for it."

My gaze cuts to her resolute expression. "Then where would you live? How would you support yourself?"

Alanna's flat is in a beautiful beachside building, and has an efficiency unit attached to it that she rents out during the season to support herself for the entire year. It's her only security—and the last place where she lived happily with Hal. I can't let her sacrifice that.

"I'll live on the street if that's what it takes to get

Summer back in one piece. I'll sell every goddamned thing I own. We don't have a choice, Indy."

I swallow the lump in my throat and feel a million times worse than I did creeping out of the casino. Alanna and Summer were both counting on me, and I failed them.

Before I can flay myself with guilt, my cell phone buzzes in my clutch. Alanna stares at my hand as I pull it out. The screen reads Unknown Number.

We both go still. The men who have Summer called from an unknown number.

"Answer it! It could be them!"

I tap the screen twice, engaging the speaker so Alanna can listen. "Hello?"

"Ms. Baptiste, it's very disappointing to hear that you are not bringing me my money tonight." The voice, rough with an accent I haven't yet been able to place, is the same one that told me what my sister did and her fate should I fail to pay.

"Excuse me?" I ask, hoping he'll slip and tell me how he knows what the hell happened tonight. No one should know what happened . . . unless one of the players, Jean Phillippe, or Armand leaked the information.

A cold weight settles over my body, chilling me to the core. *Who told?*

"You lost the most important game of your life, Ms. Baptiste. Even more important than the poker tour final you lost. Does your sister not matter to you at all?"

"Who told you?"

His laugh crackles, like the connection isn't very good, and again, I wonder where the fuck they're holding Summer. My guess is they're somewhere in

Northern Africa, but they could be next door for all I know.

"You think I don't know every move you make, Ms. Baptiste? Let that be a reminder to you. If you think about going to the police or Interpol, I won't even bother to sell your pretty sister. I'll send her back to you in a box for you to reassemble for burial. Then we'll come for you and Mrs. Clark."

Alanna slaps a hand over her mouth, muffling her groan.

"Ah, Mrs. Clark. Good that you hear my warning, so I don't repeat myself. Maybe you can remind India exactly how much time she has left."

"Six days. I know exactly how much time. I'll get you your fucking money."

"Yes, you will. Because you don't want to think about what is going to happen to Summer if you do not. Don't lose again, Indy. We're waiting."

The call ends, and Alanna's bottom lip trembles as tears slide down her cheeks.

"We have to get the money. We have to." She drags in two more deep breaths. "I'm selling my flat. I'll call the agency tomorrow."

I shake my head. "It'll take too long. We can't risk waiting. I'll find another way. I promise. I won't let you down again."

Her wiry arms wrap around me. "You didn't let me down, Indy. You're human. An incredible human. You'll find a way. I know it. In the meantime, I'm going to start the process to sell my flat. I can't do nothing. That's not the way I'm built."

I meet her blue gaze, and even though the thought makes my stomach churn like the waves crashing along the shore, I tell her, "Give me a few days. I might have another option. Just . . . I need some time to figure out the details. Okay?"

"*I* hope you enjoyed yourself tonight, Forge, because that's the last fucking time you're ever getting near Indy."

I pause midstride in the casino lobby as de Vere brushes off a brunette standing next to him near the door. Goliath stiffens beside me, on the verge of hulking out at his taunt.

Just seeing de Vere's face makes me want to rip the bottle of booze out of his clenched fist and beat him with it. Hot, fiery rage races through me, and it takes years of self-imposed iron control to lock it down and not show a shred of emotion.

You will have your vengeance, Isaac. I swear it.

"Care to make a bet on that, de Vere? I'm happy to take more of your money tonight, especially since I already had her."

His nostrils flare, and a vein throbs in his forehead. He hasn't learned to school himself. Not surprising.

De Vere is a spoiled little bitch riding through life like

it's one big party while he tries to spend all of Mummy and Daddy's money. He's the epitome of everything I hate, even if he hadn't killed the only person who meant a damn thing to me in this entire world. *While he was fucking drunk.*

"You didn't have her. She told me," he says with a condescending chin lift, and my fists clench at the thought of him cornering her after Goliath intruded. *Not happening again.* "You can try to take every fucking thing from me, Forge, but you won't get her. Not unless it's over my fucking dead body."

The predictable answer would be *that can be arranged*, but I take another avenue. One that will piss him off even more.

"How long's it been since she spread those long, tanned legs for you? Because I could swear I saw God tonight."

De Vere lurches toward me, liquor spilling onto the marble floor from the open bottle. "Go fuck yourself, Forge. You ever talk like that about her again, and I'll shove the words back down your throat with my fucking fist."

He sways on his feet, and I wonder if he's defending her honor because he's drunk or if he's really this hung up on her. No woman I've taken from him over the years in my effort to make him miserable has seemed to care much about him, nor him about them. They've all been quick fucks, party favors, or toys. He's never given a damn when he saw them on my arm or they stopped taking his calls.

But India Baptiste is different. That's the only reason

he's kept his interest in her so quiet for so long. He's kept her off my radar on purpose.

Not any longer.

"You care about her, don't you, de Vere? She's not like the others."

He bares his teeth. "She's mine, Forge. I'm not fucking letting you have her."

My chest shakes before I unleash a few waves of laughter. "You don't *let me* do anything." I take a step closer to him. "You should've kept your secret under tighter wraps. Now you've got something to lose that actually matters, and all you'll be able to do is dread the day I take my final revenge. You won't see it coming, but you're going to spend every minute until then wondering when it will happen." I flash a smile at him as his lips flatten into a thin, hard line.

"Try and take her. I'll kill you myself."

I glance up to one of the bubbles in the ornate gold-leaf ceiling, concealing the casino's surveillance. "I've got your death threat on film now. I'll add that to my compilation of everything that'll have you rotting in prison if anything ever happens to me."

"Fuck you, Forge."

I shake my head. "I'd much prefer to fuck India Baptiste. And I will. Repeatedly. Maybe I'll even keep her. Make her my mistress." I jerk my chin toward Goliath. "Get the car. I'm done with him." Goliath strides ahead of me, and I turn to follow.

"She won't fucking touch you. We're getting married."

I spin around and take in the smug, almost victorious expression crossing de Vere's features. *What the fuck?*

But I say nothing. I study him to look for tells that he's bluffing. None are apparent.

His smirk widens. "No answer? That's what I thought. Check and mate, Forge. Check and mate."

I reach out a hand and clasp his shoulder, settling my thumb just over his windpipe, and then I squeeze hard until he coughs.

"You don't understand how this works, de Vere. Check and mate means one of us is dead."

He coughs again, his fingers wrapping around my hand. To the cameras watching us, it looks like we're having a friendly moment, which is exactly what I intend.

"India Baptiste would be better off as my whore than your wife. In fact, that's exactly what's going to happen."

INDIA

I don't sleep at all, and I know Alanna doesn't either because I hear her tossing and turning all night in my spare room. By the time the sun rises, I've replayed everything that happened last night dozens of times.

My sum total of new ideas to get the money to sit the game in Monaco? Zero.

I'm not taking it from Bastien . . . if I can come up with any other solution.

Right now, those solutions include loan sharks, bank robbery, and cat burglary—none of which I have any experience with, but I'm not going to rule them out just yet.

I unearth an espresso capsule from my hidden stash and prepare to brew some coffee so I can find the necessary energy to go back to the hotel and collect my things from the room. I still can't believe Forge threw me out.

Lucky, Indy. That was luck. It doesn't matter that it didn't feel lucky at the time, and the sting still hasn't completely faded.

The Nespresso machine finishes heating when Alanna enters the kitchen, wearing her same clothes from the night before. The dark shadows under her eyes tell me that I was right about her not getting any sleep.

I'm so sorry, Alanna, I think. *I wish I could have come home with better news.*

"Good morning." I inject a cheery note into my voice that I certainly don't feel, but it's the best I can do.

Instead of responding in kind, Alanna looks at me with her lips trembling like she's on the verge of sobbing. "I emailed the agency this morning. They're closed until tomorrow, but I'm going to sell the flat. You can't talk me out of it."

"Alanna . . ." I rush over and throw my arms around her. "Please, just give me some more time. I'll find a way."

Tears tip over her lids. "It's just a place to live. That's nothing compared to Summer's life."

It won't help to remind her that a half million in cash in a couple of months won't do anything to save Summer, so I nod and try to change the subject.

"How about poached eggs for breakfast? I can even make hollandaise."

Alanna straightens her shoulders and wipes away the tears. "That sounds lovely, dear."

Twenty minutes later, I'm blending the sauce when someone knocks on the door. My spine stiffens, and Alanna and I stare at each other.

Is it them? Are they coming to collect early?

The fear I see on her face is no doubt reflected on mine. I silence the blender and move toward the door, but the nimble older woman beats me to it.

"Alanna!"

She peers through the peephole and gasps.

Sweet fucking Christ. No.

I run toward her, not giving a single damn that the eggs are going to be ruined.

"What?" I ask, skidding to a halt beside her.

Alanna pulls back from the peephole, her eyes wide. "There's a giant at the door."

"A giant?"

She points to her head. "With dreadlocks."

A giant with dreadlocks. I need exactly one guess to know who fits that description—the man who interrupted Forge and me last night.

What the hell is he doing here?

I peer through the round hole, and he stares into it like he can see inside and knows I'm watching him. He reaches out with a beefy arm and knocks again. A small black duffel bag dangles from his other fist.

My stuff?

"Do you know who he is?" Alanna asks.

"Yes," I tell her. "It's okay. Just . . . check the eggs, please. I'll handle this."

I know she doesn't want to move from my side, but thankfully, Alanna backs away toward the kitchen.

I take a steadying breath before opening the bolt. I might be making a huge mistake, but if he brought my things, I'm not letting pride or fear stop me from taking them. Given the fact that I went from millionaire to broke overnight, I don't exactly have many other options.

Just in case, I open the door with the chain still

attached and peek out. The giant's attention locks onto my face, and he holds up the bag in front of him.

"Your things, Ms. Baptiste."

The bag is too large to push through the gap between the door and the doorjamb, so I hold up a finger before shutting the door in his face. When I open it the second time, he's still standing there, expressionless.

I reach out to take the bag from him, but he doesn't release it.

Oh no, I'm not playing this game. I yank on the handle of the bag, but his beast-like grip is impossible to break.

"I have a message for you from Mr. Forge."

"Don't care."

"You would be wise to listen, Ms. Baptiste."

I tug harder. "Still don't care. Shockingly enough, I have bigger problems to deal with than your boss. Now, give me my shit and I'll thank you, and we can both pretend like none of this ever happened and move on with our lives."

He lets go abruptly and I stumble backward, nearly landing on my ass on the tile floor.

"The message is in the bag. I suggest you read it, or you'll be unprepared for when he comes for you."

When he comes for me? Um . . . Hell. No.

I right myself and stare at the dreadlocked giant. "Listen to me carefully, whatever-your-name-is, because you're going to want to tell your boss what I said—I don't owe him a goddamned thing, and if he thinks I do, he can go fuck himself."

Digging into my deep well of attitude, I salute him

with two fingers before flipping him off and slamming the door.

That felt pretty damn good. *I just hope I'm not going to regret it.*

I stare down at the bag and debate whether I should dig for the note.

Nah. I don't think so.

Hopefully, I don't regret that too.

THE EGGS TURN out less than ideal, but since we both push them around our plates in a show of eating instead of actually consuming them, it doesn't matter.

Alanna and I talk about the weather, tourists, the weather, and tourists some more, but before we can go through another round of saying the same things to each other, there's another knock on my door. She and I both jerk our gazes toward the open slider that leads from the tiny patio of my flat to the door.

"Do you think it's him again?" Her voice shakes as she squeezes her hand into a fist around her butter knife, holding it like a dagger.

I lay my fork on the small table and slowly rise.

"I don't think you should answer it, Indy. Please. It can't be good."

She's probably right. The only visitors I usually have who arrive unannounced are Alanna and Summer. Obviously, they're both out of the running.

"Stay here. I'll handle this."

"Indy . . ."

I squeeze her shoulder and smile. "I'm sure it's fine. Nothing happened last time."

She gives me a small nod but doesn't lay down her knife. If there's a threat outside that door, I wouldn't put it past her to use it.

As I take measured steps through the open-floor-plan flat, I flip through the short list of people who could be outside the door.

Forge's man.

Forge himself.

Bastien.

Someone delivering a threat about the money I need to pay to save Summer.

Basically, no one I'm interested in seeing for the rest of my life.

Whoever it is pounds on the door again. "Indy? You in there?"

The sound of the building manager's voice coming through the door triggers a wave of relief. *Thank you, Jesus.* I stop in front of the door and remove the chains, then slide the bolts before pulling the door open a few inches.

"Miguel? Is something wrong?"

Miguel Herrera, a retired football player from the age before they made bajillions of dollars, greets me with a tight smile on his tanned face. "I don't know, but I thought you could tell me if there was."

"What do you mean?"

"There were men here a few minutes ago, asking questions about you. I told them they had the wrong address and I'd never heard of you."

"A large man with dreadlocks?"

Miguel's brow creases with confusion as he shakes his head. "Dreadlocks? No. No dreadlocks."

The apprehension that drained away when I heard his voice comes back with a vengeance. *It had to be the men who have Summer.* They said I had ten days, and I have six days left. Did they lie?

Of course they would lie.

Now, more than ever, I'm glad I had the presence of mind to be concerned about my privacy when I joined the poker tour. My lease is in the name of a company I used for the sole purpose of renting the flat, and there's no label on my buzzer. *But that didn't stop them from finding me.*

"Did they give names? Any information at all?" My brain is going wild, thinking of how I could possibly use the information to track down where Summer is being held, and maybe get her back without paying a ransom if I can somehow morph into Liam Neeson in *Taken*.

"No. But they were Russian. Mafioso, I think."

"Ru-Russian?" I choke out the question because the man who calls me about Summer is *definitely not* Russian. "Are you sure?"

Miguel nods. "When I played in Russia, we went to a club one night, and there was a group of them from the Bratva. Scary sons of bitches. These men sounded just like them. These are not good guys, Indy. Have you gotten into something . . . bad?"

Jesus fucking Christ. Russian mafia? My breathing picks up, along with my heart rate.

"How many men, Miguel? Tell me every detail."

He grips the back of his neck as he looks up. "Two.

One who asked questions, and one who stood there like a pit bull. He had tattoos on his hand. Prison tattoos, I think."

Fucking hell.

"What did they say, exactly?"

"They said they were looking for a blonde with blue eyes who goes by the name of India."

Goes by the name of India? Like I made that shit up?

I make a split-second decision, if for no other reason than I don't know what the hell else to do. "If they come back, call the police."

Miguel's dark tanned skin pales. "I don't think you understand, Indy. The police can't do anything about men like that."

"Indy? Is everything okay?"

Alanna calls my name from behind me, and I give Miguel a nod, because there's nothing left for him to tell me.

"Thank you for the warning. If you see or hear anything else suspicious, please let me know. Be safe."

I close the door, but Miguel presses a hand to it to stop me.

"Maybe it's time for you to take a break from the island, Indy. You don't want people like that sniffing around your flat. They looked dangerous."

"Thank you for warning me. I'll talk to you later, Miguel."

He releases his grip on the door, and I close, bolt, and chain every last lock before I turn to face Alanna.

"What now?"

"Miguel says there were Russians looking for me."

Any remaining color in her face disappears. "Why on earth would Russians be looking for you?"

"I don't know. Maybe . . . maybe it has to do with Summer?"

"But . . . you said you couldn't place his accent. You would know a Russian accent."

"Maybe they're working with Russians? I don't know."

"Why would they come, though? We have more time. They can't take you too. I won't let them." Her tone borders on shrill as it rises an octave.

"They're not going to take me. I swear. It's going to be fine." I have no idea whether I'm lying to Alanna, but I hope I'm not.

Wait. Shit.

"I forgot about Belevich. He's Russian. People say he has ties to the Bratva. He played last night. I won some of his money, but I lost it all to Forge."

Alanna wraps her arms around herself. "Do . . . do you think he sent people to get his money back?"

I shake my head. "That wouldn't make sense. He plays all the time. I've never heard of him going after people before."

Not for something like this, I add to myself. I have heard one or two stories about Belevich fighting over women with other men. I know I wore my gold dress . . . but it was clear he didn't have a chance with me, or so I thought after Forge staked his claim.

"I don't like this, Indy," Alanna says.

"Me either, but I don't know what else to think. Unless

. . ." I trail off as I gather my thoughts. Maybe there's another possible reason Russians were here.

"What?"

"Maybe they followed Forge's guy here."

Alanna's hand covers her mouth. "Good God. That man probably has enemies all over the world."

I'm sure she's right, because he has plenty right here in Ibiza. What if they were trying to track me down to get some kind of leverage over him?

But that doesn't make sense, because I'm nothing but a pawn in his game to piss off Bastien. He doesn't give a shit about what happens to me. He proved that last night when he tossed me out on my ass like a hooker who'd served her purpose.

Either way, I have one more problem to add to my list . . . and Forge may be the only person who can tell me why Russians are looking for me.

I pace to where I left the bag on the sofa after his dreaded henchman left, and rip it open looking for the note.

It's right there, on top of my neatly stowed makeup. The bold handwriting is more slashes than curves, but it's legible.

You need a stake for a game.
I have a million-dollar proposition.
No one will let you play anywhere worth playing unless
you show up at La Marina Quay tonight at 8.

15

FORGE

From the helm of my newest toy, a Gamma Black Shiver that'll act as the tender to my superyacht when it returns home, my island comes into view. Not Ibiza. Isla del Cielo. The small island paradise I inherited when Bastien de Vere killed Isaac Marco.

Isaac was the father I never had. The only person I've ever fully trusted. He saved my life when I was a stowaway aboard his ship. He saw the bruises from my last beating, and instead of turning me over to the cops to deal with, he gave me a new life. He's the reason I joined the merchant marines. He taught me to be a good captain and how to make money shipping cargo. He made me the man I am today. And that fucking reckless bastard killed him— and never paid the price or suffered a goddamned punitive consequence. Taking everything from de Vere isn't even enough. He'll still never understand the pain of his actions.

If he thinks he's going to live happily ever after married to India Baptiste, he's going to receive a rude awakening.

Take her and break her.

That was my initial plan, and then I saw a glimpse of what de Vere sees in her.

The plan can't change. I'll lure her back into my web through any means necessary, starting with bribery and threats. No one has ever accused me of being a good man, especially after Isaac died.

The knot in my chest tightens every time I think about him. Ten years has dulled the sharpness of the wound, but my need for vengeance grows every day.

A stupid man would have killed de Vere outright before Isaac was cold in his grave. I may not be a good man, but I'm not a stupid one either. I knew no one would let the murder of the heir to an earldom go unpunished, which is why I'm still biding my time and taking swipes where I can.

With that vow echoing in my brain, I reach the island's dock, and two of my old crew members, Koba and Ivan, toss lines to me.

"What have you learned?" I ask as soon as I tie up the boat and step foot on the pier.

"Plenty about her, but no one knows why she needs the money."

"Keep digging. I want to know about her family, friends, and where she'd go for help next."

"Her records only go back as far as seventeen. She and her sister were adopted by an American with dual citizenship named Alanna Clark. Before that, she didn't exist, Forge."

They fall in step beside me as I make my way up the path toward the cliffs and the house that Isaac built and was only able to enjoy for a year before he was murdered.

"What the hell do you mean, she didn't exist before she was seventeen? You have every resource at your disposal. How can you not find records?" I look from one man to the other.

Koba shrugs. "Could she have gone by a different name? India Baptiste doesn't pop up on radar until adoption proceedings started. Before that, she was a ghost."

"What about her sister?"

"Same. Summer Baptiste doesn't exist until age eight. She almost dropped out of high school, but somehow she managed to graduate and then go to university, where she majored in fashion design. She also tried to join the poker tour but didn't make the cut. She doesn't have the skill at cards her sister does, and from all evidence, it seems she prefers partying to working."

I file the facts away for later use. "And the adoptive mother?"

"Nothing interesting. Widow who rents out part of her beachfront flat for income. She's been here almost twenty years. Rarely leaves the island and lives a quiet life."

We climb the stairs carved out of the rock and reach the top where the low-lying white villa sprawls beyond the blue water of the pool.

"What about debts? Who does India owe? Who does her sister owe?" There's something they're not finding. I may not know her well, but I know there's no way in hell India would willingly offer herself up unless circumstances were dire.

"The sister parties and plays cards. She could owe

people, but nothing on record. No one has seen her in a few days, so she might be off the island."

"All signs point to this being related to her sister then." I stare up at the brilliant blue sky and try to piece together the puzzle. It would make sense that India would take bigger risks and be more desperate if her sister is in trouble. I can't fault that kind of loyalty.

"Dig deeper on the sister. If she has debts, find out who holds them. I want leverage over this woman before she arrives. You have three hours."

Both men nod and split off to head for the staff quarters, which are on the other side of the island, allowing us all our privacy while living on one of earth's most remarkable places.

It doesn't even occur to me that India may not come.

She needs money.

I have money.

That's how the world works.

I glance skyward one last time before heading inside. *I will get revenge for you, Isaac. I swear it.*

16

INDIA

I reach the quay ten minutes after the appointed time, mostly because I was hoping I could talk myself into not going. Unfortunately, telling Alanna about the note led to the opposite effect I had intended.

"You don't have to do anything but listen to him, Indy. If there's a chance . . ."

Her well-intentioned logic lasted until she left my flat about an hour before I needed to leave. I spent that time scouring the internet for underground poker games like the one that got Summer into trouble, but they don't post schedules like the poker tour. Not shocking, I know.

Finding absolutely nothing, I resigned myself to the fact that Alanna was right. If there's a single chance I can get what I need from Forge without selling my soul in the process—and stop him from making me persona non grata at every casino in Europe—I have to hear him out. Even more than that, I have some questions of my own about the Russians sniffing around.

A sleek, dangerous-looking boat floats at the end of the

pier. The massive dreadlocked giant stands beside it, which tells me that I've reached the right place.

"Good evening, Ms. Baptiste."

"Maybe it's good from where you're standing, but I have other opinions on the subject."

His expression doesn't change as he gestures to the boat. "Mr. Forge doesn't appreciate tardiness."

I spare him the sharp reply that begs to leap off my tongue, deciding that I'm better off keeping my hostility in check until we reach the man who summoned me.

Think of Summer. She's all that matters.

With a deep breath, I step onto the boat that floats on the gently lapping waves. It looks more like something the military would use than a civilian, but for some reason, that doesn't surprise me. Jericho Forge is a billionaire. It's probably one of a long list of extravagant toys he owns.

A list he probably wants to add me to. What else could a million-dollar proposition mean? After being thrown out by him last night, I don't know what to expect. The man doesn't follow any set of rules I've ever encountered, and apparently just makes up his own.

The perks of being ridiculously rich, I'm sure.

As soon as the giant boards, he points to a seat and I take it. I'm not going to quiver and protest like a helpless damsel in distress, regardless of how in distress I actually am.

I just want to get this over with, which means reaching Forge as quickly as possible and then getting away from him even more quickly.

Thanks to Forge's infamy, I already know exactly where we're heading—his private island that's less than ten minutes from here. The internet held a wealth of information about how he grew a shipping company with a fleet of twenty into two thousand. The world is literally at his fingertips, and he's one of the wealthiest men on the planet.

He wouldn't even notice ten million missing.

Except I'm not a thief, no matter how much I wish I had those skills right now. Which again shows how low desperation will take you.

As we approach the island rising out of the ocean with its sheer cliff faces and staggering beauty, I can't help but wonder what it must feel like to know it's yours.

Or maybe when you have enough money to own an island like this, you take it all for granted. Which is so much worse.

Why the hell am I even wondering this crap? I snap myself out of my awestruck reverie as I catch sight of a man standing near the edge of one of the cliffs, his figure imposing even from here.

I don't need a second guess to know it's Forge, watching his dreaded beast deliver me according to his bidding. His broad-shouldered frame and wind-swept black hair make it impossible for it to be anyone else. No matter what he's expecting tonight, I can promise I won't comply, if for no other reason than the man puts me on the defensive simply by existing.

Two other men, one blond and the other darkly tanned, approach the dock. Both are large enough to make me question why I agreed to a meeting on Forge's turf, where I wouldn't have a prayer of being able to swim to shore.

As the giant and one of the men tie up the boat, the other man holds out a hand to me.

"Ms. Baptiste. If you'll come with me."

I use the stairs that lead up the side of the boat and hop onto the dock without his assistance, thankful that I chose flat gladiator sandals rather than heels. My azure-blue sundress with its shoulder-baring design and puffed sleeves circling the tops of my arms doesn't show even a hint of the cleavage that I displayed in full force last night.

From his actions, Forge proved that he's not a man to be swayed by tits and ass. I can only assume that he gets a wealth of them shoved in his face at every opportunity. Gold-digging party girls are a dime a dozen in Ibiza. All you have to do is sit by the pool at one of the swanky resorts for less than an hour to see them begging to be invited to private cabanas to drink with the men on stag weekends.

The thought of bachelor parties reminds me of how Bastien and I met, and how he is ultimately responsible for me standing here right this moment. The animosity between him and Forge is legendary, but rumors can't substantiate what caused it. Only that it's very real.

I follow the blond up the path and toward the stairs that will take me to Forge. The other man trails close enough behind me that I can feel his presence.

Apparently, hospitality isn't their forte, because nothing about this reception feels *welcoming* at all, and I highly doubt that will change when I see Forge. With each step, I feel like I'm being led to the gallows, but there's not a damn thing I can do about it now. *There he is.*

"Ms. Baptiste." He says my name and nothing else. No

greeting. No false warmth. Nothing but a man carved from rock, just like the island on which we stand.

"Mr. Forge," I reply in kind.

"Follow me." He turns on his heel and walks toward the massive white villa fronted with floor-to-ceiling windows, just beyond the turquoise waters of the swimming pool.

My gaze darts from the house to the landscape to the man, trying to gauge all of my surroundings at the same time. My attention zeroes in on Forge because he's clearly the most dangerous.

Instead of being dressed in a somber suit like he was last night, he's in tan linen trousers with a white linen shirt, billowing open in the wind as he makes his way to a table that's been set for two beside the pool.

"You're joining me for dinner. You're having the fish I caught earlier," he says without turning around.

I stop short beside the table. "Did you poison it?"

His head swivels to face me, one eyebrow raised as his dark hair catches on his collar. "Why would I go through all this trouble to get you here to kill you?"

"Can't blame a girl for wondering, under the circumstances." He has to know I'm referring to the feud between him and Bastien.

Forge pulls out the chair that's sure to give the best view of what promises to be a spectacular sunset this evening. "Sit, India."

And there he goes barking orders at me like I'm a mutt again. Or a bitch, as he put it.

Before I can snap out a reply, the wind picks up and

my skirt lifts. I slap it down against my thighs before dropping into the seat.

"You didn't have to stop it on my account."

I flick my gaze at Forge as he studies me in his indolent fashion. "You didn't seem impressed the last time my dress disappeared."

"Martyrs don't turn me on. Pissed-off women who would prefer to chance drowning in a swim to shore rather than fuck me do."

How the hell can he read my mind? I have no idea, but keeping my emotions masked at this table has become more important than any poker game I've ever played.

"There's something seriously wrong with you. You should probably seek psychiatric help."

Forge takes the seat next to mine. "Last I checked, they can't get me revenge, but mouthy women distract me from it." His dark gray gaze dips to my chest before rising back to my face.

Really? He's checking out my boobs in the cleavage-less dress when he couldn't manage to spare a glance when they were on full display? I don't know why that pisses me off, but it does.

"Cut the shit, Forge. Why did you summon me, and what the hell is this million-dollar proposition? Dinner isn't necessary to say what you have to say."

He lifts the cloth napkin off the plate in front of him and shakes it out before placing it on his lap. I don't know if it's a signal of some kind, but one of the men from earlier approaches with a carafe of water in one hand and a decanter in the other. I watch them both as he fills the glasses in front of us without asking me if I want anything.

Forge lifts the lowball glass of liquor in salute. "Here's to a productive business discussion."

Business discussion?

"What the hell are you talking about?" I ask him in lieu of raising my own glass.

"You and I are about to make a deal, India. So, drink up. You'll probably need it to help loosen your tongue into saying yes."

FORGE

I thought of a hundred different ways I could play this. How I could entice her to take the money I know she desperately needs and lock her down so that Bastien can never have her. After last night, there's no question that she's a proud woman. Luckily for me, pride goeth before a fall.

"Make a deal? Are you already drunk?"

The smile that tugs on my lips is something that only seems to happen when I'm around her. She entertains me, which is a bonus, considering I'm going to own her.

I tip my glass against my lips and sip the sixty-two-year-old liquor. My tastes have changed drastically as my fortunes improved, but there's one thing that hasn't—my appreciation of a beautiful woman with a mind to match.

When I replace the glass, I lean my elbows on the table and steeple my fingers. I notice she can't stop her gaze from dropping from my face to where my shirt gapes open, exposing my chest and abs.

She's not immune to me in the fucking slightest. It's

gratifying to confirm that I didn't exaggerate her attraction last night.

"First drink of the day."

"Then what the hell are you talking about?"

"You need money. I have money. Did you know that concept, in large part, is what makes the world go 'round?"

She rolls her eyes, but it doesn't make the unique blue color that matches her dress any less striking. "Spare me the deal bullshit if you're about to tell me about the oldest profession in the world, because I already told you I'm not a whore. You can take your money and—"

Before she can finish her sentence, I pull a piece of paper out of the breast pocket of my shirt and hold it out to her.

"What is that?"

"Something I was going to wait to show you until after dinner, but as your striptease last night indicated, you're an impatient woman."

A blush colors her cheeks, and I find it fascinating that she still has the ability. Most women I encounter can't even fake it. There's an innocence Ms. India Baptiste tries to downplay, but she can't hide it from me. Soon, she'll find out she can't hide anything from me.

"You blew your chance last night. So unless that's a check for a million dollars made out to me, I don't give a single fuck what it is."

My grin splits as I burst into a low chuckle. "Ah, Ms. Baptiste. No wonder you're such a good poker player. You see through paper."

Her blue eyes go wide with shock. "What?"

When her hand reaches out, instead of pulling the

check back, I let her snatch it from my fingers. She's the kind of woman who won't believe it until she sees it.

She unfolds the paper, and her lush bottom lip drops open far enough that I could slide my cock right into that hot little mouth.

My dick jerks up at the thought, and I push the visual away. All in good time.

"What the hell is this?"

"I believe I just told you, and your capability for reading has confirmed it."

She lowers the check to her lap. "But that doesn't explain why you're offering me a million dollars."

"Not offering. Giving."

She swallows, and again, my dick tingles, because there's nothing more I'd like to do in this very moment than push her to her knees to show me how far she can take it down her throat.

"No one gives someone a million dollars for nothing. What's the catch?"

"Catch?"

India shoves to her feet, the metal of the chair scraping the concrete patio. "If this is a joke, it isn't funny. Tell me what the hell you want from me, Forge." She holds the check up in the air so that it flaps in the breeze. "Or I let this fucker fly and the sea can have it."

"That'd be unfortunate for you, wouldn't it? Since there's only one thing I ask in exchange, and it's something I'm pretty sure you already want to do."

"If this is your way of telling me you think I want to ride you like a Jet Ski, I don't give a shit. I need cash, not a fuck buddy."

And the poker player doesn't even realize she's showing her hand.

I lay both palms flat on the table and rise. "I don't pay for sex, Ms. Baptiste. Never have. Never will. You're not a whore, and I'm not a john. The only thing I want in return for my million is a promise."

Her blue eyes narrow. "What kind of promise?"

"An easy one."

"No promise that merits a million-dollar payment is easy."

"But what if it were, India? Are you still letting that check go?"

"I don't understand you," she says, lowering herself back into her seat as she tucks the check under the plate in front of her, preventing it from blowing away.

"You don't need to understand me. In fact, you couldn't. You don't know what it's like to have billions of dollars at your disposal. A million is a lot to a millionaire, such as you . . . *were*. But it's not shit to a billionaire."

Her flinch tells me my dig stings, but she stays silent for a moment.

"Tell me about this promise you want me to make, then." All the skepticism she's feeling in this moment pervades her words.

"All you have to do is swear you'll never have contact with Bastien de Vere ever again."

18

INDIA

"Jndy! I almost thought you weren't going to show."

Bastien greets me with a smug smile as he strides across the tarmac I shouldn't be standing on. I should be literally anywhere else but here, especially given the check in my purse.

Bile rises in my throat when I think about what I'm doing, but I inhale slowly and exhale out any concern for playing by someone else's rules.

Does that make me a bad person? I don't actually care. People with options are the ones who can have existential crises and soul-searching moments. I have a sister to save, and that's all that matters right now.

"Bastien? Who's this?" a gorgeous woman with auburn hair and diamonds at her ears and wrists asks as she clips toward us on Jimmy Choos.

Wait. One. Second.

Did Bastien really propose marriage to me and then bring another woman with him when he figured I wouldn't come? I don't even know why I'm surprised. There's nothing I wouldn't put past Bastien.

He doesn't reply to her immediately. Again, not a surprise. How exactly is he going to explain this?

The woman's haughty stare drops to my feet, making me glad I threw on my Prada pumps and packed all my most expensive couture for Monaco. I may have eaten from trash cans, but this woman won't make me feel like something *less* with her condescension that doesn't even require words.

"Poppy, this is a friend of mine."

"One of your whores? Really, Bastien?" She huffs out a sound of disgust.

"I'm sorry, if I'm one of his whores, what does that make you?"

Poppy skewers me with her stare. "His sister, you bitch."

Fuck. Fuck. Fuck.

Bastien steps between us. "Claws sheathed, ladies. There's more than enough room on the jet for all of us."

"I'm not getting on my own damn jet with your slag. She can walk right back to where she came from. Probably back to your bed," Poppy says with a toss of her mane of what looks like freshly blown-out hair.

"For the record, I haven't been anywhere near your brother and a bed at the same time in almost a decade."

Her stare turns from disgusted to razor sharp. *What the hell did I say wrong now?*

"*You.*" She steps toward me, bumping into Bastien's shoulder. "You're the one who embarrassed our entire family and ruined my debut."

"Poppy, it's not the same—"

I shouldn't even be surprised when Bastien tries to lie, but his sister clearly doesn't believe him.

"Yes, it is. I remember Mother showing me her picture from the investigator. She looks exactly the same, just older."

"Guilty as charged. Older and wiser, one would hope."

Poppy's auburn-tinted eyebrows wing upward. "Clearly not wiser, if you're here. What did Bastien promise you? A luxe holiday so you could feel like that hooker in *Pretty Woman*?"

Bastien takes a step toward me and wraps an arm around my shoulders. "Watch your fucking mouth, Poppy, and pretend you're a lady. India is the future Mrs. de Vere, and one day, the Countess of Carlisle."

Just hearing the words out of his mouth are almost enough to make me toss up the few bites of toast I managed to force myself to eat before I left my flat.

All the color drains from his sister's face as she stares at us both.

This is going to be a fabulous flight.

19

FORGE

"Mr. Federov, you have the ability to build the ships I need without going to China like my competitors, and I have the money to buy them. Why are we still discussing whether or not you're going to take my money?"

I'm losing patience with my discussions with Grigory Federov, a Russian oligarch who refuses to negotiate like a reasonable person, or even a rational unreasonable person. I'm close to dropping the efforts completely, but I don't want Chinese steel. I want Russian steel, and I always fucking get what I want.

Holding the phone, I stare out at the blue expanse of ocean beyond the glass separating my office from the outside as I wait for his response.

"Mr. Forge, I don't think you understand my position. I'm an old man. Business is good, but what I want can't be bought."

"Then tell me what else you want in addition to money to make this deal happen?"

As per usual, the Russian remains cagey. "Information."

"What kind of information do you want?" Glancing at the clock, I wonder how long this is going to take and if I should cut my losses now.

"First . . . let me tell you a story, and then we can discuss terms."

———

WHEN I HANG up with Federov, my life has taken an unexpected and more complicated turn. I stare out the window, working through the deal he offered as I watch the yachts and sailboats glide along the water that's more home to me than this piece of rock.

What the fuck am I going to do now?

I don't know why I bother asking myself the question. There's only one outcome I will accept.

I hit a button on my phone and wait two minutes for a knock to come at my office door. "Enter."

Koba pushes open the door and steps inside. "Information from the airport just came in. Another passenger was added the manifest of de Vere's flight to Monaco before it departed, just like you said."

That traitorous bitch. She did exactly what I thought she would.

"Call the pilot. Fuel the jet."

"We're going to Monaco, sir?"

"Yes." I lean back in my chair and steeple my fingers as I stare out at the sea. "It's time to retrieve my property."

20

INDIA

"What do you mean, it's been declined? This is an unlimited card. Do you know what that means? It's literally impossible for it to be declined." Bastien speaks to the clerk at the Casino de Monte Carlo like he's an idiot.

"I suggest you call your bank, sir. Perhaps they can explain the mistake I've surely made."

The clerk is trying to allow Bastien to save face, but Bastien isn't taking the lifeline. Instead, he snatches the card out of the man's hand and stalks away, passing me as he leaves the private office.

"So sorry for the inconvenience, madam," the clerk says to me.

"Don't worry about it. It's not your fault. I'm sure there's some kind of red tape. I mean, how often does someone try to get $2 million as a cash advance on a credit card?"

The clerk's shrug gives me the impression that this might not be such an unusual request, even though he doesn't voice it. I'm not sure why I'm surprised. We're in one of most exclusive casinos in the entire world. Citizens of Monaco aren't even allowed in the door of the Casino de Monte Carlo, with its overload of gilt and crystal decor.

I leave the office and search for Bastien, wondering if I've made a horrible error in judgment by coming here.

Beggars can't be choosers. Even when they're playing both sides of the game.

I find Bastien on his phone as he paces the lobby, and spot his sister off to the side, glass of champagne in hand, watching with a catlike smile on her face.

It doesn't take a genius to figure out his little sister is extremely satisfied with the current state of affairs. Bastien is the black sheep of the de Vere family, but somehow that never stopped his ever-flowing fount of money before, which makes me wonder why now . . .

Fuck.

Me.

That's why now.

She turns her gaze on me and the mirth doubles. "How do you like him now that he's a pauper? Gold diggers like you are all the same. You'll be out that door faster than he can find out that he's been disowned. Don't worry, I already made sure to tell the casino manager. He's doted on me since I was a little girl."

The knot that's been my companion since the moment I got the call about Summer twists in the pit of my stomach.

This bitch has no idea what she just did. Because if Bastien doesn't have a stake to sit the game, *then there is no game for me either*. Even with my reputation from the poker tour and the million-dollar stake I got from Forge, no one will give me a seat at a table in Monte Carlo with a pot big enough to win what I need. I don't belong to the old boys' club of the rich and powerful. I don't have Bastien's connections.

And now, he doesn't have his connections anymore either.

I just took the biggest risk of my life getting on Bastien's jet—defying Forge's direct order—and it was for nothing.

Fuck. Fuck. Fuck.

I thought I was being so smart by playing them both. Taking Forge's money and using Bastien's contacts to get in the game so I could save Summer.

Visions of my sister being bought by some man with more money than morals crash through my brain, sending more stabbing pains into my stomach.

I'm so sorry, Summer. I'm going to find a way. I promise. I'll play a smaller-stakes table here and gamble until I find someone who knows how to get me into a private game nearby. Yes. That'll work. I will find a fucking way, Summer. I swear it.

"You can't cut me off! Not because of this!" Bastien's hair stands up on end as he yells into his phone, creating a scene for the gathering crowd. I want to melt into it and disappear.

I take one step back when a deep rumble of laughter echoes in the lobby. I whip my head around to face the source of the sound.

No. Not possible.

How in the hell did Forge find us so quickly?

The percussion of his slow clap draws the attention of the onlookers who have assembled near Bastien.

"This is fucking priceless. The family finally cut you off and derailed the gravy train."

Bastien lowers his phone and bares his teeth before rushing forward and launching himself at Forge. Poppy screams as the two men collide in a flurry of fists and black-and-white formal wear.

I walk toward her slowly, my Prada pumps clicking against the floor. I knew I shouldn't have worn them. They're still carrying the bad luck from my game at La Reina.

When I stop in front of Poppy, her hand covers her red lips as she gasps. "Someone has to stop them. Now. Right now. He's going to hurt him."

"I thought that was your goal? Hurt your brother in any way possible?"

She jerks her attention to my face. "I just didn't want him marrying the same slut who ruined his wedding before."

"For your information, your brother arranged that scene all by himself. I didn't know he was engaged. In fact, I'm pretty sure someone drugged me that night, and I don't remember a goddamned thing. I don't even know if he *slept in the same bed as me.*"

Poppy's eyes bulge, but a loud *smack* of flesh on flesh drags our attention back to the fight. Security bears down on both men.

Oh shit. No. No. No.

This can't be happening. If they get kicked out . . . there won't even be a small-stakes game for me to play, and my silent promise to my sister will be completely worthless.

My breathing turns shallow as my body trembles so hard, my hands shake.

I can't lose this chance. I can't lose this chance.

I back away slowly, attempting to fade into the crowd, but Poppy wraps her hand around my arm and calls out to security.

"She's with them too. Don't forget to throw her out!"

That fucking cunt.

One of the security guards comes toward me as Forge shoves Bastien off him and straightens the lapels of his tux before his gaze sweeps over the gawkers. *Looking for me.*

The security guard motions for me to leave, and I consider bolting to avoid both Forge and Bastien, and maybe even have a shot at disappearing into a game before anyone can catch me. It won't be any use, though. They'll tackle me to the floor and then throw me out.

If I have to go down, I'm not going alone.

I grab Poppy and give her wrist a hard yank. "She's with them too."

At the sound of my voice, Forge's dark gaze locks onto my face.

Shit. Shit. Shit. He's fucking pissed. A wave of apprehension sweeps over me as he surveys me from head to toe.

I knew this was a risk. I took it willingly. But the risk seemed inconsequential compared to the immediacy of needing to save Summer. Now . . . the risk is staring me right in the face with gray eyes promising retribution.

I glance over my shoulder, again calculating my odds of disappearing into the casino.

It'll never work.

"Ms. Baptiste." Forge's voice cracks like a whip. "I believe we have matters to discuss."

He's wrong. We don't have a damn thing to discuss, because *I just lost my next best chance to save my sister.*

"All of you, please leave the premises immediately." More security guards have joined the first responders, attempting to disburse the crowd as both Forge and Bastien walk toward the door.

Salt-tinged air hits my face as I'm shown outside the casino, and my entire body trembles with the reality of my situation. *I have to get back inside. I can't lose this chance. Alanna is going to be devastated.*

Spinning around, I dart back toward the building, but a large hand clamps over my wrist, stopping me before I take two steps.

"You're not—" Forge says, but I fucking lose it.

With a jerk of my wrist, I scream, "Let me go! I have to get back inside! I have to play!"

My entire body shakes, but his grip holds firm. With what little energy I have left, I swing around to slap at his arm with my purse.

"Let me go! You don't understand!"

21

FORGE

ears spill down India's cheeks, and her screams turn piercing. For a moment, I think she's pretending, but the tremors rippling through her body tell me otherwise. Unless she's a great actress, India Baptiste is coming unhinged.

She smacks me with her hand before tugging at my grip again and lashing out with her clutch. It narrowly misses the mirror of my Bugatti that's parked by the valet.

"India, *stop*," I tell her, but she's unable to be reasoned with as she dissolves into sobs. Her hair tangles in front of her face and her knees bend, on the verge of giving out.

Her arm whips out again, and I release her wrist. She starts to crumple before I wrap my arms around her from behind and pick her up off her feet.

"Enough, Indy. Enough."

"No! You don't understand! I can't—" Whatever she's going to say is choked off by a sob.

"Let her go, Forge! Fucking let her go!" de Vere yells

at me as he disentangles himself from the hold security has on his arm.

"Leave her, Bastien. You've done enough damage already," de Vere's sister screeches as the casino guests pour outside to continue watching the scene.

"Get me away from them. Please." India's request is low and barely audible, but I don't need to hear it twice.

I set her on her feet and wrap an arm around her shoulders. She's pale and trembling and looks like she's been through hell and back. I don't know what the fuck happened before I arrived, but she looks like she's about to pass out.

"Don't you dare—" de Vere's threat gets lost in the crowd as the valet rushes forward with the keys to my black-and-silver Bugatti.

"Fuck off, de Vere. She's not yours to worry about anymore."

The valet opens the passenger door for India, and I help her inside as the LED lights illuminate the black-and-white leather interior.

Once I'm inside, the Chiron roars to life with all of its 1500 horsepower, and I check the mirrors before peeling out from the front of the casino and down the drive. One glance at the rearview shows de Vere staring at us as we speed away.

I always win, de Vere. You should know that by now.

In the passenger seat, India fumbles along the door panel, searching for something, and I hope it's not the door handle so she can jump out.

"What do you need?"

"Air. I can't . . . I can't breathe."

Fuck. "Do you need a hospital? Did he hurt you?"

Her chin snaps toward me. "Hurt me? No. I just . . ." Her chest rises and falls faster and faster, and a thought occurs to me.

"Are you having a panic attack?"

She presses both hands to her face, and her entire body shakes.

"Calm down, Indy. Just calm down."

She drops her hands. "I can't calm down! I'm running out of time!"

I take the turn toward the harbor, grateful that Monte Carlo isn't large or crushed with traffic tonight, and a few moments later, I turn down the quay. The rear hydraulic door of the yacht is open, waiting for me to drive aboard.

Koba rushes toward the stern, gun drawn, likely from the roar of the Chiron's engine and the speed at which I approach. It wouldn't be the first time I've had to make a quick getaway from somewhere. But tonight, I have completely different reasons, and they all have to do with India Baptiste.

As soon as she realizes we're driving off the quay and onto a ship, her eyes dart from window to window. "What the hell are you doing?"

I shut off the engine as the door lifts behind us and turn to her.

"Kidnapping you."

22

INDIA

*K*idnapping me?

He can't be serious. At least, if he were anyone else, he wouldn't be serious. But with Jericho Forge . . . I have no idea what to expect.

He exits the car—one that looks like it's straight out of a futuristic movie—and rounds the long hood.

My head buzzes as the passenger door swings open.

Why did I ask him to take me away from the casino? My brain isn't functioning right, because I can't even answer my own question.

I trip as I try to climb out, and he catches me around the waist with both hands. Before I can speak, my feet leave the ground as he lifts me into his arms.

"Put me—"

"Shut up, Indy."

A woozy feeling washes over me, and I comply, but only because I'd prefer not to puke on a tux that no doubt cost more than my rent.

As he carries me through the bowels of the boat, my

body relaxes against him almost against my will. As much as I hate to admit it, having his solid arms holding my weight gives me a sense of safety I haven't felt since I got the call from the men who have Summer.

But it shouldn't. He's just as dangerous. Maybe even more so, because I still can't figure out what he wants from me.

"Why did you follow me?"

He glances down at me with those unreadable gray eyes. "We had a deal, and you broke your word. That's a cardinal sin."

He's right. I did. I knew I was going to the moment his henchman with the dreads delivered me back to the pier from his island.

"I had no choice."

"You always have a choice, Indy."

It's the second time he's said my nickname, and it sounds strangely good coming from his lips. *Because I'm losing my goddamned mind.*

My hands shake as he carries me to a glass cylinder that parts as we approach. As soon as we step inside, the doors close. When we begin to rise, I grip his shoulders tighter, like I'm afraid I'll fall.

"It's an elevator. Calm down," Forge says as we soar up to a silver-and-white hallway, broken up by modern art. The doors slide open, and he steps out.

This is ridiculous.

Another set of double glass doors slide open, and he steps inside what looks like a main salon. Planks of reclaimed wood line the floors beneath the white leather furniture and navy and gray accents. A white granite sideboard, shot with threads of silver, holds a plethora of matched decanters. Strips of LED lights give off a warm glow, inviting someone to sit down rather than run away, because it appears too fancy for the average human.

I don't know why I'm surprised we just *drove onto a superyacht*, but I am. Forge is a billionaire who throws around checks for a million dollars like they're pennies, so why wouldn't he own one.

When he sits me down on a surprisingly cushy sofa, I squeeze my eyes shut and try to concentrate on something other than how screwed I am right now—and not just because my brain is reminding me how much I like the smell of his skin.

Pull it together, Indy.

I open my eyes to the sound of ice clinking in a glass, and Forge watching me out of the corner of his eye as he pours amber-colored liquid over the ice at the sideboard.

"I don't need—"

"You don't know what you need right now."

My mouth drops open at such a high-handed comment. "Excuse me?"

"You're acting like a gambling addict desperate for a game, so clearly you're not making good decisions. You took my million and then walked right to de Vere. Only someone stupid or desperate goes against my orders."

"I did what I had to do," I say as I push up off the sofa.

"Sit the fuck down. You're not going anywhere."

I whip the check he gave me out of my purse and tear it to shreds, letting them fall to the wood floor like confetti. "There you go. I didn't cash your check, so you don't have a goddamned thing to say about what I do. I'm walking off this fucking boat and going to find someone who'll stake me, and then I'm going to play."

My voice trembles as I speak. I have no idea where I'm going to find the resources to make my bold words into truth . . . especially now that my best shot at having a stake is now scattered on the floor.

Shit. Why did I do that? Why don't I think before I act when he's around?

Forge crosses the room, carrying the glass, and grabs my fisted hand before I can take a single step. He peels my fingers open and wraps them around the tumbler.

"You aren't getting off this boat without my permission. Drink your fucking whiskey while I decide what the hell to do with you."

"You can't keep me here. I'm not a fucking prisoner."

His roughly carved features shift, breaking into a roguish smile. "Did you think I was joking about the kidnapping? Because I wasn't."

He's fucking impossible.

"You want me to drink? Fine." I drain the contents and shove the glass back at him. "Done. Now I'm leaving."

His grin fades. "Sit. The. Fuck. Down. If I have to tell you again, you'll be facedown over my knee, with my handprint burning on your ass."

The dark edge to his threat gives me pause, and I plop down. He's the only person who has ever threatened to spank me in my life, and just like the last time, a flare of heat ignites between my legs. This *should not* turn me on.

It has to be the alcohol. *Another lie.*

Forge's fingertips brush over my hand as he takes the glass from me, sending shivers of pleasure up my arms that shoot straight to my nipples. They pebble into hard points, pressing against the thin fabric of my red dress. Forge misses nothing. His stormy gray eyes dip before meeting my gaze again, as if daring me to disobey and give him a reason to follow through on his threat.

My breathing catches as he stares at me like he's once again trying to read my mind.

If he knew what I was thinking, would he sit down beside me and flip me over his lap, pull my dress up, and find out just how wet I am before he spanked me?

Banked fire smolders as he takes a step away from me. Then another. And another. He doesn't break eye contact until he reaches the sideboard and pours another measure into my glass, and more into a second one.

When he turns around, his expression is blank once more.

I swear, this man has a split personality for how well he can control his emotions. *A talent I wish I had right now.*

He takes a sip of his drink, and my pulse kicks up as he continues to stare. Finally, he speaks. "Why do you need money so badly?"

"I can't tell you."

He reverses his path from before, taking one measured step toward me at a time before pressing my glass into my hand. "You're not leaving this boat until you tell me."

I curl my fingers around the drink and lift it to my lips without breaking his stare. I drain it and embrace the warm punch of the liquor rushing through my system. For a moment, the crushing anxiety that gripped me outside the casino seems to subside. I stand again on semi-steady legs and silently turn in a circle to survey the decadent wood, granite, and leather interior of the ship, because it's definitely nothing so pedestrian as a *boat*.

For a single moment, I let myself pretend that I could escape from all my problems here. Even if it was just for a day.

"Maybe I'd be okay with that." I stop my circling to meet Forge's stare. The smolder is back, and I immediately regret my words.

He moves toward me as he speaks. "Women are only on this boat for two reasons—to fuck or to serve. Which role are you taking?"

His vulgar statement reminds me of how he turned me down Saturday night in my room at the casino hotel.

"You don't want to fuck me, so I guess that leaves only one option."

"Who says I don't want to fuck you?" His dark gaze travels over my body, leaving tendrils of fire everywhere it touches.

"You did."

With his glass dangling from his fingers, he takes another step toward me. "I didn't want a martyr laid out like a cold fish. When I fuck you, you'll be a full and willing participant."

"When?" I laugh, trying to take another sip from my already empty glass. "You're arrogant as hell." For some reason, when I say the words, my gaze drops to his crotch, and through the thin material of his tux pants, there's no mistaking the bulge.

"Call me whatever you want, but first, you have a story

to tell me." Forge spins around to snag the decanter and crosses the room to refill my glass again.

I know I shouldn't drink it, but right now, my capacity for good decision making is shot. For one night, I want to forget that my sister is being held—

No. Stop.

I take another sip of the liquor and let it lie on my tongue, appreciating the flavor. *Forge's mouth would taste the same way.*

Nope. Not thinking about that either.

"I need money. End of story."

"Quit lying, Indy, and maybe you'll find that I'm a good ally. Because whatever you need, I have." His full lips tempt me not only to tell him what he wants to know, but also to lean up and taste them.

No. I tear my gaze away from his mouth, trying to break the spell. It doesn't work, so I go with the only thing that I know will—some of the truth.

"If I tell you, I'm risking someone's life, and I can't take that chance."

Forge moves closer, and I want to soak up the heat radiating off him. "Whose life?"

"I can't tell you."

His fingers lift my chin, forcing me to meet his gaze. "This yacht has the latest technology available. No one will hear a goddamned thing you say while you're on board. It's routinely swept for bugs. You might as well be trapped in a snow cave in Siberia."

With every word out of his mouth, he's seducing me into trusting him, but I know I shouldn't.

DEAL WITH THE DEVIL

His thumb sweeps along my cheek. "India Baptiste, you are an extraordinary woman with immense talent . . ."

The compliment and his touch do something to me. My body moves toward his instinctively.

"But you're also extraordinarily stupid not to tell me right now."

I jerk away from him. "And you're a fucking dick."

His gaze drops to his crotch, and mine follows again.

Did the bulge get bigger?

"I might be a dick, but I'm a rich dick, and there isn't a problem you have that I can't throw money at to fix. Tell me what I want to know now, or I'm going to get you drunk, seduce you, and then you'll tell me every secret you've ever kept."

I choke out a laugh at his overconfident statement. "You can't expect me to fall in line with your plan when you tell me in advance."

"I always get what I want."

I press my lips together before taking another sip. Lack of food since breakfast makes the liquor go to my head faster than it normally would, so I retake my seat on the sofa. I rarely have more than one drink because I need my wits about me at the poker table.

But something in my gut tells me to lay it all out and let Forge help me solve the problem I'm facing. Of all the people I've met in my life, he may be the one man who actually could.

I know I can't do this alone. I've already tried and failed, and the days are ticking away. No doubt I'll get another call from the unknown number telling me how disappointed they are in my failing to sit a game in Monaco, and threaten Summer's life again.

What if they lose their patience? What if they won't wait the entire five days I have left for the money? Am I really willing to gamble my sister's life on their word? Am I willing to gamble it on Jericho Forge's?

Bastien said something to me Saturday night that echoes through my head now. *At least I'm the devil you know.*

In this moment, Forge is that devil, because Bastien can't help me anymore.

I take another sip and close my eyes, unable to believe what I'm about to say. "You can't tell anyone. I can't go to the police or Interpol. It is literally a matter of life and death."

"You have my word."

With a deep breath, I let it all spill out. "I need $10 million in five days or my sister is going to be auctioned off to the highest bidder by sex slavers."

Forge's dark gaze turns flinty. "Who has her?"

"I don't know. They call from an unknown number."

"When and how did they take her?"

"Five days ago. She was . . ." I pause, not wanting to share the humiliating part of the story.

The sofa dips beside me from Forge's weight as he sits. "If you don't tell me everything, I can't help you."

I tell him as I stare into the remains of my whiskey. "She was playing in an underground poker game. She was losing, so she cheated. They caught her. It was a $5 million pot, and they want double to get her back. They said if I told anyone . . . they'd kill her. And me. And Alanna."

I flick my gaze to the side to get a read on his reaction. Neither his posture nor his expression change. I decide to take that as a good sign.

"Do you have a recent picture of her? Or a video? Something?"

I nod. "Yes. Both."

"Give them to me." He holds out his hand.

"They're on my phone. Give me a minute." I sit my glass on the floor and flip my clutch open, trying to hold back the relief bursting to life in my chest. "You're really going to help me get her back?" I ask as I tap the code to unlock my phone.

He doesn't answer until I meet his gaze. "I'm going to investigate the situation."

Okay, that's not a yes, but also not a no . . .

"But I don't do anything for anyone without getting something in return."

I should have expected him to say that. My heart hammers harder as I study the austere lines of his face, softened only by the stubble that seems to permanently color his jaw.

"What do you want?"

One eyebrow rises. "From you? For $10 million? You should already know the answer to that." The corners of his mouth lift until his expression is the picture of sheer triumph. "Every-fucking-thing."

23

INDIA

*E*very-fucking-thing. The word vibrates through my body, hardening my nipples further and intensifying the thrumming pulse between my legs.

"At the risk of repeating what happened at La Reina, I'm keeping my clothes on," I tell him, my voice sounding husky, even to my ears.

"Good, because when I want them off, I'll strip you myself."

A shiver rolls down my spine. *How can words affect me so much?* But it's not just the words. It's the man.

Forge turns on the sofa and reaches toward me. I flinch when his thumb strokes the pulse point fluttering in my neck. He pauses, his dark gaze penetrating mine.

"You're afraid of me."

My lips press together as I think of a way to answer without sounding stupid. I decide to go with the truth. "I'm not used to being touched. Not . . . not like this."

His gaze intensifies as he caresses my skin and curls

his other fingers around the side of my throat. "You can't say things like that to a man like me."

Slickness gathers between my legs, and I'm moments away from climbing him. *It's the alcohol. Right?*

Whatever the reason, I've never been drawn to a man as powerfully as I am to Jericho Forge. He's like a black hole, and I'm helpless to resist the gravity sucking me in. *Because I'm an idiot.*

Even that knowledge doesn't dim the effect of the warmth radiating off him or the delicious salty fresh scent of man that surrounds me. Every brush of his fingertips across my throat is intoxicating.

"Why can't I say things like that?" I whisper.

"Because then I'll want to do this."

He shifts his grip and pulls me onto his lap. My knees spread, one landing on either side of his thighs as he cups the back of my neck with one hand and slides the other down to palm my ass.

With a rough tug, he yanks me against his body until my every curve is pressed against rock-hard muscle hidden beneath his tux. Except one part isn't hidden at all. The bulge is an iron rod, and I can't help but shift against it. Forge's mouth hovers over my lips for a second, and I stare at him as his gaze pierces straight through me.

One heartbeat. Two. Three.

I don't know what he's waiting for, but I'm dying to feel his lips on mine. His expression changes just before his mouth crashes down.

This is no soft, sweet kiss. It's a storming of the gates, and my defenses are already in shambles. He demands entrance and my lips part, letting his tongue charge through.

Just like I thought earlier, the whiskey tastes even better mixed with him.

I release a low moan as he grips my ass tighter and lifts me to press harder against his cock. He's a marauder, plundering just like the pirate I thought he was the first time I saw him. He takes without permission or apology.

And I love it.

I rock my hips, and lust lights up every nerve ending. I need this. Need him. Want him. With a desperation I haven't felt in . . . well, ever.

The kiss goes on and on, and the liquor goes straight to my head, releasing me from my inhibitions as I bury my fingers in his hair. I tug at the long strands, pulling him closer. Begging him silently to kiss me harder. To take more. To make me forget this mess I've found myself in, even if it's just for a few minutes.

My body is primed and ready. Wetness soaks my panties. I've never been so hard up for a man in my life.

And then he stops.

Like he flipped a switch, Forge's body stiffens, and his hands leave my neck and my ass to go to my hips as he sets me away from him on the sofa and rises to his feet.

What the . . .

I stand up, reaching out to grab him by the lapels, but he holds me at arm's length.

"Sit down, Ms. Baptiste."

"Why? What the fuck, Forge?"

"This isn't happening. Not here. Not now." His roughened voice tells me he's not as unaffected as he wants me to believe.

My attention drops to the massive hard-on testing the strength of the thin material of his pants.

"You're turning me down again? Are you serious? Because your dick has a severe problem with your decision."

He narrows his eyes on me and then nods to the floor. "Then feel free to take care of it, but I'm not fucking you."

The heat burning through my veins turns to anger, and my hands clench into fists. "Oh, hell no. You can fuck right off, Forge. What the hell is wrong with you?"

His gaze turns heavy-lidded as he studies me.

I know he wants me. *So, why isn't he taking what he wants?*

Forge's hands drop away from me, and he steps back. He touches a finger to a glass panel next to the sideboard, and one square illuminates with blue light. Ten seconds later, a man enters the room.

"Get Ms. Baptiste dinner," Forge says without looking at him.

Dinner? He thinks I want food?

"I don't—"

Forge's chin cuts toward me, silencing my protest. "You'll eat, and then you'll send the photos and videos to the email Koba gives you."

With his final order delivered, he turns and walks out the same doors the other man just walked in.

That motherfucker.

Before he disappears from sight, I catch a glimpse of his hands flexing into fists and releasing.

What the hell is Jericho Forge's game?

24

FORGE

*T*he feel of her skin sears my palms. I shouldn't have touched her. Shouldn't have kissed her. Not yet. Not like this.

I have plans for India Baptiste, and while I should be glad she has no aversion to fucking me, I can't allow myself to be distracted.

And, holy fuck, is she distracting.

I've had some of the most beautiful women in the world throw themselves at me, and not a single one has affected me like she does. Not even my most skilled mistress could turn my dick rock hard so fucking fast.

It's not just the curves of India's body that I want to learn every inch of, or her stunning face. It's her. Her attitude. Her grit. Her determination. *Her loyalty to her sister, even though the girl fucked up.*

If I'm being honest with myself, there's nothing that could suck me in faster than that.

Which means I have to be vigilant. I can't let myself see her as more than a means to an end. But my cock has other ideas. I try to think of anything to deflate it as I head for my office on board, but nothing works.

I'm too old, and honestly, too fucking rich, to take care of my hard-on by jacking off in the shower. It was on a whim that I told her she could handle it herself, but I don't know what I would have done if she'd dropped to her knees right there in the salon.

Bullshit. I know exactly what I would have done.

I would have unzipped my pants and watched her blue eyes go wide when she caught sight of my dick. I'd have let her lick and suck and try to swallow me down until she gagged on it with tears streaming from her eyes.

Then I would have gripped her by the nape of her neck, tilted her head back, and taught her—

Instead of going down, my dick hardens to the point of pain.

Fuck. Fuck. Fuck.

I need to concentrate, and not on how much I want to bend her over and fuck her mouth, her pussy, and her ass.

I walk into my office and shut and lock the door before heading straight into the attached bathroom.

Fuck it.

Within seconds, I've stripped, and the water from the shower pours over my shoulders. I wrap my hand around my cock and tug hard enough to punish myself for letting her steal my ironclad self-control.

With my head bowed, I brace myself against the wall as I jerk my dick, picturing her plump pink lips, and how fucking tight they're going to wrap around my cock while I show her exactly how I'd like to fuck her face.

God, I want to see that.

The picture becomes even clearer in my mind, and I would swear it's the most provocative sight I've ever had in my brain.

India Baptiste is another level.

Jesus, fuck.

My balls draw up, and I know it won't take long to shoot my load all over the shower wall.

I shouldn't come this fast. But there's no denying that I'm going to blow before I'm ready.

I don't bother to muffle my roar as lightning shoots down my spine, and I picture India swallowing every single drop of cum that spills out of me.

I stumble backward and crouch on the floor of the shower, letting the water rush over me, like it's going to erase the traces of what I just did. But nothing will. India Baptiste is under my skin.

Fucking hell. I knew she was going to be a problem. I knew it. I also know exactly what I'm going to do next.

INDIA

I'm alone in the salon when a noise that sounds like a wounded, enraged animal rumbles through the ship.

Was that Forge? I stand up and whip my head around, waiting to hear pounding footsteps of people running to the rescue, but there's no sound at all until the blond guy returns with a tray and sets it on the round table in the back corner of the salon.

"Did you hear that sound?"

He looks at me blankly. "I'm paid not to hear anything, Ms. Baptiste."

Um. That's awkward and weird. Now I want to know about all the things he's been paid "not to hear."

"So, just to be clear, you did hear it, or you didn't hear it?" I ask.

"I hope you enjoy your dinner, ma'am."

I manage to stem the urge to roll my eyes. "I said I didn't want anything."

"Mr. Forge said you're eating, so you're eating."

With a mulish set to my jaw, I cross my arms. "Not unless Mr. Forge plans to force-feed me."

It may be the new glass of whiskey I helped myself to that's making me so impertinent, or it could be the fact that I really despise being told what to do by strangers.

"Mr. Forge is otherwise engaged at present, but he'll be quite unhappy if he finds out that his orders haven't been followed."

"Then that's his problem," I say as I walk to a sofa in the opposite corner of the salon from where he placed the tray.

My snappish comment is fueled by the fact that the man left me with a heinous case of female blue balls, and now all I need is a goddamned orgasm so I can clear my head and figure out what the hell my next step is if Forge can't or won't help me get Summer back.

The man holds out a business card. "Send any pictures and videos of your sister to this email address."

So the blond guy is Koba. Got it.

I reach out and snatch it from him. It's a black card with nothing but an email that's a long string of numbers followed by a domain I don't recognize.

"That, I can do. But you might as well take the food away. It's going to go to waste here."

"I follow orders, regardless of whether you like them. Enjoy your meal, Ms. Baptiste."

Well, that makes one of us, I think as Koba turns and leaves the room.

I move to the decanters and top off my drink, but decide to send the pictures before I sip. My capacity for doing anything useful is disappearing with every taste of whiskey.

After opening my email, I attach pictures of Summer and a video I have of her dancing around Alanna's flat last Christmas. I type in the email address, checking it three times to make sure I got it right, and hit SEND.

With my glass in hand, I toss my phone on the sofa and take a long pull of the whiskey. Delicious scents emanate from the covered tray, and against my will, my stomach growls.

Goddammit. I'm not hungry.

Curiosity gets the better of me, and I lift the lid to see a succulent piece of white fish on what looks like mashed sweet potatoes, topped with sliced almonds, edamame, and a lemony butter sauce.

Seriously? Someone just threw together a gourmet meal for a late-night snack? Then I remember where I am. A superyacht owned by a billionaire. Gourmet is probably all that's on the menu, regardless of the time of day.

I take another deep breath, and the glass of whiskey in my hand wobbles. Maybe it'll blunt my hangover in the morning if I eat . . .

With that reasoning in mind, I sit down and take a single bite. It melts in my mouth. Before I know it, the plate is clear.

"I knew you would eat."

Koba's voice comes from the doorway, and I whip my head around.

"Jesus Christ. You scared the hell out of me."

He comes forward to retrieve the tray. "Mr. Forge told me to keep an eye on you."

"Where did he go? He and I need to have a discussion." I toss my napkin on the silver lid before he moves it out of range.

"Busy," Koba says before leaving the way he came. As he steps through the sliding glass doors, he adds, "I'll return to show you to your cabin shortly."

I don't bother to reply. Instead, I help myself to enough whiskey to make me forget I have a single care in the world.

INDIA

*B*right light stabs my eyeballs like spears of fire as I open them. "Oh God. Turn off the light."

When there's no answer and no dimming of the surface of the sun beating down on me, I shield my eyes and roll over on the silky-smooth sheets of the bed.

Wait. What bed?

I sit up with a start and clasp the sheet to my chest, even though I'm still wearing my dress from last night.

I don't remember leaving the salon. I certainly don't remember getting into a king-size bed and curling up under the sheet fully clothed.

Rising from the bed, I slowly take in the massive cabin. It has the same reclaimed wood floors as the salon, but the walls are dark gray and the sheets are navy blue. It's dark and masculine.

This is Forge's cabin. All I have to do is breathe in deeply to catch the hint of sandalwood and fresh man-scent I smelled on him the night at La Reina.

I check the pillow beside the one I used. It shows no

signs of being disturbed. *Forge didn't sleep here.* Where is he?

My bladder protests that his whereabouts doesn't matter right this moment, and I glance around and spot a door across the room that I hope leads to the facilities.

I push it open, and instead of finding a luxurious en-suite bathroom, I find an office with a large desk and computer monitors mounted on it. I turn to leave, but I catch sight of something on the desk that shouldn't be there.

My phone.

It's connected to a laptop with a cord.

What the hell?

I stalk over to it and pick it up. Sure enough, it's mine. I tap the screen, and instead of bringing up the lock screen, it opens without a password.

He hacked into my phone. What. The. Fuck?

I yank out the cord and storm out of the bedroom, propelled by fury. The next door I yank open leads to the bathroom. *That works too.*

After making quick work of the facilities, I try the rest of the doors in the cabin until I find the one that leads to a bright white hallway that extends in acres of wood in both directions.

Forge is somewhere on this damn boat, and when I find him, I'm going to rip him a new one for invading my privacy. I sent him the damn pictures. What else did he need that he had to hack my phone?

"Ms. Baptiste, can I help you?" a woman with dark hair slicked back into a tight bun asks. She's wearing what must be the ship uniform of a navy polo with a silver logo in the shape of a stylized *F* on the breast, paired with white slacks and deck shoes.

"Yes, I'm looking for Mr. Forge. Can you take me to him?"

The woman's expression stays completely placid. "I'm afraid he's unavailable right now, Ms. Baptiste."

"You don't understand. This is an urgent matter. It can't wait." I clutch my phone in my hand, and even though I want to show her and explain exactly why I need to see the hacking bastard, I don't.

"I'm sorry—" she says, starting to apologize and give me another excuse.

"Can you at least tell me if he's on the boat?" I watch her face for any flicker of information that might be helpful.

"In a matter of speaking."

"What does that mean?" I glance around like he's going to pop out of the ceiling. He doesn't.

"Ms. Baptiste, if you'd please come with me to the salon, we have breakfast waiting for you. Mr. Forge will join you at his leisure."

At his leisure? I repeat silently. My temper begins to rear its ugly head, but I remind myself it's not this woman's fault that he stole my phone and hacked into it. Forge is the only one who needs to answer for that.

"If you follow me, you'll be one step closer to speaking with him." The woman spins on her deck shoes and moves efficiently down the hallway.

I have two choices, and pouting like a child isn't going to get me anywhere. Besides, the more ground I can cover, the more likely it is that I'll find Forge. It may be a massive boat, but there are only so many places the man could hide.

We reach the salon, which I remember from last night, despite the throbbing in my head from too much whiskey. Beyond the sliding glass doors, there's nothing but blue ocean, even though the boat isn't moving.

What the hell? We left Monaco?

"Where are we?"

The woman, whose name I still don't know, follows my gaze out the window. "The Mediterranean."

I blink repeatedly, but the view outside doesn't change. "The *middle* of the Mediterranean?"

She shrugs. "Not exactly the middle."

"Where are we going?" I ask as I step closer to the windows.

"I'm afraid I'm not at liberty to share that information with you right now. But if you'll wait for Mr. Forge, I'm sure he'll answer your questions."

My brain spins in a hundred different directions as I stare out at the gorgeous blue sea, and the only thing I can think is that with every nautical mile this boat has moved, I'm farther away from getting my sister back.

"Where the hell is he?" I turn to find that I've asked the question to an empty room, and there's nothing but silence as a reply.

I tap the screen on my cell phone to see if I have service, but of course, I don't. My wireless package doesn't exactly include middle-of-the-ocean capabilities.

That's when I hear a splash from somewhere beyond the large sliding glass doors at the rear of the salon.

I rush through them and find myself on a massive teak

sundeck, complete with white wooden loungers with navy-and-white striped cushions. In the middle of the deck is a pool. But that's not where the splash came from, because it's completely empty. I hurry to the side of the boat and spot someone with dark hair cutting through the water, stroke after strong stroke.

Forge.

It has to be him. I follow the railing of the boat to the stern to get a better look at the man.

Of course he'd get his exercise swimming in the middle of the goddamned ocean like he's Aquaman. Suddenly, visions of Jason Momoa flash through my mind, and the uncanny resemblance between the two men hits me. No wonder I think Forge looks like a pirate, because he's built like someone who plays a warrior superhero in movies.

Before I can open my mouth to yell at him, he dives underwater and disappears.

I count to sixty before panic filters into my system, overtaking the anger. *Where did he go? He can't drown. I need him!*

I grab the railing, craning my neck right and then left, looking for any sign of the man. When I see nothing, I spin around, looking for help. The sundeck is empty but for me.

Two sets of wide white fiberglass stairs curve down to the giant swim platform, and I pick one, stumbling in my haste. There's what looks like a large hidden door, which I would put money on is the one we drove into last night in the Bugatti.

But that doesn't help me. I need a life ring or something.

I scan the spotless white wall of fiberglass until I notice a raised white cross on another panel. With no idea how to actually open the thing, I take my chances and shove it with the heel of my hand. Hydraulics pop it open, and inside are life jackets and the orange floaty thing that you see the lifeguards use on *Baywatch*.

I yank it out of the compartment and turn . . . to see Forge hauling himself out of the ocean on a ladder that disappears down into the water from the swim platform. His broad shoulder muscles ripple as he pulls himself up, revealing his well-developed pecs and washboard abs.

I didn't think men over thirty could have abs like that. I was wrong.

And then he takes another step up, and I see a whole hell of a lot more. Jesus Christ. My mouth drops open as his cock comes into full view.

Blessed mother of all things holy. He's naked. Totally, completely naked.

And his dick is massive. And the ocean can't be super warm. Which means . . .

"It's like someone unleashed the Kraken," I whisper as he moves toward me, his dick bouncing from side to side with each step.

My gaze is glued to his cock. I have zero shame. I can't stop staring. It's . . . it's just *perfect* hanging there in all its glory, fresh from a dip in the Med.

"The Kraken?" Forge's entire body shakes as booming laughter tumbles from his lips.

But I'm not looking at his lips. I'm still watching his dick as it bobs when he laughs. It's also getting *bigger*.

"Are you going to look at my face or just stare at my dick?"

"I've seen your face before," I tell him, not looking up. I got caught staring; I might as well make the most of it.

When a navy towel with a silver monogram suddenly covers the object of my attention, I'm forced to glance up . . . at the most beautiful grin that has ever crossed a man's face.

Why is he so attractive? It's not right. Money, abs, a big dick, and drop-dead gorgeous? If I needed any more proof that life is definitely unfair, it's standing right in front of me. Even his laugh is perfect.

Stop, Indy. Get down to business. He hacked your phone.

"Stop laughing. This isn't swim time. This is *tell Indy why the fuck you hacked her phone* time, and *what the hell you want from me to get my sister back* time."

Forge doesn't stop laughing, though. He scrubs himself dry for several moments while chuckling.

My concentration is tested, because while he's doing that, I get little peeks of his beautiful cock every few seconds.

Stop acting like it's been a decade since you've seen a dick. Except it nearly has been, and I'm hard up.

I thought it was the whiskey last night, but it wasn't. It's Forge. He's the reason I can't keep my wits about me.

Start fixing that right now then, Indy.

I take a deep breath and drag my attention from his groin to his face. He's still smiling, and he needs to stop, because I can't handle those straight white teeth grinning at me when I know there's a monster cock hidden beneath that scrap of fabric. I'm just not built to withstand that kind of temptation. I don't have that kind of self-control.

But I will find it, I vow.

Forge knots the towel around his waist before his gaze darts behind me to where the cabinet is open and the lifeguard float is halfway yanked out of its storage space.

"Were you worried about me, Ms. Baptiste?"

Not willing to admit anything I've thought in the last five minutes, I press my lips together and try to come up with a decent-sounding lie.

"I thought I needed protection in case I had to beat you off. It would've been self-defense."

His lips curl up again in a way that I really, really need him to stop. "I don't know how you ever bluff in poker, because your lying skills need work."

"Oh, fuck off, Forge. My bluffing is superb."

I pin my attention to his right shoulder, where there's a hint of black ink snaking over from his back. *Sweet Jesus, he can't have tattoos too. That's just not fair.*

"If either of us needed to beat someone off, I'm guessing it'd be me. Did you get a good enough look, or do you want me to lose the towel?" He grips the knot with one hand, and part of me wants to tell him to drop it and then mount him right where we stand.

"I've never been a fan of the Kraken. Too angry."

His eyes close for a beat as his chest shakes again with laughter, and I remind myself why I tracked the man down before I got distracted by the beast between his legs.

"Why the hell did you hack my phone? I sent you—"

"Nothing. You sent me *nothing*. I assume you had a few too many drinks and couldn't manage the email address. Instead of losing precious time waiting for Sleeping Beauty to wake, I did what needed to be done. You can thank me later." He walks past me toward the staircase on the right. "I'm hungry. If you want to talk, you're going to have to do it while I eat."

This fucking arrogant bastard.

"Why the hell did we leave Monaco? You can't really kidnap me!" I yell as I follow him up the stairs. He stops at the top and I skid to a halt, barely missing running into his back.

Yep. That's a tattoo. A traditional sailor's anchor that does nothing but highlight the slabs of muscle that make up his back. I shove down the unfairness of it all as he turns to face me.

"You're free to leave anytime you'd like, Ms. Baptiste." Forge gestures to the open ocean. "Go right ahead."

"Unlike you, I don't swim like a fish."

"Probably because no one has ever tossed you off the side of the boat and asked if you wanted to live," he mutters under his breath as he walks toward the automatic glass doors, and I barely catch it before the ocean breeze whips it away.

"What did you say?"

He doesn't stop until he takes a seat at the table in the salon. "If you have special requests for the chef, feel free to relay them to Dorsey. She's been assigned to meet all of your needs while you're on board," he says as he shakes out a white napkin and drops it onto his lap.

"The chick with the navy polo and dark hair who

wouldn't tell me a damn thing?" I ask as I approach the table.

Forge pours himself a glass of what smells like freshly squeezed orange juice and takes a long drink before replying. "She doesn't need to tell you anything to do her job, which is to make sure you have what you need."

"What I need is some goddamned information. Did you find anything out about my sister? Are you going to help me get her back?"

Forge gestures to the chair across from him. "Sit. Eat."

"Why are you always trying to feed me?"

His dark gaze travels up my body, skimming every single curve still on display from the daring red dress I wore last night. "Do you really need to ask? I like tits and ass, and I wouldn't want you to start losing yours because I didn't keep you properly fed."

My mouth drops open as he lifts the lid off a steaming platter of scrambled eggs and moves half of them onto his plate.

"If you don't want answers to your questions, then don't sit and eat. Your choice, India."

I drop into the chair across from him with a huff.

Am I being a brat? Probably, but this man is maddening. I have no idea how to navigate this situation, and I'm doing the best I can.

I'm not the type of girl to roll over when life throws me a curveball, but that doesn't mean I know how to handle a man like Forge. He's attracted to me, that much I know, but he can turn it on and off like the flip of a switch. Obviously, he has self-control that I don't.

Adds SELF-CONTROL *to my mental list of things to work*

on, ten thousand lines below GET MY SISTER BACK BEFORE SHE'S AUCTIONED OFF AS A SEX SLAVE.

Forge eats his eggs with the assistance of a slice of crusty bread that looks absolutely divine.

So what if I'm capable of being both dick-struck and carb-struck. Sue me. I have weaknesses. I'm talking my pride into allowing me to steal a piece of bread when Forge speaks.

"You should really choose a more difficult pass code for your phone. Your sister's birthday is a pretty obvious choice. It wasn't hacking so much as getting it right on the second try."

I glare at him. "Aren't you smart. Do you want a cookie?"

"No, but I wouldn't turn down a blow job from your smart mouth."

My eyes widen, and I lock down the shock that must be reflected on my face.

"Are you always so crude?" I ask as I reach across the table to grab a hunk of the bread I was eyeing.

"I was raised on a ship full of men who fucked everything in sight as soon as we hit port. What do you think?"

I take a bite of the bread and chew the crunchy outer edge and soft middle of nutty deliciousness before replying. "You're American, aren't you?"

He watches me for a moment before nodding. "And you?"

"According to my passport, German. Which is funny, because I don't speak a word of the language."

His gaze narrows on me. "What about your sister? Does she have a German passport too?"

"No, she was born in Amsterdam. Our mom basically dragged us around Europe."

"What did she do?"

I shrug. "What didn't she do? If you asked her, she'd say she was a burlesque dancer, but mostly she just stripped and did peepshows and whatever else paid the bills. She taught me how to pick pockets when I was eight and she got pregnant with Summer. She thought she wouldn't be able to make rent. But it turns out, everyone has a kink, and you can make decent money stripping as a pregnant chick."

"This isn't the mother who was at your flat when Goliath stopped by." It's a statement rather than a question.

"Why would you assume that?"

"Because you don't sound like you have a whole lot of respect for the woman you said dragged you around Europe."

"Alanna's our adopted mom. She found us when I was sixteen and Summer was eight. She wouldn't leave us alone until I agreed to let her feed us."

"I think I'd like her," he says with a quirk of his lips, and I assume he's referencing the fact that he's always trying to feed me too. "What happened to your birth mom?"

I reach for another chunk of bread, even though I know it's going to go straight to my already curvaceous love handles. "Don't know. She left one night, a few months after we came to Ibiza, and never came back."

"When you were sixteen?" he asks before taking another drink of orange juice.

"Fifteen, almost sixteen. We made it about six months

on our own, and then Alanna came into the picture." I reach for the pitcher and pour myself a glass. I take a sip, and it's just as sweet and fresh as I hoped.

"That's not an easy life for a kid, especially trying to take care of a sibling."

"I did my best. I picked pockets. Learned to play cards. Then Alanna happened." I set the glass down and wave my hand around at the interior of the salon. "I'm guessing despite all of this, you didn't exactly have it easy as a kid either, did you? That's why you're such a hard-ass."

He chews a bite of his eggs and toast but doesn't answer my question. I feel like that's because I'm right.

Regardless, it doesn't matter. Only one thing does.

"What did you find out about Summer?"

He washes the food down with the remains of his orange juice and reaches for the carafe to refill his glass and mine. "Your sister got herself into a hell of a mess."

"I know. Trust me, *I know.*"

"Is that normal for her?"

My hand stills as I reach for my OJ. I glance up at Forge's unreadable expression. "Does it matter?"

"It is if she's constantly expecting her big sister to bail her out of trouble," he replies before lifting his napkin to his lips.

"She's my only family, Forge. I'll always do whatever I can to help her."

He puts his napkin down and leans both elbows on the table. "Even sell your own soul to do it?"

I swallow a lump in my throat. "If I have to."

Something flickers in his dark gaze, but I have no way of reading him.

"Good. Then you'll have no problem agreeing to my proposition."

"What proposition?"

He rises. "I'm going to shower, and I expect you to eat some protein. You have a busy day ahead of you."

"What do you mean, busy day?"

But he's already striding out of the room, the towel flapping around his calves . . . until it slips down, revealing a tanned and muscular ass you could bounce a quarter off.

Sweet Jesus.

Life is so unfair.

FORGE

J wrap my fist around my dick, one hand pressed to the wall of the guest shower. I haven't jacked off twice in twenty-four hours since I was fourteen fucking years old. But give me a woman in a rumpled red dress from the night before with a smart mouth and sassy attitude, and I'm harder than a steel beam.

She wants me to release the Kraken? She can have it anytime she wants.

My laughter echoes in the shower, and I stop what I'm doing for a moment to rest my head against the tile.

When was the last time someone made me laugh like that? I don't have an answer for the question, but as soon as her face pops back into my head, I finish myself off in record time, shooting my load down the drain.

Next time, I'm coming down her throat.

I make that promise to myself, but I also know there's no way in hell I'll take something that isn't offered. And after today . . . there's a good chance India Baptiste is going to want my head on a pike.

She'll get over it. Eventually.

Means to an end. That's all that matters.

I scrub the salt off my skin and think of how she was going for the rescue buoy, assuming I was drowning in the ocean. When was the last time someone was actually concerned about my safety when they weren't on my payroll?

No one since Isaac.

All lightness flees from my mind as I remind myself why we left Monaco—because de Vere was still there, and I wasn't taking a chance that he was going to attempt some last grand gesture to try to get the girl.

Not that I think de Vere is capable of grand gestures, but he's capable of fucking my life up beyond recognition. Which he's already done once, and I'm not giving him the opportunity to do it again.

I dress in khaki shorts and an unbuttoned white linen shirt I had Dorsey retrieve from my cabin. When I return to the salon, it's empty.

I press a button on the intercom panel to contact Dorsey. She responds immediately.

"Where is she?"

"Changing, sir. I'll escort her back to you as soon as she is finished."

"If you hear a splash, assume she jumped overboard and call out the crew."

"Yes, sir."

I move away from the intercom and check my phone. Fatigue from a night with no sleep might bother most people, but I'm used to it. However, I wasn't ready for the temptation of having India Baptiste asleep in my bed.

After I slid her under the covers, I left the room and forbade myself from returning. Because if I had . . .

Not thinking about that now. I don't have time for another shower.

A few minutes later, India follows Dorsey into the salon.

"Is your entire crew under orders not to share anything helpful with me?" India asks, frustration underlying her tone.

She's wearing clothes left on board by another female guest, which would no doubt piss her off, so I have no plans to tell her. The top definitely doesn't fit her quite the same way, because her tits are damn near about to fall out of it. I'm not complaining, however. She looks incredible, which shouldn't be possible in cast-off clothes and no makeup.

The corner of my mouth tugs upward, which happens all too often in her presence. This time it's because India Baptiste is a little liar. She made a big production out of the mess in her hotel room and how high-maintenance she is, but she looks even more entrancing fresh faced from the shower.

"The crew's orders are to see to your comfort. Information isn't necessary," I tell her.

"Information *is* necessary, Forge. Because if you don't tell me what your plan is or what the hell you want from me, I'm about to jump ship, and I'm not joking."

I look to Dorsey. "Leave us, please."

The steward nods and disappears.

India watches her leave and then looks back to me. "Cut the shit, Forge. It's time to lay out our cards."

INDIA

*H*is black hair is wet from his shower, and I can't help but wonder if he knows that I used the fancy showerhead in his bathroom to get myself off. I checked for cameras before I climbed in the shower, and then I realized how stupid I was being. It's *his* sanctuary. He wouldn't allow anyone to see anything in there.

I also poked through his cabinets and drawers, trying to find some insight into the man I'm dealing with. Other than high-end products and cologne that I might have thought about stealing, there was nothing useful to be learned.

After that, I tried to use his computer, but unlike me, his shit is impossible to hack into. None of the creative passwords I tried worked either, including *bigdickswinging69 and releasethekrakenwithindy*.

He stands before me now, his arms crossed over his chest, studying me like he's coming to some sort of decision.

"What, Forge? Just tell me already."

He's silent for another moment before he replies. "I'll bring your sister back to you safely, but in return, you have to do something for me, no questions asked."

That gives me pause. "What kind of something?"

He looks skyward, and I wonder if he's trying to find the patience to deal with me. He meets my gaze again, but this time, there's no humor in his expression at all.

"No questions asked, India. Do you understand what that means?"

I bite my lip because I have at least seventeen questions ready to fire off at him.

"I will tell you, though," he says, "it's not sexual in nature, but it is something that will be financially beneficial to me."

Not sexual in nature, but financially beneficial? Neither of those clues gives me any kind of assistance in solving the riddle that is Jericho Forge and what he wants in return for saving the person who matters most to me.

"Yes or no, Indy. You have sixty seconds to decide."

My eyes widen, and I blink several times in quick succession. "What? Sixty seconds? That's—"

"How it's going to be. It's not a hard decision. You shouldn't need more time to decide. After all, you did say you'd do anything, even sell your soul, to get your sister back, didn't you?"

I grit my teeth, because I want to say so many things, but none of those things are going to change the situation.

He glances at his watch. "Forty-five seconds."

I wait, on purpose, until he hits fifteen. "Fine. I'll do it. Whatever *it* is. *I'll do it.*"

I expect a victorious smile to spread over his features, but instead, he just nods without even a hint of humor.

"Come with me to the bridge."

"Yes, *sir*. Right away, *sir*," I say, my mocking quips not lost on the man, at least I assume not given his raised eyebrow before he leaves the salon.

I follow him outside, along the side of the yacht, through a single glass door and then up two curving flights of stairs through another set of double doors.

The captain and Koba both stand near the massive steering wheel of the yacht.

"Captain, can you confirm for me that we're in international waters?"

What the hell does that matter? Is he going to start diving for treasure and pull $10 million out of the ocean?

"Yes, Mr. Forge. We are indeed."

"And this ship is registered under the flag of a country that allows marriage at sea?"

What in the actual fuck is he talking about?

The captain nods again, but with confusion this time. "Yes, sir. That's correct."

"Excellent. Then you can do Ms. Baptiste and me the great honor of marrying us."

Forge did not *just say that.*

The captain looks just as shocked as I'm sure I do. "Sir?"

"Are you questioning my order, Captain?"

"No, sir. I just wanted to confirm that you, in fact, want me to perform a wedding ceremony right now. Between you and Ms. Baptiste?"

"Yes."

The captain looks around the room, as if to buy himself time to respond. "We'll need a second witness."

"Dorsey is on her way up with the marriage license."

Forge looks at me, as if waiting for me to say something. But for the first time in maybe my entire life, I'm speechless. Completely speechless. I don't know what to say or what to think. Nothing makes sense.

Am I still drunk? Am I dreaming? I reach down and pinch my arm, but the sting tells me I'm wide awake.

"Nothing to say, Ms. Baptiste?"

I stay quiet, watching him like he's about to sprout a second head at any moment.

Jericho Forge wants me to marry him? Why on earth could he possibly want to marry me? I recall his words in the salon.

"It is something that is financially beneficial to me."

I can buy that, but *why me*? I desperately want to ask the question, but I agreed to no questions. It takes everything I have to keep it inside.

Dorsey enters the bridge carrying a file folder and a pen. She hands them both to Forge. He flips the folder open and signs his name to a document.

"Where the hell did you get a marriage license?"

"Friends in high places."

I shake my head at him. "There is something severely wrong with you. Possibly a mental defect, because this isn't normal."

I take the pen from his hand and the piece of paper that reads CERTIFICATE OF MARRIAGE on the top. My hand hovers over the line waiting for my signature.

I glance up at Forge. "You're sure you want to do this?"

"No questions asked, Ms. Baptiste. That was the stipulation."

"I'm not asking for your reasons, Forge. I'll do it. I don't have a choice. But I need to know you're sure that this is the only way."

Something in his expression softens for a beat. "I'm sure." He presses his lips together and adds, "But you always have a choice with me, Indy. Choose wisely."

I study his face, looking for any semblance of a reason that he'd want to marry me, especially after he pushed me away last night.

All I see is unreadable dark gray eyes, and a face that haunts my waking and sleeping hours.

I bite my lip and make my decision.

I don't know whether it's the wise choice, but I scrawl my name on the signature line right below his.

He planned this. Last night, while I was asleep. Jericho Forge planned our goddamned wedding.

But why?

I hand him the license back, and he tucks it away in the file before reaching down to grab my hand and pull me next to him in front of the captain.

"Now, if you'll proceed, Captain."

I DON'T RECALL a single word the captain spoke. They all blurred together like I'd been plunged underwater. Then

Forge slides a ring onto my finger, bringing everything into laser-sharp focus.

It's a silver band with a big fat diamond in the middle. So, probably not silver. More likely platinum.

How does he have a ring? And how does it fit perfectly?

As the captain says, "You may kiss the bride," Forge's dark eyes lock onto my face as his mouth descends toward mine. Our lips collide, and it's no chaste kiss. No, it's possessive and hungry and all-consuming. His fingers curl around my upper arm and his hand presses against my lower back, moving me closer to his body.

Every shred of confusion and lingering question about why he secretly arranged a wedding disappear from my brain as I learn his taste and spar with his tongue. My fingers tangle in his long dark waves, and I pull his head down harder against mine. He nips at my bottom lip, and a bolt of pleasure shoots lower until I'm squeezing my thighs together to fight off the urge to mount him right here, right now.

And in a split second, it's over. He pulls back and sets me away from him. My disengaged fingers hang limply between us like I'm still reaching for him.

Forge turns to the captain. "Thank you."

Then he turns to leave the bridge as I gape after him.

He pauses at the door and holds out a hand. "Come, India."

I'm still deciding how to respond to his Jekyll-and-Hyde personality switch when I hear a distinctive *whap-whap-whap* sound.

Forge cranes his neck to look toward the sky before looking back to me. "Come on. They're here."

I move to him and look up at the chopper approaching the boat.

What the hell?

"Who's here?"

"You'll see." Forge takes my hand and pulls me toward another stairway that leads to the top deck, which I now realize is a helipad.

The chopper sets down and the door opens. A man gets out, followed by a slim woman with blond hair whipping in the wind created by the rotors.

Summer.

I've never seen so wide an array of emotions flash over someone's features with such clarity. *Shock. Disbelief. Confusion. Relief.* And then something I've never seen on Indy before.

Pure joy. It lights up her entire countenance.

All the stress and worry and panic I've seen on Indy's face since the first time I stepped foot in the card room at La Reina give way to bliss. I didn't think it was possible for her to look any more beautiful, but apparently, I was wrong.

Stop. Don't get soft. And what the fuck was that kiss? Get yourself together, Forge.

"Summer!" Indy yells as she drops my hand and speeds toward her sister, who looks like a younger version of the woman I just married.

As I watch the two collide in a grapple of a hug, I let what I just did sink in.

I married her.

I can't stop the wave of possessiveness that charges

through me at the knowledge that she's *mine*. It's fierce and primal and goes beyond the knowledge that I've removed her from de Vere's orbit permanently.

I married her . . . and I haven't even fucked her yet.

Tears stream down both their faces, and they look like the perfect reunion of long-lost siblings.

I shut down the emotion and remind myself why I did this. I didn't just buy her loyalty today. I bought *her*.

Everything else will play out in good time. For now, I need to get my head straight and get back to work. This is just the beginning.

INDIA

"Oh my God. Oh my God. Are you okay? Please tell me you're okay." I run my hands all over Summer's shoulders and arms before she grabs my wrists.

"I'm okay. I swear. No one hurt me."

"You're okay. Thank God you're okay." I cup my hands around my little sister's cheeks and tilt my face until our foreheads touch.

"Thank you," she whispers. "Thank you for getting me out of there. I was so scared that I . . ." Summer trails off and lifts her face to meet my eyes.

"I know."

She shakes her head. "You don't. You never should know. I'm so sorry, Indy. I fucked up bad, and that's on me. I'm so fucking sorry. I won't ever touch another deck of cards as long as I live. I swear to God, I won't. I'll . . . I'll . . . get a job waiting tables or scrubbing floors. I'll never—"

I drop my hands to grip my sister's shoulders and

squeeze her. "Just breathe, Summer. It's going to be okay. You're home now. Everything's going to be fine."

I'm saying it just as much for myself as for her as I pull her against me and hug her hard. For long moments, neither of us moves.

Finally, Summer releases me and looks around. "Where the hell are we?"

I glance over my shoulder, expecting to see Forge, *my new husband*, standing behind us and watching intently, but he's nowhere to be found.

Dammit, Forge. I have a million questions right now, for both him and my sister, but it's clear I won't be getting any answers from him.

"Indy?" Summer asks as I go silent.

My gaze returns to her dirt-streaked face. It looks like someone gave her a mostly clean towel to wipe off the grime.

"We're safe and everything is fine." Just the thought of what she must have gone through makes me choose my words wisely.

I've always protected Summer. When our mother brought her home from the hospital, she made it very clear that Summer's health and safety were my responsibility. I was eight at the time, but I took the vow I made in that trashy little flat very seriously.

I won't let anything bad happen to her.

At that time, it meant her dirty diapers were changed and her bottles were the perfect temperature. I can count on two hands how many times our mother took on either task, and still have plenty of fingers left over.

It's not a responsibility an eight-year-old should have

to bear, but I did it gladly. Summer was the one person in my life who loved me unconditionally and depended on me for everything. She was *mine* in a way nothing and no one ever has been, before or since.

And now I'm married to a man I don't know because that's what it took to save her life . . . Except how the hell did he get her out so fast? I just told him the truth last night.

My joy at seeing my sister still burns just as brightly, but a sliver of confusion and resentment stabs into me.

He already had his plan underway when the captain pronounced us man and wife.

What the hell is Forge's game? There's no way he would have married me unless it was *extremely* "financially beneficial." He's already a billionaire, and he made it clear that mere millions are the equivalent of pocket change. I have to find out what his motives are and why he maneuvered me into this situation.

"I thought I was going to die there," Summer says, her shoulders shaking as she breaks into a sob.

Every other thought in my head evaporates as I wrap my arms around her. "You know I would never let anything bad happen to you. Ever."

Her body shakes harder as tears soak my shirt. "I can't believe I was so stupid. I shouldn't have gotten involved. I knew better. And all I could think was—Indy is going to be so mad at me." She lifts her face, and I wipe away the tears dripping down her cheeks with my thumbs.

"I'm not mad at you. I promise. In a few years, I might want to shake the crap out of you and ask what the hell you were thinking, but right now, I'm just so glad to have you back."

My sister flings her arms around me and squeezes me even tighter. "Thank you. Thank you so much, Indy. I swear I'll pay you back. I promise. Even if it takes me the rest of my life, I will."

That's when it hits me. Forge paid $10 million to save my sister . . . and now I have to go thank him and find out *why*.

But first . . . a tear slides down my cheek as Summer cries on my shoulder, and I send up a prayer to anyone who may be listening.

Thank you for saving my sister. Please protect me from whatever is coming next.

Bad luck has always come in threes in my life, and I have no doubt that this isn't completely over.

FORGE

I'm in my study on a call when I hear a knock at the door.

I gave orders not to be interrupted. Which means . . . it could only be one of the two people on this boat who didn't receive those orders.

The knock comes again. "Forge?"

It's India. *My wife.*

That rush of possessiveness keeps taking me by surprise. I never planned to get married. Never realized how the knowledge that a woman belonged to me and only me would affect my brain and body.

Even now, blood rushes to my dick at the sound of her voice. *Fuck.* Now I can't stop picturing her kneeling between my legs, showing me exactly how fucking grateful she is that her sister isn't being sold off as some perverted fuck's toy.

I end the call with a terse excuse.

"Enter."

As soon as I say the word, the door swings open and India stands there with her wind-ruffled hair and tearstained face. Instead of her poker face in place and her guard up, her emotions are easy to read.

Just like I thought before I made myself walk away from the reunion scene—she's never looked more fucking beautiful.

Maybe that's because she's mine.

More blood rushes to my dick at the thought, and I force myself to stop thinking about it. Or at least I attempt to.

"What do you need?" My tone comes out clipped, but it doesn't faze her.

She steps into the office and closes the door behind her, not realizing she's entering the den of the beast. I'm approximately thirty seconds away from ripping her clothes off, bending her over my desk, and mounting her to get rid of this fucking fascination I have with her and her luscious body.

She takes another step forward, and I wrap my fingers around the arms of my chair to prevent myself from leaping up to do exactly that.

This woman doesn't have a fucking clue, and for some reason, I like that way too goddamned much.

"I don't need anything," she says, sounding more hesitant.

Well, that makes one of us. Because I need to blow my load in your tight cunt and show you who owns you.

I clench my teeth to keep from saying what's on my mind. She'd be fucking terrified if she had a clue. For some reason, a smile tugs at the edge of my mouth. *Maybe I want her terrified. Maybe I want to hear her beg.*

I'm a ruthless motherfucker, and up until this very moment, women have been disposable objects. Fungible goods, each one no different from the last. But India Baptiste—*correction, India Forge*—is the exception to the rule.

Because she's the only woman I'll ever give my name.

Forcing back the urge to smile like a fucking madman, I raise an eyebrow. "If you don't need anything, then why are you here?"

I sound like a dick, and that's not an act. I am a dick. Life is easier when people don't know you give a fuck about them.

India's brief attempt at timidity sheers away, and she bristles with the confidence that never fails to fire my blood. She crosses her arms over her chest, lifting her tits deliciously, and stares me down.

"I came to say thank you. I don't know what your motive is, but regardless, you did something that I can never repay, and I need to thank you."

I study her carefully. "Who says you can't repay it?"

Her blue eyes go wide. "It'll take me years to—"

I shake my head, cutting her off. "I don't want money from you. I never have."

India's lips flatten into a thin line. "I thought you also said you knew I wasn't a whore."

I spread my legs and lean forward. I choose the crude words that follow purposely, because I know she'll tell me to fuck off, and it'll keep the distance between us that I need to retain my focus on the endgame.

"You're not a whore. You're my *wife*. I think we both know exactly how I'd like for you to repay me." I nod to the floor between my feet. "If you'd like to show some of that gratitude, feel free to start right now."

32

INDIA

Is he fucking serious?

All my warm and fuzzy feelings of appreciation disintegrate as soon as Forge throws down his gauntlet.

I came in here to thank the man for getting my sister back safely—with genuine gratitude—and he throws it back in my face.

What did you think you were getting into by marrying him, Indy? The voice in my head asks the rhetorical question, because it clearly doesn't require an answer.

But me, in my desperation and moment of naivete, didn't expect *this*. But I should have. Because he's a man, and they're all the same.

I know I'm out of my league with Forge, despite the fact that we're married, but that won't stop me from trying to hold my own in any way I can.

I straighten my shoulders and stare him down with my *don't fuck with me* gaze, the one I normally only pull out in a room of misogynistic poker players. "You played me."

His lips quirk, but not quite far enough to be labeled a smile. "Call it what you want."

"Why?" His dark stare is the only answer he gives, so I keep going. "You're not even going to pretend that this wasn't all part of your premeditated plan, are you? You knew I'd do anything to get her back, and you put the whole operation into action before you even offered me the solution, because you were so damn sure I'd say yes to it."

His expression stays static, but heat burns in his eyes. "You're not stupid, India, so why are we having this discussion when you've clearly already figured everything out?" Forge's drawl takes on a mocking edge.

It's clear this man I married not even an hour ago thinks he has me figured out on every level, but he forgot that I live and breathe strategy. When I sit down at a table, I take the emotion out of the game. I don't just play the hand; I play the people. I fucked up at La Reina. I let emotion get to me—specifically, fear that Forge would fuck everything up—which is exactly what happened. It was a self-fulfilling prophecy, and I won't make that mistake again.

It doesn't matter that my fuckup actually saved my sister's life. Because now I'm in debt to a man I'll never be able to repay. When I said "I do" and became another one of Jericho Forge's possessions, my life changed irrevocably. My only shot at not losing myself completely in these new, uncharted waters of being tied to an infamous billionaire is to go back to basics.

Play the man. I can't let him best me, which is exactly what's going to happen if I'm predictable.

Jericho Forge may think he has me figured out, but he has no idea who he's fucking with—or who he married.

My every instinct tells me to run, but instead, I take a step forward. "Right here? Are you sure you're not too busy?"

One of his dark eyebrows rises arrogantly as I take another step toward him. "I'm never too busy for my wife to suck my dick."

Rage, the likes of which I haven't felt in years, boils up inside me, and my decision is made.

I'm going to break Jericho Forge.

33

FORGE

She closes the distance between us, her steps no longer hesitant, and more blood rushes to my dick.

Anger burns in her eyes. Rage rolls off her. My plan to keep her away failed spectacularly, and now she'd rather kill me than wrap her mouth around my cock. If I were a careful man, I'd keep my distance.

But I've never been a careful man. I take risks that sane men call crazy, but when I walk away with a prize that's bigger than anything they've ever conceived in their limited imaginations, I feel their envy.

Having India Baptiste on her knees, choking on your dick, is something any man would envy. *Yet no man but me will ever know what that feels like from this moment on.*

The thought shakes my composure for a second. I never planned on keeping her, but watching this fire-breathing dragon of a beauty walk toward me with murder on her mind while she's still willing to go to her knees changes everything.

She's fucking magnificent.

If she can suck dick half as well as she can make me hard just by breathing, I may have found my newest addiction.

She stops, and I wonder if she's partly bluffing, but the determination in her gaze says no. I was before, but I'm sure as hell not bluffing now either.

I reach for the button on my shorts and flick it open before tugging down the zipper. "I'll let you take it from here, *wife.*"

The sharp slice of her blue eyes could cut a man to shreds, but it only makes my dick harder.

"You're an asshole," she says.

"Don't talk about assholes unless you want me to fuck yours."

Her pretty mouth drops open to form a little *O*, and my cock throbs. Her reactions to my obscene language only make me want to tell her more of the depraved things I've imagined doing to her, simply to watch her shock.

"Second thoughts? If so, feel free to show yourself out." It's my last offer to let her walk out.

She bares her teeth at me, which should be a sign to tell her to *get the fuck away from my dick*, but I won't.

"No teeth," I tell her.

India bends forward, laying a hand on each of my knees, and stares at me point-blank. "You are either a very brave or a very stupid man."

I can't help but smile at her actions and words. There are grown men, CEOs of billion-dollar companies, who have a hard time looking me in the eye.

I reach out and grasp her blond hair in my fist. "You

don't have a single clue what kind of man I am, India, but you're about to find out."

With a tug, I bring her to her knees between my legs, and revel in the shocked breath that escapes her lips.

Fuck, taming her is going to be fun—or the death of me.

34

INDIA

*M*y knees hit the plush pile of the carpet, and the only thing I can think is that he has a dickless death wish. Or he's just that arrogant.

I curl my nails into the muscles of his thick, hard thighs, and my resolve doubles down. *I'm going to bring* him *to his knees. He'll never know what hit him.*

It's a vow that I would sign in blood, but Jericho Forge's grip moves to my neck, squeezing just enough to let me know that he's in control.

Bullshit. I'm in control. This is my choice, not his.

He may think he's won this battle of wills, but it isn't even close to being settled yet. Any other woman in her right mind would probably decide she's going to give him a half-assed blow job just to get the hell out of here, but not me.

Fuck no. I'm going to blow him better than any woman who has ever come near his cock. *Why?* Because when you own a man's dick, you control him. Since I just married this man, it's time to stake my claim, especially before he can stake his.

"I hope you're ready for this."

"Darlin', I was born ready."

I roll my eyes. "Cliché much?"

A wolfish smile spreads over his face but then disappears in an instant. "I didn't marry you for your opinions. Those lips, on the other hand . . ."

I glare, but reach into his fly and wrap my hand around his monster of a cock. "What about these hands?"

I stroke him hard, once and then again, gripping the smooth flesh over steel. His dick responds with a jerk, and I keep my eyes on his as I lower my mouth to circle the head with my tongue.

He attempts stoicism, but I catch the shift in his hips as he spreads his legs to make more room for me, and the upward buck of his hips he tries to fight.

Sorry, Mr. Forge, this is my game. You don't make the rules here, but feel free to beg.

I circle the head again, flicking my tongue at the clear precum that beads on the tip. I lift my head slowly, my gaze never leaving his, and lick my lips and moan. "You taste delicious."

His brow furrows as his gaze narrows on me. "Tease me at your own risk."

I huff out a laugh. "If you think this is teasing . . . just wait."

I break our eye contact and lick him from base to tip before taking him deep. His hips lift and his hand tenses on my neck, just enough to tell me that it's killing him to let me be in control. He wants nothing more than to hold me where he wants me and to fuck my face until he shoots his load down my throat.

Heat blooms between my legs, despite the fact that it should piss me off.

I try to tell myself I'm only doing the unexpected to keep him off guard, but the wetness slicking my thighs tells me I'm a liar.

I lift my gaze back to Forge's and pull my mouth off the end of his dick with a *pop*. "I have three words for you, Mr. Forge."

His brows dive together, his expression turning angry. "If you tell me to go fuck—"

I shake my head, cutting him off. Then I deliver my coup de grâce by holding up one finger at a time as I say the words.

"Fuck. My. Face."

35

FORGE

*J*esus fucking Christ. Who is this woman?

I don't have time to answer that question because I'm too busy complying with her order, something I *never* do.

With one hand wrapped around the back of her neck and the other alongside her cheek, I shift both of our positions so that I can get the right angle, and then I do exactly that.

Thrust after thrust, I plow between those pillowy lips, fucking her gorgeous face. She tilts her head back when I hit the back of her throat, no doubt adjusting to her gag reflex. I give her a moment to recover when I see unshed tears forming in her eyes, but she gives me a nod to keep going, and there's no fucking way I'm about to stop now. Not when I've just found heaven.

My cock disappears down her throat as she breathes through her nose and there's no hesitation. Pump after pump, I fuck her face like it's her cunt. Her hands grip my thighs, and I watch the tears streak down her cheeks.

Fucking beautiful.

I swipe my thumbs along her skin to catch them as they fall. Another thing I've never done before. Then again, I've never been married before either.

Another thought follows. *She's too fucking good at this.*

Something akin to rage that she's had enough practice to perfect the art of having her face fucked sends me spiraling. I lose my rhythm, fighting the urge to come.

She digs her nails into my legs, almost like she's encouraging me to keep going. With a harsh breath, I flex and pump between those lips until I'm about to blow my load. Just before I come, I pull out.

"Don't you dare come on my tits, Forge. Don't you fucking dare."

She releases her grip on my thighs and wraps her hand around my cock, stroking before she closes her mouth over the head of my dick. Then she sucks and strokes, and her other hand finds my balls.

Fuck.

I can't hold it back another second. I blow hard, and she swallows every drop as I come down her throat.

When my cock softens in her mouth, she retreats, using my knees to push herself to her feet as she wipes her fingers across her grin with triumph lighting those vivid blue eyes.

"What the fuck are you smiling about?" I ask, my tone low and deep.

"Wouldn't you like to know? I'll see you later, Forge. I'm sure you know how to find me."

And with that, my fucking wife turns on her heel and walks out of my study, leaving me with my dick out and a fuck-ton of questions about what the hell I really got myself into.

"This boat is insane. How the hell did you end up on here? With *him*?" Dressed in a cute pink blouse and white shorts provided by Dorsey, my sister braids her hair, wet from the shower, as she looks around the salon where I retreated after my encounter with Forge.

My husband. I still don't know how I feel about that.

I haven't told my sister yet. She's been more than a little distracted since she got off the helicopter, which is probably the only reason she hasn't noticed my ring and started asking a million questions. Thankfully, the shower seemed to have washed away most of the terror from her ordeal—or she's pretending it never happened, which is a skill we both picked up during childhood.

"We need to get in touch with Alanna and let her know you're okay. She's been worried sick," I say instead of answering her questions.

Summer's brows go up. "I already did. That chick gave me a sat phone when she showed me to the cabin for my shower." My sister pauses, her voice lowering. "Alanna told me what happened with Forge. That you played him in a game and you *lost*."

Dammit, Alanna. She didn't need to know.

Now what the hell am I going to tell Summer? You'd think the truth would be the obvious answer, but I've spent so many years telling my little sister half-truths and white lies to shield her from the harsh realities of life, the truth isn't my go-to reply.

"It's a long story, and the only thing that matters is you're here and away from those awful people."

"You're deflecting, Indy. If you don't want to tell me, don't. But I don't need you to try to protect me from this. I'm an adult, not a kid. I got myself into this situation, and now I need to figure out how to get you out of whatever mess you're in because of me. I owe you that much."

I paste a smile on my face, because Summer's like a dog with a bone. She won't let go of this.

"Let's go find some food, and I'll avoid your questions over lunch. Sound good?"

Summer rolls her eyes. "Fine. But you know I'll find out eventually, even if I have to ask Forge himself."

Normally, I'd beg her to leave it alone, but in this case, I don't think it's necessary. Letting her question Forge would be like letting her talk to a granite rock face. All she's going to get is hard looks and silence in return.

"Knock yourself out. Now, come on, let's eat."

I lead the way to the sundeck, following the scent of food. Even all these years after our stint of living on the street, my nose is still highly attuned to such things. It hasn't steered me wrong yet.

Under the massive fiberglass roof, we find a teak table

set with linens that match the navy and white uniforms of the workers on the boat. Fresh fruit and vegetables are set out, along with salads and pastas and a plate of thinly sliced meats and cheeses.

Summer's stomach growls. "I think I've found paradise," she says as she pulls out a chair and drops into it. She grabs an olive and pops it in her mouth. "I might eat this whole damn spread."

I look around for a sign of Dorsey or another person to ask if they mind if we eat, but I see no one, so I take a chair as well. Forge is always trying to feed me, so it's not like he's going to object.

Why am I looking to him for approval? That has to stop. I make a mental note and grab my napkin.

"How do you know where we are?" I ask Summer.

Her hand pauses as she reaches for the olive platter. "Am I not supposed to know?"

"I was just curious. Did they tell you on the chopper? Do you know where you were being held?"

She scoops up a handful of olives and drops them on the silver-rimmed white china plate emblazoned with the stylized *F* logo in front of her.

"Not exactly. I just know it was hot, sticky, and dusty, and no one spoke English. I heard some French and Arabic and Italian, though."

A thought strikes me, reminding me I never asked Forge about the Russians who were looking for me.

"No Russian?"

Summer frowns. "I don't think so. Why?"

"Miguel said there were guys sniffing around the

building, looking for me, and he thought they were Russian mobsters."

The color drains from Summer's tanned face. "Those are some serious bad dudes, Indy. I would never get involved with people like that."

"Russians weren't running the poker ring you played?"

"I don't think so. Although, I don't really know anything for sure. My contact was Spanish."

"But you didn't say anyone spoke Spanish where you were being held."

She pauses in mid-chew. "They didn't. They handed me off to some other guys who kept me blindfolded and gagged and tied up." Tears fill her eyes. "I thought I was going to die, Indy. I knew that if there was anyone who could save me, it would be you . . . but I thought I finally did something that couldn't be undone. I'm so sorry. I will never stop apologizing for it."

"Good."

Forge's deep voice comes from behind us, and we both whip our heads around to look at him as he crosses the sundeck. He's wearing black slacks and a dress shirt, like he's going to a meeting instead of standing on a boat at sea.

"Thank you, Mr. Forge. You have my undying gratitude. If there's anything I can ever do to repay you, I'll do it."

Forge's cursory gaze sweeps over my sister before shifting to me. "I didn't do it for you. I did it for my wife."

Summer's eyebrows climb up her forehead as she looks from Forge to me and back again.

"Wait. Wait just a freaking second. You're saying . . ."

She jerks in her seat as she catches sight of the ring on my finger. "What in the actual fuck happened while I was gone?"

My lips press together because I have no idea how I'm supposed to handle this. Forge and I never discussed what story we'd give people, because the chopper touched down with my sister. Then again, Forge is the one who raised the subject, so he can deal with the explanations.

Except he *doesn't.* He's totally silent, watching us both.

Seriously, man? He just unleashed a tidal wave of curiosity, and he isn't even going to toss me a life raft?

Wait. Maybe this is some kind of test?

"Indy?" My sister's eyes widen, and her voice rises.

"It was a whirlwind. I can barely believe it myself." I glance up at Forge, unable to read his blank expression. "We just . . . clicked, and . . . one thing led to another."

"You don't even like men," my sister says.

"I like men just fine!" My retort comes out a tad bit defensive.

"Really? Then why have you been under a dick embargo since I've been old enough to know what dick was?"

A fiery flush creeps up my cheeks, and there's nothing I want to do more than hug my sister so tightly she can't speak, and maybe muzzle her.

Forge's laughter booms out, and he moves to stand behind my chair. His big hands, the ones that held me by the hair and throat when I was on my knees in front of him, curl around my shoulders possessively.

"She was waiting for the right dick to come along."

I can't see his face, but the grip of his fingers on my

skin lights up my body in all the places I just managed to calm down. *I can't let my nipples get hard sitting at lunch with my sister. Just, no.*

With shock stamped on her features, Summer stares at us in silence for several beats. "I don't even know what to say."

"Congratulations would be a good place to start," Forge says.

Summer presses her lips together, and I know she sees through the game we're playing. She knows me. Knows that I never intended to marry anyone, and I'm pretty much allergic to romance, especially the whirlwind kind. "If you forced her . . ."

Forge's fingers tense on my shoulders, and I know I have to make this convincing, or Summer is going to raise hell and probably call the police and tell them I was coerced. Which is ironic, considering she's the one who put me in this position.

I reach up and lay my palm over the back of his wide hand and squeeze. "Really, Sum? Would someone have to force you to marry a gorgeous billionaire who would do anything for you? Including sending out the rescue team to save your sister?"

All tension in Forge's touch disappears, and I wonder if I've shocked him. My sister, on the other hand, still doesn't look quite convinced . . . at least, not until she bursts out laughing.

"You finally got the good dick." She shakes her head. "I get it. I really do. But damn, Indy. At least hold out a few months so you can make him pant after you."

Mortification rushes over me, and I'm grateful that

Forge is behind me where I don't have to look him in the eye.

"Ms. Baptiste, I suggest you refrain from speculating about the reasons your sister had for marrying me. I can assure you, I was very, very persuasive."

"I have no doubt. But I still don't believe this whirl-wind-romance bullshit. I'll have to see that for myself first."

One of Forge's hands leaves my shoulders to slide up to my throat. His fingers wrap loosely around the column of my neck as he tilts my head back. "She's the most unique woman I've ever met. How could I not want to make her mine?" His dark gray eyes spear into me with an intensity exclusive to him.

I'm so struck by his words and expression, I sit stunned while he leans down to press his lips against mine. It's barely a kiss. More of a brush against my mouth with his. But something about it knocks me off-balance enough to open a crack in the wall I built a decade ago to protect myself from men.

This isn't real, I remind myself. *He married me for some kind of tax break or something. Not because he actually thinks I'm unique and wanted me. Right?*

Forge releases me and steps away from my chair, and Summer watches us with her mouth hanging open. I suppose that's one way to take her mind off being kidnapped. I'm praying she bounces back as quickly from this as she does everything else. It's one of her talents I've always envied. She just lets the bad roll off and moves on with life.

"Damn. Okay. I guess I'll just sit here and wish my own bajillionaire would look at me like that."

"Start by staying out of underground poker rings, Ms. Baptiste," Forge tells her as he takes the seat next to mine at the table.

Summer swallows and nods. "Got it. Which means . . . I need to find an actual job."

"I've already secured you one. You start next week."

"What?" Summer and I both ask as we turn to look at the man I married.

"You got me a job?" My sister blinks as though she's trying to comprehend the words in some foreign language.

"Yes. I understand you have a degree in fashion marketing. I have a close friend who could use an executive assistant knowledgeable in the business. She's quite talented and needs the help. She's agreed to take you on for a probationary period to see if you're a good fit."

This time, I'm the one with my jaw practically sitting on the table. "When did you do that?"

"Ten minutes ago," Forge replies, his dark gaze saying more than his words.

After I blew him in gratitude, he got my sister a job. Arousal stirs between my legs again, and I shouldn't be turned on by this.

A silent conversation passes between us. *You give me what I want. I give you what you need.*

I swallow and shift in my seat, hoping I'm not leaving a wet spot on the fabric of this borrowed skirt. *I am so fucked.*

"Wow. Thank you," Summer says, oblivious to the

tension mounting at the table. "Who is she? Is it someone I've heard of?"

"Juliette Preston Priest." Forge drops the name of one of the most sought-after celebrity designers who keeps a villa on Ibiza and has made a massive splash on the international fashion scene in the last few years. *A woman whose name I've seen linked with his in the press.*

A close friend is how he described her.

Jealousy rips into me like a lightning strike, catching me completely off guard.

When Summer asks, "Didn't you date her?" I grit my teeth because I don't want to show a single shred of my emotions that are rising due to the subject of this conversation.

I don't care who his close friends are. I don't care who he dated. I don't care who he ever dates in the future.

All lies.

No. No, they can't be lies because this marriage isn't real. He can be with whoever he wants, whenever he wants, and I don't care. I got my sister back, and that's all that matters.

As Forge picks up his napkin and drops it on his lap, he replies to my sister. "Date? Men like me don't date, Ms. Baptiste."

Men like me don't date. I repeat his words in my head, and I know what he means. Men like him just—

"Was she your mistress?" Summer says, cutting off my thought.

My heartbeat roars in my ears, and I can't believe I'm listening to this. Even more, I can't believe I care that I'm listening to this. I'm not a jealous person. I've never felt a sliver of jealousy in my life when it comes to a man.

But you've never been around a man like him before either, Indy.

Forge helps himself to the food on the table rather than answering, but it doesn't deter Summer in the least.

"Did you break it off, or did she?"

"Summer," I say as a warning, my tone clipped.

"What? Just because you don't want to know who else got the good dick doesn't mean I don't, especially if I'm working for her. I need to know if she's going to secretly hate me because my sister snagged the prize she wanted."

Summer's ability to state the truth without bullshit, even in front of Forge, is probably something I should applaud her for, but all I feel is humiliation.

"Ms. Priest and I parted ways on amicable terms. She wouldn't do me this favor if that weren't the case."

"Well, that answer gives me exactly nothing to go on, so I'll have to assume that you left her with a giant string of diamonds like those British lords used to do when they decided to offload their aging courtesan for a younger model."

I should be glad she's not cowering in the corner after her ordeal, but still, I groan and drop my forehead into my hands. "Just stop. Please. For the love of God."

"What? You're the one who told me to read books. I happen to love historical romance. Besides, it's not like your new hubby is going to go sniffing around his left-overs. Isn't that right, Forge? Because then you'd have a pissed-off little sister to deal with, and I might be half your size, but I'm meaner than I look."

"Your threat is duly noted, Ms. Baptiste. I will inform Ms. Priest that you'll be reporting for duty on Monday as agreed upon." He pauses, shooting Summer a meaningful stare. "Don't fuck this up. I know you've been through a lot, but you get only one chance from me. Is that clear?"

Any levity on Summer's face disappears with the serious tone of his voice. "Clear as crystal, Mr. Forge."

The table goes quiet for several minutes as we eat in awkward silence.

I can't stop thinking about Juliette Preston Priest, and why he didn't choose her to marry if all he needed was a bride. Or was I just the only one who was desperate enough to agree to a no-questions-asked request? Was that a test too? Why does this man have to be such an enigma? I still have no answers when Summer speaks up again.

"Where are we headed? Back to Ibiza?"

"Yes. We'll be passing by the French Riviera today."

I whip my head toward the starboard side of the boat, and sure enough, there's a shadow of land in the distance.

"You mean . . . Saint-Tropez?" Summer asks, and I know exactly where this conversation is going.

My little sister has had an obsession with Brigette Bardot since childhood when our mother let us watch *And God Created Woman* way too early in life. More accurately, I should say she left us and the movie to keep us busy for a while. This is why I tried to turn Summer on to books instead. Apparently, that wasn't a good plan either.

"Yes. We should be less than an hour away at this point. We should dock in Ibiza tomorrow morning."

"Can we stop?" Summer asks, and the excitement in her tone sounds almost childlike. "I've always wanted to see Saint-Tropez. Our mom refused to take us there when she was working in Cannes, even though we were so close. It's on my bucket list."

I expect Forge to shut down her request without a second thought, but he doesn't. He turns to look at me.

"That's up to your sister."

I study him, trying to determine if this is yet another test, but I find no answers on his rough-hewn face.

"Indy, please . . . You know how bad I've always wanted to go there. Please."

I tear my gaze from him to glance at Summer and then back to Forge. "Don't you have to get back?"

"Not if my *wife* wants to stop in Saint-Tropez."

My inner muscles tense every damn time he says the word *wife*, and I can't help but wonder what I'm going to owe him in return for this favor. Or rather . . . what I'll be willing to do to thank him for making my sister smile so soon after her near-death ordeal. I already know I can't say no to her, because I've been unable to before.

"I would love to see Saint-Tropez," I tell him.

Forge nods and pushes back from the table. "I'll inform the captain."

FORGE

Saint-Tropez isn't on the schedule I handed the crew this morning before I dove off the boat to try to forget the woman sleeping in my bed.

I need to get back to Ibiza. My self-imposed timeline doesn't include flexibility for unplanned excursions. So, why the fuck am I telling the captain to drop anchor off the coast of France, and to ready the tender to take the two women and Goliath to shore?

Because I can't fucking help myself with her.

The lure of India Baptiste is more potent than anything I've ever felt. Every time she shifted in her seat at lunch, it took all my self-control not to rip her out of her chair, throw her over my shoulder, and take her downstairs to my cabin to fuck the hell out of her.

She wants me. That's not in doubt.

She also probably hates me. But I can live with being hated as long as her tempting body bends to my will. And the way she looked at me in shock when I said yes? I liked it. I want to see that expression on her face again.

"It's just as beautiful as the pictures," Summer says from the deck below as I turn to leave the bridge.

"That doesn't mean you should've asked for him to stop. Seriously, Summer. You can't treat him like he's a normal guy. He's not," India says, unaware I can hear them.

Which makes me pause and wait to see what else they have to say. Do I give a damn that I'm eavesdropping? Not at all. I only wish I could see them as well.

"Just because he's gorgeous with a billion dollars doesn't mean he's not a normal guy."

Summer's words parrot how India described me earlier when she was dancing around how to explain our hasty wedding to her sister. I found it very interesting that she kept the truth from Summer without me directing her to do so. I assumed my wife's instincts were good, and her response reinforced that assumption.

"That's not what I'm talking about," India says.

"Then what the hell are you talking about? He's not normal because you married him? Therefore, he's officially the only guy in the world who could bag Ilsa, the *Frozen* princess?"

I don't know who Ilsa the frozen princess is, but I get Summer's jibe. I could see India as an ice queen.

"No, I just mean . . . don't be so familiar with him."

I step closer to the railing and catch a glimpse of the two blond women below, one more gold and the other more platinum, as they move out from under the covered portion of the sundeck. I pull back just enough to stay out of sight without obscuring my view.

Summer, the platinum head, turns to face India. "He's

family now, Indy. How the hell else would I be with him? Besides, you should be thanking me for trying to find out about his mistress. I mean, don't you want to know which bitches are going to want your head for stealing their man?"

Summer's comment almost makes me smile. Every woman who has been part of my life has known full well that marriage was never part of the deal. *Ever.*

Will some of them be surprised when it gets out? Absolutely. Do I give a fuck? Not a single one.

I wait a beat for India to respond, but she doesn't. I take a step forward but pause when Summer speaks again.

"Wait a minute. Are you worried he's going to go back to his mistresses? That he won't be faithful?"

India looks out toward the Saint-Tropez coastline as she crosses her arms. "I've been married for approximately five minutes, Summer. Can you not talk about my husband cheating on me already? We know they all do. Some are just better at hiding it, and a billion dollars gives you the ability to hide plenty."

Interesting . . .

I hadn't even considered the idea of fidelity because I've been too focused on acquiring the woman in question. Knowing she expects me to stray and hide it confirms one very important thing about her.

She doesn't trust me or any other man.

Now, I have a new goal. Win her trust . . . and make her want me as badly as I want her.

"Are you seriously sending him with us as a bodyguard?" I glance at Goliath, the large man with dreads who brought my bag back to my flat, who waits near the smaller boat in what I've learned is called the *toy compartment* of the yacht, where the boat can literally drive right out of a hydraulic door in the hull.

"Goliath is captaining your tender. Koba will be your security."

The blond man who fed me the night before exits the elevator in a suit, joining us on the webbed rubber mats.

I glance from him to Forge. "This is really unnecessary. We don't need a babysitter. I'm plenty capable of taking care of myself."

"You're the wife of a billionaire," Summer says, stealing my attention. "Welcome to the world of being a big fucking deal, sis."

I could punch her in the arm for the wink she shoots me.

"If you want to get off this boat, then Koba goes with

you. The only concession I'm willing to make is that he'll give you some space, but he won't be far. I suggest you get in the tender before I change my mind."

Seawater laps at the sides of the floating boat and turns the white interior walls an otherworldly blue as I choose how I want to respond.

Before I can speak, Summer grabs my hand. "We're going. We have no objections. He can help carry our bags when they get too heavy, because there's no way I'm not shopping in freaking Saint-Tropez."

I squeeze my sister's hand as she moves toward Goliath. "You don't have any money, Summer. You don't even have a purse or a cell phone."

My sister looks up at Forge. "Like he's going to let you go anywhere without some fancy black card with no limit. Isn't that right?"

"Summer . . ."

Forge's gaze lands on me and he reaches into his pocket. Instead of pulling out a black card, the likes of which I've seen Bastien use, he pulls out a clear piece of plastic. There's no name or numbers on it. Only a silver chip at one end.

He holds it out to me. "For every item your sister buys, I expect you to buy something for yourself."

The order makes me want to refuse the card completely, but Summer snatches it from his hand. "Don't worry, I'll make her."

Forge nods to Goliath and Koba before walking toward the elevator and stepping into the clear glass tube. He tucks his hands into his pockets, and his gaze stays fixed on me as it lifts him into the main cabins of the boat.

Even out of sight, I can feel his stare. Before I can ask myself why, Summer speaks again.

"What is this? It must be some crazy card no one but people with sheikh money can get." She holds the card up to the light and tries to bend it. "Holy shit. It's not plastic. It's some kind of glass. This is *awesome*. Shopping spree!"

I turn away from the elevator and wonder if Forge is setting me up to add more to what I already owe him. I snag the card out of Summer's fingers and toss it on the stand behind me that houses the controls for the door.

"We're not spending his money."

She tilts her head to the side. "Isn't it *your* money too? Or did you sign a wicked-bad prenup to snag that beast of a man?"

Her question hits me like a punch to the gut. Jericho Forge is a billionaire who won't let me leave the boat without a security guard like it's standard operating procedure. Why didn't he have me sign a prenup? My heart pounds in my ears, drowning out the roar of Goliath starting the tender's engine.

"Come on, let's go." Summer grabs my hand and pulls me toward the boat, but the question is still firmly fixed in my mind.

What is your game, Forge?

I can't believe we're finally here."

Summer's excitement is contagious once we're standing amongst the bustling tourists on the quay in Saint-Tropez. The beautiful provincial architecture and old-world charm is preserved here like nowhere else I've ever been. My sister is practically bouncing beside me, no doubt mapping out exactly where she wants to go first, but my mind is on something entirely different.

My husband. There's something he's not telling me. Actually, if I were placing bets, I'd say there's a metric shit-ton he's not telling me.

Summer charges through the crowd, and I know if I don't keep up, she'll be long gone. I glance over my shoulder to see Koba melting into the crowd, his gaze scanning constantly before locking on me.

What kind of threat do we need to be worried about? That's the new question bouncing around in my brain, along with: *Did Forge pay Summer's ransom, or did they steal her back?* Is that why he's worried about our security? Why didn't I ask him?

"Summer, hold on a second," I say as I rush forward and grab her hand.

"What?"

"Please . . . be aware."

My sister looks at me like I'm crazy. "I'm the one who just got rescued from being kidnapped. If I'm not paranoid, why are you?"

"I don't know, but . . . I just don't want to take any chances. Let's be smart."

I wish Forge were here. It's another stray thought in my head, but one that I can't get out. I didn't realize it until this moment, but for some reason, when I'm around him, I feel safe in a way I'm not sure I've ever felt before.

My whole life has been a series of close calls. Almost starving to death. Staying out of the hands of the cops when I shoplifted and picked pockets. Nearly getting kidnapped myself one night before Alanna took us in. *Almost losing my sister . . .*

I'm always waiting for the next bad thing to swing through and upset the balance. But when I'm with Forge, the only thing I'm scared of is myself. How he makes me question my sanity because of the way my body responds to him. How he taunts me into becoming a sex kitten I don't recognize. How he makes me fearless.

And now that he's out at sea and I'm here, all my old insecurities and worries are coming back like bad habits I wish I could drop for good.

"Come on, let's go to Gucci," Summer says, pulling me along like I didn't just tell her to watch her back.

"With what money?"

My sister throws a look over her shoulder and then holds up the clear credit card I left on the control unit. "With this."

"Dammit, Summer. I told you—"

"And I decided your idea was stupid. I like pretty things, especially when I'm not paying for them."

I take a deep breath to calm myself and think of reasons I shouldn't strangle her. The primary one is that I just tethered myself to a man I don't know to save her, so killing her would be counterproductive and probably wouldn't help me get an annulment.

Wait. Do I want an annulment?

Summer pulls me through the crowd until we reach the door of Gucci, and when we walk inside, I still haven't been able to answer the question.

It shouldn't be that complicated. But it is.

What does Forge want from me? How long does he expect this marriage to last? How long will it take for him to get his full financial benefit before he cuts me loose?

Those are the only things on my mind as Summer struts through the store in borrowed clothes that no doubt look better on her than on their original owners. Clerks rush toward her like they have some special ability to identify people holding unlimited credit cards.

"Can we help you, ladies?"

"Oh, definitely," my sister says.

The shopping expedition takes over, and my questions fall by the wayside.

TWO HOURS LATER, we're loaded down with bags, and we don't look much different from the other tourists walking along the cobblestone streets of Saint-Tropez. I search the crowd for Koba, but I don't see him. *Where the hell did he go?*

"My arms are tired."

"Then stop buying shit."

She shoots me another *are you stupid* look and then stops in her tracks. "Oh my God. I didn't realize she had a store here. We have to go in."

I look up at where Summer is pointing, and there's a Juliette Preston Priest sign painted in azure blue, which is her signature color, said to be inspired by the waters surrounding Ibiza.

"We don't need anything else."

"Call it research to prep for my new job. You do want me to succeed, don't you?"

"Summer . . ."

My sister ignores me and heads for the door, leaving me to hustle behind her and catch up.

Dammit. This is the last place I want to go because I'm going to be faced with the gorgeous creations made by a woman who has shared my husband's bed. Or as Summer would say, someone who's had the good dick . . . when I still really haven't.

Not that my sister knows that, nor will I ever tell her. She will question everything even more critically than she already is if she knew Forge and I have never slept together.

Against my will, I open the door to the store and see the gorgeous and flowy blue, cream, and white clothes that have made Juliette Preston Priest's designs so sought after in havens for the rich and bored.

Summer is already holding a white bikini against her body. "This would look way better on you. Try it on." She shoves the wooden hanger toward me.

"I don't want anything from this store."

A woman steps out from a door camouflaged by the blue-and-white mural on the wall. "I believe that's the first time I've ever heard someone say they didn't want anything from my store."

Fuck my life. It's her.

Juliette Preston Priest.

Shouldn't she be in Ibiza? Why the hell is she in Saint-Tropez?

"Don't listen to my sister. It's an honor to meet you." Summer steps forward and holds out a hand. "I'm Summer Baptiste. I'm going to be your new executive assistant."

Juliette's hawk-like gaze sharpens on us. "Isn't this quite the happy coincidence then? I didn't expect to meet you until next week when Jericho said you'd be back on Ibiza."

She calls him Jericho. I don't know why that rubs me the wrong way, but the hair on the back of my neck stands up like I'm a dog cornered in an alley.

Summer is completely oblivious, as always, and keeps talking. "I wanted to see Saint-Tropez. Brigette Bardot is my idol."

Juliette assesses my sister and nods. "You'll do just fine then. We all owe Ms. Bardot a debt of gratitude for bringing attention to Saint-Tropez, and for her advances in fashion." Her attention shifts to me. "So that makes you the woman Jericho is willing to pull in favors for. What was your name again, darling?"

It's official. I don't like her. The condescending way she says *darling* makes me want to tear her hair out. But I'm not jealous. At all.

"India Forge." I don't know what possesses me to say my new name, but it's totally worth the shock value.

Juliette's composure slips, and her eyes widen in disbelief for a beat before she covers it. She lifts her chin even higher as she surveys me more closely.

"Clearly Jericho is keeping secrets from me. *Interesting.*" Her tone takes on an insouciant quality, but I can tell she cares *very much* about the bomb I just dropped on her.

"He said you're old friends?" Summer asks, catching on to the tension rising between us.

Juliette smiles. "Very good old friends. But apparently not good enough to be invited to the wedding, though. I'll have to take him to task for that. I never thought I'd see the day that he settled down for one woman." She tilts her head and studies me like I'm a bug under a microscope. "You must be very special for him to give up his legion of admirers."

Legion? Now she's throwing around the word legion. *Oh, hell no.*

Before I can think of something sophisticated and yet cutting to reply, she taps a finger to her lips and steps toward me. "I recognize you. Why do I recognize you?"

"She's the legendary India Baptiste. Poker player extraordinaire," Summer supplies helpfully.

Juliette snaps her fingers and points at me. "That's it. I've heard Bastien de Vere mention you . . . quietly, of course. Probably because he didn't want Jericho to steal you away. Too bad for him, I suppose. But then again, Jericho always wins."

The fact that she knows about Bastien doesn't sit well with me.

"That explains everything," Juliette says with a self-satisfied smile.

"What do you mean?" Summer asks, and I'm back to wanting to shut her up any way possible.

"The vendetta. Jericho's sworn to take everything he can from Bastien. He wants him to feel the same pain Jericho did when Bastien murdered Isaac. He would never have married you otherwise. But this way, he owns you, and Bastien has to watch as he parades you around as his newest possession for everyone to see."

Murder? That's why Forge hates Bastien? My stomach drops to the floor when I realize that their bad blood stems from something much worse than I could ever imagine.

I'm trying to keep my expression blank, but Summer turns to look at me, her eyes wide.

"Is that true, Indy?"

"It's complicated, Summer." I'm praying she'll drop it, especially in front of her new boss, and somehow, she hears my subliminal begging.

"There's nothing complicated about how he looks at you, Indy. Even I can see that. Plus, he gave me explicit orders to make sure you're spoiled today." She turns back to Juliette, and I want to hug her for not making the situation worse. "He even gave us his credit card to buy whatever we wanted, but only if Indy buys as much as I do."

Instead of wiping the smile off Juliette's face,

Summer's words cause it to turn even more smug. "I'm sure he did. He likes his women to be walking perfection because it reflects better on him." She circles a hand around in the air near her left ear. "Who do you think helped me start my label? There would be no JPP brand without Jericho investing in me and my dream."

I force a bright smile onto my face. There are a million things I want to say right now, but every single one of them will end up costing my sister this job, which could actually set her on the right path and keep her out of seedy underground poker games. So instead, I keep it as civil as I possibly can.

"He's very generous, and it appears none of us are above his charity."

"Very," Juliette says, dripping with condescension. "Now, why don't I pick out a few pieces for each of you that'll suit your figures and send you back to him looking better than you ever have. Unless, of course, you already own my designs?"

"That would be amazing," Summer says, bright and cheery. She holds up the white swimsuit in front of me. "Wouldn't Indy look incredible in this?"

Juliette studies me, and again, I feel lacking. "I have something better for her silhouette. Us well-endowed girls need a little more support than that offers."

She turns and walks away to a rack, pulling out a blue suit that is so beautiful, I hate it immediately. "I designed this one specifically for myself. Of course, I rarely wear the top, as I prefer fewer tan lines."

Of course. Of course she goes topless, because she

probably doesn't feel the least bit self-conscious walking around with her perfect boobs that defy gravity.

"I think I'll pass. I'm really shopped out at the moment."

"I insist," Juliette says. "You'll never find a better swimming costume. I promise. You can ask Jericho, and he'll tell you I'm never wrong about things like this."

Every time she says his name, I grit my teeth together, and I hate that.

I shouldn't care that she once laid claim to the man I'm married to, and no doubt knows him better than I ever will, because this isn't even a real marriage. I shouldn't care about any of it.

But I do.

And when I try the suit on, it's perfect, and I hate that too.

"I THINK THAT WENT WELL, don't you?" Summer says as we leave Juliette Preston Priest's store and the summer heat closes in on us. The sea breeze is blunted by the rows of stone buildings and the growing crowd of people.

"I'm not speaking to you. Maybe ever again."

"Come on, Indy. She was nice. She's going to be my boss, and she found you the perfect suit."

"Not speaking to you," I say, not caring that I sound like a toddler about to throw a tantrum.

"He fucked her. Who cares? He *married* you."

My mouth drops open, and I swing around to look at my sister.

Before I can reply, a man's shoulder knocks into mine, and I stumble. A burning slash of pain lights up my side, and I fall forward. The cobblestone street rushes upward, and my knees slam into it before I can untangle my arms from our shopping bags.

"Indy!" Summer screams as she staggers sideways, almost landing on top of me. My sister rights herself, bracing her hand on my shoulder before reaching out to pull me up.

"Are you okay?" she asks.

I reach down to touch my side, and my hand comes away with smudges of red. "He cut me."

I look down at the mess of bags I dropped to the ground. Well-versed in dealing with creative pickpockets on Ibiza, mostly because I've been one, I immediately notice what's missing.

My purse. Damn it, I just bought that!

"Oh my God. We need to get you to a hospital. You're bleeding." Summer's tone edges on hysterical, but my brain locks down the pain.

"No, I need my damn purse." I bounce to my feet and whirl around to catch a glimpse of a man jostling the crowd to slip around a corner.

I see you, asshole.

"Stop him! He stole my purse," I yell just before bolting after the thief. I don't bother to wait for Koba, who I see fighting through the crowd to get to me from the opposite side of the street.

The thief is out of sight, but pedestrians point in the direction he went as they check to make sure he didn't grab any of their property. I shove through the crowd, weaving in and out as Summer yells for Koba and the police.

By the time I turn the corner, I assume the guy will be long gone. But he's not.

I skid to a halt when I see an enraged dark-haired man holding the thief up by his throat, pressing his back against a wall.

"Give me one good reason to turn you over to the police instead of taking you out to sea and watching you drown," Forge growls, terrifying the man who claws at the hand wrapped around his neck.

What the hell is he doing here?

He jostles the man again. "You think you can steal from my wife and get away with it? Do you have a death wish? Answer me."

The man shakes his head and starts mumbling words in a mishmash of French and English.

"That's right," Forge says. "You're fucking sorry. Drop the goddamned purse."

The man complies, and my purse hits the cobblestones.

Forge looks toward me, scouring every inch of my body. His gaze stops on the hand I have pressed to my side.

"He hurt you." It's not a question.

"He cut through the strap of my purse and caught some skin."

"Show me."

I lift my palm off my wound, revealing the spot where the sliced fabric is now rusty red.

Pure, unadulterated fury sweeps over Forge's features, transforming his already murderous expression into one even more lethal. His nostrils flare as he turns back to the man he's holding against the wall with one hand.

"You made her bleed." His grip tightens on the thief's throat. "You'll fucking die for that."

"Oh my God, he's really going to kill him." Summer's voice comes from behind me. "And the police are going to see it because they're right behind me."

"Boss." Koba's voice joins the fray. "They're sixty seconds out. No more."

Shit. Shit. Shit.

The man's feet kick in the air as his face turns even brighter red and his eyes bulge. Forge pulls the man's back off the wall before slamming him harder against the brick.

"You made her bleed, and I'll make you bleed. Eye for an eye."

Police yell at pedestrians to move out of the way as they come closer.

I step forward, my hands out like I'm approaching a wild beast and hoping not to get eaten. "Forge, please. Put him down. The police will take care of him."

The man I married, the man who looks like he has no problem killing this thief with his bare hands, looks at me once more. The rage is gone and his dark gray gaze ices over.

"Give me one good reason."

"Because I don't want to visit my husband in prison. The idea of conjugal visits creeps me out."

Something flits over his features. Slowly, he releases his grip on the man's throat, and the guy hits the ground in a crumple of limbs. Relief washes over me, and I feel like the woman who is able to talk down the Hulk when he's angry and green. I'm not sure why that kindles a warm sensation in the pit of my stomach, but it does.

I release a long breath, and the pain in my side fires up again. Forge grabs my purse off the ground and strides toward me.

"Are you okay?" he demands, but my question comes at the same moment.

"What are you doing here?"

Before either of us can reply, two police officers turn the corner, followed by Juliette.

"Good Lord, Jericho. Now you're apprehending criminals too?" Juliette says from just beyond my sister. "I know you're a man of many talents, but that's a new one."

Forge doesn't even look at her. His gaze stays pinned on me and my wound. "We need to get you to a hospital."

"I'm fine. It's just a scratch. I've had worse."

His expression darkens further as he pulls me carefully into his side. "Never again. I won't allow it."

"That's the guy," Summer says to the police, who walk toward us as she points to the man on the ground.

The police move toward him as he stumbles to his feet. They charge him before he can take a step to escape.

"Get his ID," Forge orders. "I want to know who the fuck he is."

"Sir, we'll need to take statements from all of you," one officer says.

"My wife's bodyguard will provide a statement," Forge replies, pointing at Koba.

"We'll need to speak to your wife as well," the officer says.

"She'll provide you a statement in writing, as will I."

Forge tightens his arm around my shoulders. "Right now, she needs medical care, and Saint-Tropez has lost its appeal for us."

"I can give a statement," I say, but Forge shakes his head.

"You're going back to the boat." He turns me to face my sister and Juliette. "Summer, do you need help with the bags?"

My sister shakes her head. "I got them."

"You dropped this one, Summer," Juliette says, holding up the tiny one containing the bikini I purchased in her store against my will. My reluctance feels ridiculous in the face of actual problems.

"Thank you, Juliette. I'll certainly be enjoying my wife in whatever she purchased."

Juliette's mouth turns into a little pout. "And here you swore you'd never marry."

My entire body tenses.

"That's because I hadn't met Indy yet."

40

INDIA

*F*orge brushes off the police with an impressively small amount of effort before shifting his grip on me and lifting me into his arms.

I whip my head around to look at him. Our lips are only a breath apart. "I can walk. I'm not that hurt."

"I'm done taking chances with you."

"Indy, look at your knees. Shit." Summer points to the small rocks embedded in my skin, and they immediately sting.

"Thanks, sis. Didn't realize that—"

Forge takes a step, carrying me with ease, cutting off my words.

Crowds clear a path before him like he's Moses at the Red Sea. It's crazy and impressive, and I have absolutely no idea how he does it. It's presence and authority and alpha-male pheromones.

Summer follows us back to the quay where Goliath is waiting in the tender. As soon as he sees us, he jumps up. His eyes widen at the sight of blood on my shirt and hands.

"Hospital?" he asks.

"Back to the boat," Forge replies. "And then we're underway to Ibiza."

"Yes, sir." Goliath holds out his arms, as if offering to take me from Forge.

"I can get on the boat myself. I'm not an invalid," I protest before he can hand me off.

Forge doesn't reply or take Goliath's offer of assistance. Instead, he steps on board carefully before lowering me into one of the white leather captain's chairs. He places a hand on each arm and lowers his head until his nose almost brushes mine.

"I've just made you a target for the entire world, and I didn't protect you well enough. That's my fault, and I'll never make the same mistake again. You have my word." His granite gaze and solemn tone send chills down my spine as he makes his vow.

"Why would I be a target?"

Forge stares at me, not answering for several moments. Finally, he says, "I have enemies, and now, so do you."

"What kind of enemies?"

"We'll discuss it later. But I will keep you safe in whatever way I deem most effective, and you won't fight me on it. Understood?"

I blink twice. "No. Not understood. You have to—"

He leans forward and presses a kiss to my lips, silencing me.

When he pulls back, he nods at Goliath.

"Let's go."

41

FORGE

*I*ndy argues with me again as I lift her into my arms to carry her on board the yacht, but my actions override her protests.

Never in my life have I felt such a cold, killing rage settle over me as I did the moment I saw her blood.

No one touches what's mine. No one hurts the people I claim. If Indy hadn't stopped me, I would have ripped out his throat.

I've never met anyone who had this kind of effect on me. How fiercely I feel about her safety and well-being is as shocking to me as the possessiveness I can't shake.

She's not just a means to an end anymore. She's mine. And I take care of my own.

It's an unexpected turn of events, but one I can't regret.

"Forge, put me down."

She wiggles in my arms, but I'm not ready to let her go yet. I walk us to the master bath attached to my cabin and sit her on the counter.

"I'm fine. I swear. He just got a little carried away with his knife when he cut the strap."

My anger rises to the surface again when she says *knife*. "He shouldn't have had the chance, and that's on me and Koba."

I reach for the hem of her shirt and pull it up.

Indy slaps her hands over mine. "Stop. What are you doing?"

"Taking care of you."

Her hands go limp, and I shake them off. I try not to focus on the fact that I've never said those words before in my life.

"Well, you can ask a girl before you take her shirt off," she says, the words muffled as I pull the ruined tank over her head, leaving her in a bra.

"You're not a girl. You're my wife." I toss it to the floor before crouching to assess the injury. She's right. It's a surface wound and not as bad as the blood would suggest, which is helpful, because now I don't have to chopper out a surgeon to stitch her up.

"A fact you didn't share with your mistress when you talked her into hiring my sister. Why is that, I wonder?"

India's smart mouth is going to get her in trouble, but that doesn't bother me in the least. I know exactly how I'll handle her. But right now is not the time to paddle her ass.

"She's not my mistress." I surprise myself again by giving Indy this information. I don't explain myself to anyone. I never feel the urge. But for some reason, she has me breaking all the rules.

"But she was, wasn't she?" Indy asks as I grab a wash-cloth and wet it to wipe away the crusting blood.

"Does it matter?" I open the cupboard to pull out the first aid kit and find an alcohol swab. I tear open the package as she fires back at me.

"Why do you always respond to a question with a— Ouch! That hurt." Her shoulders bunch around her ears as she hisses in pain, and it's like a stab to the heart.

I blow on the cut, wanting to allay the discomfort I caused.

Fuck. This woman is going to be the end of me.

"It would've been worse if I'd warned you."

I meet her gaze from beneath hooded lids as I stem the urge to apologize. *I never apologize.*

"You have a shitty bedside manner," she says as her eyebrows knit together.

"Good thing I don't usually get called on for nursing." I pull out the tube of antibiotic ointment, and she flinches. *Another stab.*

"This won't hurt." I wait for her to nod before using a sterile gauze pad to spread it over the wound.

"You're avoiding my question. Why didn't you tell me you got my sister a job with your mistress?"

I grit my teeth. "She's not my mistress. I don't have a mistress. I have a fucking wife."

"Who you've never slept with, and I know enough about men to realize if they're not getting it at home, they're getting it somewhere else."

"We've been married less than a day. Do you really think I'm out getting it somewhere else?" I place my hands on her thighs, above her abraded knees. She glares at me as I expected. "Unless that's an invitation?"

"Go back to nursing, Forge. Your seduction game needs work."

The bathroom fills with the sound of my laughter, and India's glare sharpens.

"You should be afraid of me, and yet you taunt me at every turn."

"The only thing I'm afraid of is what you're going to pour on my knees to clean them."

I don't reply until her side is covered with a large bandage to protect the two-inch-long slice. I grab the bottle of peroxide from under the sink and hold it up in front of her.

"You'll survive. I promise. The cobblestone was fairly kind to you."

"The only way I won't scream while you clean my knees is if you tell me about you and Juliette."

And now she's bargaining with me. *Emotional blackmail.* Borderline extorting information from me. The negotiator in me approves.

"Is that right?" I say as I lift her off the counter and set her in the shower. Shockingly, she doesn't make a fuss over being manhandled.

"Yes. Those are my terms."

I reach for the movable showerhead and turn the water on, letting it run for a few moments before it reaches an acceptable temperature.

"What makes you think you get to set the terms of this negotiation?" I ask, my tone more curious than anything.

"Because you have a tell."

This makes me stop and look up at her, my eyebrows raised. "Is that right?"

"You don't like seeing me in pain." She smiles like she's discovered the map to the holy grail.

"And you think I'm willing to bargain with you to avoid seeing you in pain?"

Her grin widens, and there's not much I won't do to keep that smile on her face, as opposed to a grimace.

"Yep."

"Take off your skirt if you don't want it to get wet."

This time, her eyebrows go up. "Wait . . . What?"

I lay a hand on her hip, tucking a finger into the waistband. "Your skirt. Off or on. I promise I won't be moved to ravish you at the sight of your panties."

"I'm sure that's what all the pirates tell the girls to get them naked."

"What did you say?" I ask, truly confused this time.

Indy's cheeks turn pink. "I didn't mean to call you a pirate out loud."

Ah . . . "You're not the first person to call me a pirate. I'm sure you won't be the last." I tug the waistband of the skirt, and Indy slaps her hand over mine.

"I'm also not wearing panties, so . . ."

My attention cuts to her face as heat that has nothing to do with the steam filling the shower floods my body.

"You were out in public. In a skirt. Why the fuck weren't you wearing panties?"

"I didn't exactly pack for this trip."

My fist clenches around the showerhead. "Then you should've bought some."

"From who? Your mistress?"

"*She's not my mistress.* And if you say that again, I'll show you exactly where I'm getting my satisfaction."

Instead of quailing at my tone, Indy smiles and shoves her skirt over her hips, revealing her bare pussy.

Fuckkkk.

"Good," she says. "I don't like sharing, even if I don't have a fucking clue why you married me."

INDIA

I'm standing in front of my husband, in the shower of his bathroom, naked except for a strapless bra. My words and tone may sound confident, but that's only because I have a great poker face. My heart hammers harder as his gray gaze skims over my body, moving down until it locks on the little silver bead peeking out from between my lips.

"Where the hell did that come from?"

A surge of power rushes through me. "My piercing? It's been there the whole time."

Wetness slicks my thighs at his shock.

He studies my face, and I have absolutely no idea what he's hoping to find. But like someone waved a wand, he banks the fire and returns to ice. "I'll try not to hurt you."

The warm water washing over my knees stings, even though he's covering the needles of spray with his hand to trickle the water over my road rash.

"When did you meet her?" I ask, trying to keep my mind off it.

"None of your business."

"When did you break it off with her?"

He brushes a washcloth gently over one knee, and I look down to see the skin turning pinkish-red, but most of the grit that was clinging there is already gone.

"Long before I met you," Forge says, and I'm shocked he gave me even that much information.

"We literally only met a few days ago, so that's a pretty vague answer."

"Do you have another question, or are you going to fixate on Juliette, who is completely irrelevant other than the fact that she's giving your sister a job?"

He's giving me an opening, and there's no way I'm going to waste it on Juliette. I choose my words while he turns off the water and reaches for the peroxide. He uncaps the bottle and looks up at me, as if asking for approval before he causes me more pain.

I grip his shoulder with my hand, not caring that I'm essentially dragging his face closer to my pussy, and I strike while he seems the most vulnerable.

"Why did you marry me?"

The peroxide splashes against the abraded skin of my knees, and I tense.

"Because I had to have you."

The words tear through me, blunting any pain as I stare down into those storm-cloud eyes.

He lowers the bottle of peroxide, and I can feel my heart beat in my nipples and between my legs. *This isn't normal. I shouldn't feel like this.*

But Forge is a force of nature. A rogue wave, crashing into my world and leaving it completely unrecognizable.

Why should I be shocked that my body reacts to him like no one else before?

He rises slowly, his fingers trailing up my bare, wet skin. "What do you need from me, India?"

I press my lips together, refusing to say everything swirling in my mind. He already has the upper hand. I can't give him all the leverage. But I also want him to touch me so badly that I can't think of another goddamned thing right now.

But it doesn't matter that I don't voice my needs, because Forge can read me better than anyone ever has before.

"You want me to touch you. Take your mind off the pain. Make you come." All statements. No questions.

I stay silent.

Forge holds out a hand. "I won't make you say it. All you have to do is take my hand."

4 3

FORGE

*S*he shields her inner turmoil well. Her pride wars with her needs. I'm a gambler too, and I know exactly where I'd lay my bet.

On us.

Indy's fingers shake as she raises her hand. She'll either grasp mine or slap me across the face. When her palm slides across my calloused skin, my grip tightens on her like I'm afraid she'll change her mind. I'm not giving her that much time.

"On the bed. Bra off. Spread your legs. Show me that pretty cunt and the piercing you've been hiding." My orders come out like I was born to give them to her.

Indy's cheeks darken with a blush, but her nipples pebble against the thin material of her bra. She likes it. She wants it.

With her lips pressed together, she slips around me in the bathroom, and I release her hand.

I force myself to wait a solid sixty seconds before

following her. And when I do, it's to see pure fucking heaven laid out for me.

Her legs are barely spread, and I wonder if she's shy or just disobedient. I'll take either. I'll take anything from her.

"You look like an offering to a pagan god."

Her blush spreads to her neck and down her chest, almost reaching her pink nipples.

I stop at the end of the bed, where her feet hang over the edge. I grasp her ankles and lift them, bending her knees and pressing her feet flat on the duvet.

Her eyes widen as her pussy lips part, revealing everything to me, including that little silver piercing that dangles right over her clit. Wetness slicks between her thighs, and the beast inside me demands to taste her. Touch her. *Fuck her.*

When she squeezes her eyes shut for a beat, I can't help but wonder if she's less experienced than I assume.

"Are you a virgin?"

Her eyes flick open. "No. Of course not."

"Then why do you look as terrified as you are excited?"

She swallows and turns her head toward the windows.

"Indy, I'm about to finger-fuck your pussy and eat you until you scream, so I think we're past the point of embarrassment here."

Her gaze snaps back to mine. "It's been a long time, okay?"

I kneel on the bed between her spread legs, careful to avoid her knees. "How long?" I ask as my palms slide up her thighs.

"Long enough."

I pause with my thumbs an inch from her pussy lips. "Answer me, and I'll give you what you want."

Her lips flatten again, and I stroke the pad of my thumb along her slick pink skin. She releases a quiet moan, and my cock turns rock hard.

"Ten years."

The admission hits me like a sledgehammer, and I stare down at her in shock.

"Ten years?"

"Touch me, dammit."

"How is that even possible? You practically ooze sex. You're a fucking siren. Every man who sees you wants to make you his." I swipe my thumb between her pussy lips and flick her piercing. "But they can't have you because you're fucking *mine*."

*H*umiliating admission? Check.

Already on the edge of orgasm from one touch and Forge's possessive words? Also check.

My inner muscles clench as he spreads me open with his thumbs and bends forward to swipe his tongue from bottom to top.

Holy. Shit.

"Fuck, you taste good."

His grip on my thighs tightens, and any feeling of pain or discomfort from this afternoon disappears when pleasure cascades through my body.

He eats me like he's been starving for the entire decade I've been abstinent. When he flicks my piercing with his tongue, the one I got just for *me*, it sends me hurtling toward the edge faster than ever before.

And then his tongue does something I've never even thought of before in my life—it moves over my ass, teasing that very virgin territory. I squirm away, trying to escape the unfamiliar feeling, but his hand clamps down and makes me take it.

And, holy hell, does it feel good.

I writhe against his mouth as he moves to suck my piercing between his lips and bites down on my clit.

"Ah!" I screech as my orgasm shatters me.

Forge takes that moment to push his thumb against my asshole and suck harder on my clit. Wave after wave of pleasure threaten to drown me. My head thrashes back and forth on the bed as I bury my hands in his hair.

"I can't. I can't." I huff the words, but he doesn't stop.

The tip of his thumb penetrates my back hole while he continues to suck and lick and *feast.*

"Again." He growls the word against me and my body complies, even though my brain fights to regain control.

I can't stop. My legs spasm, and the vibrations from Forge's mouth undo me completely.

I scream out my orgasm, not caring who might hear. My fingers yank at his head, pulling him up from between my thighs, because I don't know if I can take any more.

"You're not—"

Someone pounds on the door, interrupting whatever Forge was about to say.

"Go away," he barks, but I struggle to sit up and the tip of his thumb slips from my ass.

I didn't even know I liked that kind of thing.

"Indy? Is he torturing you? I will fucking kill him, even if he saved me."

It's my sister's voice, and I'm not sure if I'm thankful for the rescue or if I want to kill *her* for interrupting.

"Ms. Baptiste, please come with me."

Goliath's voice comes through the door next, and mortification sweeps over me.

They all heard me. And turns out, right this moment, I do care.

I reach for the blanket and yank it out from under Forge so I can cover myself.

"I'm fine!" I call out, but it's a lie. I don't know what just happened in this room, but I'm not fine. I'm fucking terrified that I just made the biggest mistake of my life.

I let my husband make me come.

And I loved it.

45

FORGE

"*H*oly shit. You're having sex," Summer says through the door, giggling uncontrollably. "I didn't even think with Saint Indy . . . Sorry, guys!"

"Ms. Baptiste, come with me."

I can picture Goliath dragging a laughing Summer away from the door, but it's already too late. My wife is wrapped up like a goddamned burrito in the blanket, and closed down like a fortress.

"I'm sorry," Indy says. "I shouldn't have . . ."

"Why the fuck are you apologizing?" My reply comes out harsher than I intended.

Her gaze flicks from my face to my obviously hard dick. "I . . . I don't know. It was the adrenaline. I think I was just—"

I hold up a hand to silence her. "If you don't want me touching you, I won't fucking touch you. I'm not a goddamned monster."

I shove off the bed, wondering how the hell this perfect fucking moment went sideways.

As I head for the bathroom, I say, "Unless you want to watch me take a cold shower, I suggest you stay in here."

With the devil riding my shoulder, I step into the master bath and leave the door open. The shower water comes on, and I want to torture her just as badly as I feel tortured right now.

She wants me. That's not a question. But the fact that it's been ten years since she's been fucked . . . that explains a lot more. *Except it doesn't explain why she hasn't had a man in so long.*

I strip and step into the warm spray. As it beats down on my bowed head, I take a fist to my cock, imagining how tight her pussy is going to be when I finally earn that prize from her.

Stroke after stroke, I jerk it harder, picturing the tears that ran down her cheeks as I fucked her face. She looked so goddamned beautiful. But it's the more recent memory of the clench of her ass around the tip of my thumb that makes me blow my load all over the travertine wall.

The bathroom door slams shut, and my gaze cuts to the closed door.

She watched me.

My dick gets hard all over again. That naughty fucking wife of mine is going to be the death of me. She's going over my knee for this.

I dry off as quickly as possible, my dick hard like I didn't just come, and step out into the bedroom . . . to find her reaching for the door handle.

"Stop."

Indy freezes, her shoulders stiffening, and I note she's

wearing a bikini that I'm guessing came from Juliette's store.

"Turn around."

"I'm just going—"

"You're not going anywhere."

She turns around slowly to face me. I stand naked and proud with my cock rising between my legs.

"I just wanted to grab—"

"You wanted *me.*"

She swallows as I walk toward her, and her nipples pucker against the top of the suit.

"You shouldn't have even bothered getting dressed, because we're not done."

"But—"

"You could've walked out of this room, but you didn't. You wanted to see me with my hand wrapped around my cock, picturing you while I blow the load that belongs in your tight little cunt all over the wall."

Her mouth drops open.

"Unless you'd rather I fuck your face again?" I shake my head. "No. I think we'll save that for later. I want you, and I want you now."

Indy shifts her weight from foot to foot, and her chest rises and falls faster with each breath.

"And you want me just as fucking bad."

"I don't want anyone to hear. I can't—"

"Goliath will have removed everyone from being able to hear, especially if you learn how to keep those screams in. But I don't care if you do. I don't care if the whole fucking world hears." I stride to the bed and sit. "Come here."

Dozens of emotions sweep over Indy's face as she tries to talk herself out of following my orders, but she won't. She wants this as much as I do. Maybe more, if it's been ten fucking years.

My dick jerks between my legs at the thought of her near-virgin status. I already felt possessive over her, and now it's more acute.

Triumph rises inside me as she releases the door handle and walks toward me, pausing a few feet away.

"Closer."

She takes two more small steps, and careful of her wound, I grip her around the curve of her hips and drag her the rest of the way forward.

"Over my knees." I nod down at my spread thighs.

Indy stares at my dick and then looks back to my face, wide-eyed. "What?"

"Your ass needs my hand, and I'm going to give you what you need."

"Excuse me?"

"I gave you an out, and you didn't take it. You know what that tells me? Everything you're not willing to say out loud. You want me? You get me."

She squeezes her thighs together, and I guarantee she's still wet and getting wetter. Her top teeth scrape across her bottom lip.

Christ, she's fucking beautiful.

"The only decision you'll regret making is walking out of this room. I swear it to you."

Indy fights through her battle of wills, and one inch at a time, she bends, laying her body over my spread thighs.

My hand cups one of her ass cheeks, which are almost completely exposed by the bikini bottom.

"You were going to let everyone else see this ass? I don't think so. Not until I've staked my claim properly."

She inhales sharply as I sweep my fingers under the scrap of material that runs between her cheeks. The sound tells me everything I need to know. *She was made for me.*

"You liked my thumb in your ass, didn't you?"

I stop over the whorl and press against it until she clenches. *I don't think so.* I pull my hand free and tug down the bottoms, baring her completely. I take a few seconds to appreciate her pale skin before landing the first strike.

Her gasp is followed by a moan.

"That's what I'll give you when you try to lie to me about what you want."

"I didn't—"

Smack.

Indy shifts over my thighs as my cock presses against her stomach. I reach between her legs and find her soaked pussy.

"You're so fucking responsive. You were going to leave me hard while you walked out with a wet pussy? Bad little wife."

I pull back and land another slap on her left cheek before sliding a finger inside her.

"Oh God . . ." Indy moans as her inner walls clamp down on me.

"Fuck, you're tight. My cock might not even fit inside this snug little cunt."

I pull free and slide a second finger inside, stretching her. Indy bucks against my touch.

"You like that? Being filled up with my fingers? Loosening you up so my big fat cock fits inside you?"

"Please," she whispers. "Don't stop."

"Not a fucking chance."

Thrust after thrust, I finger-fuck her as she grows wetter and wetter, slickness dripping down my hand. It's goddamned glorious. Her pretty little asshole teases me from between her round cheeks, and I think about how she writhed against me when I took my tongue to it.

I pull my fingers free and dip my thumb into her slickness to lube it up. Slowly, I circle her pucker. "Don't tense."

She does, and I smack her on the hip. She relaxes immediately.

"I'm going to tease your pussy and your asshole until you come, and then I'm going to fuck you until the entire world hears you scream my name."

46

INDIA

*H*is words shouldn't affect me like this. His touch shouldn't affect me like this. But that doesn't change the fact that I'm a slave to Jericho Forge.

His thick fingers stretch me and my body relaxes for him, letting him go deeper and faster with every stroke. *I want more.*

My nipples bead so tightly that they ache. I want his mouth on them, biting down on the sensitive skin to add an edge I never knew I needed.

When his thumb caresses my ass again, every nerve ending lights up.

"I'm going to fuck you here someday," he says, his voice a deep growl as he increases the pressure. "We're going to take our time stretching you out so that when the head of my cock slides inside this tight hole, you'll feel pleasure like you've never known existed. I'll finger your pussy with my cock in your ass, and you'll beg me until your voice goes hoarse."

He has no idea how close to begging I am right this minute. He pushes the tip of his thumb inside, and my hips rock against him. I don't know how much longer I can hold back until I throw myself on his mercy and plead for him to give me what I need.

You'd think I didn't come less than fifteen minutes ago. But I'm learning that Jericho Forge is even more addictive than any drug on the planet, and I'm moments away from admitting I'm a junkie.

His fingers pull free of my body, and he teases my piercing and my asshole at the same time until I'm poised to fly over the edge. When I shatter, he doesn't stop. He keeps demanding more and more and more.

The wall I've built is crumbling because he's burrowed under it and made me realize what I've been missing in my life—this. Him.

When my climax finally subsides to the point where I can think, he lifts me up to cradle me against his body. When he stands, he turns us toward the bed before laying me on my back on the edge, leaving my ass nearly hanging over.

"I think it's time I fuck my wife."

He moves to the nightstand, removes a condom, and rolls it over his cock before returning to stand between my spread legs.

"Wrap your legs around me."

I follow his orders and send up a prayer of thanks for tall bed frames, because his cock head now presses against my entrance. And then I remember his words.

Will it fit?

I look up at him, a tendril of hesitation blooming inside me, and Forge locks onto my shifting emotions.

"I'll fit. I promise."

With a hand under each of my smarting ass cheeks, he pulls me forward just far enough for his cock to breach my opening and groans.

"Fuckkkk . . ."

My mouth drops open, and I suck in a breath as sensations ripple through me. I may as well have been a virgin, because it's never felt like this before.

"More." I whisper the request, and the expression on Forge's face morphs into one of complete and utter possession. If I thought he looked like a pillaging pirate before, I was wrong—because that's exactly how he looks now.

"Fuck my cock. Show me you want it," he says as he pushes inside a little further. I lift my hips, pushing forward and forcing him deeper.

"Oh God. Oh God. Fuck." My head whips from side to side as I mumble incoherently.

"Fuck me, Indy. Use my cock to take what you need."

The fingers of one hand curl around my ass, and he presses one against my asshole. I buck upward, fucking him just like he ordered.

"Fucking magnificent. Give me more."

I do it again and again until I feel like I'm coming unglued, and still, he's not seated all the way inside me.

"Give it to me. All of it," I beg through broken moans.

"All you ever had to do was ask." He pushes forward, burying his cock inside me to the hilt, and my silent scream kicks me over the edge into devastating bliss.

Forge tunnels into me over and over and over. He

moves his other hand so he can tease my clit and keep the orgasms rumbling over me. My blood roars in my ears, and my heart beats hard enough to merit an explosion.

When Forge roars out his orgasm, his cock pumping inside me, my body goes limp and I let go.

INDIA

J wake up not knowing what the hell happened, but I'm still wearing my bathing suit top and am tucked under the covers.

Forge is nowhere to be seen, but the boat is rocking as it charges into choppy seas. I grab the discarded bikini bottoms, and pulling them up my legs reminds me of what Forge said.

"You were going to let everyone else see this ass? I don't think so. Not until I've staked my claim properly."

Every part of my body feels claimed by him now, and for some reason, that scares the living hell out of me.

I've never given a man any kind of control over me.

When I leave the cabin, I tiptoe around every corner, expecting him to pop out and take me by surprise. He doesn't, and I hate to admit that a part of me is disappointed.

Not that I need to see him, because I can still feel the ache left behind throbbing between my legs.

What the hell does this mean for us? Does it change

anything? I have absolutely no idea. And now, we're heading back to Ibiza, and I have a feeling if I try to go back to my flat, Forge is going to have something to say about it.

I find my sister on a chaise on the upper deck, which is otherwise empty, watching the sunset.

"So he really is the *good, good* dick!"

"Summer. Drop it," I snap.

"It's not like it's a big deal, Indy. Everyone has sex. I mean, except you. At least, until now." My sister levers up on her elbows to stare at me.

"I don't want to talk about it, okay?"

She stares at me in shock. "Why in the hell not?"

"I'm not having this discussion with you right now. Or ever."

She shakes her head, and the breeze catches her hair like she's posing for a magazine. "He's your husband. He's gorgeous. He clearly has some talent between the sheets if he can make a nun like you come, so why feel bad for banging him like a steel drum?" She winks. "See what I did there? Steel? Forge?"

I cover my face, wishing I could unhear that. "Please, just shut up, Summer."

"Fine . . . but it's nothing to be ashamed of. Goliath hustled me out here so I couldn't hear any more. I'm just enjoying the fabulous scenery now." She lays back against the cushion and gathers her hair up into a perfectly messy bun.

"Did he tell you when we'd be back in port?" I ask, looking out over the shimmering water surrounding us.

"Tomorrow morning. They let me use the phone to call Alanna again too."

I jerk my attention back to Summer. "You didn't tell her I got married, did you? Please tell me you didn't."

"No. I figure that's your mess to explain, and I'm not getting involved. But you better tell her before she finds out from anyone else, because she's going to have a fit."

"Who would . . ." I plop onto the lounger beside her as I think of any way Alanna could possibly find out.

"I don't know if Juliette is the gossiping type, but this is juicy news. One of the world's most eligible billionaires getting hitched after he publicly swore off marriage? When it gets out, it's going to spread like wildfire."

I sigh and stretch out on the thick cushion, letting my head drop back onto the pillow.

How the hell am I going to handle this?

J avoid Indy and my cabin until the sun rises over the islands ahead of us. I didn't trust myself to lie in bed next to her without keeping her up all night, and she needs time before she's ready for everything I want from her. Instead, I spent the entire night working on everything I've let slide since she shifted into the center of my world.

As soon as we drop anchor, I allow myself to close my laptop and make my way to the salon.

"You're coming with me," Goliath says to Summer.

"What about me?" Indy asks.

They all look at me as I enter. Indy's cheeks turn pink, and I can't help but hope she can still feel me with her every step. Maybe that's fucked up, but I don't care.

"You're coming home with me. Where you belong," I tell her.

"But I need to see Alanna too," she argues.

"We'll bring her out to the island tomorrow and tell her

the news." I shoot a look at her sister. "You say nothing about this when you see her. Understood?"

Summer nods as Indy's shoulders stiffen.

"But she needs to know. She's going to wonder why the hell I'm not with Summer."

"Summer will make your excuses, and Alanna will understand as soon as you tell her tomorrow." Indy will keep arguing until she runs out of air, so I try to preempt what's coming out of her mouth next. "I'd like to spend the afternoon showing you our home. And then this evening . . . I have something special planned for you." I reach out to grab her hand as her mouth snaps shut.

Argument over. I glance back at my new sister-in-law.

"Summer, your job starts Monday. Someone will make sure you have the information you need about where to go and when."

"Thank you, Forge. Really. I know I haven't said it enough, but . . . you saved my life and went above and beyond. I can't thank you enough."

"It's nothing."

"But—"

I wave her off as my new favorite boat approaches the yacht. "Go with Goliath. Enjoy your freedom, Summer. Don't fuck up."

INDIA

*a*s I lose sight of Summer and Goliath, I can't help but wonder what is going to happen when I get to Forge's private island. He didn't come to bed last night, and he was completely MIA until minutes ago.

Why is he avoiding me?

I'm not sure about anything right now, least of all how *I* feel about all of this. The last time I was on his turf, he made me a deal and I broke it in the most appalling fashion —I ran straight to Bastien.

I've been telling myself that since I didn't use Forge's million, the deal was null and void and there can be no further consequences to my actions. Whether he agrees with me is yet to be determined. It's not like I'm about to bring up the subject.

When the military-looking black boat that I rode on out to his island before ties off to the yacht's expansive swim platform, Forge leads me down the stairs. He jumps aboard and says something to the captain before returning to the side to help me on.

"Sit here." He points to the chair adjacent to the helm, and the captain gives him a nod.

"Enjoy, Mr. Forge."

"What the hell is he doing?" I ask when the captain hops off the black boat and unties it from the yacht.

"What I told him to do. Find his own way back. You and I are getting some lunch. Goliath told me you didn't eat breakfast."

I turn to look at him sharply. "Wait, if we're going for lunch, why didn't we go with Summer? I thought—"

"You'll see."

Forge takes the wheel and with an expert hand, he guides us away. As soon as we're a safe distance from the yacht, he guns it in the direction of the island, but not toward the dock I used before.

Wind whips my hair, and I quickly pull it back into a low ponytail as the boat speeds around the cliffs to the other side, which I've never seen before. It's almost a straight drop-off down a sheer rock face. It's utterly breathtaking.

We slow to a stop, and Forge turns off the ignition.

"What are you doing?" I ask as he reaches for the hem of his shirt.

He peels the polo off and tosses it over the seat. "Going fishing," he says, sidestepping me to open a compartment. He unearths a dive mask and a spear gun.

"Wait, what?" I step back as he climbs up onto the large sun pad on the back of the boat, looking like freaking Aquaman again, and slips the mask over his face.

"You'll see." He picks up the spear, turns, and steps off the side, holding the mask against his face.

"Forge!" I rush to the side of the boat to look, and he flips his body. All I see are his toes before they disappear beneath the surface.

I may have spent a lot of my life living on an island, but that doesn't mean I'm a big water lover. As a result, I'm not a strong swimmer. I can dog-paddle enough to get by, but that's about it.

And now I just watched my *husband* throw himself overboard with a freaking spear.

What in the actual fuck?

"Oh my God. We're not anchored." I don't know why I bother to say it out loud because no one's around to hear me. The boat bobs on choppy waves, no doubt drifting away from where he dove in.

What if something happens to Forge? I can't save him. I'm not a lifeguard. I scan the surface of the water, but I see nothing.

Wait, when did I get so concerned about making sure Forge is safe?

Probably about the time I realized he's the only man who hasn't tried to take something from me I didn't want to give, or use me in a way I didn't sign up to be used.

Does this mean I actually like *my husband?*

Bubbles break the surface before I can answer the question. And, *praise Jesus,* Forge's head comes next.

"Watch out," he yells, and I jump away from the side of the boat as he tosses something over the edge.

"Holy shit!" A spiny beast flops around on the deck. I turn to yell at Forge, but he's already gone again.

He did not just catch a lobster with his bare hands. But the prehistoric-looking creature crawling around the floor of the fancy boat tells me I'm mistaken.

Another sixty seconds pass before my panic levels rise again. *I really don't like wondering if he's going to come back up.*

But he does. This time with another lobster. He tosses it over the side, ignoring my "What the fuck are you doing?" and dives again.

He really is Aquaman.

Except he's not an actor playing a role. Forge is the real deal.

Indy, you need to watch yourself, the voice in my head says. *Don't go getting dick-struck by him because he released the Kraken on you.*

Before I can tell the voice to shut the hell up, he surfaces a final time and swims around to the back of the boat. Just like the morning I saw him climb out of the Med off the coast of Monaco, Forge's dripping-wet body is a sight to behold. How can a man who should work at a desk have all those abs? But judging by the fish skewered on the spear, nothing about Forge is normal.

I was right when I thought he was a pirate.

"I hope you like sea bream."

I'm still watching with my mouth hanging open. "You just . . . jumped off the boat."

He stares at me like I'm stating the obvious, which is fair, since I suppose I am.

"And caught lobster and speared a fish."

"Do you know how to cook?"

One of the lobsters' antennae hits my foot and I screech. "Fuck no!"

I jump onto the nearest high surface and out of the reach of the spiny little bastard. Losing my balance on the sun pad, I wobble dangerously close to the edge.

Forge's arm wraps around me, steadying me and keeping me from falling overboard. "Careful," he says, and the chuckle in his voice sounds like he's trying not to laugh at me.

I look down at him. "I don't like live lobster running loose."

His lips twitch, and I poke my finger into his chest.

"Don't you dare laugh at me. I didn't know what the hell you were doing, and then you just start tossing creatures in the boat." His smile widens, and I poke him again. "No laughing."

He reaches up to curl a hand around my neck and guides my head lower until his mouth slides across mine. My lips open and he slides his tongue inside, tasting me and tempting me in equal measure.

By the time he pulls away, I'm not only wet from the water dripping off his tanned skin.

With a knowing smile, he says, "I guess I'm cooking lunch then."

THIRTY MINUTES LATER, my jaw hangs open in shock again. Not only did Forge dock the boat and tie it off by himself, he carried both lobsters and the fish up to the outdoor kitchen and cleaned them all. Now he's manning the grill like he cooks for himself every day.

"Shouldn't . . . shouldn't someone be doing this for

you?" I gesture to the grill. "I mean, you must employ a bazillion people."

He meets my gaze with one brow raised. "Don't trust my cooking?"

"No, it's just . . . it seems weird. I didn't figure billionaires cooked for themselves," I say as I shift on the stool he told me to take unless I wanted to clean fish. So, on the stool I sit.

"You forget, I wasn't always a billionaire, but I've always liked to eat. That means I know how to cook."

As the sun moves higher in the sky, it dries Forge's hair into a wavy black mane brushing his shoulders. He really shouldn't be allowed to cook, because he's already too devastating it is.

You're already married to him, so what does it matter if you drool over him a little more?

My inner voice has a point. After all, I can still feel the pulse between my legs from yesterday.

He checks the temperature of the lobster with a meat thermometer and uses tongs to set them on two red plates. A few minutes later, he puts a chunk of the freshly grilled fish and wedges of lemon on them as well.

"Let's eat."

I follow him to the table where he offered me the check for a million dollars, and that's when the surreal nature of this meal hits me.

How did I even get here? The last week has been a crazy whirlwind, and now my life is completely unrecognizable. I left this table India Baptiste only days ago, and now I sit here as India Forge.

Never in a thousand years would I have predicted this.

I watch the man across from me as he digs into the food he caught and cooked. When he realizes I'm not eating yet, he pauses.

"Something wrong with your food?"

"No. I'm sure it's great. I'm just . . . overwhelmed, I guess."

"By?"

My teeth dig into my bottom lip until I work up the courage to tell him the truth. "You."

The corner of his mouth tilts at my admission. "You'll get used to it. Eat."

I'm three bites in and trying to control my urge to moan over the freshest lobster and fish I've ever eaten when a buzzing sound comes from near the grill.

His phone.

Forge rises and walks over to it. When he looks at the display, he swears under his breath before looking back at me. "I have to take this. Don't wait for me."

Without waiting for my reply, he walks toward the house before answering with a gruff, "What?"

I keep eating, but I'm more curious about who he's talking to than I am hungry. He didn't sound happy to get the call.

I take my time, but my plate is clear but for fish bones and destroyed lobster shell when Forge comes out of the house, dressed in a suit and tie.

"Whoa. I didn't expect the dress code to change so drastically."

His expression is grave. "I have to go. I'll be back when I can."

"Like . . . in an hour? Tomorrow? Next year?"

"Make yourself at home. Someone will find clothes you can wear, or your things will be brought from the yacht," he says, specifically not answering the question I asked.

"Is everything okay?" I push up from my seat, unease creeping along my spine. This Jericho Forge isn't the smiling one who looked proud that he caught lunch. This Jericho Forge looks like the man who took every penny I had at the poker table with ruthless and cold-blooded determination.

"Do whatever you want, but don't try to leave the island," he says, then turns and heads for the stairs that lead down to the pier.

"Forge!"

He pauses to look back at me.

"I'm not ready to be a widow yet."

Something flits across his expression, and he gives me another nod.

As soon as he disappears, I push back the chair from the table and hurry to the edge of the patio to watch his confident, long-legged stride take him to the boat. He unties it, climbs aboard, and then he's gone.

I watch the boat for as long as I can keep track of it.

And I'm now alone. On an island.

I clean up the remains of the meal, putting the shells and bones into the bag he used for cleaning the lobster and fish. I wash the dishes, close the grill, and look out at the stunning view before me.

This place may be beautiful, but when there's no one else around to share it with, it feels awfully lonely. *Does*

Forge ever get lonely? I immediately dismiss the question as silly.

With the bag of fish and lobster scraps in hand, I take the same path my husband took down to the pier, hoping that they would normally toss them back into the ocean to be recycled by nature. Or maybe I'm littering, but whatever.

I sit on the end of the dock, letting my legs hang over, and toss in the first lobster carcass. Immediately, a big fish rises to the surface to steal it away. The second one attracts another fish.

Well, that's kinda cool. I haven't fed fish since . . . Lord, I don't even remember how old I was. Our mom took Summer and me to Italy for a couple of months, and we stood on the shoreline after eating pasta. Summer begged her to let us bring the bread from dinner to feed the fish.

I'm so engrossed in rinsing out the empty plastic bag when I'm done that I don't notice the speedboat roaring toward the island until it's almost to the pier.

It's red. Not black like Forge's.

Whose boat is that?

Immediately, I pop up and scuttle backward, preparing to run back up the stairs to the house, but I pause when I see messy blond hair blowing around the man's head like a tarnished halo.

Bastien.

Shit. Shit. Shit. Nothing about this can possibly be a good situation.

He pulls up to the dock and tosses me a line.

"What are you doing here?" I ask as I squeeze the rope,

not sure what I'm supposed to do with it. I can't tie up Bastien's boat at Forge's dock. He won't just spank my ass for that. He might drown me.

"Did you marry him?"

The wind catches the plastic bag and rips it from my hand as Bastien's green eyes pierce me.

I have no idea how he found out, but I press my lips together for a beat. "Yes."

"Fuck! It was a setup." Bastien's tone turns harsh.

"What are you talking about?"

"Your sister's kidnapping. It was all bullshit. He played you."

Blood rushes in my ears as I stare at him in disbelief. Nothing he's saying makes sense.

"No. No. That's not possible."

Bastien looks over my shoulder, and I hear someone shouting my name from the top of the cliffs.

"Forge only cares about the money. He doesn't care who he hurts, especially you."

"I don't believe you. You have to leave." I glance behind me and see two men rushing down the carved rock stairs toward the dock.

"Think, Indy! Why the fuck would he marry you? He had a reason. You don't know who you really are."

"What the hell do you mean, *who I really am*?" My chest rises and falls faster and faster as I wonder what the fuck I've gotten myself into.

I trusted Forge. He got Summer back . . . *and he did it before we were even married.* I was so grateful that I didn't push harder for an explanation.

"Forge is using you to get what he wants from your father."

"My father?" My entire body shakes as I blink repeatedly.

Bastien looks beyond me again and thrusts out his hand. "I'll tell you everything, but you have to come with me now."

Footsteps pound down the pier behind me.

With trembling fingers, I reach out, and Bastien grabs my hand.

"Good girl. Let's go."

Indy and Forge's story continues in *Luck of the Devil* and concludes in *Heart of the Devil*.

ALSO BY MEGHAN MARCH

ABOUT THE AUTHOR

Meghan March has been known to wear camo face paint and tromp around in the woods wearing mud-covered boots, all while sporting a perfect manicure. She's also impulsive, easily entertained, and absolutely unapologetic about the fact that she loves to read and write smut.

Her past lives include slinging auto parts, selling lingerie, making custom jewelry, and practicing corporate law. Writing books about dirty-talking alpha males and the strong, sassy women who bring them to their knees is by far the most fabulous job she's ever had.
She would love to hear from you, connect with her at:

Website: meghanmarch.com
Facebook: /meghanmarchauthor
Twitter: @meghan_march
Instagram: @meghanmarch

NEUTRON PHYSICS

G. E. Bacon – University of Sheffield

DISTRIBUTED BY

 Springer-Verlag New York Inc.
175 Fifth Avenue, New York, N. Y. 10010

 WYKEHAM PUBLICATIONS (LONDON) LTD
(A subsidiary of Taylor & Francis Ltd)
LONDON & WINCHESTER
1969

Cover illustration—Instrument used for obtaining neutron diffraction patterns—by courtesy of the U.K.A.E.A.

Printed in Great Britain by Taylor & Francis Ltd, 10–14 Macklin Street, London, W.C.2.

85109 020 6

World-wide distribution excluding the Western Hemisphere, India, Pakistan and Japan by Associated Book Publishers Ltd., London and Andover

PREFACE

NEUTRON PHYSICS is a subject which is at first sight rather remote from the school laboratory but nevertheless draws on relatively simple principles learnt in optics, mechanics and electricity. Not only is the neutron an essential particle for building nuclei but a beam of neutrons can serve as a powerful tool for investigating the properties of solids and liquids.

In this book an attempt has been made to show the sixth-former how the facts and theories of physics which he learns at school are actively used in research which is extending the boundaries of our knowledge. Success will have been achieved if some of the fascination which is felt by those who engage in this kind of work becomes transmitted to the reader.

With the aim of encouraging the reader to gain a feeling for the orders of magnitude of the physical quantities discussed in this book, and to give him confidence in having grasped the essential principles of the subject, we have included some numerical questions. These are inserted within the text, rather than at the ends of chapters, in order to encourage the reader to check his understanding as he proceeds. As a rule the answers are given to two significant figures and any necessary physical constants are generally given in the question to a sufficient accuracy. For convenience these constants are also collected together on page 135 and we list on page xi symbols for those physical quantities which we have used frequently. Inevitably, in seeking to accord with conventions, some of these symbols have more than one identity, but in these cases the context should avoid any risk of ambiguity.

As in many branches of science, there is a closely-knit comradeship amongst those who work in neutron physics and the author is indebted to many of his friends who have permitted him to use illustrations from their papers. Finally he is greatly indebted to his schoolmaster collaborator who has assisted in so many ways to make this book more understandable.

Edale   G. E. BACON
July, 1969

To William

CONTENTS

Science and Technological

UNITS

S.I. units are used throughout this book and we list below those of the basic and derived units, together with multiples and sub-multiples, which we have often employed. These are followed by a list of other units which are in regular use in neutron physics. Interatomic distances and wavelengths of radiation are conveniently expressed in terms of the nanometre (10^{-9} m) but in order to simplify the task of any reader who consults earlier books or the original papers we also quote values in Ångström units (10^{-10} m).

BASIC AND DERIVED S.I. UNITS

ampere	A mA $= 10^{-3}$ A	magnetic moment	J/T or Jm^2 Wb^{-1}
		metre	m
density	kg/m^3		km $= 10^3$ m mm $= 10^{-3}$ m
frequency (hertz)	Hz kHz $= 10^3$ Hz		nm $= 10^{-9}$ m pm $= 10^{-12}$ m
		second	s
joule	J		ms $= 10^{-3}$ s μs $= 10^{-6}$ s
kilogramme	kg g $= 10^{-3}$ kg μg $= 10^{-6}$ g	volt	V kV $= 10^3$ V
magnetic flux density (tesla or weber per square metre)	T or Wb/m^2	watt	W kW $= 10^3$ W Mw $= 10^6$ W

OTHER UNITS

Ångström unit	$\text{Å} = 10^{-10}$ m $= 0.1$ nm
atomic mass unit	$u = 1.66 \times 10^{-27}$ kg
barn	10^{-28} m^2
curie	Ci mCi $= 10^{-3}$ Ci μCi $= 10^{-6}$ Ci
electron-volt	eV $= 1.60 \times 10^{-19}$ J keV $= 10^3$ eV MeV $= 10^6$ eV meV $= 10^{-3}$ eV
mol	mole (newly defined in terms of the number of atoms in 0.012 kg of ^{12}C, but here the molecular weight expressed in g).
k mol	$= 10^3$ mol ; or molecular weight expressed in kg

SYMBOLS

A	mass number
b	neutron-scattering amplitude (nuclear)
C_v	specific heat at constant volume
c	velocity of light *in vacuo*
γ	magnetic moment of neutron in nuclear magnetons
d	interplanar spacing
e	electronic charge
E	energy
ε	scattering vector
θ	(usually) Bragg, glancing, angle; $2\theta =$ angle of scattering
Θ	Debye temperature
g	acceleration due to gravity
h	Planck's constant
h, k, l	Miller indices
I, I_0	intensity
$\mathbf{K}$	magnetic moment vector
k	Boltzmann's constant
λ	wavelength
m, M	mass
μ	magnetic moment
μ_B	Bohr magneton
n	refractive index
N	number of atoms per unit volume
N_A	Avogadro's number
ν	frequency
p	magnetic-scattering amplitude
$\mathbf{q}$	magnetic interaction vector
q	wave-number $\equiv 2\pi/\lambda$
σ	cross-section
S	spin quantum number
u, v, V	velocity
ω	angular velocity
Z	atomic number

CHAPTER 1

introduction

I<small>F</small> any justification is required for a study of neutron physics then it must come from a realization of the leading dual role which the neutron plays. First, the neutron is a primary unit of construction for the nuclei of atoms. Secondly, it proves to be, in the form of beams of neutrons, a unique tool for investigating the structures of atoms, molecules, solids and liquids. Although its existence had been predicted earlier it was not actually discovered until 1932, largely because its great ability to penetrate materials without undergoing any reaction makes its detection difficult, in spite of its substantial mass.

The implications of this discovery, as viewed by the progress and understanding of physics during the succeeding five or ten years were enormous. For example, earlier attempts to explain the behaviour of the nuclei of the atoms by postulating that they were constructed of protons and electrons had failed, because several predictions from this idea were wrong. For instance, it had been found from very careful studies of spectra that nuclei behaved like spinning-tops, having an angular momentum and also a magnetic moment, but quantitative predictions about both of these properties in terms of what was already known about protons and electrons were quite incorrect. On the other hand, the experimental data were fully consistent with prediction when the nucleus was assumed to be built of protons and neutrons, with Z of the former and A–Z neutrons, where Z, A are the atomic number and mass number respectively for the nucleus. Subsequent study and measurement have justified the picture of the nucleus as an assembly of ' nucleons ', i.e. protons and neutrons, in motion. They will have angular momentum of two kinds : first, that associated with an orbit in space within the nucleus and, secondly, from what we can picture as an intrinsic spin about the particle's own axis. These angular momenta are quantized in units of $h/2\pi$ and $\frac{1}{2}h/2\pi$ respectively, where h is Planck's constant, in a corresponding way to that in which the more familiar angular momenta of the atom's electrons outside the nucleus are quantized.

The neutron itself is far from being a featureless object having a mass but no charge. It is radioactive, with a decay time of about 12 min, and itself possesses a magnetic moment—in spite of having no charge. These properties both contribute interest to the study of the particle itself and lead to certain features in its behaviour which make the neutron useful at a more practical level.

A second, and quite different, example of the impact of the neutron's discovery was the support which it gave to the concept of the dual nature of matter in terms of particles and waves. In 1936, only four years after the neutron's first discovery, experimental techniques had developed sufficiently to permit a demonstration that neutrons could be diffracted as waves. It is true that electrons had been diffracted nine years earlier, in 1927, but in many ways the diffraction of a relatively massive particle, with a mass roughly equal to that of a hydrogen atom, is a much more striking demonstration of the reality of the wave-particle concept. It is also true that diffraction effects had been demonstrated earlier with heavier particles, hydrogen molecules for example, but in the case of neutrons the concept has led to an experimental technique which, as we shall show, has made some unique contributions to our understanding of the properties of solids and liquids. The wavelength of a neutron, or any other particle, is h/mv, where m, v are its mass and velocity, and we shall show that it is particularly easy to obtain neutrons whose wavelengths lie in the useful range of values roughly equal to the average separation distances of atoms in solids. The reader will certainly find, as he follows our account of the properties and uses of neutrons, that its wave and particle aspects are fully intertwined. Broadly we may say that when we are considering the interchange of energy between a neutron and some other particle, or even with a macroscopic solid, then its particle aspect will be uppermost. At the other extreme, when we consider how a well-defined beam of neutrons becomes distributed in space when it impinges on the periodic arrangement of atoms which exists in a solid, we shall find that the wave nature of the neutron is all-important for our understanding. We shall see that it is mainly the nuclei of the atoms which act as the scatterers of the neutron waves, in contrast to the outer electrons which scatter X-rays and the electric potential within the atom which determines the scattering of beams of electrons. Quantitatively there is not a lot of difference in the extent to which atoms scatter X-rays or neutrons but an atom will scatter *electrons* much more readily, so readily in fact that a beam of electrons can only be used to examine the surface of materials. Neutrons, on the other hand, are extremely penetrating and solids and liquids of quite large dimensions can be studied.

From a historical point of view, we must emphasize the significance of the discovery of nuclear fission in 1938, leading as it did to exploitation of the chain reaction which permitted the continuous conversion of mass into energy in the nuclear reactor. This has two particular consequences from the viewpoint of this book. The reactor provides the beams of neutrons which we use to probe the structure of matter and, at the same time, it enables the neutron to provide both credibility and practical application for Einstein's relation $E = mc^2$.

We shall find it necessary to use familiar terminology from many branches of physics but we have tried to explain those concepts with which the reader may not be thoroughly familiar. We draw particular attention here to the distinction between a *nuclide*, which is a specific nucleus with both a given atomic (or proton) number and a given neutron number, and an *isotope*, which is one of a group of nuclides each having the same atomic number. We also mention, and we shall emphasize this later, that atomic masses are measured in terms of the *unified mass unit* u, which is $\frac{1}{12}$th of the mass of the carbon nuclide ^{12}C and numerically equals 1.66043×10^{-27} kg.

Finally, in trying to gather together the concepts on which we shall have to call in the succeeding chapters, we emphasize that when we are describing the way in which neutrons behave and how they interact with matter we are working mainly in terms of ' probability '. The young student often finds it hard to adjust his outlook from the certainty of macroscopic physics (in which the idea of probability does appear, but chiefly associated with error) to the statistical approach which is essential to the study of matter at the microscopic level (where the idea of probability is rather extended). Neutron physics provides an excellent opportunity to see how probability, in an understandable and simple sense of ' working out the odds ', really does come into physics at the atomic and nuclear level. We shall find in our study that the neutron, like other particles and radiations, can, in a given situation, behave in a variety of different ways. Thus, if we allow a beam of neutrons to fall on a fragment of solid then many different reactions will appear to take place at the same time. Some neutrons will traverse the solid without change of velocity or direction : some will suffer a change of velocity, some a change of direction and some will suffer both. Others will lose their identity completely, being absorbed by the nucleus of one of the atoms in the solid, followed perhaps by ejection of some other particle : indeed, one neutron may enter the nucleus and two or three will emerge, if nuclear fission has taken place. The point which we wish to emphasize is that *any one* of these reactions might take place. For a given set of experimental conditions we cannot predict in advance the fate of an individual neutron but we can state, after investigation, the percentage or fraction of occasions, or encounters, for which each mode of reaction will occur. Accordingly, for each mode of behaviour we can state the ' probability ' of occurrence and if we add up these ' probabilities ' they will add up to unity. We assume of course that we include the probability that the neutron will proceed without change, and indeed it will do this very often in many experiments because of its great power of penetration to which we have already referred.

3

CHAPTER 2

discovery of the neutron

THE periodical *Nature* dated 27 February 1932, included a " Letter to the Editor " entitled " Possible Existence of a Neutron " from J. Chadwick of the Cavendish Laboratory, Cambridge, and written ten days previously. At the time, this letter was seen as the culmination of many years of thought and practical experiment, going back to at least 1920 when E. Rutherford in a lecture to the Royal Society had speculated on the possible existence of a fundamental particle of unit mass but no charge. Chadwick's experiment and the associated work of his colleagues were in the established tradition of simple and elegant experiments in physics. At the same time the foundations

NATURE [FEBRUARY 27, 1932

Letters to the Editor

[*The Editor does not hold himself responsible for opinions expressed by his correspondents. Neither can he undertake to return, nor to correspond with the writers of, rejected manuscripts intended for this or any other part of* NATURE. *No notice is taken of anonymous communications.*]

Possible Existence of a Neutron

IT has been shown by Bothe and others that beryllium when bombarded by α-particles of polonium emits a radiation of great penetrating power, which has an absorption coefficient in lead of about 0·3 (cm.)$^{-1}$. Recently Mme. Curie-Joliot and M. Joliot found, when measuring the ionisation produced by this beryllium radiation in a vessel with a thin window, the ionisation increased when matter containing was placed in front of the window. The be due to the ejection of protons mum of nearly 3 × 10^9 cm.

This again receives a simple explanation on neutron hypothesis.

If it be supposed that the radiation consists quanta, then the capture of the α-particle by Be^9 nucleus will form a C^{13} nucleus. The m defect of C^{13} is known with sufficient accuracy show that the energy of the quantum emitted in process cannot be greater than about 14 × 10^6 vol It is difficult to make such a quantum responsi for the effects observed.

It is to be expected that many of the effects o neutron in passing through matter should resem those of a quantum of high energy, and it is not e to reach the final decision between the two hy theses. Up to the present, all the evidence is favour of the neutron, while the quantum hypothe can only be upheld if the conservation of energy a momentum be relinquished at some point.

J. CHADWICK

Cavendish Laboratory,
Cambridge, Feb. 17.

of a new tradition were being laid. In the same laboratory J. D. Cockcroft and E. T. S. Walton had built the first nuclear-physics machine and during that same week in February wrote a paper describing how they had accelerated protons through a voltage of 710 kV. A few months later they were able to announce that these protons had achieved the first purely man-made transmutation of an element, by converting lithium into helium. In retrospect, the discovery of the neutron and the advent of nuclear technology may be said to have set science on the road to becoming a primary instrument in determining the fate of nations.

In the years which immediately preceded Chadwick's discovery several groups of research workers had been studying the effect of bombarding some of the lighter elements with α-particles from radioactive sources. Beryllium had become a particularly interesting case because it was found to emit what appeared to be an exceptionally penetrating radiation. This radiation was detected by the ionization which it produced in a chamber containing air at high pressure and was found to be considerably more penetrating than any γ-radiation which was then known : when passed through a centimetre of lead its intensity was only reduced by 20%. A diagram which shows the radiation source and the ionization chamber appears as fig. 1. When a sheet of paraffin-wax was placed in front of the counter it was found that the number of deflections recorded by the oscillograph increased considerably. It was deduced from this that the radiation was ejecting particles from the paraffin-wax and it was found that these were protons. Samples containing other elements were exposed to the radiation and gases were also studied by incorporating them in the ionization chamber. In all cases extra deflections were produced and they were attributed to recoiling atoms of the various elements produced by the impact of the radiation.

This production of recoil atoms was thought of as similar to a process which had been discovered by A. H. Compton ten years

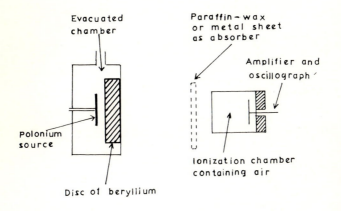

Fig. 1. Chadwick's original apparatus for demonstrating the production of neutrons when α-particles from polonium fall on a disc of beryllium.

earlier, in which loosely bound electrons are detached from atoms by X- or γ-rays. In this process the electron leaves the atom, carrying

5

away some of the incident quantum of energy, so that the photon is deflected from its incident path and takes up a longer wavelength. Broadly the collision between the electron and the energy quantum which represents the radiation is like a collision between two billiard balls and both energy and momentum are conserved. The basis of the calculation is indicated in fig. 2 and when it is carried out it is found that the maximum energy which a recoiling electron, or other particle, of mass m can carry away is:

$$\frac{2}{2+mc^2/h\nu}\,h\nu, \qquad . \qquad . \qquad . \quad (2.1)$$

where h is Planck's constant, ν is the frequency of the incident radiation and c is the velocity of light.

In the experiment with the beryllium radiation it was found that the ejected protons had velocities up to 33×10^6 m/s. From this value we can deduce by using expression (2.1) that the quanta of radiation have an energy of 55×10^6 eV. On the other hand, when a similar calculation was done for recoiling nuclei of nitrogen it was found that the incident quanta had to be 90×10^6 eV. It was equally disappointing to find that when a calculation was made of the intensity

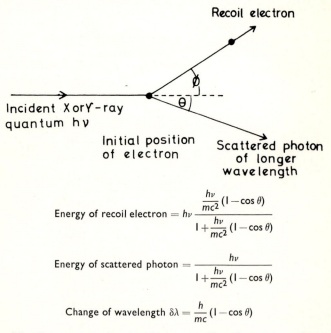

Energy of recoil electron $= h\nu\ \dfrac{\dfrac{h\nu}{mc^2}(1-\cos\theta)}{1+\dfrac{h\nu}{mc^2}(1-\cos\theta)}$

Energy of scattered photon $= \dfrac{h\nu}{1+\dfrac{h\nu}{mc^2}(1-\cos\theta)}$

Change of wavelength $\delta\lambda = \dfrac{h}{mc}(1-\cos\theta)$

Fig. 2. The Compton process in which a recoiling electron, or other particle, removes energy from an incident quantum of radiation, thus increasing the wavelength of the latter.

of scattering which might be expected for radiations of such an energy
—which could be done fairly accurately at that time—it was found that
the observed scattering was many thousand times greater than that
predicted. Both of these considerable difficulties disappear if we
assume that the emission from beryllium is *not* a quantum radiation
but a stream of particles which have a mass which is very similar to
that of a proton. We also have to assume, in order to account for the
extreme penetrating power of the radiation, that these particles carry
no net electrical charge. Chadwick proposed that these particles were
' neutrons ', supposedly a proton and electron in very close combination. Rutherford in 1920 had already speculated on the possibility

---

Question 1. *Calculate in electron volts the kinetic energy of a proton
of velocity $3 \cdot 3 \times 10^7$ m/s, given that the mass of a proton
is $1 \cdot 67 \times 10^{-27}$ kg and 1 eV $= 1 \cdot 6 \times 10^{-19}$ J.*
              Ans. $5 \cdot 7 \times 10^6$ eV.

Question 2. *In an exchange of energy by Compton scattering of
radiation, a proton of velocity $3 \cdot 3 \times 10^7$ m/s is ejected in
the forward direction from an atom. Calculate the
energy in a quantum of the incident radiation.*
              Ans. 52×10^6 eV.

---

that such a particle might exist. He had discussed it as an ' atom '
with very novel properties, which would be able to move fully through
matter and which it would be impossible to contain within a sealed
vessel. Chadwick's idea was that the α-particles from the polonium
source were knocking neutrons out of the beryllium nuclei and these

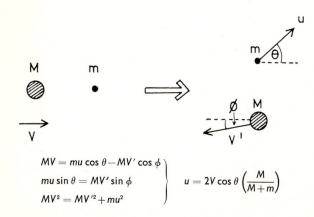

$$MV = mu \cos \theta - MV' \cos \phi$$
$$mu \sin \theta = MV' \sin \phi \qquad\qquad u = 2V \cos \theta \left(\frac{M}{M+m} \right)$$
$$MV^2 = MV'^2 + mu^2$$

Fig. 3.   The collision between an oncoming particle of mass M and velocity V
   with a stationary particle of mass m, showing the equations for conservation of momentum and energy and the value of u, the velocity given
   to the stationary particle.

7

neutral particles in their turn were knocking protons out of the paraffin-wax and ejecting the nuclei, such as nitrogen, from the other materials. With this interpretation the mechanics of the collision process are rather different and, indeed, much simpler, as indicated in fig. 3. If the oncoming particle has a mass M and velocity V it can be shown that the maximum velocity which it can give to a stationary hydrogen nucleus of mass 1 unit is:

$$u_{\mathrm{H}} = \frac{2M}{M+1} V, \qquad . \qquad . \qquad . \quad (2.2)$$

whereas the maximum velocity which would be communicated to a nitrogen nucleus of mass 14 units is :

$$u_{\mathrm{N}} = \frac{2M}{M+14} V. \qquad . \qquad . \qquad . \quad (2.3)$$

Chadwick and his colleagues were able to deduce the maximum velocities of both the protons and the nitrogen nuclei by observing the amount of ionization which they produced in a cloud chamber and found values of 33×10^6 and $4 \cdot 7 \times 10^6$ m/s respectively. By taking the ratio of these two velocities it follows from expressions (2.2), (2.3) that

$$\frac{M+14}{M+1} = \frac{33 \times 10^6}{4 \cdot 7 \times 10^6}, \qquad . \qquad . \qquad . \quad (2.4)$$

giving a value of M equal to $1 \cdot 15$ units, with a probable error of 10% due to uncertainty in fixing the velocities of the recoiling atoms of nitrogen. It was therefore clear that the mass of the ' neutron ' was quite close to the unit mass of the proton. A more precise estimate a little later gave the mass as lying between $1 \cdot 005$ and $1 \cdot 008$ units.

Question 3. *Calculate the maximum fraction of energy which can be lost by a proton when it collides with (a) another proton and (b) a carbon nucleus.*

Ans. (*a*) 100%, (*b*) 28%.

Before leaving our examination of Chadwick's original experiment we must emphasize one detail. When the beam of neutrons passes into the ionization chamber the *direct* ionization is completely negligible. The small response which is observed in the chamber, in the absence of the sheet of paraffin-wax or other material, is due to the *secondary* ionization produced by the nitrogen atoms in the air which are set in motion by the impact of the neutrons. This point is important and we shall show later on that different kinds of instrument, other than ionization chambers, are required for the efficient detection of neutrons.

CHAPTER 3

sources of neutrons

THE different kinds of source which can be used to provide beams of neutrons range as widely in physical size and complexity as in the intensity of neutron beams which they produce. At one extreme we have the nuclear reactor, and the very specialized technical installations which necessarily accompany it, and at the other are the small radioactive sources closely similar to the source which was used by Chadwick in his original experiments. In every case it is a *nuclear* reaction which leads to the appearance of the neutrons.

The small sources in common use are mixtures of beryllium with either polonium (atomic number 84) or radium (atomic number 88) and the α-particles which are emitted from the radioactive element eject neutrons from the beryllium according to the following equation :

$$\mathrm{^{9}_{4}Be + {}^{4}_{2}He = {}^{12}_{6}C + {}^{1}_{0}n + 5.7 \text{ MeV.}} \qquad . \qquad . \qquad (3.1)$$

These sources can be prepared in various ways, but their design is considerably determined by the health hazards which exist during their manufacture because of the danger of personnel coming into actual contact with the radioactive material. It cannot, of course, be over-emphasized that even in their completed form radioactive sources require to be handled extremely carefully, in precisely controlled and monitored conditions as laid down by the Code of Practice which prescribes their use. In one type of polonium source a pellet of material is prepared by compressing and drying a mixture of beryllium powder and a solution of polonium. An alternative method is to deposit a film of polonium electrolytically on a piece of platinum foil and then mount it between two sections of beryllium metal. Many of the nuclear reactions which produce neutrons are also accompanied by γ-rays, which are troublesome to the experimenter, but the polonium–beryllium reaction has the advantage that the accompanying γ-rays from an alternative mode of disintegration of ^{210}Po are very weak. On the other hand, there is a drawback because the decay of the polonium, which is changed into lead when the α-particle is emitted, takes place rather quickly. Half of the polonium atoms decay in about 136 days, so that the polonium–beryllium source will have only a limited life as a source of neutrons. In contrast to this behaviour, the life of a radium–beryllium source is extremely long. The half-life of radium, which decays to the gas radon when it emits an α-particle, is 1620 years. Unfortunately however the Ra–Be

9

source emits not only neutrons but an intense and very penetrating γ-radiation, which arises from the later decay products of the radon and this means that special precautions have to be taken by the operator who handles one of these sources. In particular they have to be placed in position by using a long handle rather like a broomstick, thus utilizing the effect of distance to reduce the intensity of any radiation. A typical way of manufacturing the radium source is to compress a mixture of beryllium powder and radium bromide. It is found that the number of neutrons which are ejected per second from each gram of radium increases steadily as the amount of beryllium is increased to about 10 g, but there is no significant increase in neutron output if more beryllium is used. At this stage the emission of neutrons is about 2×10^7 particles per second for each gram of radium : sources are rated according to the number of disintegrations which occur per second, and originally the unit of strength, called the 'curie' and abbreviated as Ci, was defined as that number per second which occur for 1 g of ^{226}Ra, which is about $3 \cdot 7 \times 10^{10}$/s. However, this form of definition meant that as measurements of the rate of α decay of radium were made more and more accurately the precise size of a curie changed. Accordingly the curie was redefined as that quantity of any radioactive nuclide in which the number of disintegrations per second is $3 \cdot 700 \times 10^{10}$. A source of this size is too large for many purposes and millicuries (mCi) and microcuries (μCi) provide suitable sub-units. We have already mentioned that polonium decays very much faster than radium—about 4500 times faster in fact —so that a curie-size source of polonium will contain that many times fewer atoms and will weigh only a little more than 0·2 mg. It is found to yield about 2×10^6 neutrons per second. A sketch of one of these sources, indicating the dimensions, is shown in fig. 4. The neutron outputs which we have just quoted are rather low, but the sources have the advantage of being small enough to be portable and easy to calibrate. Moreover, their output is either constant, for a radium source, or varies in an accurately known manner for polonium.

Question 4. *The half-lives of radium and radon are* 1620 *years and* 3·82 *days respectively. Calculate the mass of* 1 *Curie of radon.*

Ans. $6 \cdot 45 \times 10^{-6}$ g.

So far we have not said anything about the velocities with which the neutrons are ejected from the beryllium atoms. We can study the distribution of velocities by examining the implications of equation (3.1). According to this equation there would be 5·7 MeV of energy to be distributed between the neutron and the carbon atom, if the initial beryllium nucleus and α-particle did not possess any kinetic energy. In fact the α-particles from polonium have a kinetic energy of about 5·3 MeV and those from radium and its subsequent

10

decay products have energies lying between 4·8 and 7·7 MeV. Consequently there is more than 10 MeV of energy to be distributed between the neutron and the carbon atom. These energy values are, however, upper limits to the energy which will be available, because

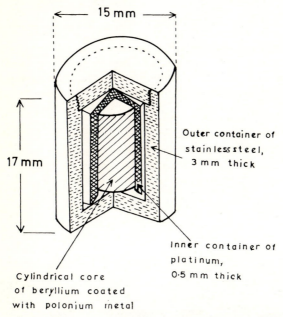

Fig. 4. Sketch of a polonium–beryllium source (courtesy U.K.A.E.A.).

many of the α-particles will lose some of their energy by colliding with other atoms in the source material before they reach their target atom of beryllium. The result is that there are wide variations in the overall amount of energy which is made available to the emerging particles. Moreover, the distribution between neutron and carbon nucleus has to be consistent with the conservation of momentum as well as energy and this means that the velocity of the emitted neutron will depend on the direction in which it emerges from the atomic nucleus. The overall result, when the neutrons emitted in all directions are considered, is that there is a wide range of energies extending from zero up to about 10 MeV. An experimentally measured distribution curve for a radium–beryllium source is shown in fig. 5. By equating the energy values to $\frac{1}{2}mv^2$ it can be shown that the neutron velocities range up to about 50×10^6 m/s. We shall see later on how it is possible to reduce further the velocity of the neutrons, by surrounding the source with a ' moderating ' material thus yielding ' slow neutrons ' which are more useful for some kinds

11

of experiment. We shall also consider in due course how the velocities of the neutrons may be measured.

Question 5. *Calculate the velocity of a neutron which has an energy of* 10 MeV.   (1 eV = $1 \cdot 6 \times 10^{-19}$ J, $m = 1 \cdot 6 \times 10^{-27}$ kg.)
Ans. $4 \cdot 4 \times 10^7$ m/s.

Surpassing these simple radioactive sources in their output of neutrons come the electrostatic accelerating machines. Several different nuclear reactions can be used in these machines, but one of the most useful and convenient is that in which a beam of deuterons,

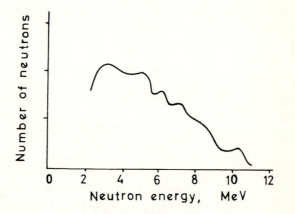

Fig. 5. The energy distribution curve for the neutrons from a radium-beryllium source (from the results of Thompson and Taylor, *Nucl. Instrum. Meth.*, **37**, 307, 1965).

nuclei of the hydrogen isotope of mass 2, is used to bombard a target of tritium, which is a hydrogen isotope of mass 3 which is radioactive with a half-life of about 12·5 years. Tritium is now relatively easy to obtain and suitable targets, capable of lasting for a few hundred hours of machine operation, can be purchased commercially. The reaction which takes place is :

$$^2_1H + {}^3_1H \rightarrow {}^4_2He + {}^1_0n + 17 \cdot 58 \text{ MeV.}$$

This reaction gives its maximum yield of neutrons when the initial deuteron particles are accelerated through a potential of about 150 kV, and the distribution of energy between the α-particle and the neutron is such that the latter leaves the target with an energy of about 14 MeV. The accelerating potential is provided by a small electrostatic generator and it accelerates the deuterons in a vacuum tube, at one end of which

12

they fall on a target of zirconium or titanium into which tritium gas has been allowed to diffuse. In a later arrangement, which extends the life of the target, a mixed beam of deuterium and tritium ions falls on a target which is coated with a mixture of erbium tritide and deuteride.

Photographs are shown in fig. 6 of an apparatus in a form designed particularly for carrying out neutron activation analysis, which is a technique which we shall discuss in Chapter 6. The output of neutrons can be increased up to about 10^{11} neutrons per second, i.e. several thousand times greater than what can be obtained from a Ra–Be source, but this maximum value can only be obtained for short pulses of time if rapid deterioration of the tritium is to be avoided.

Nuclear reactors provide the most intense sources of neutrons, depending for their operation on the process of nuclear ' fission '. This is the term used to describe one way in which a heavy atom, such as uranium, responds when it is struck by a neutron : it may split into two roughly equal portions, corresponding perhaps to krypton and barium or to zirconium and tellurium, together with two or three further neutrons. These elements have atomic numbers of 36, 56, 40 and 52 and their respective mass numbers are approximately 84, 137, 91 and 128. We shall see later that this fission process can lead to a self-sustaining reaction which yields a copious supply of neutrons. First of all it is interesting to see just how this process of nuclear fission was originally discovered, for it offers an instructive example of the use of combined physical and chemical methods. The discovery arose from experiments whose aim was to try to produce ' transuranic elements ', i.e. elements which have an atomic number greater than 92, the value for uranium which was the heaviest element which occurred naturally. When uranium was bombarded with neutrons it was evident that a number of different atomic species had been produced, because of the way in which electrons of several different velocities were emitted by the product and by the complicated way in which the activity of the product subsequently decreased with time. This decrease was interpreted as being the resultant of several curves, each one of which corresponded to a radioactive product with its own well-defined value of ' half-life '. In spite of the fact that the activities of these products can be measured very accurately they do correspond to very small masses of material, of the order of 10^{-12} g, and these were much too small to be isolated directly by chemical methods. However, they could be separated by addition of a ' carrier ', that is some chemical substance which would behave in the same way as the sought-for trace element but in a different way from the original uranium. A suitable carrier usually belongs to the same sub-group of the periodic table. Thus barium acts as a carrier for radium, and lanthanum for actinium : subsequently the trace element can be separated from its carrier by repeated fractional crystallization

13

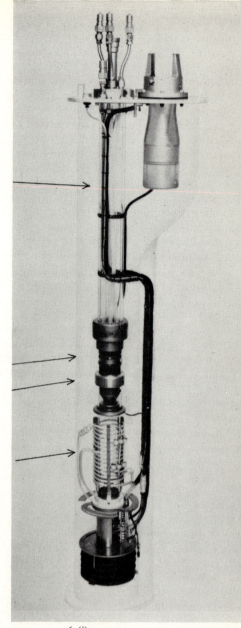

Sample transfer
system for
loading specimens
for activation
analysis

Position of
sample
for neutron
irradiation

Target position

Radio-frequency
ion source

6 (i)

Fig. 6.   A commercially manufactured neutron generator of the deuterium–
tritium type, designed for the irradiation of samples for neutron-
activation analysis (courtesy of Elliott Electronic Tubes Limited).   The
facing page shows the generator in use.

14

6 (ii)

15

from solution. During the analysis of the products of neutron-bombardment of uranium atoms O. Hahn and F. Strassmann found that the active components which had been carried over by barium and lanthanum, and which they were expecting to prove to be radium and actinium respectively, could not be separated from the barium and lanthanum. Subsequent investigation showed that the activities actually belonged to atoms of barium and lanthanum, in fact to the isotopes ^{139}Ba and ^{140}La, which had been produced by fission of some of the original atoms of uranium. The interpretation was soon confirmed by O. R. Frisch and others who detected enormous bursts of ionization when a thin layer of uranium was placed in an ionization chamber and bombarded with neutrons. These bursts of ionization are very large compared with those produced by α-particles.

It would be quite misleading to suppose that there was only a single way in which a uranium nucleus could split into two pieces. When uranium is bombarded with slow neutrons it is the ^{235}U nucleus which splits and, almost invariably, the products fall into two groups, a ' light ' group with mass numbers from 85 to 104 and a ' heavy ' group with mass numbers from 130 to 149. The most common form for the ' split ' is one for which the ratio of the two masses is almost exactly 3 : 2. At least sixty primary products have been detected so that the uranium atom is able to split in at least thirty different ways, each providing its own pair of fission products. Many of the primary products are themselves unstable and decay to other nuclei, which are stable isotopes of the same mass number, by the successive emission of electrons and γ-rays. An example of such a decay chain is :

$$^{99}_{42}\text{Mo} \xrightarrow[\text{66 hours}]{} {}^{99}_{43}\text{Tc} \xrightarrow[2 \cdot 2 \times 10^5 \text{ years}]{} {}^{99}_{44}\text{Ru}.$$

This is a particularly interesting example because it includes a long-lived isotope of the element of atomic number 43, technetium, an element which is not found in nature. The successive changes which occur in these chains make the problem of identifying the initial fission products a difficult and tedious one. However, it has been shown that for ^{235}U the initial products are distributed in mass number according to the curve shown in fig. 7 which emphasizes that a division into two equal fragments occurs extremely rarely.

Further experiment revealed that our view of the fission process has to be modified in a very important way and in a manner which is of very great practical significance. Soon after the first discovery of the fission process it was shown that when a ^{235}U nucleus captures a bombarding neutron it does not simply break up into two large pieces : it also emits some more neutrons, usually two or three. A typical break-up would be represented by :

$$^{235}\text{U} + {}^{1}_{0}\text{n} \xrightarrow{\hspace{1cm}} {}^{236}\text{U} \xrightarrow{\hspace{1cm}} {}^{95}_{42}\text{Mo} + {}^{139}_{57}\text{La} + 2{}^{1}_{0}\text{n}.$$

16

The molybdenum and lanthanum nuclei are the final stable products at the end of the two chains of electron emission which start from the primary fission products. As we have already said, the ^{236}U nucleus may break up in at least thirty different ways and these will generally be accompanied by either two or three neutrons. The average number can be measured directly by experiment and is found to be $2 \cdot 5 \pm 0 \cdot 1$.

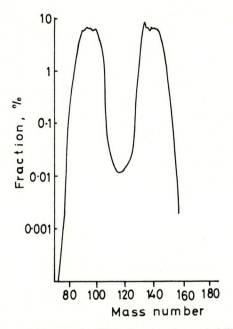

Fig. 7. The fission yield curve for ^{235}U, showing the probability that a nucleus of any particular mass number will be found in the fission products (from *The Nuclear Reactor*, Salmon: Methuen, London, 1964).

The important feature is that this number is greater than unity and this means that there is the possibility of a self-sustaining chain reaction. Assuming that a single initial neutron is forthcoming (say from cosmic rays) to break up the first uranium atom, then it will be realized that this neutron will be ' over-reproduced ' and indeed that the number of neutrons will continuously increase. Before we follow up the implications of this we will comment on a second feature of the fission process and we shall in due course see that these two features together provide the fundamental requirements for both the nuclear reactor and the atomic bomb. The second feature relates to the amount of energy which is released when a nucleus undergoes fission.

In ordinary nuclear reactions the release of energy may be 5–10 MeV but the energy released during fission is enormously greater than this and amounts to about 200 MeV. We can get an idea of the reason why it is so large by examining the curve which relates the binding energy of nuclei to their mass number. First of all, let us examine Table 1 which gives the atomic masses of certain isotopes as determined by the mass spectrograph. The neutron is included in the table. The scale of mass which is used is the one according to which the mass of the predominant isotope of carbon is taken as exactly 12 units (u). Almost all of the mass values shown in the table are known to an accuracy of 0·000001 units. This scale is not quite the same as the earlier *chemical* scale of mass which was used prior to the year 1961, because the older scale takes ordinary atmospheric oxygen to have an atomic mass of exactly 16. ' Ordinary ' oxygen contains 99·76% of the ^{16}O isotope, about 0·2% of ^{18}O and 0·04% of ^{17}O, so that the value for this mixture on the ' Carbon 12 scale ' amounts to 15·9994. Table 1 also lists quantities known as the ' packing fraction ' and the ' binding energy '. The former of these is simply the fraction by which the listed value of an atomic mass departs from a whole number : thus in the case of ^{32}S the packing fraction is $-0·027926/32$ or $-8·72 \times 10^{-4}$. We define the ' binding energy ' as representing the difference between the measured value of an atomic mass $M_{Z,A}$ and the sum of the masses of the constituent particles, i.e. protons, electrons and neutrons which are needed to build up the particular isotope. The two mass values are not the same, simply because when an atom is ' formed ' from its components there is a release of energy and, conversely, it is necessary to supply this same quantity of energy in order to break up an atom into its component parts, that is into protons, electrons and neutrons. When the atom is formed the ' binding energy ' ΔE which is released appears, taking account of Einstein's principle that mass and energy are equivalent, as a loss of mass Δm such that

$$c^2 \, \Delta m = \Delta E.$$

We can therefore write :

$$\Delta E/c^2 = \Delta m = Zm_{\mathrm{H}} + (A - Z) \, m_n - M_{Z,A},$$

where

Z = atomic number,

m_{H} = mass of a neutral hydrogen atom, i.e. proton + electron,

m_n = mass of a neutron,

A = mass number,

$M_{Z,A}$ = measured atomic mass, as given in Table 1.

If we insert the values of m_H, m_n from Table 1 and express the value of ΔE in MeV, by using the fact that 1 unit of atomic mass ($u = 1.66 \times 10^{-27}$ kg) is equivalent to 931.48 MeV, we find that

$$\Delta E \text{ in MeV} = 931.48[1.007825Z + 1.008665(A - Z) - M_{Z,A}].$$

Table 1
Atomic masses, packing fractions and binding energies for some of the stable isotopes

Nuclide	Number of		Mass u	Packing fraction (units of 10^{-4})	Binding energy (MeV)	
	Protons	Neutrons			Total	Per nucleon
${}^{1}_{0}$n	0	1	1.008665			
${}^{1}_{1}$H	1	0	1.007825	78.25		
${}^{2}_{1}$H	1	1	2.014102	70.51	2.2	1.1
${}^{4}_{2}$He	2	2	4.002603	6.51	28.3	7.1
${}^{7}_{3}$Li	3	4	7.016004	22.86	39.5	5.6
${}^{9}_{4}$Be	4	5	9.012186	13.54	58.0	6.4
${}^{12}_{6}$C	6	6	12.000000	0	92.1	7.7
${}^{14}_{7}$N	7	7	14.003074	2.19	104.6	7.5
${}^{16}_{8}$O	8	8	15.994915	−3.18	127.5	8.0
${}^{19}_{9}$F	9	10	18.998405	−0.84	147.7	7.8
${}^{27}_{13}$Al	13	14	26.981539	−6.84	224.8	8.3
${}^{28}_{14}$Si	14	14	27.976930	−8.24	236.4	8.4
${}^{32}_{16}$S	16	16	31.972074	−8.72	271.6	8.5
${}^{56}_{26}$Fe	26	30	55.934937	−11.62	492.0	8.8
${}^{63}_{29}$Cu	29	34	62.929592	−11.17	552.1	8.7
${}^{86}_{38}$Sr	38	48	85.909285	−10.55	749.6	8.7
${}^{95}_{42}$Mo	42	53	94.905839	−9.91	821.6	8.6
${}^{116}_{50}$Sn	50	66	115.901745	−8.47	988.2	8.5
${}^{139}_{57}$La	57	82	138.906140	−6.75	1165	8.4
${}^{194}_{78}$Pt	78	116	193.962725	−1.92	1537	7.9
${}^{236}_{92}$U	92	144	236.045637	1.93	1790	7.6
${}^{238}_{92}$U	92	146	238.050770	2.13	1803	7.6

As a particular example we can work out the value of ΔE for an atom of sulphur with a ^{32}S nucleus. Using the values of $A = 32$, $Z = 16$ and $M_{Z,A} = 31.972074$ we find that ΔE is equal to 271 MeV. It is convenient to express this binding energy in terms of the energy per nucleon, where by the term 'nucleon' we mean the individual protons and neutrons which we regard as the building blocks of the nucleus. For the ^{32}S isotope there are thirty-two nucleons so that the binding energy per nucleon will be 8·5 MeV. This value is shown in Table 1 and if we plot the variation of this binding energy as a function of mass number, for all isotopes including the many which are not included in Table 1, we obtain the curve which is shown in fig. 8.

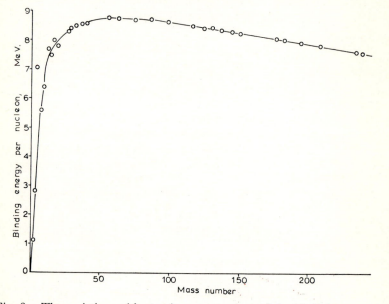

Fig. 8. The variation, with atomic mass number, of the binding energy per nucleon.

Question 6. *From the mass values given in Table 1 calculate the packing fractions for (a)* ^{16}O, *(b)* ^{116}Sn.
Ans. (a) $-3\cdot18 \times 10^{-4}$, (b) $-8\cdot47 \times 10^{-4}$.

Question 7. *Calculate in* MeV *the energy produced by conversion of a mass of* 1 u. (1 eV = $1\cdot60 \times 10^{-19}$ J.)
Ans. 931 MeV.

Question 8. *From the mass values given in Table 1 calculate the binding energy, in* MeV, *for* ^{27}Al.
Ans. 224 MeV.

It is possible to derive a semi-empirical formula which will give the values of the isotopic masses $M_{Z,A}$ to an accuracy of a few parts

20

in 10^5, when $A > 15$. This formula is:

$$M = 0 \cdot 99394A - 0 \cdot 00084Z + 0 \cdot 014A^{2/3} + 0 \cdot 000627Z^2 A^{-1/3}$$
$$+ 0 \cdot 083[Z - (A/2)]^2 A^{-1} + \delta \quad \text{mass units.}$$

δ is an empirical constant which has the following values:

$$\delta = 0 \quad \text{for } A \text{ odd}$$
$$= -0 \cdot 036A^{-3/4} \quad \text{for } A \text{ even and } Z \text{ even}$$
$$= +0 \cdot 036A^{-3/4} \quad \text{for } A \text{ even and } Z \text{ odd.}$$

The essential feature of the curve in fig. 8 is that it has a flat maximum in the region of mass numbers 50–100 and then decreases steadily towards large values of A. It is this latter variation which is important in relation to nuclear fission: on the other hand, the rapid fall in ΔE towards small values of A is of primary importance in the understanding of *thermonuclear* reactions. Because of the steady fall in ΔE as A increases beyond about 80, there will be a substantial release of energy when a uranium nucleus splits into two large fragments as a result of fission. Let us take the example which we considered earlier, whereby the ^{236}U atom, produced from ^{235}U and the incident neutron, splits into atoms of molybdenum, $^{95}_{42}$Mo, and lanthanum, $^{139}_{57}$La, and two neutrons. It can be found from Table 1 that the combined mass of the products is 235·829 units whereas the mass of the ^{236}U atom amounts to 236·045 units. This means that 0·216 atomic mass units have been converted into energy for each fission which takes place. Since a mass unit is equivalent to 931 MeV it follows that 198 MeV of energy is liberated in each atom which undergoes fission, thus confirming the statement which we made earlier. We have made this calculation for just one of the many ways in which the uranium atom may split, but it will be found that the excess of mass is roughly the same in all cases and 200 MeV is a good average value for the release of energy. The enormous magnitude of this energy release may be appreciated better if we express it in different terms. If we can carry out fission of 1 g of ^{235}U each day, then we shall have a power source of 1 MW, i.e. a source sufficient to run 1000 one-bar electric fires continuously. Alternatively, in terms of explosive power, we may say that the energy released from the 1 g of ^{235}U is about equal to that available from the explosion of 20 tons of TNT. The liberated energy from fission has to be distributed between the fission fragments, the emitted neutrons and any electrons and γ-rays produced in the decay chains, but it is found that the great majority of the energy is carried by the fission fragments, divided between them in such a way that momentum, as well as energy, is conserved. In a typical case the two fission fragments, together, would have an energy of about 170 MeV.

21

Question 9. *Calculate the power of an energy source in which each atom in* 1 kg *of* ^{235}U *splits, via the compound nucleus* ^{236}U, *into* ^{95}Mo *and* ^{139}La *and two neutrons over a period of a year.* (1 eV = $1\cdot60 \times 10^{-19}$ J.)

Ans.   2·62 MW.

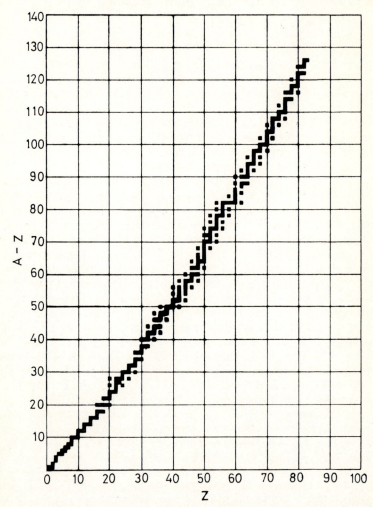

Fig. 9.   Segrè chart showing the relation between the number of nuclear neutrons and the atomic number, for the stable nuclides (from *Nuclear Physics*, Second Edition, by Irving Kaplan, 1963, Addison-Wesley, Reading, Mass., U.S.A.).

If for all the elements we make a plot which indicates the number of neutrons in the nuclei of each of their stable isotopes, in relation to the atomic number, then it will be found to have the form shown in fig. 9. Such a diagram is known as a Segrè chart and shows that for a given atomic number only a few different neutron numbers, and consequently mass numbers, are observed. We can consider therefore that the neutrons which are emitted during the fission process arise because a simple split of the uranium nucleus into two pieces would result in fragments which contained too many neutrons, relative to protons, to provide a stable atom. Stability is then achieved by emission of a neutron, generally accompanied by a γ-ray, and this happens extremely rapidly, probably within 10^{-14} s of the fission.

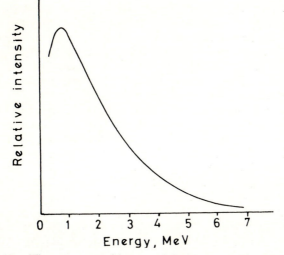

Fig. 10. The spectrum of 'prompt' fission neutrons from ^{235}U.

There are also a number of groups of 'delayed neutrons' whose emission can take place shortly after the fission process, with a delay of up to a few minutes. Numerically these are very insignificant, amounting to less than 1% of the neutrons from ^{235}U, but each group has its own half-life, as does every radioactive process, and these half-lives range from about a second to a minute.

We have developed this discussion of the process of nuclear fission at some length in order to understand the role of a nuclear reactor as a source of neutrons. Before we can attempt to establish this we have to clarify one further detail concerning the neutrons which are emitted in the fission process, namely the spectrum of velocities which is produced. The energy spectrum of the 'prompt' neutrons, namely those which are emitted effectively instantaneously with the nuclear fission, is a continuous one of the form which is shown in fig. 10 for ^{235}U. As will be seen, the peak of the fission spectrum occurs at an energy of about 1 MeV and the average energy of all the neutrons which are emitted is about 2 MeV. The spectra from other fissile nuclei are very similar to this, with slightly different values for the numerical constants which define the exact shape of the curve. The fission spectrum is practically independent of the energy of the incoming neutrons which initiate the reaction.

We have already mentioned that the possibility of a self-sustaining chain reaction rests upon the fact that the average number of neutrons liberated for each nucleus which undergoes fission is greater than unity. We have, however, to satisfy an important requirement before a chain reaction can be built up : we must ensure that neutrons are not lost from the chain for other causes. First, we must make sure that neutrons do not escape outside the reacting material before they have an opportunity to initiate another fission : this means that there will be a minimum size for the reacting mass, below which no chain reaction can be sustained. Secondly, we must ensure that the neutrons are not able to take part in other reactions as an alternative to fission. This is a very real danger, particularly in the case of ordinary uranium. In ' ordinary ' uranium, as it occurs in nature, only about one atom in each 140 is the ^{235}U isotope. The vast majority of the metal consists of ^{238}U which has quite different nuclear properties from those of the ^{235}U isotope. For the latter isotope the probability that fission will take place increases rapidly as the bombarding neutron velocity decreases. For ^{238}U, on the other hand, fission can only be caused by fast neutrons and, even then, only with a low probability : moreover, many neutrons in the range of energy between 5 eV and 2 keV are captured by ^{238}U atoms without any fission taking place. The simplest way therefore of making sure that most of the neutrons will be able to produce a further fission in a ^{235}U nucleus is to slow them down as quickly as possible after their first appearance. This ' slowing-down ' of the neutrons can be achieved by mixing the uranium with a ' moderator '. We shall show that an effective moderator is a material which contains only ' light atoms ' such as hydrogen, beryllium or carbon, with the proviso that the atoms which we choose will not be ones which are likely to remove the neutrons by other processes such as absorption. There are many different ways in which the mixture of uranium and moderator is arranged in practice. In one much-used design, rods of uranium are placed in long cylindrical cavities in a block of graphite. This is typical of many *heterogeneous* arrangements and it may be contrasted with a reactor which uses an aqueous solution of a uranium salt, where the uranium atoms and the moderating hydrogen atoms in the water molecules form a homogeneous mixture.

We can easily justify the choice of light atoms for the moderating material by making a calculation which is similar to that in the familiar problem in dynamics which investigates the collision of two elastic balls. In fig. 11 an oncoming neutron of mass *m* and velocity

24

v_0 collides with a stationary atomic nucleus of mass M. After the collision the two particles separate with velocities v, V respectively and in the directions defined by the angles α, β. If we write down the conditions for the conservation of energy and momentum in the collision, we have the following three equations :

$$mv_0 = MV \cos \beta + mv \cos \alpha, \qquad . \qquad . \quad (3.2)$$

$$mv \sin \alpha = MV \sin \beta, \qquad . \qquad . \quad (3.3)$$

$$mv_0{}^2 = MV^2 + mv^2, \qquad . \qquad . \quad (3.4)$$

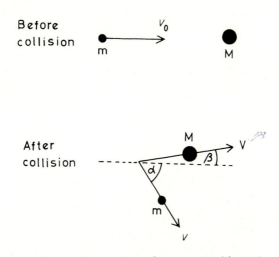

Fig. 11.   Collision of oncoming neutron of mass m ● with stationary nucleus of mass M ● in moderator.

from which α, v may be eliminated to give the result :

$$V = v_0 \frac{2m}{M+m} \cos \beta. \qquad . \qquad . \quad (3.5)$$

The energy which the neutron loses in this collision will be the amount transferred to the nucleus, i.e. $\frac{1}{2}MV^2$, and this will constitute a fraction x of the initial energy given by :

$$x = \tfrac{1}{2}MV^2 / \tfrac{1}{2}mv_0{}^2. \qquad . \qquad . \quad (3.6)$$

It follows from equation (3.5) that

$$x = \frac{4Mm}{(M+m)^2} \cos^2 \beta. \qquad . \qquad . \quad (3.7)$$

3

25

From this expression we see that when $\beta = 90°$, x will be zero. This is simply a ' glancing ' collision for which the velocity V imparted to the nucleus is zero and the neutron is not deflected from its initial path. On the other hand, we get maximum transfer of energy when $\beta = 0$ and in this case a fraction $4Mm/(M+m)^2$ of energy is given to the nucleus. For a head-on collision of this kind we get a specially interesting case if $M = m$, since this will make the fraction of energy lost equal to unity, so that the neutron loses the whole of its energy. This means that in a head-on collision with a proton the neutron would lose the whole of its energy in a single collision. For any particular value of the angle β equation (3.7) leads to the conclusion that as M increases the value of x decreases. This is clearly seen by noting that when $M \geqslant m$:

$$x \to 4(m/M)\cos^2 \beta. \qquad . \qquad . \qquad . \quad (3.8)$$

As an example we can take the case of carbon, for which $M = 12$ and for which equation (3.7) states that the maximum energy transfer in a collision is 28% : the approximate formula (3.8) gives 33%.

Question 10. *Calculate the maximum fraction of its kinetic energy which a neutron may lose when it collides with (a) a proton, (b) a deuterium nucleus, (c) a ^{12}C nucleus.*
Ans. (a) 100%, (b) 89%, (c) 28%.

As a result of the ' slowing-down ' collisions with atoms of the moderator the velocity of the neutron will fall below the range at which absorption in ^{238}U is likely to occur and within the range for which fission of ^{235}U is likely. The chain reaction is therefore enabled to continue and we have produced a nuclear reactor. So far as the present book is concerned we are interested in this simply as a source of neutrons, rather than as a source of power. An immediate consequence of the mechanism whereby the moderator has enabled us to build up a self-sustaining reaction is that the spectrum of neutrons within the reactor is quite different from the distribution which we showed in fig. 10. The presence of the ' fission spectrum ', which this figure shows, will be almost completely hidden by the large number of slowed-down neutrons, since the logical outcome of the moderating process is that the neutrons will be gradually slowed down by successive collisions until they have about the same energy as an average atom of the moderator itself. This energy will depend on the temperature of the moderator, and the calculation of the velocity–distribution curve for the neutrons is a problem to be solved by the kinetic theory in the same way as the distribution curve for the velocities of gas molecules is computed. It can be shown that the number of gas molecules which have velocities which lie between a value c and $c+dc$, where dc is a small increment, is proportional to :

$$T^{-3/2} \exp\left(-mc^2/2kT\right) c^2 \, dc,$$

where T is the temperature in Kelvin, k is Boltzmann's constant and m is the mass of a molecule.   This expression gives a distribution curve which is plotted in fig. 12 for several different temperatures, for the

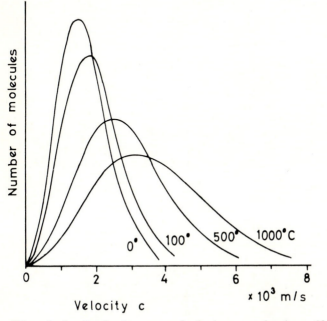

Fig. 12.   The velocity distribution curves for hydrogen molecules at 0°, 100°, 500° and 1000°C, calculated according to the kinetic theory.

case of hydrogen, by inserting for m the mass of a hydrogen molecule. As the temperature gets higher the peak moves to higher velocities and the distribution becomes broader.   It can be deduced from the above expression that, at a temperature $T°$K, the root-mean-square velocity of the molecules will be given by :

$$\tfrac{1}{2}mv^2 = \tfrac{3}{2}kT. \qquad . \qquad . \qquad . \quad (3.9)$$

Exactly the same equation will apply for the root-mean-square velocity of the moderated neutrons if we insert the mass of the neutron for m.   For a temperature of 20°C this equation leads to a neutron velocity of 2·2 km/s, which is equivalent to an energy of 0·027 eV.   This energy is vastly smaller than the energy at the peak of the fission spectrum in fig. 10.   When we express the moderated neutron spectrum as a function of energy we shall therefore have to

27

use quite a different scale for the abscissae from that which we used in fig. 10. Such a spectrum is plotted in fig. 13. This figure shows two curves which we can explain with the aid of fig. 14, where we illustrate a lined hole whose sides are assumed to be not penetrable by neutrons and which extends into the moderator of the reactor. If we could take a representative sample of neutrons at the point A and then measure the velocity of each of them, then we should obtain a

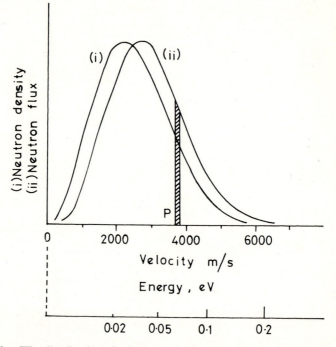

Fig. 13. The distribution of velocity, and energy, among the neutrons (i) within a moderator, and (ii) emerging in a collimated beam. The shaded area indicates a suitable choice of 'monochromatic' neutrons for a diffraction experiment.

distribution curve $N(v)$ like that labelled (i) in fig. 13, which has a peak at the velocity for which $\frac{1}{2}mv^2 = kT$. We emphasize that this is the velocity which gives the peak of the distribution curve, i.e. the most probable velocity, in contrast to the velocity specified by equation (3.9) which is the root-mean-square velocity for neutrons which are in equilibrium at temperature T. On the other hand, we get a different result if we study the neutrons which have travelled down the lined hole and emerged at B, having assumed that the end face of the hole at A is penetrable. If we measure how many neutrons with velocities within a given small range are crossing a unit area at B each second, it will be proportional not to $N(v)$ but to the product $vN(v)$. The shape of this distribution is shown as curve (ii) in fig. 13 which has a peak at the velocity for which $\frac{1}{2}mv^2 = \frac{3}{2}kT$. Later in this book we shall show how we can select from this distribution those neutrons whose velocities lie within a small range, such as is indicated by the narrow band at P in fig. 13. For the present we will simply emphasize again the difference between the 'thermal spectrum' and the 'fission spectrum'. The former can be measured quite easily by sampling the neutrons outside the reactor, at the position B in fig. 14. In order to measure the fission spectrum it is easiest to do

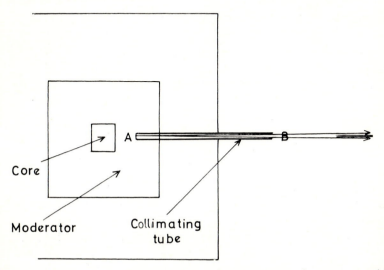

Fig. 14. The use of a collimating tube to produce a beam of neutrons outside a nuclear reactor. Measurements at A sample the 'neutron density': those at B sample the 'neutron flux'.

a subsidiary experiment outside the reactor, by letting the thermal beam fall on a thin foil of uranium. The secondary neutrons which emerge from this foil will then have the normal fission distribution.

Question 11. *Calculate the root-mean-square velocity and the energy in eV of neutrons which are in thermal equilibrium with a moderator at 100°C. What is the 'most probable' velocity of these neutrons?*
Ans.   3·04 km/s, 0·048 eV, 2·48 km/s.

Question 12. *Calculate the value of the velocity at the peak of the velocity distribution curve for the neutrons which emerge from a collimator which leads from a moderator at a temperature of 100°C.*
Ans.   3·04 km/s.

We may mention one other type of neutron source, known as a ' neutron booster ' which combines certain features of an accelerating machine and a nuclear reactor. Many different nuclei will emit neutrons when they are irradiated with γ-rays but all except deuterium and beryllium require γ-rays of very high energy. The threshold energy for the reaction is about 19 MeV for carbon and falls to about 10 MeV for very heavy elements. The neutron booster starts off with a beam of electrons from a 45 MeV linear accelerator and these are allowed to fall on a stream of liquid mercury from which they

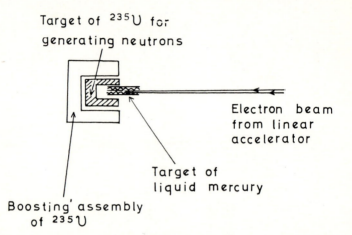

Fig. 15. Diagram to illustrate the principle of the neutron booster.

generate γ-rays. The advantage of using a stream of mercury as the target is that it can also carry away the enormous amount of heat which is developed : up to about 30 kW of power have to be dissipated in a few cubic centimetres of target. The γ-rays are then propagated mainly in the forward direction where, as illustrated in fig. 15, they impinge on a further target of ^{235}U. The interaction with the ^{235}U nuclei ejects neutrons which are then greatly multiplied in number by surrounding the target with a further assembly of ^{235}U, in which nuclear fission takes place in the manner which we have already discussed. Sufficient fissile material is used to ensure that a chain reaction develops, but not enough, of course, to reach a critical size. In practice, a multiplication of about tenfold is achieved by the boosting process and the mean output of neutrons is about 10^{14} per second. In fact the output of electrons from the accelerator exists only during short pulses of about 1 μs in length and over this period the neutron output is as high as 10^{17} per second.

Somewhat similar in concept is a Canadian proposal for an intense neutron source which uses the phenomenon known as ' spallation ' (which means a breaking-up of nuclei by the splitting off of small pieces). When beams of particles such as protons of very high energy, greater than 50 MeV, are used, very complicated reactions may occur in which a wide variety of fragments of the nucleus are emitted as separate particles. It is as though the oncoming particle shared its energy with only a small part of the nucleus, rather than with the nucleus as a whole which is what happens when fission takes place. The variety of ejected products varies considerably with the initial energy and fig. 16 gives an idea of the distribution of mass numbers

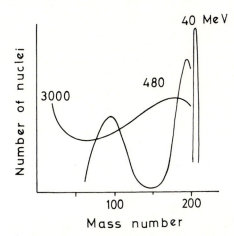

Fig. 16. The distribution of heavy mass numbers in the products of a ' spallation ' reaction when bismuth is bombarded with protons accelerated by various voltages.

among the heavier products when bismuth, $A = 209$, is bombarded with protons. At an energy of 40 MeV the products all have mass numbers not far below 209. At 480 MeV the range of mass numbers has extended down to about 160 and at the same time fission is also taking place, dividing the nucleus into two roughly equal parts ranging from about 60 to 130. At the highest energy shown, 3000 MeV, the two groups of particles merge together. The Canadian proposal, which is at present under consideration as a possible practical scheme, is to utilize the neutrons which are also produced during these reactions. A beam of protons, accelerated to have an energy of 500–1000 MeV and constituting a current of 65 mA, would fall on a stream of a liquid alloy of lead and bismuth as shown in fig. 17. The liquid alloy serves not only as the target but also as a coolant to carry away the enormous heat which is developed in the reaction. It has been calculated that a machine of this kind would produce a continuous stream of 10^{16} thermal neutrons per second. This is about ten times

31

as large an intensity as has been achieved by any other method and would revolutionize the scope of experiments which use neutron beams to study solids and liquids in the way which we shall describe in later chapters.

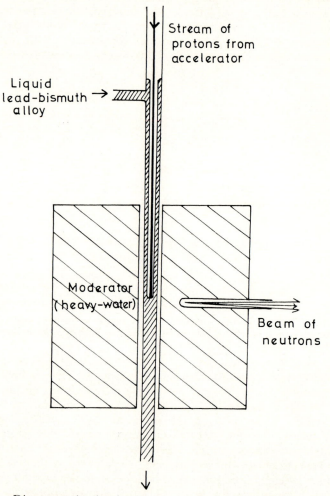

Fig. 17. Diagrammatic sketch of neutron generator employing impact of accelerated beam of protons, at 500–1000 MeV, on lead–bismuth target (from *Physics Today*, July 1968, p. 69).

Question 13. *Calculate the power conveyed as kinetic energy by a current of* 65 mA *of protons which have been accelerated through a potential difference of* 1000 MV.
                                        Ans. 65 MW.

32

properties of the neutron

OUR discussion of the basic properties of neutrons will depend on experimental measurements of their behaviour and will therefore presuppose that accurate methods of detecting and counting them are available. Later on we shall give some details about methods of detection. For the present we shall merely comment that, because they are neutral particles, neutrons cannot be detected directly and observation of them invariably depends on looking for the effect of secondary particles which the neutrons release when they pass through matter. There has indeed often been speculation whether the electric charge of a neutron is exactly zero. Soon after its initial discovery by Chadwick, it was calculated by P. I. Dee that the charge could not be greater than 1/700 of the charge on an electron : this was a deduction from an experimental conclusion that when a neutron passes through air it produces less than one pair of ions for each 3 m through which it travels. Much lower limits of charge have been postulated by considering the possible charges which so-called ' neutral ' atoms possess. If we accept an estimate that an atom such as caesium has a net charge which is less than 10^{-10} of the electronic charge, then it is likely that both the charge on the neutron and the difference between the charges of a proton and an electron are less than 10^{-12} of the electronic charge.

A typical and very commonly used method of neutron detection depends on the high efficiency for capturing neutrons which atoms of boron possess. This is a consequence of the reaction :

$$^{10}_{5}\text{B} + ^{1}_{0}\text{n} \rightarrow ^{7}_{3}\text{Li} + ^{4}_{2}\text{He}. \qquad . \qquad . \qquad (4.1)$$

Boron forms a gaseous compound, boron trifluoride BF_3, and an ionization chamber filled with this gas, enriched in the ^{10}B isotope, forms a convenient detector. The neutrons are absorbed by ^{10}B nuclei and the helium ions which are liberated according to equation (4.1) produce intense ionization of the gas in the chamber, leading in turn to electrical pulses which can be recorded and counted. In this way we are able to detect the arrival of individual neutrons and, accordingly, measure the intensity of a beam of neutrons.

4.1. *The mass of the neutron*

Of primary importance is the value of the neutron mass. The value which is accepted at the present time is 1·0086665 u. The unit of mass, written as ' u ', is defined by saying, as we described in the previous chapter, that an atom of the ^{12}C isotope is exactly 12 units. We have to distinguish this unit from an earlier ' atomic mass unit ', written as a.m.u., which was defined as 1/16 of the mass of the ^{16}O isotope : in older literature masses will of course be quoted in this earlier unit. In fact 1 u is equal to 1·0003179 a.m.u., or 1·660437 × 10^{-27} kg. The value for the mass of the neutron which

---

Question 14. *Calculate Avogadro's number from the information that* 1 u *is equal to* 1·66 × 10^{-27} kg.

Ans. 6·02 × 10^{23}/mol.

Chadwick gave at the conclusion of his first experiments was only about 0·2% less than the value which is now accepted, and from many points of view this would be regarded as satisfactory agreement. However, for many purposes in nuclear physics much greater precision is necessary, particularly because mass and energy are equivalent and it is often necessary to deduce changes in velocity from known changes in mass. It becomes especially important to know very accurately the difference in mass between a proton, a neutron and a neutral atom of hydrogen. One very exact experiment for determining the mass of a neutron, carried out by R. E. Bell and L. G. Elliott, depends on utilizing the precise knowledge of the masses of hydrogen and deuterium which can be obtained by using a mass spectrometer. These workers studied the production of γ-rays when neutrons and protons are in collision, according to the equation :

$$\mathrm{{}_0^1n + {}_1^1H \rightarrow {}_1^2H} + h\nu.$$

Very slow neutrons can be used and the kinetic energies associated with the different particles in the equation can be neglected. The experimenter has therefore to determine only the energy of the γ-ray, and this can be done very accurately by measuring its wavelength. In this way the energy was found to be 2·230 MeV, which is equivalent to 0·002394 u. Accordingly we can get the mass of the neutron by subtracting the mass of the proton from the deuteron and then adding 0·002394 u, i.e.

neutron mass = 2·014102 − 1·007825 + 0·002394

= 1·008671.

From a variety of experiments of this type it is concluded that the mass of the neutron is 1·008665 u.

It would be quite wrong to suppose that the neutron is no more than a featureless body, simply having the mass which we have just determined. It possesses an angular momentum, consistent with the assumption that it is spinning about an axis through its centre of mass, and also a magnetic moment. The existence of the latter suggests

34

that although the neutron has zero *net* charge, yet it must contain identifiable positive and negative charges. These will be equal in numbers (to the accuracy which we have already mentioned) but distributed differently in space. We know also that the neutron plays an important role in building up nuclei and is also believed to be involved in the process whereby β-particles are emitted from radioactive nuclei. There are several reasons for supposing that electrons cannot exist separately in nuclei and the emission of electrons during radioactivity can be accounted for by demonstrating that neutrons are able to decay into protons and electrons. A full understanding of the detailed structure of a neutron, and even more so, the structure of more complicated nuclear particles, is still awaited. We emphasize that this understanding of nuclear structure is the final, and most difficult, stage in the three-stage description of matter. A macroscopic piece of material is built up of a regular arrangement of atoms and each of these is an assembly of a nucleus and outer electrons : the nucleus, in turn, is a complicated assembly of nuclear particles whose detailed role and behaviour are steadily being disentangled. There must be intense, very short-range forces between neutrons and protons which hold the nucleus together. For the present we will merely give a more detailed account of the measurement of some of those properties of the neutron which we have already mentioned.

4.2. *The magnetic moment of the neutron*

There are many different physical measurements, particularly a study of the precise details of spectra, which can only be interpreted by assuming that the nuclei of atoms have the characteristic properties of both spinning tops and magnets—on a very minute scale, of course. In order to explain the quantitative details of spectra, for example, it is necessary to assume also that the constituent particles which build up the nucleus, i.e. the protons and the neutrons, also possess these characteristics of a spinning motion and a magnetic moment. It turns out that a neutron behaves as though it were spinning about an axis through its centre of mass with such a velocity that it possesses an angular momentum equal to $\frac{1}{2}h/2\pi$, where h is Planck's constant, and this quantity amounts to $5 \cdot 2 \times 10^{-35}$ J s. We can picture this angular momentum as arising simply because the neutron has a finite size and mass and is spinning about its axis, like the solid sphere in fig. 18. If the sphere in this figure had been intended to represent a cloud of electric charge (ii), then its rotation would have been equivalent to a circular current (iii) which we know, from elementary electrical theory, is equivalent to a magnetic shell or a small magnetic dipole. Indeed, *nuclei*, which we know of course to be electrically charged, do behave in this way and their magnetic moments can be measured by experiment. The very surprising thing, from the point of view of our present discussion, is that the *neutron* has a magnetic moment—in spite of the fact that it carries no net charge. This moment has important practical consequences, although the reasons for its existence are not properly understood. They must depend on details of the neutron's internal structure which we cannot explain properly at the

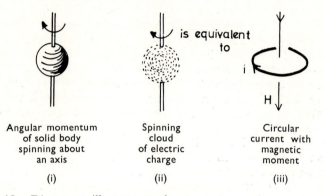

Angular momentum of solid body spinning about an axis	Spinning cloud of electric charge	Circular current with magnetic moment
(i)	(ii)	(iii)

Fig. 18. Diagram to illustrate angular momentum and magnetic moment.

present time. It is usually considered that the neutron spends part of its existence dissociated into a proton and a negatively charged π meson, according to the equation :

$$\text{n} \xrightleftharpoons{} (\text{proton})^+ + (\pi \text{ meson})^-.$$

During the dissociation period there could be a relatively concentrated positive charge surrounded at a somewhat greater distance (a few times 10^{-15} m) by a cloud of equal negative charge. Estimates of from 10–50% have been made for the fraction of time for which the neutron exists in this form. However, whatever be the ultimate truth of these speculations we can measure the magnetic moment μ by practical experiments and thus determine not only its magnitude but its sign : it is found that the sign is negative so that, in fig. 18, the neutron is behaving as though it is a *negative* charge which is rotating in the direction of the spinning top.

Question 15. *Calculate the magnitude of the angular momentum $\frac{1}{2}h/2\pi$ which the neutron possesses by virtue of its spin.*
$$\text{Ans.} \quad 5\cdot27 \times 10^{-35} \text{ J s.}$$

The principle of the measurement of μ can be understood from fig. 19 where we have placed a neutron in a magnetic field. The neutron will display its characteristic of being a spinning magnet and we have to ask therefore what will happen to a spinning magnet if it

36

is placed in a magnetic field. The magnetic field exerts a couple on the magnet which tries to align the magnet along the field direction, but a movement of this kind would involve a change in direction of the neutron's angular momentum. The result is that the axis of the neutron's spin *precesses*, just like a top or gyroscope does when a

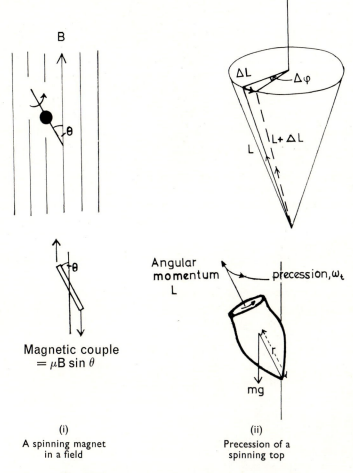

(i)
A spinning magnet
in a field

(ii)
Precession of a
spinning top

Fig. 19.   Precession of neutron in magnetic field.

mechanical couple acts upon it. The precession of both the spinning-top and the neutron can be computed with the aid of fig. 19 (ii). It can be shown quite easily that for the spinning-top the angular velocity of precession is :

$$\omega_t = \frac{mgr}{\text{angular momentum}},$$

and for the neutron in the magnetic field :

$$\omega_n = \frac{\mu B}{\text{angular momentum}}.$$

As we have already indicated, the angular momentum of the neutron is equal to $h/4\pi$, so that

$$\omega_n = 4\pi\mu B/h \text{ rad/s}.$$

We note that this value does not depend on the inclination θ of the axis about which the neutron is spinning. The *frequency* of precession will equal $\omega_n/2\pi$, which amounts to $2\mu B/h$ and this is usually called the frequency of ' Larmor precession ' in the field B. If, while the neutron is precessing in this way about the direction of the steady magnetic field B, we also subject it to the action of a small alternating field of suitable high frequency, then we can develop for ourselves an experimental method of determining the value of μ. The important condition which we have to satisfy is that the frequency of this second field is the same as that of the Larmor precession which we have just discussed. Under these circumstances the precessing neutrons can absorb energy and turn themselves end for end in the field. There are several ways in which we can detect that they have done this (one of them consists in noting how the transmission of the neutrons through blocks of magnetized iron varies) and we are able, therefore, to establish at what frequency of applied field the ' resonance ' twist-around occurs. L. W. Alvarez and F. Bloch, in 1939, were the first to carry out an experiment of this kind and they obtained consistent results in a series of measurements in which the steady field B, and necessarily the frequency ω_0 of the alternating field which produced resonance, varied over a tenfold range. The value which they deduced for the magnetic moment of the neutron was $-1\cdot93 + 0\cdot02$ nuclear magnetons†. These early experiments were made with a beam of neutrons produced by bombarding a target of beryllium with deuterons, thus utilizing the reaction

$$^9_4\text{Be} + ^2_1\text{D} = ^{10}_5\text{B} + ^1_0\text{n}.$$

In more recent times the precision of the measurements has been greatly increased by using nuclear reactors as sources and employing much more refined techniques for establishing the resonance condition. As a result of these experiments the accepted value of the neutron moment is now :

$$\mu_n = -1\cdot913148 \pm 0\cdot000066.$$

† The fundamental unit in *atomic* magnetism is the Bohr magneton, equal to $eh/4\pi m$, where e, m are the charge and mass of an electron, which amounts to $9\cdot27 \times 10^{-24}$ J m² (Wb)⁻¹ or J/T. By analogy, the magnetic moments of *nuclear* particles are expressed in units of $eh/4\pi M$, where M is the mass of a proton. This unit, which is 1836 times smaller than a Bohr magneton, is called a nuclear magneton and is equal to $5\cdot05 \times 10^{-27}$ J m² (Wb)⁻¹ or J/T.

Question 16. *In an experiment to determine the magnetic moment of the neutron, resonance absorption is obtained with alternating field of frequency 1843 kHz when the flux density of the steady magnetic field is 6.22×10^{-2} T. What is the magnetic moment of the neutron in terms of the nuclear magneton?*

Ans. 1·94.

4.3. *The decay of the neutron*

One of the familiar features of radioactivity is the emission of β-particles. For example, radium C is produced from radium B by emission of a β-particle, and these β-particles were identified as long ago as 1902 as electrons. Investigations showed that they were emitted with a continuous spectrum of energies ranging from comparatively slow particles to very fast ones. On the other hand, there was no corresponding range of energy among the product nuclei, such as RaC. The only way in which these experimental facts could be reconciled with the conservation of energy was by the assumption that some additional, and effectively non-observable, particle was emitted at the same time. The particle must be uncharged and have a rest mass which is practically zero, but it would be able to carry energy. This explanation of the difficulty was first suggested by W. Pauli in 1931 and he originally proposed that the particle should be called a *neutron*. However, this name was subsequently taken over in 1932 by Chadwick's 'real' neutron of unit mass and zero charge. Later, when E. Fermi, in 1934, elaborated the theory of β decay he proposed the new name of neutrino—which means in Italian 'a small neutral one'—for the particle which has zero, or nearly zero, rest mass.

In terms of the model of an atomic nucleus as consisting of an assembly of neutrons and protons the process of β decay could then be visualized as the break-up of a neutron into three components, namely proton, electron and neutrino. Since the rest mass of the neutrino is negligible it follows that the total mass of these components will be the sum of the masses of proton and electron and will therefore (neglecting a small ionization energy) be equal to the mass of a hydrogen atom, namely 1·007825 u. Now we have already discussed the precise value of the mass of the neutron and we have found that it is substantially *larger* than this quantity, namely by about 0·00084 u, which amounts to 0·78 MeV of energy. This means therefore that if a free neutron were converted into a proton, electron and neutrino then there would be a liberation of energy as well; we should therefore expect that such a conversion would be able to take place spontaneously. If this were the case, then we should be able to regard the neutron as being the simplest example of a radioactive nucleus. The truth of this speculation was demonstrated in 1948, and in 1950 the 'half-life' of the neutron, i.e. the period of time which has to elapse in order that a neutron has a 50 : 50 chance of having decayed was measured experimentally by J. M. Robson and found to be about 12 minutes.

The experiment was done with the apparatus which is illustrated in fig. 20. A beam of neutrons from the nuclear reactor at Chalk River in Canada was passed into an evacuated tank : about $1 \cdot 5 \times 10^{10}$

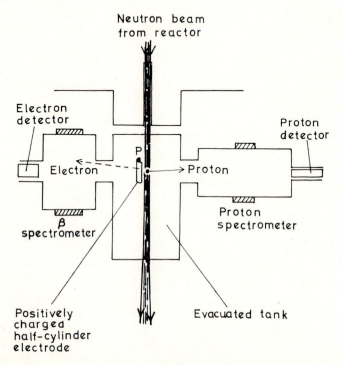

Fig. 20. Robson's apparatus for studying the radioactive decay of the neutron.

neutrons, with thermal velocities, and forming a beam about 30 mm in diameter, passed through the tank per second. Near the front of the tank were two openings, one on each side and connected to spectrometers which were suitable, respectively, for detecting and measuring the energy of electrons and protons. Let us suppose that protons and electrons are produced from those neutrons which have decayed during their travel along the line of the neutron beam. The protons have only low energies, of about 1 keV, and it is therefore necessary to insert a positively charged electrode (13 kV) at P in order to push all of them into the proton spectrometer. The electrons, on the other hand, are liberated, in all directions, with very high energies : they are travelling far too fast to be influenced by the

40

13 kV on the electrode P and just those electrons which are moving in the correct direction will enter the β spectrometer on the left of the diagram. It is possible to demonstrate, by using suitable electrical circuits, that each arrival of an electron is accompanied by simultaneous production of a proton, assuming that the necessary small correction is made for the slower journey of the proton from the point of origin P to the proton detector. It is then possible, by making a measurement of the total volume from which protons are collected and knowing the rate of entry of neutrons into the tank, to determine the probability that a neutron will disintegrate. The experimental conclusion was that the ' half-life ' of the neutron, i.e. the period of time which elapses before 50% of the neutrons have disintegrated into protons and electrons, was $12 \cdot 8 \pm 2 \cdot 5$ min. A later determination by some Russian workers has given a more precise value of $11 \cdot 7 \pm 0 \cdot 3$ min.

Question 17. *In the experiment illustrated in fig. 20 it was observed that 630 neutrons per minute disintegrated into protons, from each cubic centimetre of the beam. The number of neutrons present in each cubic centimetre was $1 \cdot 16 \times 10^4$. Calculate the half-life of the neutron.*

Ans. 12·8 min.

We mentioned at the beginning of this chapter that any net charge which the neutron possesses must be extremely small and is less than 10^{-12} of the charge on the electron. We have shown, however, that there must be a *distribution* and circulation of the equal positive and negative charges in such a way as to be compatible with the observed magnetic moment of the neutron. At the same time we can speculate whether or not the mean positions of positive and negative charges are exactly the same : if they were not in quite the same place, then the neutron would behave as a tiny electric dipole, with a moment equal to qx, where x is the distance of separation of the equal and opposite charges $\pm q$. Certain nuclear theories suggest that some small dipole moment should exist and in recent years extremely precise experiments, of various kinds which we cannot examine in detail, have attempted to measure the moment directly. At the present time the conclusion is that if we express the dipole moment in the form ex, where e is the *electronic* charge, then the value of x is less than 2×10^{-24} m.

CHAPTER 5

neutron detection and measurement of energy

When particles and radiations such as α, β, γ-rays are passed through a gas, ions and electrons are produced and a measurement of the amount of ionization serves both to detect and to measure the intensity of the radiation. In the case of α, β-rays, which are charged particles, electrons are split off the atoms because of the electrostatic force between the electron and the positively or negatively charged incident particles. In the case of X- or γ-rays some electrons are removed from the atoms by the Compton effect in which the X- or γ-ray simply loses a little of its energy, but of much more importance is the process of fluorescent absorption in which the X-ray quantum is totally annihilated, with transfer of its energy to an electron which is ejected from the atom. This electron, in its turn, will then produce secondary ionization in the gas in exactly the same manner which we have just mentioned for β-rays. In either case, for particles or for electro-magnetic radiation, the outcome of these reactions is the production of positively charged ions and electrons.

The simplest form of detector for α, β, γ-rays is the 'ionization chamber' such as is sketched in fig. 21. A difference of potential is maintained between the two electrodes and this produces a flow of the ions and electrons to the electrode which has the potential of opposite sign. With a potential of about 200 V the ions and electrons will reach the electrodes before they have a chance to recombine, thus giving a negative voltage pulse across the resistance R in the associated circuit, and this can be amplified and detected. Developments of the simple ionization chamber have yielded detectors with various characteristics and sensitivities. In particular, if the voltage is increased, then the electrons may be accelerated sufficiently on their way to the anode to acquire enough energy to produce further ionization, giving an output pulse which is much larger than, but proportional to, the primary ionization. With further increase of voltage, or reduction of the pressure of the gas, photo-ionization produces additional multiplication of the ionization and the size of the pulse becomes quite independent of the initial ionization and the sensitivity is so high that single pairs of ions produced by weakly ionizing radiation can be detected. Indeed, special quenching agents, such as bromine, have to be added to the gas in the counter in order to prevent the avalanche of ionization from being prolonged up to the arrival of the next ionizing particle. This mode of operation is that displayed by the Geiger–Müller counter which, with a quencher such as bromine and a primary filling gas of argon at 0·1 atmospheres' pressure, can operate satisfactorily with a potential of 450 V.

However, none of the above methods is suitable for the detection of neutrons, simply because neutrons do not produce ionization when they pass through a gas. Unlike α and β-particles they possess no

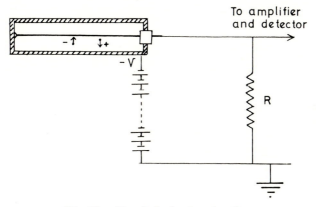

Fig. 21.   Simple ionization chamber.

charge and, indeed, as we mentioned earlier, it was deduced that the charge could not be greater than 1/700 of the charge on an electron from the observation that a neutron produced less than one pair of ions for each 3 m of path in air. In fact a beam of neutrons will pass through considerable thicknesses of even solids without undergoing any significant reactions but, fortunately, there are some materials which offer an exception to this and it is these which provide methods of detection. All these methods are essentially indirect. The neutron takes part in some reaction with an atomic *nucleus* and it is the *products* of this reaction which can be detected.

There are four distinct types of nuclear reaction which can be utilized in this way, giving rise to different kinds of detectors whose individual advantages and disadvantages depend very much on the nature of the neutron beam which is being examined and especially on the energies of the neutrons themselves. We can list the four underlying kinds of reaction as follows :

(1) The neutron is absorbed by an atomic nucleus with immediate emission of a charged particle. An example of this is the absorption by a boron nucleus of mass 10, followed by emission of an α-particle, i.e.

$$^{10}_{5}\text{B} + ^{1}_{0}\text{n} = ^{7}_{3}\text{Li} + ^{4}_{2}\text{He} + 2\cdot7 \text{ MeV}.$$

43

(2) The neutron is absorbed by a nucleus which becomes radio-active. The radioactive emission from the resulting product can then be detected and measured in a subsequent experiment. An example is the manganese isotope ^{55}Mn, which captures neutrons to give ^{56}Mn which is radioactive and emits β-particles.

(3) The neutron collides with the nucleus of a light atom, such as hydrogen in solid paraffin-wax or polyethylene or in some hydrogenous gas. The *recoiling* protons or other light nuclei cause ionization which can be measured.

(4) As a rather special case of (1) the neutron can collide with a nucleus such as uranium which undergoes fission. The fission fragments then produce intense ionization.

The first type of reaction is the basis of several different kinds of neutron detector which are particularly suitable for slow or thermal neutrons because the absorption coefficient for this kind of reaction is proportional to $1/v$, where v is the neutron velocity. Figure 22 illustrates the boron trifluoride counter in which a cylindrical chamber is filled with BF_3 gas and an electric potential of about 2·5 kV is maintained between the axial wire and the body of the counter which forms the cathode. The α-particles which are produced when the boron nuclei capture neutrons cause ionization in the gas, leading to the production of electrical pulses which can be amplified, detected and counted. Depending on the particular experimental require-ments, these counters may be up to 50 mm in diameter and 0·15–0·6 m in length, containing gas at pressures in the region of $\frac{1}{2}$–1 atmosphere. They are usually constructed of thin copper which gives negligible absorption of the neutron beam. They have a high efficiency of detection for neutrons of thermal energy and efficiencies of 80% can easily be obtained with long counters. Figure 23 shows how the efficiency of detection will vary with the energy of the neutron, and how a high efficiency is attained by using the ^{10}B isotope, for a counter of length 0·60 m and with a gas pressure of some 400 mm Hg. An important advantage of the BF_3 counter is that it is insensitive to γ-rays. The size of the output pulse is directly proportional to the energy of the neutron which is absorbed in the counter.

Question 18. *Estimate from fig.* 23 *the percentage efficiency of detection for a counter of length* 0·6 m *filled with* BF_3 *gas at a pressure of* 400 mm Hg (*a*) *for ordinary boron*, (*b*) *for* ^{10}B, *when used for the detection of neutrons of velocity* 2·2 km/s.
Ans. (*a*) 45%, (*b*) 95%.

BF_3 counters have been very thoroughly developed over a period of more than twenty years and are now produced commercially in a variety of sizes. More recently a similar type of counter has been

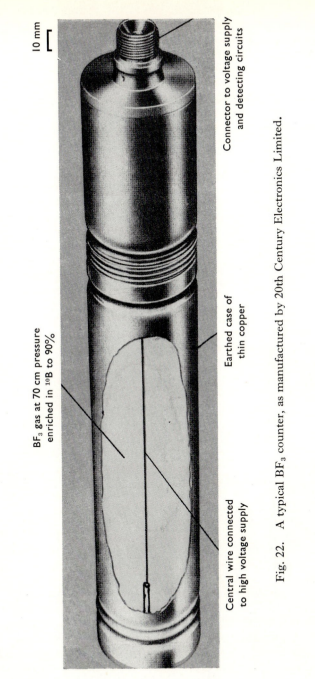

10 mm

BF₃ gas at 70 cm pressure
enriched in ^{10}B to 90%

Central wire connected
to high voltage supply

Earthed case of
thin copper

Connector to voltage supply
and detecting circuits

Fig. 22. A typical BF₃ counter, as manufactured by 20th Century Electronics Limited.

developed in which the filling gas is the helium isotope of mass 3, which can be produced by irradiating ^{6}Li in a nuclear reactor : the first product, ^{3}H, subsequently decays to ^{3}He. The use of ^{3}He as a neutron detector is based on the reaction :

$$^3_2He + ^1_0n = ^3_1H + ^1_1H,$$

and it is the ionization produced by the resulting hydrogen nuclei which produces the electrical impulses which are amplified by the detecting circuits. The advantage over the boron trifluoride counter

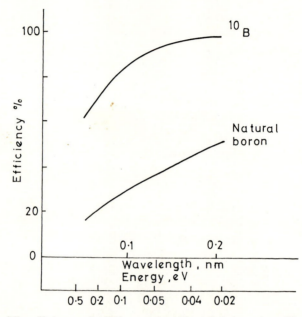

Fig. 23. The efficiency of a BF$_3$ counter of length 0·6 m when filled with gas at a pressure of 400 mm mercury, using natural boron and ^{10}B respectively.

is that the efficiency is slightly greater, for the same length of counter and gas pressure, and, at the same time, the operating voltage is substantially lower. Voltages of 1500, compared with about 2500 V for BF$_3$, are adequate, so these counters have some promising advantages.

An alternative way of making use of the reaction with boron is involved in the scintillation counter which is illustrated in fig. 24. The neutrons fall on the scintillator which is made of alternate layers of a solid containing boron, such as boric oxide, and zinc sulphide. The latter produces scintillating flashes of light when struck by α-particles and the light is amplified in the photomultiplier tube which

46

is attached to the phosphor. In this tube the initial light pulses eject electrons from a metal foil and these are steadily increased in number as they eject secondary electrons from a series of metal grids, through which they are accelerated by the application of electric potentials. In this way a single α-particle may eject from the zinc sulphide a photon which yields several million electrons at the collecting anode.

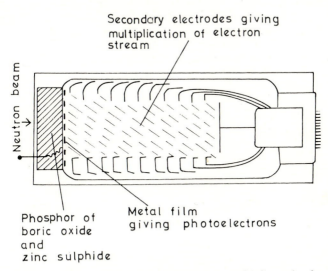

Fig. 24. B_2O_3/ZnS scintillator attached to photomultiplier tube for neutron detection.

Yet a further way of using the boron reaction is to incorporate the boron in a special emulsion on a photographic plate. The ionization of the silver bromide grains which is caused by the emitted α-particles renders these grains developable when the plate is processed photographically.

The general principle of the *second* method of neutron detection is that a thin foil of some suitable material is exposed to the neutron beam for a known length of time and it is then removed from the beam so that a measurement of its induced radioactivity can be made. The main requirements for the material are, first, that it shall have a sufficiently large capturing power for neutrons so that it can produce an adequate number of radioactive nuclei during the exposure to the beam. Secondly, the lifetime of the radioactivity must be sufficiently long to allow for the inevitable time interval between exposure and measurement, but not so long that the rate of decay is so low that it cannot be measured accurately. It will often be found that the capturing power of particular chemical elements is a sensitive function of neutron energy and may be exceptionally large at some ' resonance ' energy. This can be put to advantage when measurement is being sought of neutrons within some particular energy range, but it can otherwise be an inconvenient feature. Table 2 lists the properties of a number of metals which have proved useful for this activation method of detecting neutrons. It is convenient, while we are considering this table, to explain the term 'cross-section' which is used to describe the 'capturing power' of the metal atom for neutrons. We can indeed assign a 'cross-section' to describe quantitatively the probability that any particular kind of interaction between a neutron and an atom may occur. Let us consider, as in fig. 25, that N neutrons impinge upon a sample of material which is of unit area of cross-section and thickness dx and which contains n atomic nuclei per unit volume.

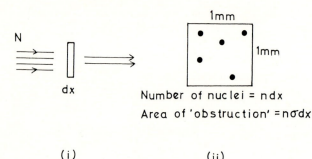

Number of nuclei = ndx

Area of 'obstruction' = nσdx

(i)   (ii)

Fig. 25. Representation of cross-section σ, which describes the probability that a neutron will undergo a particular reaction in traversing a material.

Imagine that each nucleus offers an area σ to the oncoming beam, such that if the neutrons pass within this area then a reaction (of the specified type which we are considering) will occur. It follows from the silhouette of fig. 25 (ii) that

$$\frac{\text{number of neutrons undergoing reaction in distance } dx}{\text{total number of neutrons in beam}} = n\sigma\, dx/1,$$

since there will be $n\, dx$ nuclei within the sample. Hence the change dN in the number of neutrons when N neutrons traverse the sample of thickness dx is:

$$dN = -Nn\sigma dx,$$

i.e.

$$\frac{dN}{N} = -(n\sigma)\, dx,$$

so that $n\sigma$ is what we should regard as the linear absorption coefficient for loss of neutrons by this particular reaction, thus providing a means of measuring σ, the 'cross-section' of the nucleus for this reaction.

48

Table 2 shows that these cross-sections are measured in units of 10^{-28} m² so that we can regard the atomic nuclei as having a radius of about 10^{-14} m, so far as their chances of being hit and made to undergo this particular reaction are concerned. The unit of area 10^{-28} m² is conventionally called a ' barn '. The cross-sections given in the table refer to neutrons with a velocity of 2·2 km/s.

Table 2

Properties of some metal foils suitable for the detection of slow neutrons

Element	Isotope	Abundance %	Cross-section (for 0·025 eV)	Half-life of product
Manganese	^{55}Mn	100	13×10^{-28} m²	2·6 hour
Rhodium	^{103}Rh	100	11	4·4 min
			139	42 s
Silver	^{107}Ag	51·8	45	2·3 min
	^{109}Ag	48·2	3·5	270 day
			89	24 s
Indium	^{113}In	4·3	8	50 day
			3	72 s
	^{115}In	95·7	157	54 min
			42	13 s

A particular advantage of the activation method of detection is that the detecting foil can be quite small, perhaps 1 or 2 cm² in area, so that the method can be applied to determine the way in which the intensity of a neutron beam varies over an extended area of volume. For example, the variation of neutron intensity in different parts of a nuclear reactor can readily be investigated.

The *third* method of detection, involving a collision with the nucleus of a light element which then recoils, is of particular value in detecting neutrons with very high energies. High-energy neutrons can be detected only very inefficiently by the two preceding methods. For example, the cross-section for *absorption* by the boron isotope of mass 10 is equal to 3830×10^{-28} m² at a neutron velocity of 2·2 km/s (which corresponds to 0·025 eV) but it has fallen to $2·6 \times 10^{-28}$ at an energy of 1 MeV and to $1·5 \times 10^{-28}$ at 10 MeV. In the same way we find that the *activation* cross-sections of most nuclei have also become very small, usually about $0·1 \times 10^{-28}$ m², for neutron energies greater than 1 MeV. Fortunately, the cross-section which expresses the probability that a neutron will collide with a hydrogen atom and make it recoil, remains quite substantial even for large values of

49

neutron energy. Figure 26 shows how σ for this reaction varies over a very wide range of energy. At low, thermal energies it is equal to about 20×10^{-28} m² and it has only fallen to 4×10^{-28} for an energy of 1 MeV and is still as large as 1×10^{-28} for an energy of 10 MeV.

Detectors which measure the ionization produced by the recoil protons can be made in two ways, either by filling an ionization chamber with a gas such as methane under a few atmospheres' pressure

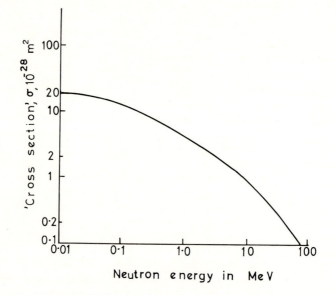

Fig. 26. A logarithmic plot of the variation with neutron energy of the probability of collision with hydrogen.

or by incorporating thin sheets or a window of a solid such as poly-ethylene. It is also possible to place the hydrogenous material in a cloud chamber or to incorporate it in a nuclear emulsion.

With *reduction* of neutron energy the recoil detectors become increasingly ineffective and they fail at low energies because the protons have insufficient energy, since this energy cannot be greater than that of the incoming neutron. As a result the electrical impulses are insignificant compared with those produced by any background of γ-rays and cosmic rays. We have to contrast this behaviour with that of the boron detectors: the latter are able to produce extensive ionization with very slow neutrons simply because the interaction with the boron liberates 2·7 MeV of energy which is carried away by the lithium and helium nuclei and which can therefore produce extensive ionization.

50

In our *fourth* type of detector, the ' fission chamber ', the ionization pulses caused by the fission fragments are very large but the tracks produced are of short range, thus leading to the possibility of making rather shallow detectors. These are particularly useful for monitoring the intensity of a neutron beam which is to be used in a subsequent experiment, and in this case the incident beam is passed through a thin counter, which, when connected to suitable recording circuits, maintains an adequate record of the intensity without causing much absorption or scattering. In these counters the fissionable nuclei can be introduced as a gas, such as UF_6, or as a metallic coating on the counter wall. By suitable choice of materials they can be made to discriminate in favour of chosen neutron energies. Thus, materials such as ^{235}U, ^{239}Pu which are fissionable by thermal neutrons will be efficient detectors at low energies. On the other hand, chambers containing only ^{238}U, which can be produced by removing the ^{235}U from natural uranium, will only be responsive to neutrons whose energies are greater than a threshold value for fission of about 1·0 MeV.

In our discussion of the different types of detector for neutrons we have emphasized how their efficiencies depend on the velocities of the neutrons which are being considered. This is a particular example of the general way in which the efficiency with which a neutron undergoes any reaction, i.e. its cross-section for a particular reaction, will vary with the neutron velocity. It is therefore convenient at the present stage in our discussion to pay some attention to some of the more important methods by which the velocities of neutrons may be measured.

It will be useful to correlate at the outset the different terms we have available for indicating the velocity of a neutron. In addition to the direct description in terms of metres per second, we shall often find it useful to specify the energy in electron volts (as we have done in much of our account of detectors). Further, we know that in terms of the wave-mechanical theory a particle also displays wave properties and we shall find that the wave nature of the neutron is an essential concept when we come to consider the way in which beams of neutrons can be diffracted by solids and liquids. Quantitatively the wavelength λ is equal to h/mv, where m, v are the mass and velocity of the neutron and h is Planck's constant. We give in fig. 27 a numerical correlation between the values of v, E and λ which will be found useful in some of our later discussion. As an example, we can say, from fig. 27, that a velocity of 2 km/s is equivalent to an energy of about 0·02 eV and a wavelength of 2×10^{-10} m. A velocity of 0·8 km/s is equivalent to an energy of 0·32 eV and a wavelength of about 5×10^{-10} m. The velocity will increase as the square root of the energy and the wavelength will vary inversely as the velocity. We have also indicated in the figure the different ranges—slow, intermediate, fast, high energy—into which the whole range of neutron

Fig. 27. Energy, wavelength and velocity correlation for neutrons. A vertical line on the diagram will link equivalent values.

52

energy is conventionally sub-divided. It must be pointed out though that the boundaries between the different ranges are not in any way precisely defined ; nor are the boundaries of the sub-divisions which are sometimes applied in the ' slow ' range, and which are also shown in the figure.

We may say rather generally that, compared with most atomic particles, neutrons are often travelling quite slowly. Even for an energy of 10 keV the velocity is only about 10^6 m/s, which is ten

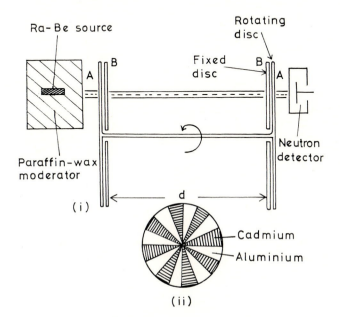

Fig. 28.   Dunning's mechanical apparatus for measuring the velocity of thermal neutrons.

times less than the velocity of α-particles and vastly smaller than that of β-particles, which approach the speed of light. It is not really surprising therefore to find that the velocities of ' slow ' neutrons, and even of neutrons which are some way into the intermediate range, can be determined by what can be described as ' mechanical ' methods. The simple device illustrated in fig. 28 was first used by J. R. Dunning and his colleagues in 1935 to measure the spectrum of velocities for the neutrons given off by a radium–beryllium source.   Two sectored discs AA, separated by a distance d of about 0·5 m and shown in more detail at (ii), are mounted on a shaft and rotated in front and behind a similar pair of fixed discs BB.   The sectors of the discs are made alternately of cadmium and aluminium, the former of which obstructs completely the neutron beam.   The whole assembly is mounted between the neutron source and a detecting counter. Imagine first of all that all the neutrons emitted from the source have the same velocity v and let us measure how the number which reach the counter varies with the rate of rotation of the discs AA. The number will be a minimum if the time taken by the neutrons to pass between the two discs, i.e. d/v, is just equal to the time taken for the discs to rotate from an open to a closed position, i.e. $\theta/2\pi n$, where θ is the angular width of an open sector and n is the frequency of revolution.

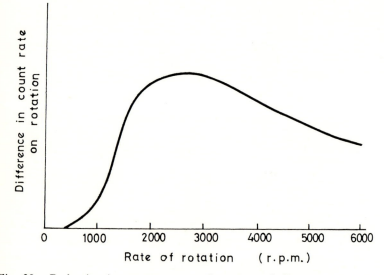

Fig. 29. Reduction in neutron count when sectored discs are rotated, as a function of the number of revolutions per minute.

In practice the neutrons which are emitted from the source will not have a constant velocity, but a Maxwellian spectrum similar to what we showed earlier in fig. 13 for the spectrum of neutrons from a reactor. Figure 29 indicates, for each rate of rotation of the discs, the reduction in the number of neutrons which enter the counter when the discs are in motion compared with the number when the discs are stationary. The maximum in the curve at about 2500 revolutions per minute indicates that the peak in the velocity distribution curve for the neutrons must occur at about 2·25 km/s. This general method of measurement of neutron velocity is usually called the ' time-of-flight ' method, because it depends on measuring the time taken by the neutron to traverse a given length of path, and it has been improved and developed very considerably. The time interval is now usually measured by an electronic method and there are two particular applications of this technique. First, when the neutron source gives

54

a continuous supply of neutrons this supply is pulsed or chopped by a rotating mechanical shutter which may provide bursts of neutrons lasting for about 20 μs and occurring perhaps 200 times per second. Secondly, the initial neutron beam may already be pulsed because it has arisen from a pulsed particle accelerator or from a nuclear reactor which itself has a pulsed output. In either case the output of the detecting counter can be fed to a series of electronic counting circuits which are themselves only made sensitive for short periods of time.

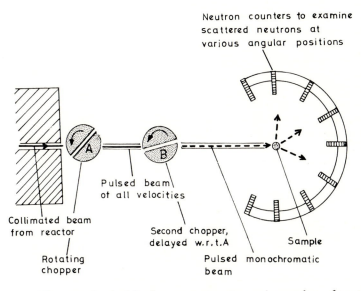

Fig. 30. The use of a double-chopper system to produce pulses of neutrons whose velocities are measured electronically after being scattered by a solid sample.

These intervals of time can be adjusted as desired, in relation to the initial pulse of neutrons, so that the neutrons are sorted out into groups according to the time which they have taken to traverse the given flight path to the detector. In a ' multi-channel analyser ' it is possible for more than 1000 groups of neutrons to be examined at the same time, so that the spectrum of neutron velocities can be measured with a high degree of resolution. These techniques have been developed to a very high level of efficiency for the production of beams of neutrons of a single velocity which, because the neutrons will also have a single equivalent wavelength, we call ' monochromatic ' neutrons. Monochromatic beams of neutrons are of great value for studying the structure and constitution of solids. Figure 30 shows one method by which such a beam can be produced. Two rotors,

55

each incorporating a transmitting slot, are phased so that the second one opens at a predetermined time after the first one, and then electronic devices are used to examine the velocities of the neutrons after they have been scattered by a sample. A large series of detectors is arranged in a circular arc so that measurements can be made simultaneously in many different directions. The aim of the experiment is to study the way in which the neutrons may gain or lose energy as a result of their encounter with the solid and we shall look more closely at this behaviour in a later chapter. With the apparatus shown in fig. 30 as many as 4000 counting channels are used, permitting the neutrons which are scattered into each of twenty detecting counters to be allocated among 200 different energy intervals.

By suitable design, such as using rotors with diameters of the order of 0·8 m and rotating them at up to 200 revolutions a second and using flight paths of up to 60 m, it is possible to use these chopper and time-of-flight techniques for producing and measuring monochromatic beams of neutrons with energies up to about 10 keV, corresponding to a velocity of 10^6 m/s. One application of this work has been to measure how the scattering and absorption properties of individual elements vary with the neutron energy. This provides important information both for the technology of nuclear reactors and for the development of the theory of nuclei. A typical example is shown in fig. 31 which indicates how the absorption of cadmium, as represented by its ' cross-section ', varies with neutron energy over the region from 1 to 10 000 eV. It will be seen that there are several sharp resonances, especially in the interval from 10 to 100 eV, and it is for this reason that the high degree of energy resolution, which can be obtained with the apparatus which we have described, is so important.

Question 19. *Calculate the velocity of a neutron which has an energy of* 20 000 eV *and the time taken by it to travel a distance of* 60 m.
Ans. $1·96 \times 10^3$ km/s, 30·6 μs.

Continued development of electronic timing methods in which intervals of time as short as a few milli-microseconds can be measured has permitted the energies of neutrons produced from pulsed accelerators to be measured into the region from 10 to 100 MeV, using flight paths of up to 1·5 m in length.

For neutrons which have energies below about 20 eV, a quite different method of measurement of velocity and energy is available. It is in this region of energy that the concept of the wavelength of the neutron becomes important. At an energy of 20 eV the wavelength is about 7×10^{-12} m and at 0·01 eV it has risen to 2×10^{-10} m. This range of wavelengths comes well within those which can be measured by utilizing the manner in which a regular succession of atomic planes, which occurs in a crystal, can function as a diffraction grating. Studies

56

of solids show that the distance between the centres of neighbouring atoms is about 10^{-10} m. For example, the distance between carbon atoms in diamond is 1.54×10^{-10} m and between copper atoms in metallic copper it is 2.55×10^{-10} m. In a similar way we find that the separation between neighbouring *planes* of atoms in a solid is also of the order of 10^{-10} m. Consequently, those who study solids on an atomic scale use a special name for this distance of 10^{-10} m or 0.1 nm. It is called an Ångström unit (Å), perpetuating a name used

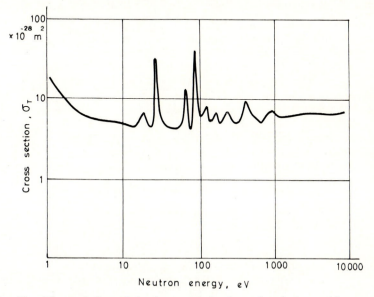

Fig. 31. The variation of the 'cross-section' σ_t of cadmium with neutron energy, drawn as a double logarithmic plot. σ_t is the 'total' cross-section and includes both absorption and scattering.

by spectroscopists in honour of a Swedish physicist, and we shall often find it convenient to use this unit in our descriptions of solids. We shall examine the diffraction process in much greater detail when we consider how the technique of neutron diffraction can be used to investigate the atomic architecture of solids. For the present we will simply note that a neutron spectrometer equipped with a diffracting crystal can measure the wavelength of neutrons in an exactly analogous way to that in which an optical spectrometer, with a conventional grating of ruled lines, will determine the wavelength of visible light. The ratio of the spacing of the grating to the wavelength of the radiation is closely similar in the two cases. Compared with the time-of-flight method of energy analysis it can be said that the crystal diffraction method has a better energy resolution in the case of low-energy neutrons.

For fast neutrons, whose energies are measured in MeV, both the time-of-flight method and the crystal-diffraction technique become difficult. With the former there is a limit to both the velocities of rotors which can be achieved and the minuteness of intervals of time which can be measured. With the latter the angle of diffraction and the change of this angle for a given change in energy become extremely small at high energies. Use is therefore made of the interaction of neutrons with protons, as in the proton-recoil detectors, to design spectrometers which determine the energy of the initial neutron by

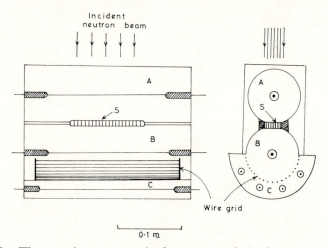

Fig. 32. Three-section counter tube for energy analysis of neutrons by study of recoil protons produced in methane (from G. J. Perlow, *Rev. scient. Instrum.* **27**, 460, 1956).

making a subsequent measurement of the energy of the recoiling proton. There are several ways in which the measurement can be made but they all depend on the equation which we derived earlier, which expresses the energy E given to a nucleus which recoils at an angle β as :

$$E = E_0 \frac{4M}{(M+1)^2} \cos^2 \beta,$$

where E_0 is the energy of the incident neutron and M is the mass number of the recoiling nucleus. In the particular case when the latter is a proton we shall have simply :

$$E_0 = \frac{E}{\cos^2 \beta}.$$

One very direct way of applying this relation is to use the triple counter tube designed by G. J. Perlow, which is illustrated in fig. 32. Each of the counter tubes is filled with methane gas and the incident

58

neutron beam is allowed to fall normally on the upper tube A. The protons which recoil in the forward direction, for which $\beta = 0$, will pass through the channels of the collimating slits S and enter the second counter. The pressure of the gas is arranged so that the proton will be stopped within B and not reach the lower section of the counter, C. The fact that this has happened can be established by suitable electrical circuits which are able to show that coincident ionization bursts have occurred in A, B but not in C. The amount

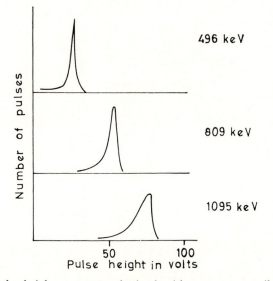

Fig. 33. Pulse-height spectrum obtained with a proton-recoil counter for neutron beams of energy 496, 809, 1095 keV respectively (from G. J. Perlow, *Rev. scient. Instrum.*, **27**, 460, 1956).

of energy possessed by each recoiling proton is then assessed by other electrical circuits which determine the sizes of the bursts of ionization. If we plot a distribution curve for the size of the bursts of ionization then a group of neutrons of constant energy will be revealed as a sharp peak in the curve. An example is given in fig. 33.

Many different kinds of proton-recoil spectrometer have been developed and are capable of giving high accuracy but they have relatively low efficiencies. A much cheaper method of analysis, though more tedious, is to measure the lengths of tracks which the protons produce in photographic emulsions, which we have already mentioned as the basis of a method of neutron detection. In this case we can actually observe the angle β between the direction of the incident neutron and any proton which is knocked out of a molecule in the photographic emulsion. Nuclear emulsions contain about

50 μg/mm³ of hydrogen. It is simplest to study protons ejected at some particular value of β, say 10°. From the results of subsidiary experiments which relate the energy of a proton to its range within a particular photographic emulsion it is then possible to plot a spectrum of the incident neutron beam. Figure 34 (i) shows a spectrum which

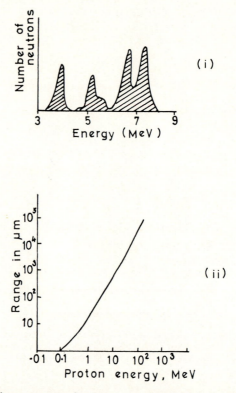

Fig. 34. (i) The spectrum of neutrons produced in the reaction ⁹Be (d,n)¹⁰B as determined by measurement of proton recoil tracks in a nuclear emulsion. Curve (ii) gives the correlation between proton track length and energy in a typical emulsion.

has been determined in this way for the neutrons produced by bombarding beryllium with a beam of deuterons. Curve (ii) in the figure shows a typical relation between proton energy and range in a convenient nuclear emulsion, such as is used to establish the neutron energies.

CHAPTER 6

reactions of neutrons

NEUTRONS are able to interact with atoms in a great variety of ways, largely because the lack of any electric charge on the neutron permits it to penetrate into the interior of any atoms which lie in its path, and thus to react with the atomic nucleus and with its constituent particles. Because there is no repulsive barrier for the neutron to penetrate in order to reach the nucleus, it follows that interactions may occur even with very slow, thermal neutrons. We have to contrast this behaviour with the situation which exists when a charged particle tries to reach a nucleus. In this latter case, even for the nucleus of a light element, which will have only a small charge, it is necessary for the charged particle to have an energy of about 1 000 000 eV before it can get through the electrical barrier and within range of the intense (but short-range) forces of nuclear attraction. We shall examine first of all the general variety of reactions and then consider the useful applications to which some of them can be put.

In order to have a pictorial model of what is happening when a neutron passes through a solid (or a liquid or gas) we can consider that there is a certain probability that the neutron will be captured by a nucleus to form a ' compound nucleus '. The latter may then break up in several ways, by re-emitting the incident neutron with its velocity unchanged in magnitude but in a different direction (which is called ' elastic scattering '), by emitting a neutron with more energy or less energy (inelastic scattering) or by emitting some other particle (or particles) or a quantum of radiation. In general there will be specific probabilities that each of these various possibilities will take place and these will depend not only on the particular atomic nucleus which has been encountered, but also on the velocity of the neutron. In quantitative terms we can describe the likelihood of any particular reaction taking place in terms of a ' cross-section ', as we have discussed previously in Chapter 5. The loss of neutrons from our beam because of any individual reaction will be controlled by the equation $I = I_0 \exp(-N\sigma_j x)$, which specifies the way in which the intensity of the beam diminishes as it passes through any material. In this equation x is the length of path, N is the number of nuclei per unit volume and σ_j is the cross-section for the particular reaction. In order to express the *attenuation* of the neutron beam brought about by all possible types of reaction we must replace σ_j by $\sum \sigma_j$, in which we sum up the cross-sections for the various reactions which can take place.

We shall defer consideration of elastic scattering until a further chapter, where we shall examine the way in which, when we consider the wave properties of the neutron, we can get superposition and interference effects between the contributions from neighbouring nuclei. These will provide us with a valuable procedure for exploring

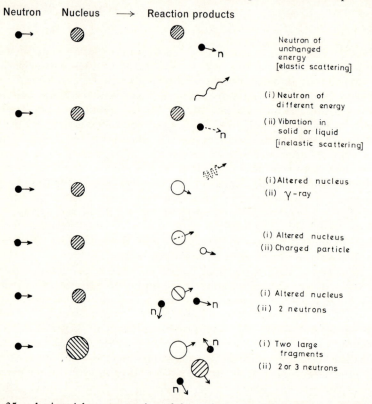

Fig. 35.   A pictorial representation of the various ways in which a neutron may interact with a nucleus.

the three-dimensional environments of atoms in solids. We can summarize the other possible interactions between neutron and nucleus as follows: (i) radiative capture, with emission of a γ-ray, (ii) ejection of a charged particle, such as a proton, deuteron or α-particle, (iii) emission of two neutrons and (iv) nuclear fission, in which the nucleus breaks up into two large fragments together with several more neutrons, in a way which we have already described in connection with the nuclear reactor. Figure 35 summarizes in a pictorial way the various reactions which a neutron may undergo.

The process of radiative capture can take place with nearly all elements and it is often more effective with slow neutrons. An isotope of the original element is produced, with liberation of considerable energy which is carried away as a γ-ray. Typical examples are :

$$\ce{^1_1H + ^1_0n \to ^2_1D + \gamma + 2.23\ MeV},$$

$$\ce{^{107}_{47}Ag + ^1_0n \to ^{108}_{47}Ag + \gamma + 7.23\ MeV}.$$

Question 20. *Calculate the wavelength of a γ-ray which has an energy of 2·5 MeV.*

Ans. 5×10^{-13} m.

As we have explained earlier, the mass equivalent of the γ-ray energy will be equal to the difference in mass between the product atom and the incident atom plus neutron. In mass units the difference in the first example above will be 2·23/931, which is equal to 0·00239 u, bearing in mind that 1 u is equivalent to 931 MeV. The spectrum of the γ-rays is not usually restricted to a single wavelength but includes several lines : the shortest wavelength which is emitted corresponds to the energy release given by the equation.

The product nucleus, which is an isotope of the original element, will have a larger ratio of neutrons to protons than is normal for stability and will generally be radioactive. It can regain stability by increasing its nuclear charge, which it can do by emitting an electron. Thus neutron bombardment of $\ce{^{23}_{11}Na}$, which is the naturally occurring form of sodium, produces $\ce{^{24}_{11}Na}$ which is radioactive and decays to $\ce{^{24}_{12}Mg}$, with a half-life of 15 hours. Bombardment of ordinary aluminium $\ce{^{27}_{13}Al}$ produces radioactive $\ce{^{28}_{13}Al}$ which, with a half-life of 2·3 min, emits an electron to produce stable silicon $\ce{^{28}_{14}Si}$. These reactions are important in providing ' tracer ' atoms which can be followed in both chemical and physical processes because of the accuracy with which they can be detected by means of their radioactivity. Moreover, they may be conclusively identified from their characteristic half-lives.

Question 21. *The half-life of $\ce{^{239}Pu}$ is 24 360 years. How many atoms decay each second from a sample weighing 1 g?*

Ans. $2·3 \times 10^9$.

The reactions of neutrons with uranium are of particular importance. By neutron bombardment of uranium the transuranic elements neptunium and plutonium are produced by successive emission of electrons from the $\ce{^{239}U}$ which is the product of neutron capture by the $\ce{^{238}U}$ isotope.

Thus :

$$\ce{^{238}_{92}U + ^1_0n = ^{239}_{92}U + \gamma},$$

$$\ce{^{239}_{92}U \to ^{239}_{93}Np} + \text{electron, with a half-life of } 23·5 \text{ min.}$$

$$\ce{^{239}_{93}Np \to ^{239}_{94}Pu} + \text{electron, with a half-life of } 2·3 \text{ days.}$$

The product nucleus $^{239}_{94}$Pu is effectively stable, having a half-life of 24 360 years as it decays very slowly with emission of an α-particle. Occasionally the first product of an (n, γ) reaction is stable. An example is $^{114}_{48}$Cd which is produced from the cadmium isotope $^{113}_{48}$Cd.

In the case of neutron reactions in which a charged particle is ejected it will be necessary for this particle to have substantial energy in order to escape from the oppositely charged nucleus. It is not surprising therefore that this kind of reaction usually only takes place with fast neutrons and also that higher energies are need in order to produce the reaction for nuclei which have large atomic numbers, and hence large nuclear charges. One important class of reaction is that in which a proton is ejected—this is usually called an (n, p) reaction—and in this case it is generally necessary for the incident neutron to have an energy of at least 1 MeV. There are three important exceptions of nuclei for which energy is *liberated* in the (n, p) reaction and in these cases the reaction will occur with slow neutrons. These exceptions are :

$$^{3}_{2}\text{He} + ^{1}_{0}\text{n} = ^{3}_{1}\text{H} + ^{1}_{1}\text{H}, \qquad . \qquad . \qquad . \qquad (6.1)$$

$$^{14}_{7}\text{N} + ^{1}_{0}\text{n} = ^{14}_{6}\text{C} + ^{1}_{1}\text{H}, \qquad . \qquad . \qquad . \qquad (6.2)$$

$$^{35}_{17}\text{Cl} + ^{1}_{0}\text{n} = ^{35}_{16}\text{S} + ^{1}_{1}\text{H}. \qquad . \qquad . \qquad . \qquad (6.3)$$

As before, for the (n, γ) reaction, the loss of a proton and the gain of a neutron mean that the product has an excessively large ratio of neutrons/protons for it to be stable and in almost all cases it will decay with emission of an electron. For the (n, p) reaction this will mean that the product of the radioactive decay will be identical with the initial nucleus. Thus in a typical case the neutron-capture reaction is expressed by :

$$^{32}_{16}\text{S} + ^{1}_{0}\text{n} = ^{32}_{15}\text{P} + ^{1}_{1}\text{H} + Q, \qquad . \qquad . \qquad . \qquad (6.4)$$

followed by the radioactive decay :

$$^{32}_{15}\text{P} = ^{32}_{16}\text{S} + \text{electron} + E_{\text{max}}, \qquad . \qquad . \qquad . \qquad (6.5)$$

where Q, E_{max} are the energies which are liberated in the two reactions. If we add together equations (6.4), (6.5) and eliminate the species which are common to the two sides of the resulting equation we have :

$$^{1}_{0}\text{n} = ^{1}_{1}\text{H} + \text{electron} + Q + E_{\text{max}}. \qquad . \qquad . \qquad (6.6)$$

This relation shows that the net result of the two reactions is that the neutron has been transformed into a proton and an electron. We have already pointed out in Chapter 4 that the energy release in this transformation, when it occurs directly, is $+0.78$ MeV. It follows therefore that for all pairs of reactions of the kind represented by (6.4), (6.5):

$$Q + E_{max} = +0.78 \text{ MeV.}$$

In most cases the value of the maximum energy carried by the electrons in a reaction such as (6.5) is greater than 0.78 MeV, so that it follows that Q, in the (n, p) reaction, is negative. In the particular case given, we find that

$$^{32}_{16}S + ^{1}_{0}n = ^{32}_{15}P + ^{1}_{1}H - 0.92 \text{ MeV,}$$

confirming, as is observed in practice, that there is a threshold of neutron energy at about 1 MeV, below which this (n, p) reaction will not take place. Above this threshold the reaction is succeeded by the decay:

$$^{32}_{15}P = ^{32}_{16}S + \text{electron} + 1.70 \text{ MeV.}$$

Thus, as we expect:

$$Q + E_{max} = -0.92 + 1.70 = 0.78 \text{ MeV.}$$

In each of the exceptional cases shown in equations (6.1), (6.2), (6.3) above, the energy E_{max} of the electrons emitted from the product nuclei $^{3}_{1}H$, $^{14}_{6}C$ and $^{35}_{16}S$ is less than 0.78 MeV and the initial (n, p) reaction can, accordingly, therefore be brought about even by slow neutrons.

Question 22. *Use the atomic masses given in Table 1, together with*
$$^{32}_{15}P = 31.973909,$$
$$^{3}_{2}He = 3.016030$$

and
$$^{3}_{1}H = 3.016050,$$

to determine the quantities of energy E_{max}, which are liberated by conversion of mass, in the nuclear reactions
$$^{32}_{15}P = ^{32}_{16}S + \text{electron} + E_{max},$$
$$^{3}_{1}H = ^{3}_{2}He + \text{electron} + E_{max}.$$
$$\text{Ans. } 1.71 \text{ MeV, } 0.02 \text{ MeV.}$$

The masses which appear in these equations are *nuclear masses*. In actual calculations they are replaced by masses of neutral atoms which are obtained by adding the masses of the outer electrons. In general these will cancel out on the two sides of the equation. Thus the reaction:

$$^{32}_{15}P \rightarrow ^{32}_{16}S + \text{electron} + 1.70 \text{ MeV}$$

means:

$$\begin{array}{ccc} \text{mass of} \\ ^{32}_{15}P \text{ nucleus} \end{array} = \begin{array}{c} \text{mass of} \\ ^{32}_{16}S \text{ nucleus} \end{array} + \begin{array}{c} \text{mass of} \\ \text{electron} \end{array} + 1.70 \text{ MeV.}$$

If we add the mass of fifteen electrons to each side of the equation we have :

$$\text{mass of } {}^{32}_{15}\text{P nucleus} + \text{mass of 15 electrons} = \text{mass of } {}^{32}_{16}\text{S nucleus} + \text{mass of 15 electrons} + \text{mass of electron} + 1\cdot70 \text{ MeV}$$

i.e. :

$$\text{mass of } {}^{32}_{15}\text{P} \begin{array}{c}\text{neutral}\\\text{atom}\end{array} = \text{mass of } {}^{32}_{16}\text{S} \begin{array}{c}\text{neutral}\\\text{atom}\end{array} + 1\cdot70 \text{ MeV},$$

and we can then use the masses of the neutral atoms given in Table 1.

When some of the light elements are bombarded with neutrons the emission of an α-particle can take place and two important reactions concerned with the detection of neutrons are of this type :

$$^{10}_{5}\text{B} + ^{1}_{0}\text{n} = ^{4}_{2}\text{He} + ^{7}_{3}\text{Li}$$

and

$$^{6}_{3}\text{Li} + ^{1}_{0}\text{n} = ^{3}_{1}\text{H} + ^{4}_{2}\text{He}.$$

These two particular reactions will take place with slow neutrons, but as the atomic number of the target nucleus is increased it is found that only neutrons of high energy will react in this manner and there is indeed an increasing probability that an (n, 2n) reaction, in which two neutrons are emitted, will occur for preference. Such a reaction has the net result of detaching a neutron from the target nucleus, and he have already seen in our discussion of fig. 8 that this requires an energy of about 8 MeV. Experimentally it is accordingly found that energies greater than 10 MeV are usually needed for producing the (n, 2n) reaction. Typical threshold energies are 12·6 MeV for $^{23}_{11}\text{Na}$ and 10·5 MeV for $^{59}_{27}\text{Co}$.

Fission is the most spectacular interaction of neutrons with nuclei and we have already seen that slow neutrons will cause fission of ^{235}U but not of ^{238}U ; fast neutrons, with energies greater than 1 MeV, may cause fission of both ^{235}U and ^{238}U but only with low probability. Thorium and protactinium also undergo fission, but only when bombarded with fast neutrons. It is interesting to note that it is also possible for nuclei to undergo fission spontaneously, without the intervention of a neutron, but this process only occurs to any significant extent for artificially produced transuranic elements which have atomic numbers greater than 96.

Our foregoing discussion has been limited to an explanation of the principles of the different kinds of neutron reaction together with some examples of each type and an indication of the importance of neutron energy in determining the relative probabilities that different kinds of reaction may occur. In fact the reaction properties of individual elements, and their isotopes, have been studied in very great detail, largely because of the importance of accurate knowledge of this kind in nuclear technology. The choice of structural materials in reactors, resulting in the use of quite uncommon elements, is based on a detailed knowledge of their neutron cross-sections, in a rather similar way to that in which the choice and use of particular metals and materials in structural engineering depend on such factors as their density and elastic properties. As we have already said, the attenuation of a neutron beam when it passes through a thin sample of a material measures the sum of the cross-sections for the different possible reactions which may occur. By making subsidiary experiments it is possible to allocate the total cross-section among the different individual reactions and this allocation and information have to be investigated for all neutron energies. In certain parts of the energy range it is found that the cross-section for the removal of neutrons from the beam varies rapidly for small changes in neutron energy. This is accounted for by the occurrence of resonance effects in the nucleus, in a way analogous to that in which electrical circuits have natural tuning frequencies and to the way in which organ pipes vibrate preferentially for sound waves of particular frequencies. These resonant frequencies will occur at different energies for each isotope and for each type of reaction, thus leading to a wide variety of cross-section versus energy curves. We conclude this chapter by showing three examples which will indicate the wide variety of behaviour which is found. Curve (i) in fig. 36 relates to the neutron properties of carbon. Practically the whole of the attenuation of a neutron beam is due to elastic scattering, with simple re-emission of the original neutron. This does not vary with neutron energy and effects due to (n, γ), (n, p), (n, α), etc. reactions are quite negligible. The variations at low energies are due to the effects of crystal diffraction which we shall discuss in the next chapter. They show up prominently in the curve for carbon because the absence of any effects due to absorption and capture permits us to use a very open scale for the ordinate in this graph, thus accentuating the effects of diffraction. Curve (ii) displays the contrasting behaviour for cobalt, which shows two particular features. At low energies there is a substantial component of cross-section which varies as $1/v$ and is due to radiative (n, γ) capture. At an energy of 120 eV there is a large peak in the curve and this can be shown to be due to a resonant effect in the elastic scattering : there is a further resonance beyond the range of the diagram, accounting for the continuing rise of the curve on the right. In curve (iii), for indium, there is a succession of resonances in the neighbourhood of 1–10 eV and these are superimposed on a large cross-section for (n, γ) capture which varies as $1/v$ at low energies.

We have commented earlier on the extremely widespread occurrence among the elements of the ' radiative capture ' type of reaction for neutrons. The extent of the reaction, as judged by the size of the cross-section and the way in which this varies with the energy of the neutron, varies widely among the elements but in each case the nature of the products, including the precise wavelength of the emitted

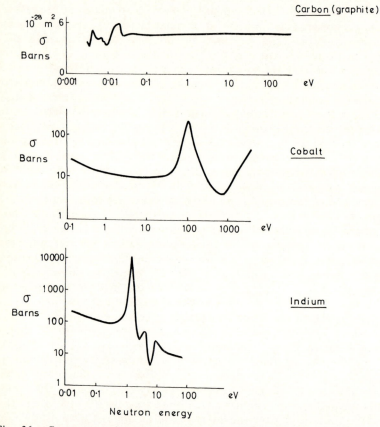

Fig. 36. Some examples of the way in which the ' total cross-section ' of elements for neutrons (including both capture and scattering) varies with the energy of the neutron (from *Experimental Nuclear Physics*, Vol. II, ed. E. Segrè : Wiley, New York, U.S.A.).

radiation, is very specific. In fact the spectrum of the radiation is a characteristic ' finger-print ' of the target element and can be used as an extremely powerful and rapid method of analysis for chemical elements in which quantities as small as 10^{-9} g can be detected. The technique is known as ' neutron activation analysis ' and consists essentially of using an automated apparatus to measure the γ-ray spectrum from a small sample which has been irradiated in a neutron beam. Particular elements can be sought by using individual channels of the detecting apparatus to assess the intensity of γ-rays of particular wavelengths. The lower limit of detection will depend on the nature of the element and the intensity of the neutron beam. Consequently irradiation in a high neutron flux in a nuclear reactor is preferable, and because of the wide range of neutron energies which is present it is essential that the quantitative measurements are done by a comparison method, in which standard samples of the same elements are irradiated and then ' counted ' at the same time as the unknown sample. If we can use a neutron flux of 10^9 neutrons per mm^2 per second, which is typical of a present-day reactor, and an irradiation time of about 1 hour, then it is possible to detect amounts of about 10^{-9} g for some seventy elements. For a sample as large as 1 g this means that concentrations down to 10^{-3} parts per million can be observed. In some cases, for those elements whose products have a long life, the minimum quantities for detection can be reduced still further by using a longer time of irradiation. For more than half the elements of the periodic system this method of neutron activation analysis is the most sensitive of all known methods of detection. The great speed of the analysis, when it is carried out with an automated series of instruments, is an equally important advantage in many of its applications. Current developments of the accelerating machines which produce neutrons from the deuterium–tritium reaction offer prospects of a much wider application of these techniques.

CHAPTER 7
using neutrons for studying solids

IN our discussion of the properties and behaviour of the neutron we have been thinking of it largely as a spherical particle and we have been able to picture a beam of neutrons rather like a stream of bullets emerging from a gun, well-defined in direction but often with a wide spread of velocities. However, when we presented fig. 27 which correlated the various ways in which we could characterize the energy of a neutron, we did mention that neutrons could show wave properties and that a wavelength λ can be ascribed to a neutron. This is of course a typical example of the way in which both radiation and matter, and the fundamental particles which constitute it, have a dual nature and different aspects of their behaviour can display one or other of these two characteristics. Perhaps the most familiar example of this duality is visible light, which in the phenomena of interference and diffraction displays its wave nature but nevertheless takes part in the photoelectric effect which we can only interpret in terms of the light particles which we call ' photons '. Broadly we can say that we use the wave picture when we are considering the way in which light is distributed in space, whether for example some particular place is bright or dark, but we are compelled to use the particle picture when we are examining the way in which light actually interacts with matter, and in doing so becomes, itself, changed in nature. Exactly the same kind of consideration applies to the neutron. In our discussions so far we have been able to picture it as a particle simply because we have been almost entirely concerned with its reactions with atoms, such as the way in which it can combine with an atom of the ^{10}B isotope to produce atoms of lithium and helium or the way in which it can share its energy with an atom of carbon in the moderator of a nuclear reactor.

The wave properties of the neutron can be revealed in precisely the same manner as for visible light, by observing how the phenomena of interference and diffraction determine the way in which a beam of neutrons propagates and spreads. In order to observe diffraction, which was first reported for neutrons in 1936, our most important need is to use experimental apparatus on the right sort of scale, appropriate to the numerical value of the wavelength of the neutrons which we are using. Again, exactly the same thought has to be given to a diffraction experiment with optical light. The familiar optical diffraction grating, which we use as a matter of course, has its rulings at intervals of about 1/500 of a millimetre, a distance which is about three times as large as the wavelength of sodium light. We should find it very difficult to do an experiment in optical diffraction if we used a grating which consisted, say ,of parallel wires 50 mm apart : on the other hand a grating of this kind would be very satisfactory if we wanted to demonstrate the diffraction of very short-wave radio-waves of wavelength 30 mm. Let us examine therefore the range of wavelengths which we are likely to encounter among beams of neutrons.

The wavelength λ and velocity v of the neutron, or any other particle, are related by the equation :

$$\lambda = \frac{h}{mv},$$

where m is the mass of the particle and h is Planck's constant which has a numerical value of $6 \cdot 63 \times 10^{-34}$ J s. The corresponding values of λ, v which appear in fig. 27 were derived from this equation.

When we were discussing the neutron spectrum from a nuclear reactor, which is the most intense source of neutrons available, we stated that the peak of the spectrum of neutrons which emerge from the reactor occurs at a velocity v for which

$$\tfrac{1}{2}mv^2 = \tfrac{3}{2}kT,$$

where k is Boltzmann's constant and T is the temperature of the reactor. If we insert the values of m, k in this equation and choose, for example, a reactor temperature of 500°K we deduce that the neutron velocity will be $3 \cdot 52$ km/s and hence, from the previous equation, the corresponding wavelength will be $1 \cdot 12 \times 10^{-10}$ m. It happens that this value is quite similar to the distances of separation of atoms in a solid. For example, as we have already stated, the atoms in metallic copper are $2 \cdot 56 \times 10^{-10}$ m apart and in organic compounds the separations of neighbouring carbon atoms range from $1 \cdot 20 \rightarrow 1 \cdot 54 \times 10^{-10}$ m and this led to acceptance of the special name of Ångström unit (Å) for this distance of 10^{-10} m ($0 \cdot 1$ nm). We should expect therefore that the ordered arrangements of atoms which we find in solids would be able to act as diffraction gratings for our beams of neutrons. In fact a rather similar line of reasoning led over half a century ago, in 1912, to an experiment in which M. von Laue demonstrated that X-rays had wavelengths of the order of magnitude of an Ångström.

Question 23.   *The density of metallic copper is $8 \cdot 9 \times 10^3$ kg/m³ and its atomic weight is $63 \cdot 5$, so that $63 \cdot 5$ g of metal will contain $N = 6 \cdot 0 \times 10^{23}$ atoms. Assume that each copper atom occupies a corner of a cube in an extended array of cubes in three dimensions and calculate the distance of separation of a copper atom from its nearest neighbours.*
Ans. $2 \cdot 28 \times 10^{-10}$ m ($2 \cdot 28$ Å).

This historical experiment is of particular importance to our present discussion because we shall see later that the unique value of neutrons in diffraction experiments arises from the extent to which they can *supplement* the knowledge which can be gained with X-rays. It may readily be realized that the technique of using beams of neutrons for experiments in diffraction is a cumbersome and expensive one, needing as it does a nuclear reactor, compared with the relative simplicity of acquiring and manipulating a beam of X-rays. We shall, however, find that neutrons can make some quite unique contributions to our knowledge of solids, and indeed liquids, so that their relative inconvenience and expense are disadvantages which are well worth accepting. We shall be able to see how some particularly useful features of solids can be revealed from experiments with neutron beams when we have compared rather more closely the way in which X-rays and neutrons are scattered, i.e. redirected, by atoms.

In the theory of optical diffraction gratings two principal facts emerge. First, the angular positions of the spectra, i.e. the principal maxima in the diffraction pattern, depend on the distance of separation between neighbouring lines in the grating. Secondly, the relative intensities of the spectra depend on the ' shape ' of the individual lines, i.e. on the way in which the transmission of light varies for different parts of the ' line '. Some examples are shown in fig. 37. In the first part of this figure we have an extremely narrow line ; it can be shown that this will produce only a slow fall-off of intensity as we proceed through the orders of spectra 1, 2, 3, ... In curve (ii) we have a grating whose lines have a ' square-topped ' shape of transmission function and for which the open and closed sections of grating are of equal width. It can be shown mathematically that for this grating orders 2, 4, 6, 8, ... are completely missing and that the amplitudes of the odd orders 1, 3, 5, ... decrease according to the factors $1, \frac{1}{3}, \frac{1}{5}, \dots$, and their intensities will therefore be as the squares of these numbers. For curve (iii), where we have chosen a line which has a sinusoidal variation of transmission factor, only the first-order spectrum occurs : all the higher orders are missing. If, as in (iv), we make a grating for which the *sign* of the transmission alters after each half-cycle (which means introducing a phase difference of π) then there will be no straight-through light or zero-order spectrum either : there will simply be the first-order spectra. From this brief discussion

72

we state that if we know how the transmission of a ' grating unit ' varies from point to point, then we can deduce the relative amplitudes and intensities of the spectra of order 1, 2, 3, ..., etc. Conversely, it can be established rigorously that if we know the relative magnitudes of these spectral amplitudes, then we can deduce the detailed nature of the transmission function of the unit.

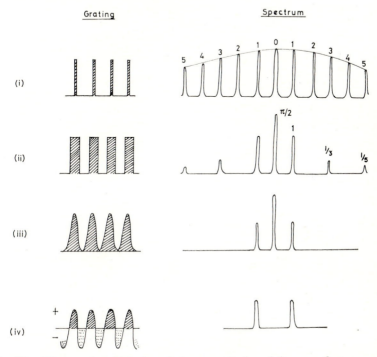

Fig. 37. The way in which the relative magnitudes of the zero, first, second, third, ... order spectra depend on the ' shape ' of the grating ' line '.

When we turn to consider three-dimensional solids as gratings for diffracting X-rays or neutrons, then the analogue of the optical transmission factor of the line will be a function which describes how the three-dimensional unit diverts or, as we say, *scatters* the radiation. We must, however, make one stipulation. When we examine the diverted or scattered radiation we are only going to consider that part of the radiation which is quite unchanged in nature by its passage through the solid. For example, if we are considering the diffraction of X-rays we are not going to be concerned with those X-rays which eject electrons from the atoms, even though this process may be succeeded by the appearance of new fluorescent X-rays. Nor in the case of neutrons are we talking of those neutrons which make inelastic collisions with atoms in the solid and necessarily proceed on their way with diminished velocity. It is the *unaltered* neutrons, the ones which have been scattered by an *elastic* collision, which will enable us to build up a picture of the grouping of atoms which form the building unit in the solid. The reason for this is fundamentally that our spectral distributions are determined by interference and superposition, which depend on the preservation of phase relations, of the wave contributions from different parts of the scattering unit. Our requirement is the same as the one which stipulates that there must be a single monochromatic source as the ' originator' in the conventional Young's interference experiment with two slits.

When a beam of *X-rays* is elastically scattered by a solid the scattering agents are the *electrons*, so that the picture of the unit of the solid which we can build up, and which we call the unit cell, will be a description in terms of electron density, measured as electrons per unit volume. For metallic copper, which we can again take as an example, the unit cell has a volume of 47×10^{-30} m³, and contains 116 electrons : for rock salt, NaCl, the unit cell has a volume of 178×10^{-30} m³ and contains 112 electrons. As a rough guide therefore we may think of the average electron density in solids as being one electron in each 10^{-30} m³ of volume. It will be noted that, in terms of our conventional unit of atomic distance, the Ångström, this means that there is roughly one electron in each Ångström cube. These electron-density pictures, which we can draw with the aid of X-rays, will of course be three-dimensional and therefore rather difficult to represent properly on paper. It is simpler to show as a typical result a two-dimensional projection, in which the electron content of the unit cell has been projected onto a plane, thus giving the appearance of a contour map. Such a projection is shown in fig. 38 (i). We emphasize that this has been obtained by *X-ray* diffraction and we have to draw attention to the fact that, although the carbon atoms are prominently shown, the picture does very little justice to the hydrogen atoms and these appear to be very insignificant. The reason for this is that so far as the X-rays are concerned the hydrogen atoms are indeed insignificant, since they have only one electron each, compared with the six which are present in a carbon atom. If the hydrogen atoms had been portrayed alongside some heavier elements, say iron or lead, then the hydrogens would have looked extremely trivial—and proportionately difficult to locate with accuracy. For comparison, the second illustration in fig. 38 is a corresponding pattern obtained with neutrons : it is not for anthracene, which has not yet been examined with neutrons, but for solid benzene. The very considerable enhancement of the hydrogen atoms, compared with those in the X-ray picture, is quite clear and arises simply because so far as the neutrons are concerned a hydrogen atom is quite a good scatterer. Admittedly

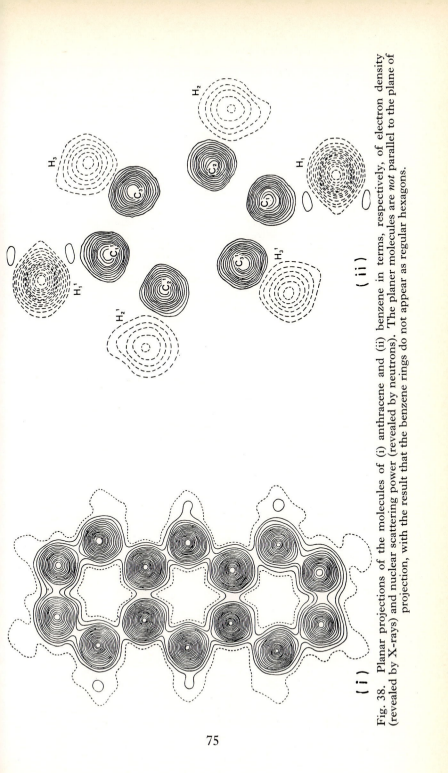

Fig. 38. Planar projections of the molecules of (i) anthracene and (ii) benzene in terms, respectively, of electron density (revealed by X-rays) and nuclear scattering power (revealed by neutrons). The planer molecules are *not* parallel to the plane of projection, with the result that the benzene rings do not appear as regular hexagons.

it does not scatter quite as much as a carbon atom (the amplitude is about 60% as large as for carbon) but if necessary a nearer approach to equality can be achieved by using the deuterium isotope in place of ordinary hydrogen, since it happens that deuterium almost matches carbon in its scattering ability.

The above example underlines one of the two fundamental advantages of using the diffraction patterns for neutrons as a way of studying solids. We may indeed say that whereas the amplitudes with which atoms scatter X-rays vary almost a hundredfold over the Periodic Table (uranium is 92 times as effective as hydrogen) the amplitudes for neutrons cover a range of only two or three times. The reason for this is that neutrons are scattered by the *nucleus* of an atom, not by the surrounding electrons, and the extent to which the nucleus scatters depends on two factors. First, it depends on the physical size of the nucleus and this is a quantity which increases relatively slowly with mass number. The important parameter is the radius of the nucleus which, because nuclear matter is of constant density, increases as $A^{1/3}$, where A is the mass number. Secondly, superimposed on this nuclear-size effect is a dependence on the magnitude of the permissible values for the energy of the nucleus or, more precisely, of the 'compound nucleus' formed from the incident neutron and the target nucleus. If the incident neutron has an energy which just raises the energy of the compound system to certain particular values, then enhanced scattering can take place, like the enhanced oscillations in an electrical circuit at a resonant frequency. The scattering amplitude is influenced over a wide range of neutron wavelength. The contribution to the scattering from this resonance effect varies seemingly haphazardly from atom to atom in the Periodic Table so that there are considerable differences of behaviour between neighbouring atoms. We should be able to predict these quantitative values if we had a full understanding of the structure of nuclei, but at present we have to rely on experimental measurements of the amplitudes for scattering. The resulting conclusions are emphasized pictorially in fig. 39 where the areas drawn for each atom represent the magnitude of the amplitude for neutron scattering. The average value of this quantity, taken over all atoms and isotopes, is 6×10^{-15} m, having the dimensions of a length. Very few atoms have values which are less than half of this average or greater than twice it. The lower half of fig. 39 contrasts the behaviour of X-rays for which, as we have already said, the scattering amplitude increases steadily and linearly with atomic number as we advance up the Periodic Table of the elements. In drawing the second section of this figure we have used a scale which is ten times smaller than that which we used for the neutron amplitudes. It will be realized therefore that in quantitative terms the fraction of an X-ray beam which is scattered by a group of atoms is about ten times as great as the corresponding fraction of neutrons.

We draw attention to some further features of fig. 39 (i) which are of practical importance. In the case of a few elements, such as hydrogen, titanium and manganese, the scattering amplitude is negative, which means that there is an additional phase change of π compared with what happens when neutrons are scattered from most elements. It will also be noticed that in two cases, for hydrogen and lithium, we have shown different values for different *isotopes* of the element: thus, for hydrogen and deuterium the values are -3.75, $+6.70 \times 10^{-15}$ m respectively and for the lithium isotopes ^{6}Li, ^{7}Li they are $+1.8$, -2.1×10^{-15} m. These are examples of what is a general feature, namely the fact that the nuclei of different isotopes of an element may scatter neutrons quite differently. Information is not yet available for all the isotopes of every element but it is clear that there are substantial differences for several elements, especially for light elements, the iron group of transition elements and the rare-earths. The cases which show large variations will be those where the values of the energy levels vary appreciably between isotopes, thus leading to substantial changes in the resonance contribution to the scattering. A very noteworthy example is nickel, for which the amplitudes for the isotopes of mass 58, 60, 61, 62 and 64 are 14.4, 3.0, 7.6, -8.7 and -0.37×10^{-15} m respectively. For 'ordinary' nickel the value is 10.3×10^{-15} m, which is the weighted average of the above values, taking into account the relative abundances of each of the isotopes in the naturally occurring metal.

The second important advantage of using neutrons is that although the normal scattering centres within the atoms are the nuclei, yet there is additional scattering from atoms which have paramagnetic properties. This extra scattering arises from the resultant electron spin which these atoms possess. It will be recalled that in the description of the electronic constitution of atoms in terms of the quantum theory, four quantum numbers are ascribed to each electron. Of these n, the principal quantum number, primarily determines the energy, l describes the orbital angular momentum, m indicates the orientation and hence the behaviour, in a magnetic field and s describes the intrinsic electron spin. The spin quantum number s can have only two possible values, either $+\frac{1}{2}$ or $-\frac{1}{2}$, corresponding to spin angular momenta of $\pm h/4\pi$, where h is Planck's constant. Detailed explanations of atomic spectra and the chemical properties of atoms, as summarized by the Periodic Table, are forthcoming in terms of these four quantum numbers if we accept the general principle stated by W. Pauli and known as the Pauli Exclusion Principle. This states that no two electrons in an atom can have the same set of four quantum numbers. It follows that most of the electrons in an atom can be grouped in pairs, whose angular momenta (due to both orbital motion and to intrinsic spin) are of equal magnitude but oppositely directed: the two members of such a pair will cancel out

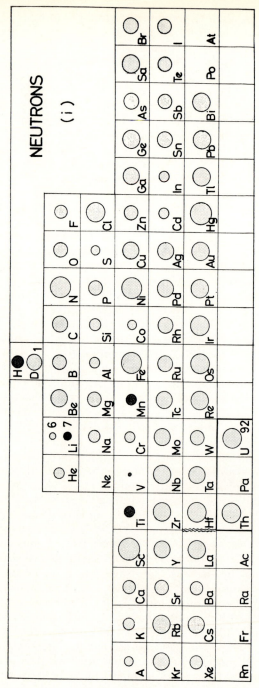

NEUTRONS

(i)

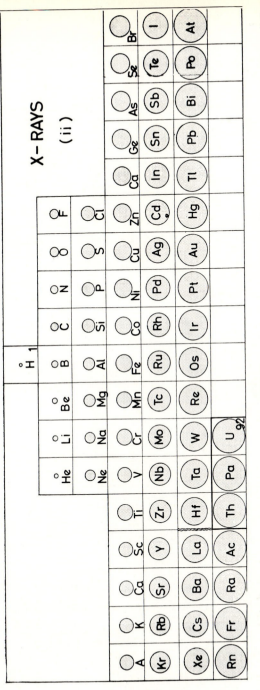

Fig. 39. The target sizes of atoms for the scattering of neutrons (i) and X-rays (ii), arranged according to the positions of the atoms in the Periodic Table. The areas which are shaded grey indicate a positive scattering-amplitude but the few black areas which occur in (i) indicate negative values.

79

each other's effects. In many atoms and ions all the electrons will be paired off in this way but in other atoms there will be a small resultant effect, amounting up to a few units of angular momentum. We say that these atoms have ' unpaired electrons ' and as a consequence of their resultant angular momentum they will have a resultant magnetic moment. Sometimes the structure of a solid is such that the orbital part of the momentum is ineffective and is said to be ' quenched ', with the result that the magnetic moment is then due solely to the intrinsic spin momentum of the electrons. Very often the resulting magnetic moments will point in random directions from atom to atom in a solid and in this case the latter will display the behaviour which we know as paramagnetism. In other cases the moment directions will line up to give ordered arrangements of which ferromagnetism is the best-known example. In either case we can ascribe a magnetic moment μ to the atom, in units of the Bohr magneton which we mentioned on p. 38, and it is these ' magnetic atoms ' which give rise to additional scattering of the neutrons. We can regard this extra scattering as indicative of the interaction between the magnetic moment of the neutron itself and that of the atom. We shall defer further discussion of this magnetic scattering, and the way in which it can be used to examine the magnetic structures of solids, until the following chapter. Meanwhile we will make a brief examination of the way in which experimental measurements of neutron diffraction patterns can be made at a nuclear reactor.

Figure 40 shows, in a diagrammatic way, the experimental arrangement for extracting a beam of neutrons from a nuclear reactor and using it to measure the diffraction pattern for a solid. Figure 41 shows photographs of two sets of apparatus in use. The first of these, (i), is a large instrument which is used mainly for examining materials which are in the form of powders or polycrystals, whereas the use of the second instrument (ii) is restricted to substances which can be obtained in the form of adequately sized single-crystals†, whose linear

---

Question 24. *In order to produce a neutron beam which is almost unidirectional the neutrons are passed down a colli-mator constructed of uniformly-spaced parallel thin steel plates of length 1·5 m. What must be the horizontal separation between adjacent plates in order to provide a beam with an angular divergence in the horizontal plane of $\pm 0·3°$?*

Ans. 7·9 mm.

---

† The term ' single-crystal ', which we shall often use, emphasizes that the whole of the sample has crystallized as a single individual in which the atomic planes (see further in fig. 44) maintain their directions throughout the sample to an accuracy of a fraction of a degree. Some substances will only grow ' properly ' in this way for a fraction of a millimetre whereas others will grow correctly for many centimetres. The ' single-crystal ' is contrasted with a ' polycrystalline ' sample which is comprised of many distinct individual crystals, often oriented completely at random.

dimensions are about 2 or 3 mm in each direction. Referring first to fig. 40, which indicates the principles of the technique, we see that the first stage in the measurement is to use a collimating tube to select a beam of neutrons which are effectively unidirectional. Ideally the neutron beam should be as unidirectional as possible, but high angular resolution can only be obtained at the expense of reduced

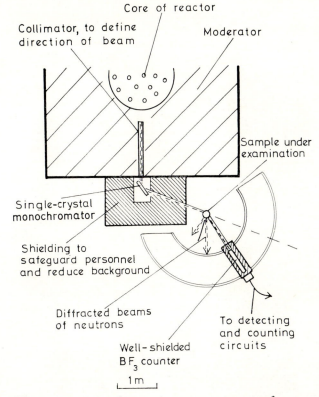

Fig. 40. The arrangement of a rotating neutron counter for recording the diffraction pattern of neutrons, at a nuclear reactor.

intensity, so that in practice a collimation of about $\pm 0.3°$ in angle has to be accepted. The neutrons which emerge from the end of the collimator are then ' monochromatized ', which means that solely those neutrons which have velocities (and, hence, wavelengths) within a narrow band are selected. This selection is made by reflecting the initial beam at the surface of a large single-crystal, which makes the selection according to the Bragg equation $\lambda = 2d \sin \theta$, where d is the distance of separation between successive planes of atoms within the crystal in a direction parallel to the crystal surface. θ is the glancing angle which the incident beam makes with the surface.

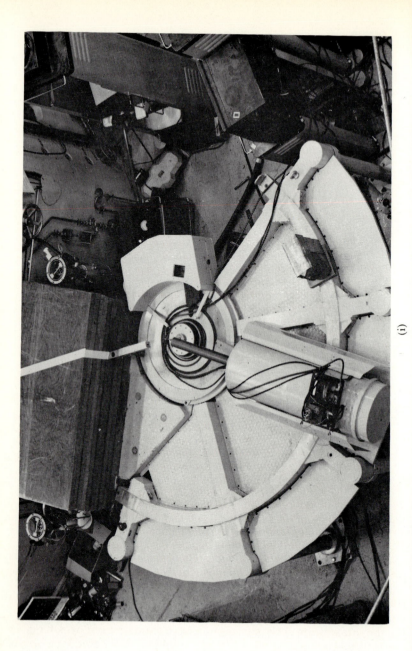

(i)

82

(ii)

Fig. 41. Photographs of instruments used for obtaining neutron diffraction patterns at the nuclear reactors at the Atomic Energy Research Establishment, Harwell. The large instrument (i) is designed for use with powdered and polycrystalline samples: (ii) is a fully automated machine for determining crystal structures from single crystals (by courtesy of the U.K.A.E.A.).

In a typical apparatus a large crystal of copper or beryllium is used as the monochromator and the geometry is chosen so that the wavelength of the reflected beam is a little greater than 0·1nm (1 Å). The spread of wavelength in the beam is due mainly to the finite spread of directions in the beam from the collimator and is equal to about 2 pm (0·02 Å). The monochromatic beam is then allowed to fall on the sample under examination and the distribution of the scattered neutrons is examined with a rotating detector. This is almost always a cylindrical counter filled with BF_3 gas which operates in the manner which we have described in Chapter 5. With a polycrystalline sample

---

Question 25. *A lead crystal for use as a monochromator is cut with its surface parallel to the* 111 *crystal planes, which have a spacing of* 0·282 nm (2·82 Å). *What glancing angle* θ *must the neutron beam make with the surface if neutrons of wavelength* 0·1 nm (1 Å) *are to be reflected?*

Ans. 10·2°.

If the incident neutron beam diverges in direction over an angular range of $\pm 0·2°$ *there will be a spread of wavelength in the reflected beam. Calculate this spread in the above case, by differentiating the Bragg equation.*

Ans. $\pm 1·9$ pm (0·019 Å).

---

there are always some fragments of the sample which are correctly oriented to give any particular diffraction spectrum, so that the intensities of the various spectra can be plotted out as the counter is rotated in the horizontal plane. With a single-crystal the procedure is more complicated, but correspondingly more informative. The conditions for three-dimensional diffraction are more stringent than those which apply to the one-dimensional diffraction from an optical grating, with the result that each individual spectrum can only be observed when the single-crystal is oriented at some precise setting with respect to the incident beam. With modern apparatus it is fortunate that the successive repetition of the processes of orientation of crystal and counter (in turn for each spectrum), followed by a period of counting, can be programmed to take place automatically. Figure 42 gives some examples of diffraction patterns obtained from powdered samples, using a counter which rotates continuously and from which the indications are fed to a ratemeter whose output operates a pen-recorder. The figure shows photographs of the original experimental records. Figure 43 illustrates the data obtained from the single-crystal apparatus when it has been programmed to advance the counter step by step through the position of a particular spectrum. Alongside the record of the printed output from the machine we show a plot of the diffraction peak. This particular plot has been drawn out by hand, but it is also possible to feed the output of the apparatus to an automatic plotter.

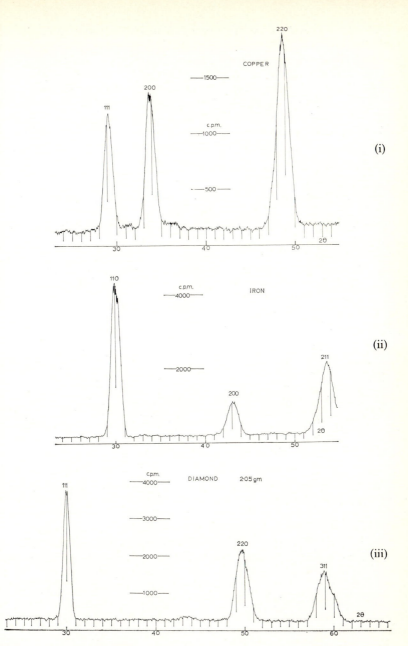

Fig. 42. Some examples of experimentally recorded diffraction patterns for (i) copper, (ii) iron, (iii) diamond, given by polycrystalline samples. The three-figure symbols, such as 111 and 220 in (iii), are the Miller indices which identify the spectra, as described in the text.

85

It will be noted that the peaks in these diffraction patterns are labelled with a set of three indices, which serve to identify the spectrum in the same way as the single numbers $1, 2, 3, \ldots$, etc. indicate the

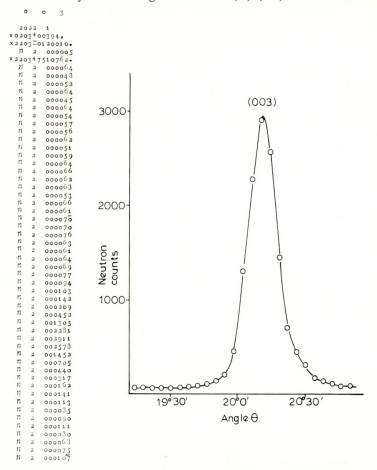

Fig. 43. On the left is shown a portion of the printed record of the diffraction pattern from a single-crystal of salicylic acid $C_6H_4OH \cdot COOH$ in the neighbourhood of the (003) spectrum. Successive lines correspond to increments of $4'$ in the glancing angle θ. The final column gives the number of neutrons counted, and this is plotted out on the right.

successive orders of spectra from a simple optical diffraction grating. In the three-dimensional crystal three conditions have to be satisfied simultaneously if a diffracted beam is to be observed. If we think of a regularly repeating crystal structure as referred to three co-ordinate axes in space, Ox, Oy, Oz as in fig. 44, then the conditions for a spectrum will be as follows : the path lengths for waves scattered by

86

consecutive equivalent atoms A, A', A" along the Ox axis must differ by $h\lambda$, for atoms B, B', B" along Oy by $k\lambda$ and for atoms C, C', C" along Oz by $l\lambda$, where h, k, l are whole numbers and λ is the wavelength of the radiation. The set of three indices hkl then describes the

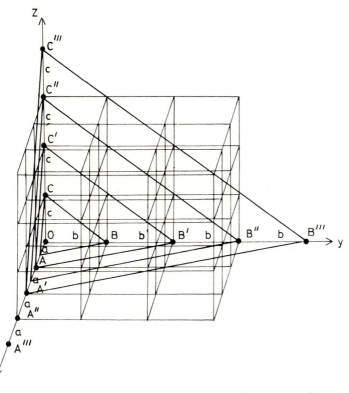

Fig. 44. A representation of the three-dimensional structure of a crystal, indicating equivalent points O, A, A', ..., B, B', ..., C, C', ... along the three co-ordinate axes. The inclined planes are the series with indices (211). The first plane in the series, proceeding outwards from the origin, intercepts the axes at the points $a/2, b, c$.

spectrum. An alternative way of regarding the spectra is that they are formed by constructive superposition of the waves contributed by members of stacks of planes in the crystal structure, such as the set drawn in the figure. It will be noted for these that the first plane outwards from the origin passes through the points $a/2$ on Ox, b on Oy and c on Oz. The conventional description is to call this particular set of planes (211) and the numbers are called 'Miller indices'. It can be shown that the three indices 2, 1, 1 are indeed the same numbers as h, k, l which we used above in our first method of considering the origin of the spectra.

Perhaps the most general application of these methods is to the determination of the atomic and molecular structures of organic materials, taking advantage of the power of neutrons to locate accurately the hydrogen atoms. There are two separate aspects of this which are important. First, it becomes possible to determine bond lengths, such as C—H and O—H, with accuracy and in this way to become certain of the types of chemical binding which exist in the solid. For example, it is possible to demonstrate directly the existence of ' hydrogen bonds ' in solids. A ' hydrogen bond ' is the name given to a very important linkage in solids in which a hydrogen atom acts as an agent which draws together two neighbouring atoms, usually oxygen, more closely than they would otherwise be. Very often it is neighbouring molecules which are brought together in this way but sometimes we have an intra-molecular bond which links together different parts of a single molecule. Figure 45, which is a projection of the nuclear scattering density of α-resorcinol $C_6H_4(OH)_2$ on a plane, indicates the way in which the predominant forces which hold together the structure arise from the spirals of hydrogen bonds which link together adjacent molecules. Another example is provided by neutron studies of hydrated crystals, such as $CuSO_4 \cdot 5H_2O$ and the alums like $K_2SO_4 Cr_2(SO_4)_3 \cdot 24H_2O$, where it is found that the hydrogen bonds which link the water molecules to the oxygen atoms in the sulphate groups play the major part in holding together the crystal. Secondly, precise information about the hydrogen atoms is of great help in assessing the thermal motion of the molecules. To a significant extent it is found that molecules vibrate as rigid bodies, although this motion is modified by the bending and stretching of individual bonds. It happens very often that hydrogen atoms are located at the periphery of molecules and therefore they will execute large movements if any molecular oscillation is taking place. Precise knowledge of the hydrogen positions and of their thermal motion, which also can be deduced from the neutron diffraction data, is therefore of great help in trying to deduce the motions of the molecules. From the point of view of the theoretical chemist these precise measurements of hydrogen atoms are especially important because it is only for a very simple atom like hydrogen that the detailed constitution can be calculated with confidence.

We have already mentioned that a nuclear reactor is needed in order to provide neutron beams of sufficient intensity for making measurements of diffraction and the scope of the technique has steadily widened since the year 1945 as beams of greater intensity have become available. We must point out, however, that even the most powerful reactors in existence are not able to provide beams which, measured in terms of the number of quanta per unit area, are anything like as intense as the beam of X-rays from a conventional tube used for X-ray diffraction. Indeed, the X-ray beam has an advantage by a factor of about 1000 times.   This means that larger samples of material have to be used with neutrons and accounts for the fact that when a single-crystal is to be studied it will usually need to have linear dimensions of about 2 mm.   This sets a limitation on the kind of material which

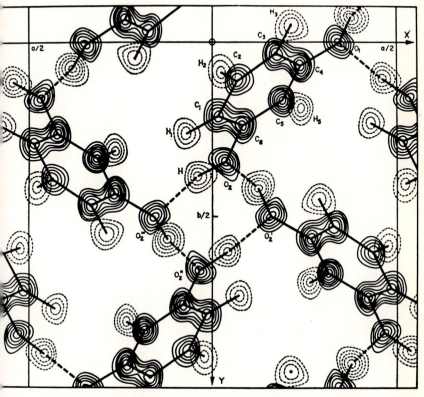

Fig. 45.   A projection of the neutron-scattering density in α-resorcinol.   The full lines represent positive contours from carbon and oxygen atoms, and the broken lines are negative contours from hydrogen atoms.   The hydroxyl groups from neighbouring molecules are linked to form infinite helices of hydrogen bonds through the crystal : in the two-dimensional projection these helices appear as the eight-sided closed circuits such as $O_2 O_2' O_2'' O_2'''$.   The molecules are inclined at $61°$ to the plane of the projection.

can be studied, although this is a limitation which is slowly becoming of less importance as the intensity of the available beams of neutron increases.   Probably the most ambitious study which has been made so far is an examination of a derivative of vitamin B_{12} which, although not so precise and complete as could be desired, was good enough to give important chemical information about certain features of this complicated molecule.

CHAPTER 8

magnetism and magnetic materials

WE have seen in the last chapter that when a beam of neutrons is diverted or scattered by the atoms in a solid, without any change in the energy or wavelength of the neutrons, it is principally the *nuclei* of the atoms which cause the scattering. This is a quite general process which takes place for all atoms, although there are some differences in the quantitative scattering powers of the atoms of different elements, as we have already shown in fig. 39. We have, however, already mentioned that extra scattering occurs for those atoms which possess magnetic moments, arising from an interaction between the magnetic moment of the atom and that of the neutron. We shall now examine this process of magnetic scattering in more detail and we shall find that it provides us with a means of studying magnetism on an atomic scale which has some immense advantages over the more conventional measurements with magnetometers and susceptibility balances, which make relatively macroscopic observations. The outcome of this type of investigation with neutrons is a realization that many solids have regular periodic magnetic structures, or a kind of magnetic architecture, and we can determine the details of these structures by making experiments with neutrons. The familiar concept of ferromagnetism, according to which the magnetic moments of the atoms are in parallel alignment throughout a domain of material, is no more than just the simplest of many possible kinds of co-operative arrangement.

We can examine the important basic features of the magnetic scattering with the help of fig. 46, in which an atom is sited at the point A. This atom has a magnetic moment, pointing in the direction **K**, and is situated in a beam of neutrons coming from the direction of the point X. The fact that some atoms have ' magnetic moments ' is a consequence of their particular electronic structures : every electron has a spin and in most atoms or ions these spins cancel out in pairs, each made up of a clockwise and an anticlockwise spin, but atoms which show magnetic properties are ones which retain a *resultant* spin. The neutrons will be partially scattered by them in all directions and it can be shown that the extra number which travel towards Y in fig. 46 (i) depends on the quantity :

$$q \left(\frac{e^2 \gamma}{mc^2} \right) Sf.$$

All the quantities in the bracketed term are constants : e, m are the charge and mass of an electron, γ is the magnetic moment of the neutron expressed in nuclear magnetons (which we discussed on p. 38) and c is the velocity of light, so that the numerical value of

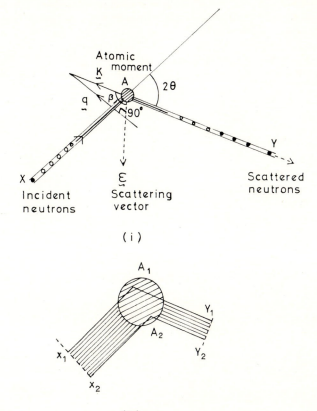

(i)

(ii)

Fig. 46. The important parameters which determine the intensity of magnetic scattering. Diagram (i) defines the vector **q** which is in the plane of **ε**, **K** in a direction perpendicular to **ε** and of magnitude $\sin \beta$, and (ii) shows the different path lengths $X_1A_1Y_1$, $X_2A_2Y_2$ for electrons in different parts of the atom, resulting in the angle-dependent form factor f.

$e^2\gamma/mc^2$ is $5\cdot4 \times 10^{-15}$ m. S is the spin quantum number which describes the magnetic state of the atom, so that the magnetic moment of the atom in units of the Bohr magneton, which we also defined on p. 38, is equal to $2S$. The other two factors, namely f which we call the 'atomic form factor' and q, called the 'magnetic interaction vector' will require some further explanation. We can see the significance of f if we recall that the linear dimensions of an atom, or more specifically of the space which is occupied by its magnetic electrons, are a few tenths of a nanometre (a few Ångströms). This distance is about the same as the neutron's wavelength and this means, as implied at (ii) in fig. 46, that there will be a significant difference of path, and hence of phase, between the neutrons which are scattered from different parts of the atom A_1, A_2 on their way from X to Y. If the angle of scattering, 2θ, is zero, then all the contributions will be in phase, but as θ increases, the net amplitude of scattering, represented by the form factor f, will fall off rapidly as shown in fig. 47.

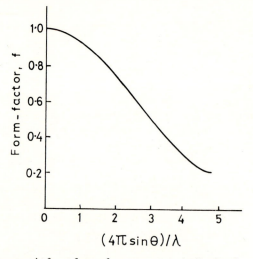

Fig. 47. The magnetic form factor for manganese, indicating how the magnetic scattering decreases as the angle of scattering (represented by the quantity $4\pi \sin \theta/\lambda$) increases.

Question 26. *A beam of radiation of wavelength 0·1 nm (1 Å) is scattered through an angle of 30° by a spherical atom of diameter 0·2 nm (2 Å). What is the extreme difference of phase of the contributions from different parts of the atom.*

Ans. $2 \cdot 07\pi$.

(Note that the answer is not exactly 2π.)

The experimental quantity which determines the rate of fall-off is $(\sin \theta)/\lambda$ because this is the factor which determines the phase differences for contributions from different parts of the atom. Finally, in interpreting the above expression, we have to explain the significance of the quantity q which is the numerical value of what we call the 'magnetic interaction vector' **q**. In some respects this is the most important quantity in the whole expression because its occurrence there enables us to use the neutron measurements to determine **K**, the directions in space in which the atomic moments are pointing. Looking again at diagram (i) in fig. 46 we state that the numerical value of **q** is the value of $\sin \beta$, where β is the angle between the vector **K** and the vector **ε**, which bisects the angle between the incident and scattered beams of neutrons and is itself called the 'scattering vector'. The *direction* of the vector **q** which, although not important to our present discussion, will be of significance to us later, is indicated in fig. 46: it lies in the plane of the vectors **ε**, **K** and is perpendicular to the direction of **ε**. We have therefore a full description of the magnetic scattering amplitude of our atom which will give us a quantitative measure of the number of neutrons which the atom will scatter in any given direction, in terms of its magnetic moment and the orientation of that moment with respect to the incident and scattered beams. Conversely we have available a means of determining both the magnetic moment and its direction, from an assessment of the spatial distribution of the scattered neutrons. We shall not attempt to justify the rather intricate details of the steps which have to be followed in deducing the magnetic structure from the experimental data, but simply take some examples which will give an idea of the clear and characteristic way in which individual types of magnetic structure manifest themselves and, therefore, can be identified.

Figure 48 relates to a ferromagnetic material, characterized by the fact that the line-up of all the magnetic moments in a single direction, as shown on the top of the figure, continues throughout domains which include many hundreds of atoms. Metallic iron would be a typical case of this kind, with the 'body-centred' structure which is shown at (iv) in the drawing. If we take a powdered sample of iron and measure the diffraction pattern in a monochromatic beam of *X-rays* we shall observe an angular distribution represented by curve (i) in fig. 48. If a neutron beam was used for the experiment the pattern would not at first sight appear very different, allowing for a change of wavelength, but careful measurement would reveal that the intensities of the well-defined peaks were greater for cold iron than for iron which is heated beyond its Curie temperature of 770°C. This is accounted for by the additional magnetic scattering of the neutrons which is produced by the aligned array of magnetic moments. The patterns at two different temperatures are contrasted in curves (ii) and (iii). The important feature is that the magnetic scattering, which is shaded bold in curve (iii), appears at the same angular positions, as the ordinary nuclear neutron, or the X-ray, scattering. The reason for this is that the 'magnetic periodicity' of structure (iv) is exactly the same as the 'chemical periodicity', i.e. the unit is a cube of side AB. These experiments give direct evidence that in a piece of unmagnetized iron all the magnetic moments point in the same

93

direction, at least throughout domains which measure between 10 and 100 nm. We can also show, by making observations at different temperatures, that the magnetic order has disappeared completely above the Curie temperature of 1043°K. Below this temperature the perfection of the order steadily increases and the magnetization

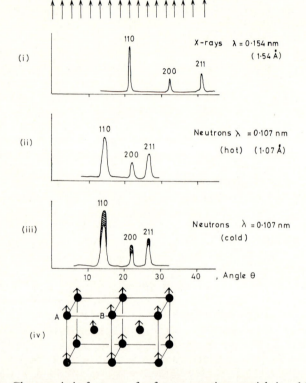

Fig. 48. Characteristic features of a ferromagnetic material, in which all the magnetic moments point in the same direction within a domain. The general features of the diffraction patterns, illustrated for iron, are the same for X-rays (i) and neutrons (ii) hot, and (iii) cold, but the latter pattern includes increased scattering shown shaded. Diagram (iv) illustrates the structure of iron. Both magnetically and chemically (the latter 'ignores' the arrows which represent the magnetic moments) the unit cell is a cube of edge AB.

is more or less complete at an *absolute* temperature which is half of the Curie temperature. It is also possible to show from the neutron intensities that when an external magnetic field is applied, then the directions in which the magnetic moments point in the various domains are all pulled around into the direction of the applied field. Indeed, it is possible to plot the magnetization-cycle loops in terms of the intensity of a diffracted neutron beam instead of by the conventional measurement with a magnetometer.

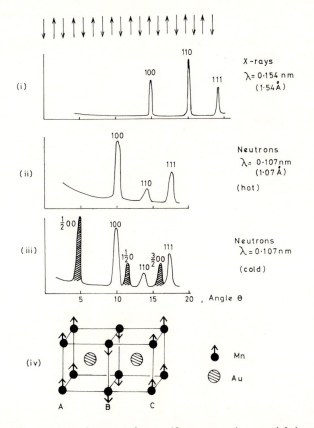

Fig. 49. Characteristic features of an antiferromagnetic material, in which the atomic moments are directed alternately up and down. For AuMn, illustrated here, the neutron pattern (iii) below 200°C shows a completely new set of spectra, shown shaded and indexing as $\frac{1}{2}00$, $1\frac{1}{2}0$, $\frac{3}{2}00$. These indicate that the magnetic unit cell, shown at (iv), is doubled along one axis compared with the 'chemical' cell. The quite different ratio of intensities of the spectra 100,110 and 111 for X-rays and neutrons arises because the scattering amplitude of manganese for neutrons is negative.

We contrast the above behaviour with what we illustrate in fig. 49, which relates to what we call an 'antiferromagnetic' material, and for which we use as an example the alloy of gold and manganese of composition AuMn. We shall see that within a domain of this kind of material the magnetic moments point alternately 'up' and 'down' or ' north ' and ' south '. There is also a dependence of the perfection of order on a characteristic temperature which is similar to that described above for a ferromagnet. In this case we call the characteristic temperature the Néel temperature, in recognition of L. Néel who was responsible for providing the first understanding of this kind of magnetic material. The neutron patterns prove to be very distinctive. For our alloy AuMn they enable us to demonstrate that below about 200°C the magnetic structure is that which is shown at (iv) in fig. 49. The magnetic moments, represented by the arrows, are carried only by the manganese atoms and they point in opposite directions in successive sheets of atoms, at A, B, C, ... This implies that the magnetic periodicity in this direction is *not* AB but the doubled distance AC and this deduction can be made very directly from the neutron pattern (iii) which includes the peaks, labelled with the Miller indices $\frac{1}{2}00$, $1\frac{1}{2}0$, and $\frac{3}{2}00$. These peaks appear in positions midway between those which showed for the nuclear peaks (ii) or the X-ray peaks (i). In particular the occurrence of the ' magnetic ' peak $\frac{1}{2}00$ means that there is a magnetic periodicity 0·64 nm (6·4 Å), twice the chemical unit distance AB, which measures only 0·32 nm (3·2 Å.) From a study of the actual intensities of these additional magnetic peaks, it is possible to show not only that the periodicity is doubled but also that the moments point in the direction of one of the axes, as illustrated in the figure. If the sample of Au Mn is heated, then this regular arrangement of magnetic moments will disappear at a temperature just above 200°C and the extra peaks will disappear. Nevertheless, although the order is broken up, the atoms do still retain their moments which now point in random directions : the material has become paramagnetic. Magnetic scattering does take place, but it is observed as a contribution to the general background of the diffraction pattern and not in any particular directions. Thus, careful measurements with the same sample would show that the background level in curve (ii) of fig. 49 was higher than for curve (iii) : the same feature would be observed in the curves for the ferromagnetic material of fig. 48. In each of these cases the magnetic contribution to the background would be found to be largest at very small angles of scattering and to decrease quite rapidly as 2θ increases ; this is a consequence of the way in which the atomic form factor f varies with angle.

The arrangements of atomic magnetic moments to produce ferromagnetism and antiferromagnetism in the way which we have described are only the simplest of the possible kinds of magnetic architecture, brought about by the way in which the magnetic forces between the atoms arrive at a position of equilibrium. Many more complicated arrangements exist and we will mention one or two further examples. Our justification for elaborating this point is that it is the measurements of the neutron diffraction patterns which have revealed the existence of these various arrangements. Indeed, these measurements offer the only known way of determining them.

Figure 50 indicates what is often called ' helimagnetism ' in which there is a spiralling arrangement of magnetic moments. If we examine the direction of the moments in the successive sheets of atoms which we have labelled 1, 2, 3, ... we see that they rotate successively

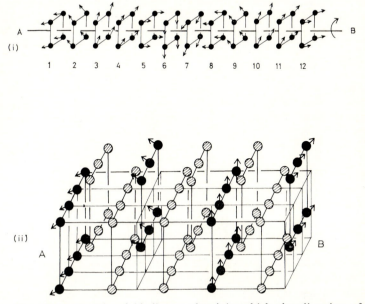

Fig. 50. The principle of ' helimagnetism ' in which the direction of the magnetic moments in successive sheets of atoms rotates steadily. In the figure (i) there is a rotation of about 50°, from sheet to sheet, in the direction of the arrow. At (ii) is shown, as an example, the structure of Au_2Mn in which double layers of gold atoms are sandwiched between successive layers of magnetic manganese atoms .

from sheet to sheet by about 50°, in the direction of the circular arrow in the figure. Thus the original direction of the moments in sheet 1 is approximately reproduced by the atoms in sheet 8. Experiments with neutrons have shown that this kind of arrangement exists in a variety of solids, though often only at reduced temperatures. The second part of fig. 50 illustrates in more detail the structure of the alloy Au_2Mn, which is of this type. The alloy has a layer structure in which double layers of gold atoms are sandwiched between layers of manganese atoms. Only the manganese atoms carry magnetic moments and the directions of these spiral around as we advance through the structure from left to right in the direction AB, changing

97

by about 50° from sheet to sheet in the manner which we showed at (i) in fig. 50. For the particular alloy $Au_2 Mn$ the spiral arrangement does exist at room temperature : its perfection is reduced as the temperature is raised and the order finally disappears at about 90°C, above which the alloy is paramagnetic. It is interesting to see that this helimagnetic structure produces a very distinctive neutron diffraction pattern which can be distinguished readily from those for ferromagnetic and antiferromagnetic materials which we showed in figs. 48 and 49. A characteristic feature is that each of the 'ordinary' nuclear spectra in the diffraction pattern is accompanied by a pair of satellites, such as we illustrate in fig. 51. One satellite appears on

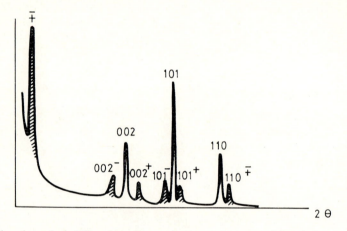

Fig. 51. A typical diffraction pattern from a substance with a helimagnetic structure. The ordinary nuclear reflections are accompanied by pairs of satellites, which index in the figure as 002^-, 002^+ and 101^-, 101^+ corresponding to a spiral axis parallel to the c axis of the structure. These satellites are shaded in the figure. For a spectral reflection such as 110, where the c index is zero, the two satellites 110^-, 110^+ overlap. Also shown shaded is the intense reflection which appears at a low angle.

each side of the ordinary reflection and from the angular separation and the magnitude of their intensities it is possible to deduce both the direction of the spiral axis, i.e. the direction which we marked as AB in fig. 50 (i), and also what is usually called the 'turn angle', i.e. the angle of rotation of the moments between neighbouring sheets. Another feature of the pattern is that an extra zero-order reflection appears at a very low angle of scattering. In the particular case of Au_2Mn this will have apparent indices of $00\frac{2}{7}$, corresponding to the fact that the magnetic unit cell is almost exactly three and a half times as long as the chemical cell. The chemical cell is in fact twice as long as the distance between two sheets of manganese atoms so that there is a rotation of about 100° between the two ends of a chemical cell : the ratio 360°/100° is very close to the value $3\frac{1}{2}$. Calculation shows that the reflection which indexes as $00\frac{2}{7}$ will occur at an angle of scattering of about 4° and it is usually necessary to employ a particularly well-collimated neutron beam in order to distinguish the reflection from the intense undeviated beam itself. It is possible to give a detailed theoretical explanation of why this spiral kind of structure exists : in very simple terms we can summarize it by saying

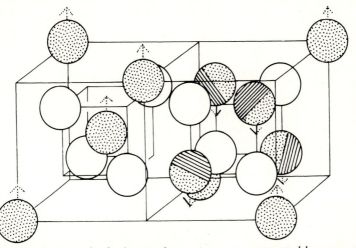

Fig. 52. A diagram of a ferrimagnetic structure, as represented by magnetite $Fe^{2+}(Fe^{3+})_2O_4$. The dotted atoms are Fe^{3+}, one per formula-unit, with upward-directed magnetic moments of 5 μ_B. The dotted/shaded atoms are Fe^{2+}, Fe^{3+} in equal numbers, arranged at random but with one of each per unit, and with downward-directed moments of 4 μ_B, 5 μ_B respectively. Thus the net moment is 4 μ_B, downward, per formula-unit. The unshaded circles represent oxygen atoms.

that it depends on the relative values of the interaction energy between atoms which are in neighbouring sheets and ones which are in next-but-one sheets. For certain values of this ratio it can be shown that a spiral structure is the one which has the minimum energy and is therefore the stable structure.

If we accept the primary concepts of ferromagnetism, antiferromagnetism and helimagnetism it may not seem surprising that structures can be found which show the characteristics of more than one of these three types. A simple combination of the first two would give what we know as ferrimagnetism, which we illustrate in fig. 52. All the moments in such a material lie parallel to a single direction and some point up and some point down, but the strengths of the moments in the two categories are different, thus giving a reduced but definite magnetization. The familiar mineral magnetite, Fe_3O_4, whose structure is shown in fig. 52, is the simplest example of a ferrimagnetic material and the class also includes all the ferrites, which are very important magnetic materials with many technical applications. Each formula weight of magnetite contains three magnetic ions : two of them are Fe^{3+} which has a magnetic moment of five Bohr magnetons which we write as $5 \mu_B$, and there is one Fe^{2+} ion with a moment of $4 \mu_B$. The structure is such that in each unit one of the Fe^{3+} ions has its moment upwardly directed, whereas the other one points downwards, along with the Fe^{2+} ion. The net result therefore is a downward pointing moment of $4 \mu_B$ for each ' molecule ' of Fe_3O_4 and this is in good agreement with the experimentally measured magnetization of magnetite when a magnetic field is applied. In the more complicated case of materials which combine helimagnetism with ferro or antiferromagnetism we can regard the magnetic moment of each atom as consising of two components, one of which takes part in the helimagnetism and the other, say, in the ferromagnetism. The directions and magnitudes of these components will depend on the environment of the atoms, for example, on the way in which the magnetic forces—and the ratio between their values for nearest neighbours and next-nearest neighbours—vary in different directions. The elements of the rare-earth group have provided a very rich field of discovery for these complicated magnetic structures. Some of them, such as holmium, thulium and erbium, display two or three different structures which appear successively as the sample of metal is reduced in temperature. Thulium, for example, shows successive changes at 56°K and 40°K. Most of these magnetic phase changes are found to occur at low temperatures because it is here that the ordering tendencies of the relatively weak magnetic forces are able to assert themselves against the disturbing effects of thermal motion which tend to break up any regular co-operative arrangement. At higher temperatures the thermal displacements destroy the regular arrangement and the material becomes paramagnetic.

As a final example of the way in which neutron diffraction studies have revealed and disentangled for the first time these complicated structures we illustrate in fig. 53 the structure which has recently been deduced for $MnSO_4$ by workers at the Brookhaven National Laboratory in the U.S.A. It is an elegant development of the not-uncommon antiferromagnetic arrangement of ferromagnetic sheets. In the figure we see that successive layers of atoms, perpendicular to the c axis, have their magnetic moment vectors lying on the surfaces of alternately upward and downward pointing cones. However, these directions do *not* remain constant for all the atoms within a sheet but rotate around in azimuth, about the cone axis, in a manner which depends on the individual atom's location along the a axis of the structure. In this way, as indicated in the figure, the structure repeats at intervals of

100

about six ordinary chemical unit cells, 3 nm (30 Å), along the *a* axis. It is likely that equally intricate structures exist in other materials and that their onset of growth at particular temperatures accounts for many so-far-unexplained anomalies in the properties of various

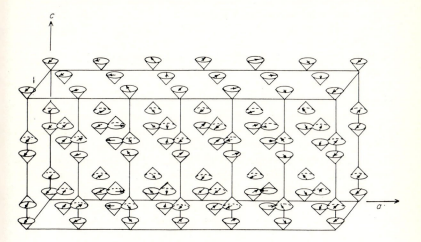

Fig. 53. A sketch of the magnetic structure of $MnSO_4$ indicating the sheets of atoms perpendicular to the *c* axis. Along any vertical line the directions of the magnetic moments, which lie on the surface of cones, are oppositely directed from sheet to sheet. The azimuthal direction on the cone rotates as we advance in the *a* direction, i.e. from left to right in the diagram, at such a rate that a ' repeat ' occurs over the six units which are included here.

magnetic materials. Their rate of discovery depends largely on the limited amount of effort and the limited number of suitable nuclear reactors, and suitable diffraction apparatus, which is available for their study.

CHAPTER 9

the dynamics of solids and liquids

IN our discussions of the previous two chapters, which have related to the way in which neutrons can be used to determine the structures of solids, we have concentrated on the picture of a solid as a completely regular arrangement in three dimensions, attained by a stacking together of identical unit cells. The dimensions of these cells have been determined by measuring the angular *positions* of the spectra which are produced when a beam of monochromatic radiation is scattered : the atomic content of the cells, and its spatial distribution, are determined by examining the relative *intensities* of these spectra and we have been especially concerned with the advantages of using neutrons as the investigating radiation for this purpose. However, this picture of a solid with its atoms firmly anchored at precise positions is only an ideal one. In fact the atoms in a solid are in motion, oscillating about their mean positions with a continual interchange of energy between potential and kinetic forms. The total internal energy, like that of the molecules of a gas which we study in the kinetic theory, is proportional to the absolute temperature. The essential point about the solid is that the atomic motions are restricted to small displacements about mean positions which them-selves form a three-dimensional array which usually maintains perfect periodicity for distances which cover some hundreds or thousands of unit cells, even up to a micro-metre. We might at first be tempted to think that the motions which the individual atoms undergo are random ones, but this cannot be the case in a solid (as distinct from a gas) since the atoms are close enough together for strong forces to exist between near neighbours. If therefore one atom is displaced from its equilibrium position, then all the atomic forces in the neighbourhood will be affected and all the nearby atoms will undergo displacement of some kind as a repercussion of the initial displacement which we postulated. This means that the motions of the atoms within the solid are not individual but collective. When one atom moves, all the atoms within the crystal are affected to a greater or lesser extent. It becomes practicable therefore to replace our picture of individual atomic motions by the conception of ' crystal vibrations '. By the term ' crystal vibrations ' we do not mean that the motion of the crystal can be described simply as a harmonic vibration at one frequency but that the resultant motion is built up by adding together a complete spectrum of vibrations, covering a wide range of wave-

102

length and different types of polarization. If the crystal contains N atoms, then there will be $3N$ different vibrations included in the spectrum, corresponding to the fact that $3N$ independent co-ordinates are necessary in order to specify the positions of N atoms. We can say that all the N atoms participate in each vibration and that each of the vibrations gives rise to a displacement of all the atoms. The range of frequency extends from practically zero up to some maximum value, which we denote by ν_{max}, which is characteristic of the particular material. As an example fig. 54 shows the frequency

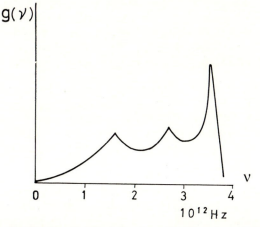

Fig. 54. The distribution function for the vibrations in sodium. $g(\nu)\,d\nu$ is proportional to the number of phonons which have frequencies in the range of numerical values from ν to $\nu + d\nu$ (Dixon, Woods and Brockhouse, *Proc. Phys. Soc.*, **81**, 973, 1963).

spectrum of the vibrations in sodium. It is usual to think of each quantum of vibration energy as a ' phonon ' in just the same way as we think of quanta of electromagnetic energy as photons. Accordingly we speak of the curve in fig. 54 as a phonon spectrum.

We have discussed this analysis of the motion of the atoms in a solid in some detail because, as we shall see, experiments with neutrons provide the only straightforward way of determining the motion by practical measurements on individual materials. In fact the information given for sodium in fig. 54 was computed from data provided by neutron experiments. Before we examine the principles which underlie these experiments, and which show us the particular value of neutrons for these investigations, it will be worth while to examine briefly the various models which have been put forward in the past to describe the crystal vibrations.

The earliest model was proposed in 1907 by A. Einstein who assumed that all the nuclei vibrated with the same frequency. A few years earlier, in 1901, Planck had put forward his quantum theory and used it to explain the shape of the spectrum of radiation which is emitted by a heated black body, in particular the fact that the energy radiated approaches zero at very high frequencies. The crucial feature of Planck's treatment was his deduction that the average energy E of an oscillator was not simply kT but

$$E = \frac{h\nu}{\exp(h\nu/kT) - 1},$$

which only approaches kT when T is large. Einstein applied exactly the same treatment to the vibrations in a solid, making the assumption that in a crystal which contained N atoms there would be $3N$ oscillators, all vibrating with the same frequency. In the light of our earlier discussion this assumption means that the vibrations of the different atoms *are* independent. Curve (i) in fig. 55 emphasizes the single-line

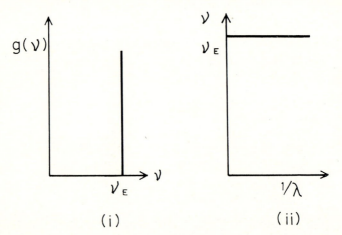

Fig. 55. Diagram (i) indicates the single-line spectrum $g(\nu)$ which is assumed in the Einstein model. As shown at (ii), the frequency is independent of the wavelength λ.

spectrum which this theory supposed, in complete contrast to fig. 54. Curve (ii) emphasizes the other feature of the theory, namely that the frequency of a wave is not dependent on its wavelength : this means that the wave's velocity is proportional to its wavelength which, again, is not supported by experiment. Nevertheless, Einstein's simple application of Planck's ideas had considerable success in explaining the variation of the specific heat of solids with temperature. The expression given above for E represents the contribution of the oscillator to the heat capacity of the solid and, therefore, the differential dE/dT will be its contribution to the specific heat, C_{v}. This differential has the shape shown by the broken line in fig. 56, approaching a constant value at high temperature, and thus satisfying Dulong and

104

Petit's law, and falling away very fast at low temperatures, as observed experimentally. However, the precise form of the variation at low temperature was not predicted correctly. Experiment had shown

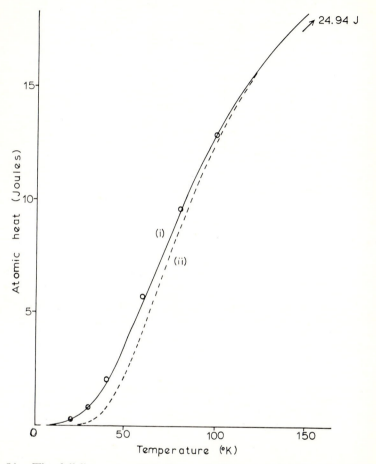

Fig. 56. The full-line curve (i) indicates the heat capacity of a gram-atom of aluminium calculated according to the Debye theory. The broken line (ii) is for the Einstein theory. The circles indicate some experimentally measured points. At high temperatures the curves extrapolate to 24·94 J.

that at low temperatures C_v is proportional to T^3. A relation of exactly this form is a consequence of the later model of a solid proposed in 1912 by P. Debye. The full-line curve in fig. 56 indicates Debye's prediction for C_v at low temperatures and this is to be contrasted with the Einstein curve.

8 105

In Debye's model an attempt was made to take into account the periodic nature of the crystal. It was again assumed that there were $3N$ independent vibrations and for simplicity it was necessary to assume that the crystal was continuous in nature like an elastic solid, as distinct from being constituted discontinuously of discrete atoms, and that its properties were the same in all directions. However, in order to take partly into account its periodic nature, as represented by the fact that waves of length less than about twice the distance

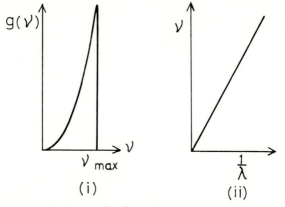

Fig. 57. Diagram (i) shows the frequency spectrum $g(\nu)$ according to the Debye model of a solid, with a sharp cut-off at a frequency ν_{max}. The proportionality between ν, $1/\lambda$ in curve (ii) indicates a constant wave-velocity (the velocity of sound) in the crystal.

between atoms will not propagate, it was assumed that the spectrum was cut off at some characteristic frequency ν_{max}. With these assumptions it follows that the frequency spectrum and the variation of frequency with the reciprocal of the wavelength should be as shown at (i), (ii) respectively in fig. 57. Curves like the latter, which indicate the relation between frequency and wavelength, or reciprocal wavelength, are often called 'dispersion curves' and the slope of such a $(\nu, 1/\lambda)$ curve at any point is equal to the velocity of the vibrations at that particular value of frequency and wavelength. In fig. 57 (ii) the 'curve' has become a straight line because the dispersion is zero. This means that the velocity of the vibrations is a constant and not dependent on their wavelength. This is the same conclusion as is found for waves on a continuous string or a solid rod, for which there are constant velocities of $\sqrt{(T/m)}$ and $\sqrt{(E/\rho)}$, where T is the string tension and m is its mass per unit length, E is Young's modulus for the rod and ρ is its density. The slope of the straight line in fig. 57 (ii) is the velocity of sound in the material.

In order to improve on the predictions of the Debye model it is necessary to take into account the precise interactions among the atoms in the material. The calculation will become more and more difficult as we assume that interatomic forces extend beyond the immediate neighbours of an atom to its second, third, fourth, ..., nth neighbours and, also, as we deal with more complicated solids which contain several different kinds of atoms. As a relatively simple case we show the result for a linear chain of nuclei which are alternately of two kinds, of masses M, m, and for which only nearest-neighbour interactions are assumed. Figure 58 shows the expected form of the

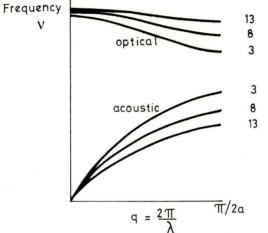

Fig. 58. The dispersion curve showing the relation between frequency ν and wave-number, $2\pi/\lambda$, for a linear chain of two kinds of nuclei, of masses M, m. There are two types of vibration, called 'acoustic' and 'optical' modes respectively, which depend on the ratio of M/m. Only the forces between nearest neighbours have been taken into account : the interatomic separation is a.

dispersion curve† for various values of the ratio M/m. The two parts, or 'branches', to the curve arise because there are two different kinds of atoms and it becomes possible, for each wavelength, to have two different types of wave, in one of which the two kinds of atoms move in the same direction and in the other they move in opposite directions. It will be obvious that although we have still restricted ourselves to a greatly oversimplified model, yet the expected dispersion curve is becoming very complicated. If we try to improve on the accuracy of the model, then the assumptions which we are forced to make about the detailed nature of interatomic forces become more and more open

† In accordance with the usual practice we use the symbol q to denote the wave-number, $2\pi/\lambda$, in fig. 58 and succeeding figures. It should not be confused with the same symbol used for the magnitude of the magnetic interaction vector in Chapter 8.

to question. Fortunately it is possible by making certain measurements of the scattering of neutron beams to deduce the actual form of the dispersion curve by *experiment*. We have therefore an experimental method for determining in some detail the nature of the interatomic forces between atoms. It is not unexpected that the experimental data become difficult to interpret in complicated structures, but for the simpler materials a considerable amount has been added to our knowledge by this kind of investigation in recent years. We shall outline the way in which the neutron scattering is indeed influenced by the dynamics of the solid.

As we have already mentioned, our studies of scattered neutrons so far have been restricted to those neutrons which have not undergone any change of energy, or wavelength, as a result of their encounter with the solid. We can describe these neutrons as ones which have been ' elastically ' scattered. We have used them to determine the nature of the material in the unit cell, from both a chemical and magnetic point of view. In our discussion we have not mentioned one fairly important feature, namely, that the intensities of the elastic spectra are reduced by the fact that the atoms undergo displacements from their ideal positions. These displacements, and the consequent reductions of intensity, increase with increasing temperature and they can be computed by observing the effect of temperature on the intensities, bearing in mind of course that other changes may be taking place as the temperature is altered. However, there is a much more direct and precise way of studying the dynamics of the crystal. When a neutron is scattered by an atom in a crystal it is *not* necessary that it should emerge from the encounter with its energy unchanged. It is possible for some of the neutron energy to be used to excite vibrations in the crystal : the neutron may ' hand over ', or equally well *receive*, the energy comprised in one or more quanta of the crystal vibrations or ' phonons ' which we have been discussing. We then have to ask ourselves what effect this will have on the incident neutron. This is a question which we can only answer usefully by first getting some quantitative idea of the size of the quanta of crystal energy in relation to the energies of the neutrons which we are using for our experiments. Referring again to fig. 57 (i), it would be reasonable to take $h\nu_{max}$, where h is Planck's constant, as an approximate measure of the energy content of a quantum of crystal energy. According to the Debye theory this quantity $h\nu_{max}$ is equal to $k\Theta$, where k is Boltzmann's constant and θ is a characteristic parameter of the solid which is known as the Debye temperature, and which can be determined by experiment in several different ways. Most substances have values of Θ of a few hundred degrees. Copper, for example, is approximately 300°K. Diamond, with a very high value of 2000°K, and lead, with a very low value of 70°K, are exceptional cases. If we take 300°K as a representative value of Θ then we find that the quantum energy $k\Theta$ is about 4×10^{-21} J, which we can express alternatively as $h \times 0.6 \times 10^{13}$ corresponding to a frequency ν of 0.6×10^{13} Hz. If we refer back to p. 29 we can recall that the energy of the neutrons at the peak of the spectrum from the nuclear reactor is $\frac{3}{2}kT$, where T is the temperature of the moderator in the reactor. When T is 500°K this energy comes to about 10^{-20} J or $h \times 1.7 \times 10^{13}$, which is two or three times as large as we calculated for a quantum of crystal energy. An immediate way of finding this ratio is to note, from the form of the expressions for the two energies, that it will be equal to one and a half times the ratio of the moderator and Debye temperatures. The

---

Question 27. *The Debye temperature of silver is* 220°K. *Calculate the value of* ν_{max}, *the maximum frequency of the crystal vibrations on the Debye model, and the energy in a quantum of these vibrations (Boltzmann's constant* $= 1.38 \times 10^{-23}$ J K^{-1}).
　　　　　　　　　　Ans. 4.6×10^{12} Hz, 3.04×10^{-21} J.

Question 28. *The expression for the specific heat per mole of a solid according to the Einstein theory is* $3Rx^2 e^x/(e^x - 1)^2$ *at temperature* T, *where* $x = \Theta/T$. Θ *is a characteristic temperature and* R *is the gas constant, which equals* 8.31 J K^{-1} mol^{-1}. *What is the value of this expression (a) when* T *is very large and (b) when* $T = \Theta/2$.
　　　　　　　　　　Ans. (a) 24·93 J, (b) 18·05 J.

---

important conclusion for our present discussion is that the neutron energy is not a lot greater than a quantum of crystal energy and, consequently, if a neutron gives up, or gains, such a quantum then its own energy and wavelength will be altered substantially and to an extent which can be accurately measured. Before describing how this can be achieved experimentally we must point out that we should have come to quite a different conclusion about the feasibility and value of such experiments if we had been considering the scattering of X-rays. A calculation of the size of a quantum of energy for an X-ray of wavelength 0·1 nm (1 Å), close to the wavelength of the neutrons which we have been considering, shows it to amount to $3h \times 10^{18}$. This is more than 10^5 times as great as a quantum of crystal energy, so that the gain or loss of a crystal quantum by an inelastically scattered X-ray would alter the latter's wavelength by less than a thousandth of 1% and the change would be extremely difficult to detect and measure with accuracy. For the neutron the measurement is quite easy to make, using the methods for measuring velocity which

---

Question 29. *Calculate the energy of (a) a neutron, (b) an X-ray photon, each of wavelength* 0·1 nm (1 Å).
　　　　　　　Ans. (a) 1.31×10^{-20} J, (b) 1.99×10^{-15} J.

---

we have already described. If the neutron gives up some energy then we say that a crystal phonon has been created. Conversely, when the neutron gains energy a phonon is destroyed. Let us therefore look at an experimental arrangement for observing the neutrons which have been inelastically scattered and for measuring their energy, thus enabling us to find the energy of a crystal quantum. We shall see, at the same time, that we are able to find the wavelength of the particular crystal vibration which has taken part in the interchange of energy. Accordingly we shall find that we can evaluate the relation between energy and wavelength, i.e. the dispersion curve, for the crystal.

Figure 59 shows the general arrangement of the experiment. We begin with a monochromatic beam of neutrons which is produced, as we have described previously, either by reflection from a single crystal or by means of a chopper. The beam falls on the sample S

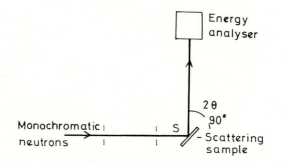

Fig. 59. An arrangement for studying the neutrons which are scattered inelastically by a solid. The incident beam of neutrons from the reactor has been monochromatized either by reflection from a crystal or by passing it through a chopper. The energy analysis of the scattered neutrons can be made either by a further crystal or, in the case of a chopped incident beam, by a time-of-flight analysis.

which is a single-crystal whose orientation relative to the incident beam can be chosen and adjusted at will. The scattered neutrons are observed at some particular angle of scattering 2θ and this is very often chosen to be 90°. If we were hoping to observe elastically scattered neutrons, there would be a negligible chance of finding any, because we have arbitrarily chosen a scattering angle of 90°, in addition to having chosen an arbitrary setting of the crystal : we have already seen that elastic spectra can only be produced by *both* setting a crystal plane at the right inclination to the incident beam *and* observing the scattering at the correct angle. However, some *inelastically* scattered neutrons will be found in any arbitrary chosen direction for any setting of the crystal—although their intensity may

110

be very low. Returning to the diagram in fig. 59 the experimental procedure is to measure the energy spectrum of the neutrons scattered at 90°. This can be done either by using a further single-crystal as an analyser, in which case the crystal functions in just the same way as our monochromator crystal, or by making a time-of-flight analysis. If we wish to use the latter method, then it is necessary that our incident beam should be pulsed, which we can achieve if we produce it by a chopper system as we discussed in Chapter 5. The energy spectrum which we obtain will be found to show several peaks. An example, for the case of a single-crystal of silicon, is given in fig. 60.

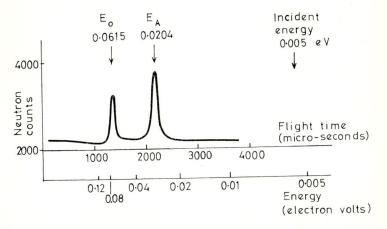

Fig. 60.   The energy spectrum of the neutrons scattered at 90° from a single-crystal of silicon, for neutrons which have an initial energy of 0·005 eV. The incident neutrons were travelling along a main axis of the crystal.

This shows that for the particular settings of crystal and detector the required conditions for conservation of momentum and energy could be satisfied by neutrons which had taken up energies of either 20 meV or 61 meV from the crystal vibrations. For either of these peaks we are able to deduce these values for the energy of the crystal quantum simply by measuring the difference of energy between the incident and scattered neutrons. We can determine the momentum of the quantum by also taking into account the change of *direction* of the neutron, thus enabling us to determine both the magnitude and direction of the ' phonon ' in the crystal. By a succession of measurements of this kind, made with different settings of the scattering crystal, we can plot out the dispersion curve of the crystal. Some results are shown in fig. 61 for germanium. The curve shows several different ' branches ', as was suggested by our earlier discussion and by the existence of the two peaks in fig. 60. Some more up-to-date results are illustrated in fig. 62 which is for aluminium and which we

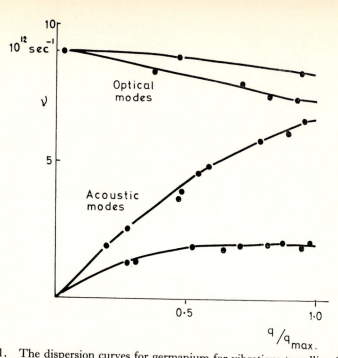

Fig. 61. The dispersion curves for germanium for vibrations travelling in the [100] directions, as determined experimentally by B. N. Brockhouse and P. K. Iyengar from observations of inelastically scattered neutrons. The abscissa is the value of q ($\equiv 2\pi/\lambda$) divided by the maximum value which $2\pi/\lambda$ may have.

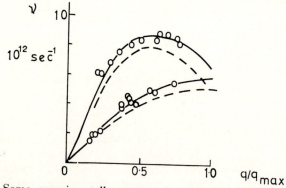

Fig. 62. Some experimentally measured points showing the variation of frequency ν, in cycles per second, with the wave vector $q = 1/\lambda$ for vibrations in a direction at $40°$ to the cubic axis of aluminium. The broken lines are the results of a calculation which takes into account only the interactions between nearest-neighbour atoms. The full lines, which are in good agreement with experiment, take account of forces as far as seventh atoms. The two sets of curves correspond to longitudinal and transverse vibrations respectively (by courtesy of G. L. Squires).

112

can use to indicate how the data are analysed. We have already mentioned that the form of these dispersion curves depends on the details of the interactions between neighbouring atoms in the solid and the curves can be calculated from a knowledge of the forces. The practical procedure is to suggest a suitable model, with various parameters to define the details of the forces, and then to refine these parameters to achieve a good fit with the experimental curves. The dotted lines in fig. 62 are for a simple model in which interactions are assumed to exist only between nearest-neighbour atoms. The full-line curves, which give much better agreement, take into account forces which extend up to the seventh neighbours.

Returning briefly to the *spectrum* of the crystal vibrations, it is possible to calculate this from experimental *dispersion* curves, such as those in fig. 62, if we have produced individual curves for many different directions in the crystal. In practice it is simpler to use the model of the crystal forces, which will have been developed to suit the dispersion curves measured in a few convenient symmetrical directions of the crystal, to compute the vibration spectrum. This is the procedure which was used for data on metallic sodium to produce the spectrum which we showed earlier, in fig. 54.

In comparison with the highly regular structure of a solid, in which the unit cells are accurately stacked over distances approaching 1 μm, or several thousand Ångström units, the structure of a liquid is rather irregular. Nevertheless, a good deal of order does exist and the liquid state occupies a position midway between the solid, which is fully regular, and the gas, in which the atomic or molecular positions are completely random. On an atomic scale liquids are much more similar to solids than their macroscopic behaviour, with its characteristic fluidity, would suggest. In a liquid the interactions between neighbouring atoms are still large and, indeed, the interatomic separations are not very much greater than in a solid, particularly in the case of simple liquids. Some comparisons of the densities of the two states for a number of materials are given below, in units of 10^3 kg/m^3,

	Argon	Sodium	Benzene	Lead	Mercury
Liquid	1·407	0·927	0·90	10·6	13·7
Solid	1·636	0·951	1·02	11·0	14·2

and these figures emphasize the point that liquids are almost as closely packed as solids. Water in fact provides an example for which the solid, ice, is less dense than the liquid and there is a temperature of maximum density at 4°C which, of course, occurs in the liquid state. The liquid state is characterized by the fact that there is a high degree of regularity in the arrangement of the *immediate* neighbours of each atom, but this regularity does not extend over large distances. If we could take an instantaneous photograph of the atoms in a liquid, then we should find that the interatomic separation for the nearest neighbours of any chosen atom was constant to within a small fraction of an Ångström unit, but for, say, the distance measured out to the tenth neighbours there would be variations having an order of magnitude equal to an interatomic distance itself.

In our studies of solids the shortcomings in our knowledge of interatomic forces are greatly compensated by the assurance that the structure of the solid is regular and repetitive over a great distance. In the case of a liquid the ' distant ' structure is completely disordered. In a gas any structure whatever is completely lacking, but in this case our ability to calculate and explain in detail the physical properties is made relatively easy by the compensating feature that the atoms or molecules are so far apart that the interactions between them may be neglected. The liquid state stands relatively intractable, both from the point of view of postulating a detailed model for it and in seeking to obtain experimental evidence which will support such a model. The most significant progress which has been achieved has come from studies in recent years of the way in which neutrons are scattered by liquids. The aim of these studies is to produce both an instantaneous snapshot picture of the distribution of atoms in a liquid and also a knowledge of how the atoms move about, that is the correlation of a series of snapshot pictures taken in sequence from moment to moment. The results are usually expressed in terms of a ' space–time correlation function ' which was first discussed by L. van Hove. It is a complicated function of both distance and time, which represents the probability that we shall find an atom within a unit volume of space at distance r and time t if we measure and count from an atom which we have observed to be at a chosen origin at a starting time $t = 0$. This probability will undoubtedly depend on the values of r and t which we are considering but, in the present state of our knowledge, we do not know just how it is determined. It is indeed the object of our studies to find out this. Meanwhile we shall simply indicate it by a mathematical symbol which draws attention to the dependence on r and t. It is usual to use the symbol $G(r, t)$ for this purpose. We can in fact regard this probability of finding an atom at distance r and time t as being the resultant of two separate probabilities. Firstly, the atom which we observe at r at time t may be the *same* one as we saw at the origin at $t = 0$ and we call this part of the probability the ' self-correlation ' function $G_s(r, t)$: secondly, it may be a *different* atom which we observe on the second occasion and this part of the probability is called the ' pair-correlation ' function, $G_d(r, t)$. In each case the form of this symbol is intended to indicate that these two quantities depend on r and t, but we do not yet know any details of the dependence.

From a more quantitative point of view there are two important parameters in this general description of liquid structure. Let us imagine that one of the atoms in the liquid passes through a fixed given point in space at time $t = 0$. As a result of this motion the density distribution at this point will be disturbed not only at time $t = 0$ but also over a certain period of *time* before and afterwards. At any given instant of time, say at $t = 0$, the disturbance will not be confined to the origin but will extend outwards in all directions, becoming ineffective as the *distance* from the point of origin increases. We can think of the size and duration of the disturbance in terms of a length r_0 and a time t_0. The ' correlation radius ' r_0 represents the distance beyond which the motion of a given atom has no significant effect on the motion of other atoms, and this distance amounts to a few tenths of a nanometre. The ' relaxation time ', t_0, which is of the order of 10^{-13} s, is the time which elapses before the disturbance produced by the motion of an individual particle is effectively damped out. We cannot express these quantities precisely but they will prove to be useful concepts in describing the behaviour of the atoms in the liquid. If a neutron is to enable us to see what is going on inside a liquid, then it is necessary that it should spend at least a time t_0 in traversing the distance r_0. In order to do this it will need to have a velocity which is not greater than about a kilometre per second. Reference back to fig. 27 shows that this is the velocity of a neutron of wavelength about 0·4 nm (4 Å), so that slow neutrons are eminently suited for making this kind of investigation. On the contrary, no useful data could be determined by observing the scattering of X-rays, which travel with the velocity of light, 3×10^8 m/s. Indeed, X-rays are only able to determine a ' snapshot picture ' of the atoms in a liquid : this will be the value of $G_d(r, t)$ when $t = 0$ and is usually written as $g(r)$. The value of $g(r)$ tells us nothing about the dynamics of the system. Its variation with r is shown in fig. 63 for the cases of (i) a monatomic gas, (ii) a single-crystal of a solid and (iii) a liquid. Curve (i) indicates that for a gas it is not possible to find a second atom within some given distance of the first one, but beyond this distance the probability increases quite quickly with increasing r until a steady value is reached, indicating that the distribution of gas molecules becomes completely random. In (ii), for the single-crystal, the completely periodic nature of $g(r)$ is the direct representation of the fact that a solid is completely regular over long distances. By contrast, in curve (iii) for a liquid, a steady value of $g(r)$ is soon reached when the value of r is increased because such order as exists in a liquid is only short-range and there is no correlation between the positions of the atomic centres over long distances.

It is much more difficult to give simple diagrammatic representations for the self-correlation and pair-correlation functions because these will vary not only with distance but also with time. We can, however, show the cases which correspond to the extremes of very short and very long times, short and long, that is, in relation to the relaxation time t_0. These two cases are shown for a liquid in fig. 64 and their study will give a clearer idea of what is represented by the two functions G_s and G_d. The two curves at (i) represent the situation very shortly after an initial observation that a particular atom A was at the origin. Curve G_s here will indicate the new whereabouts of

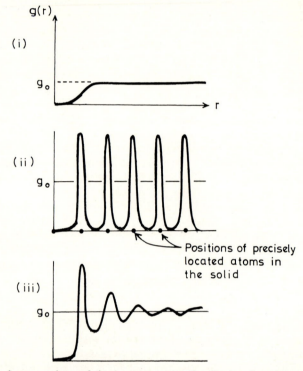

Fig. 63. A comparison of the instantaneous distribution functions $g(r)$ for (i) a gas, (ii) a solid and (iii) a liquid. The quantity $g(r)\,\delta V$ is the probability of finding a second atom within a volume δV, at a distance r from a first atom which is taken to be at the origin. The levels which are marked g_0 represent the mean density in each case.

atom A and shows, as expected, that this atom will almost certainly be still at A and cannot have moved very far away. The curve for G_d indicates the whereabouts of other atoms at this moment: as we expect this curve is almost identical with $g(r)$, giving a snapshot picture of the environment of an atom at a chosen origin. On the other hand, the curves at (ii) in fig. 64 show the situation at a long period of time after our starting instant, so that $t \geqslant t_0$. The curve for G_s indicates the fact that the atom A will steadily diffuse away

116

from its original position, but so long as the time interval is finite it is still more likely to be found at the origin, $r = 0$, than at any other particular value of r : the curve for G_d now shows that, so far as other atoms are concerned, diffusion has produced practically a uniform density, although this density will be at a minimum at the origin because there is a particular chance that the origin is still occupied by our chosen atom A.

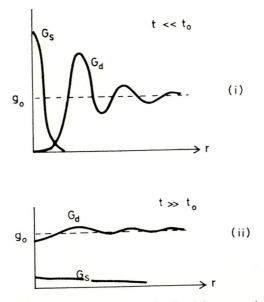

Fig. 64.   The form of the two components G_s, G_d of the space–time correlation function which describes the distribution of atoms at distance r and time t after the observation that a particular atom was at the origin ($r = 0$) at the 'starting-time' $t = 0$.   Curves (i) relate to an instant very shortly after $t = 0$: curves (ii) show the situation very much later.   In each case the level g_0 represents the average density of the liquid.

We have elaborated at some length the details of these correlation functions which describe both the 'instantaneous structure' and the 'atomic motions' in a liquid because both G_s and G_d can, in principle, be obtained directly from observations of neutron scattering, by making measurements of the scattered intensity at all angles in space, accompanied in each case by a measurement of the energy spectrum of the neutrons which are observed there.   Figure 65, as an example, shows how the self-correlation function $G_s(r, t)$ of water has been determined by B. N. Brockhouse and his colleagues for various values of t ranging from $1.5 \rightarrow 9.9 \times 10^{-12}$ s, at two different temperatures.   From these curves it is possible to study in some detail the way in which an atom (or rather a molecule in the case of water, which

117

is by no means a simple liquid) diffuses through the body of liquid. In fig. 66 is plotted, as a function of time t, the mean-square distance which the particle has moved from its position at the origin at $t = 0$. The experimentally determined points at 25°C, 75°C are shown in relation to various calculated curves. Curves are computed first on the assumption that particles behave in the same way as they would in

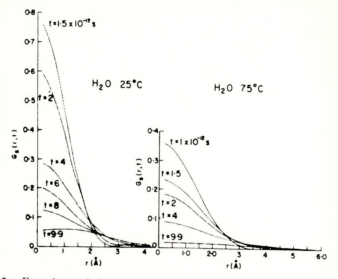

Fig. 65. Experimental data on the diffusion of water molecules at 25°, 75°C obtained by B. N. Brockhouse from observations of neutron scattering. The curves show how the self-correlation function, G_s, varies with distance at various times t, thus indicating how an atom diffuses away from an originally observed location, and with increasing rapidity as the temperature is raised.

a gas, choosing respectively particles of masses 1 and 18 and, secondly, for simple diffusion, assuming a diffusion coefficient which has been determined by making macroscopic measurements of the diffusion of water by using tracer methods. The neutron results suggest that over long periods of time the atomic motions are adequately described by ordinary diffusion theory but that this does not hold until a time of about 10^{-12} sec has elapsed, by which time a molecule has moved a distance of about 0·2 nm (2 Å), which is roughly one intermolecular separation, from its initial position.

As a further example of these methods we may mention some studies of liquid argon by B. A. Dasannacharya and K. R. Rao. Although liquid argon offers some practical difficulties in the neutron measurements it is an attractively simple liquid on which to carry out theoretical calculations. Rather similar results were obtained to those described for water, but with some indication that normal diffusion sets in a little earlier, corresponding to looser atomic binding in the argon.

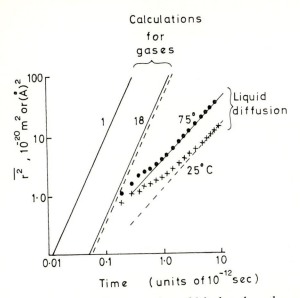

Fig. 66.   Interpretation of the neutron data which show how the molecules in water move away from an initial position.   The points ● and × represent experimental observations at 75°, 25°C.   The straight lines (on this logarithmic plot) indicate the results of calculations which assume, in turn, that the molecules behave as in a gas, with masses of 1 or 18, or according to a macroscopic view of diffusion.   In each case full lines ———— are for 75°C and the broken lines – – – are for 25°C (from Sakamoto et al., J. Phys. Soc. Japan, **17**, Suppl. B-II, 370 (1962)).

This kind of research is still at an early stage but it provides a very good example of a field in which unique information can be obtained by using neutron beams.   It is believed that as these measurements become increasingly precise and comprehensive they will lead to a detailed understanding of the nature of the interatomic forces and the atomic and molecular motions in liquids.

119

CHAPTER 10

some applications of neutron optics

WE shall describe in this chapter some further features of the scattering which takes place when neutrons pass through solids and liquids. Some of these topics are of general interest whereas others form the basis of various techniques which are used in the applications of neutron beams to the study of solids and liquids.

When a beam of radiation passes through any kind of matter scattering takes place and this is a common feature not only for electromagnetic radiation, such as infra-red, optical light or X-rays, but also for particle radiations such as electrons or neutrons. Each scattering centre sends out a secondary wave of radiation and we have been concerned with the way in which these wavelets build up identifiable beams and spectra in directions away from that of the incident radiation. At the same time the incident wave itself will necessarily be reduced and the resultant wave in the forward direction will be made up of the reduced incident wave and the scattered wavelets. Detailed calculation shows that the rate at which a mono-chromatic wave-front advances, i.e. the phase velocity of the wave, will be different from that for a wave in free space. This change of phase velocity for radiation passing through a medium, and more particularly the deviation to which it leads when the radiation impinges on the surface between two media, is what we understand by ' refraction '. The value of the refractive index, which represents the ratio of the phase velocities for free space and the medium, depends in the case of neutrons only on the atomic content of the material : it does not depend on the details of the structure of the material, i.e. the co-ordinates of the atoms in space. It can be shown that the refractive index n is different from unity by a small quantity which is proportional to the sum of the scattering amplitudes of all the atoms in a unit volume of material. The expression for n is :

$$n = 1 - \frac{\lambda^2}{2\pi} \sum_i N_i b_i, \qquad . \qquad . \qquad . \quad (10.1)$$

where the summation is made over the various types of atom $1, 2, 3, \ldots, i$ which build up the crystal. In this expression N_i is the number of atoms of type i per unit volume of crystal and b_i is the scattering amplitude, which we discussed in Chapter 7, for the particular atom. In almost all cases the value of b is positive, so that the value of the refractive index n will be less than unity. Insertion of some typical values of N, b in the expression will show that the difference from unity is only about 10^{-6} for a neutron wavelength of 0·1 nm (1 Å). However, the presence of the factor λ^2 in the expression means that $1 - n$ increases rapidly for longer wavelengths. For the few nuclei which have negative values of b, such as lithium and manganese, the refractive index of the element itself would be slightly greater than unity. At the same time it is to be noted that for X-ray scattering b always has a positive value so that for X-rays the refractive index of all materials is slightly less than unity : the value of $1 - n$ for X-rays will depend purely on the electron content of the atoms and not on the structure of the solid.

Question 30. *Calculate the value of the refractive index of metallic silver (at. wt. 107·9) for neutrons of wavelength 0·1 nm (1 Å). The scattering amplitude of a silver atom is equal to $6·1 \times 10^{-15}$ m and the density of the metal is $10·5 \times 10^3$ kg/m³.*

Ans. $1 - n = 6 \times 10^{-7}$.

The fact that the refractive index is generally less than unity for neutrons means that when a neutron beam is incident on a solid or liquid surface, in air, it will effectively be proceeding from a more to a less dense material. So the beam will be *totally internally reflected* on striking the solid when the angle of incidence is greater than a critical angle. Because n is only very slightly less than unity the critical angle i_c will be very close to 90° : thus for neutrons of wavelength 0·1 nm (1 Å) incident on copper in air the critical angle is 89° 55′. Indeed, it becomes more convenient to specify a critical *glancing* angle θ_c, which is the amount by which the critical angle of incidence falls short of 90°. In the above example $\theta_c = 5$ min and it can be shown, quite generally, that (measured in radians)

$$\theta_c = \lambda(\Sigma Nb/\pi)^{1/2} = \sqrt{[2(1-n)]}. \qquad . \qquad . \qquad (10.2)$$

Table 3 gives some values of $(1 - n)$ and θ_c at neutron wavelengths of 0·1, 1 nm for several different materials. The dependence of θ_c on the neutron wavelength means that critical reflection from a solid surface can be used as a neutron filter. Imagine that a beam of thermal neutrons, with the characteristic energy distribution shown at (i) in fig. 67, is allowed to fall on a copper sheet at the small glancing angle of 20′ which would just give total internal reflection for a wavelength 0·4 nm. The portion of the spectrum beyond this wavelength will be totally internally reflected, but at shorter wavelengths transmission can take place through the copper and the reflected component

---

Question 31. *Using the information given in Question 30 calculate the value of the critical glancing angle θ_c.*

Ans. 3·8′.

121

will decrease rapidly as λ falls below 0·4 nm. The spectrum of the reflected beam will therefore have the form shown at (ii) and is useful in experiments which require a beam of neutrons of rather long wavelength and therefore very low energy, but not monochromatic neutrons.

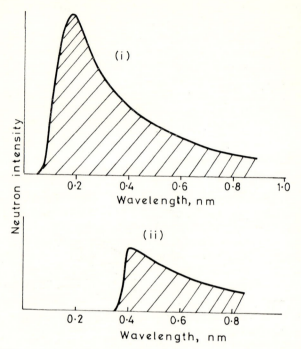

Fig. 67. The spectrum of a beam of neutrons from a reactor : (i) initially and (ii) after reflection from a sheet of copper set at a glancing angle of 20′.

Table 3

Values of refractive index and critical glancing angle

	0·1 nm (1 Å)		1 nm (10 Å)	
	$1-n$	θ_c	$1-n$	θ_c
Glass	6×10^{-7}	3·8 min	6×10^{-5}	38 min
Copper	10	4·8	10	48
Nickel	15	5·8	15	58
Rock salt	5	3·3	5	33

In a rather similar way total internal reflection may impair the properties of the collimating systems which are employed to make beams of neutrons unidirectional for use in scattering experiments. In fig. 68 (i) neutrons emerging from a point A might be expected to be restricted in angular divergence to those within the shaded cone if we pass the beam down the tube AB. However, if the angular divergence of this cone is less than the critical angle θ_c, then it is possible for additional neutrons to be guided out of the tube by total internal

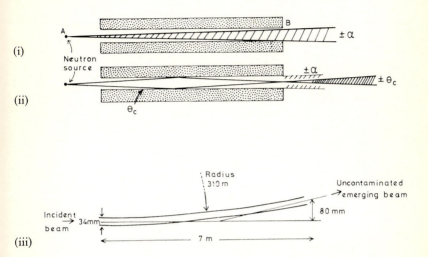

Fig. 68. Diagrams (i), (ii) indicate how the angular divergence of the neutrons emerging from a collimating tube is increased from the collimator angle, $\pm \alpha$, up to $\pm \theta_c$, where θ_c is the critical angle for reflection. Diagram (iii) gives the dimensions of a practical curved tube which utilizes the phenomenon of total reflection in order to produce a displaced beam which is free from contamination by fast neutrons.

reflection and the collimation which is achieved will not be better than $\pm \theta_c$. The second diagram (ii) in the figure indicates how the number of neutrons emerging is increased by this effect, but only at the expense of increasing their angular divergence so that they emerge over a solid angle of $4\theta_c^2$. On the other hand, this effect may be used to advantage by enabling a slightly bent tube, curved to a radius of several hundred metres, to be used to 'guide' slow neutrons to a place quite distant from the core of the reactor and, in particular, to provide a beam which is not contaminated by neutrons of high velocity, which are usually present and give a disturbing background to the scattering patterns which is not easy to remove. In a practical case, illustrated in fig. 68 (iii), a tube of length 7 m is bent into an arc of a circle of radius 310 m. The guided beam emerges displaced by 80 mm away from the line of the direct beam and this is sufficient to ensure that the contaminating background of fast neutrons is very low.

It is interesting to consider the process of total internal reflection from a *magnetic* material, instead of a surface of, say, glass or copper. The magnetic atoms will produce extra neutron scattering, as we have discussed in Chapter 8, and this will mean that the refractive index may be modified. If the material is paramagnetic, so that its magnetic moments are aligned at random from atom to atom, then the magnetic effects from the different atoms cancel out and there is no effect on the refractive index. There is, however, an important effect if we use a ferromagnetic material such as iron, with an applied magnetic field, as the reflecting mirror. It can be shown that we have to modify equation (10.2) by replacing the nuclear scattering amplitude b by $b \pm p$, where p is the magnetic scattering amplitude. The reason for this is that in the neighbourhood of the magnetic mirror the limitations set by the quantum theory require that the magnetic moment of the on-coming neutrons must be oriented in either one of two ways. The moment must lie either parallel or anti-parallel to the applied field. There is a phase change of π between the wavelets which are scattered by the magnetic iron atoms in the two cases, giving the result that the effective scattering amplitude for an upward-directed neutron spin will be $b - p$ and that for a downward-directed spin will be $b + p$. If we recall that, for a given neutron wavelength, the value of the critical angle θ_c depends on the effective value of the scattering amplitude it will be clear that θ_c will have different values for the two possible directions of the neutron spin. For example, at a wavelength of $0 \cdot 1$ nm (1 Å) the two values of θ_c are $3 \cdot 4$ minutes and $7 \cdot 1$ minutes. If we have a neutron beam which is incident at an intermediate value of the glancing angle, say $5'$, then all the neutrons with downward-directed spins will be totally internally reflected, whereas most of the upward-directed ones (which are incident at glancing angles greater than the critical angle) will be transmitted. Thus the reflected beam will be almost completely polarized. A polarized beam is particularly useful for measuring very low intensities of scattering from magnetic substances. These measurements are of great importance when attempts are made to determine accurately the size and shape of the cloud of magnetic electrons which give the atom its magnetic properties.

There is an alternative method of producing a beam of polarized neutrons which enables us to achieve more intense beams. The disadvantage of the method which we have just described is that the incident beam has to be collimated extremely well, to within two or three minutes of arc, in order that the whole of it may impinge on the magnetized mirror within the critical angle. In most experiments it is desirable to use less perfectly collimated beams, with a divergence of $\frac{1}{2}°$ or $1°$, in order to improve the intensities of the beams. We shall show that by choosing a suitable magnetized crystal as the monochromating crystal, whose function we described in Chapter 8, we can produce monochromatization and polarization concurrently. If we take a single-crystal of iron and set it up to give constructive interference between the neutrons reflected from successive crystal planes, then we shall produce a monochromatic beam for which the wavelength λ is given by:

$$\lambda = 2d \sin \theta, \qquad . \qquad . \qquad . \quad (10.3)$$

where d is the spacing of the crystal planes which are being used and θ is the glancing angle for the incident beam. If the crystal of iron is magnetized then, as before, only two orientations of the neutron spin are permissible and the effective scattering amplitudes will be $b-p$, $b+p$ respectively. For iron b, p are equal to $9 \cdot 6$, $2 \cdot 4 \times 10^{-15}$ m respectively at the appropriate value of θ, so that $b+p$ is considerably greater than $b-p$ and the number of downward-pointing spins will be much greater than the upward ones. We shall therefore produce a beam which is quite well polarized. However, we can do very much better than this by using a crystal not of iron but some other material specially chosen so that b, p are practically identical. It happens that magnetite, Fe_3O_4, is a very suitable crystal and when reflection from the 220 planes is employed it is found that the effective magnetic scattering amplitude is almost identical with the effective nuclear amplitude. In this way a beam is produced for which 98% or 99% of the neutrons have the same direction of spin. Subsidiary apparatus can be employed to 'turn over' the direction of the spins and a direct comparison of the intensities of the beams scattered by magnetized samples for upward and downward-pointing neutron spins offers a very accurate method of deducing the details of the atomic structures in a ferromagnetic material.

Finally, we will mention one other application of optical principles, to produce a roughly monochromatic beam of long-wavelength neutrons, rather similar in quality to what we showed in fig. 67, but achieving a much sharper cut-off on the short wavelength side of the spectrum. If instead of using a large single-crystal we consider the way in which neutrons are scattered by powdered material, or by a block of polycrystalline metal or other solid, then we have already seen that it will not be necessary to orient the block in any particular way in order to make sure that equation (10.3) can be satisfied. Among the random collection of crystallites which makes up the powder or block there will always be some which happen to have the right orientation to satisfy the equation. This will, moreover, happen whichever plane, with its associated value of d, that we like to consider. If we have a beam of neutrons which contains all wavelengths, like the spectrum which we showed in fig. 13, then we might at first think that from a polycrystalline block or powder there would be a complete production of all the spectra from all the wavelengths in the beam. However, there is one limitation. In any solid there is always some maximum value for the interplanar spacings. Thus, in beryllium the largest spacing which produces a spectrum is 0·198 nm (1·98 Å) and in graphite the largest spacing is that between successive layers of carbon atoms, namely 0·335 nm. It follows from equation (10.3)

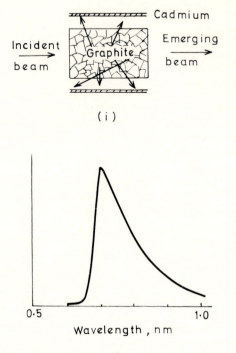

(i)

(ii)

Fig. 69. When an incident beam of neutrons with a Maxwell distribution of velocity, or wavelength, passes through a block of graphite, all the neutrons for which $\lambda < \lambda_c$ are scattered aside and absorbed in a cadmium sheet as at (i). Those neutrons which have longer wavelengths pass unhindered through the graphite to give the sharpened spectrum shown at (ii).

that, since $\sin \theta$ cannot have a value greater than unity, there is a maximum value of λ equal to twice this maximum interplanar spacing if reflection is to take place. Thus in the case of beryllium no neutrons of wavelength greater than 0·396 nm (3·96 Å) are scattered by the regular crystal structure, and for graphite no wavelength longer than 0·67 nm is scattered. Consequently when a beam of neutrons of all wavelengths falls on a block of graphite, then many of those of wavelengths less than 0·67 nm will be scattered aside and will be lost from the initial beam, but wavelengths greater than this will pass

126

through the block with undiminished intensity. We can therefore use a sufficiently thick block of graphite as a filter which, as shown in fig. 69, removes all neutrons with a wavelength greater than 0·67 nm and this produces a first approximation to a monochromatic beam, characterized by a large preponderance of neutrons of wavelength about 0·7 nm. A length of $0·1 \rightarrow 0·2$ m of graphite will serve as an adequate filter. For convenience the filter is surrounded by a sheet of cadmium which absorbs all the neutrons which have been scattered out of the beam. In the same way, a block of polycrystalline beryllium will produce a spectrum which falls off very sharply below 0·396 nm and produces a preponderance of neutrons with wavelengths of 0·4–0·5 nm. In its turn a beam of neutrons of this kind can be used to study the defects, such as displaced atoms and vacant sites, in a solid. Defects of this kind are produced when a metal is strained by cold work without a subsequent anneal or when a solid is subjected to intense beams of radiation, in a nuclear reactor for example. If we take our filtered spectrum, as shown in fig. 69, and pass it through a polycrystalline solid for which twice the maximum interplanar spacing is less than λ_c, then no constructive interference (what we usually call ' Bragg scattering ') will take place if the structure of the crystallites is perfect. However, any departures from regularity will produce scattering, and a consequent reduction in the intensity of the transmitted beam. The number of defects, and to some extent their size and nature, can be estimated by comparing the transmission of a damaged sample with that of an otherwise identical sample of perfect material. Measurements of this kind are important in trying to understand the mechanism by which damage is done to solids by irradiation, a feature of some consequence in the technology of nuclear reactors. X-rays are of little use in this kind of work because their absorption coefficients are very much greater than for neutrons and an X-ray of wavelength 0·6–0·7 nm would be unable to penetrate the material under examination to any significant extent.

CHAPTER 11

absorption and neutron radiography

RADIOGRAPHY is a technique whereby a shadow-picture of some of the inner features of an object can be drawn by exposing the object to a beam of radiation. In order to understand how neutrons can have a use for this purpose we must refer back to Chapter 6 where we discussed the various reactions which a neutron can undergo when it encounters other atoms and where we introduced the concept of a cross-section. For any particular atom there is a cross-section for each reaction which can take place, and this describes the probability that the atom will take part in this reaction when a beam of neutrons falls upon it. The value of the cross-section will depend not only on the particular atom which is being considered but also on the energy of the neutron, though some reactions are much more sensitive than others in this respect and resonance effects may occur at particular neutron energies. When a beam of neutrons passes through a material the reduction of its intensity, I, brought about by the fact that it has undergone a reaction of some kind, or has simply been scattered from its incident direction, is expressed by the equation:

$$I = I_0 \exp \left[-N \left(\sum_j \sigma_j \right) x \right],$$

which we have already stated in Chapter 6. We recall that x is the distance in the medium through which the beam has travelled, N is the number of atoms per unit volume and $\sum \sigma_j$ is the summation of the cross-sections of the various reactions which can take place. In fact the expression $N(\sum \sigma)$ defines the linear absorption coefficient of the material at the given neutron energy and I/I_0 is the fraction of beam transmitted. In the present discussion we are interested in the way in which the cross-sections vary amongst the elements.

In Table 4 we show, for a variety of elements, the cross-sections which are applicable when the neutrons have a wavelength of 0·108 nm (1·08 Å), which corresponds to 0·07 eV. The total cross-section σ_t is divided into two parts, first σ_s for cases where the neutron is simply scattered and re-emerges as a neutron and, secondly, σ_a for cases where it is truly absorbed, with the production of a quantum of radiation or some other particle. For comparison we show in the final column of the table the corresponding total cross-sections which are applicable to X-rays of about the same wavelength. In general these latter cross-sections (which are almost entirely due to true absorption with

128

production of photoelectrons and followed by emission of fluorescent radiation) show a steady increase with atomic number, or atomic weight, although there are some discontinuities which provide a sharp fall in the absorption at the absorption edge of an element. For the wavelength which we have taken for our example, 0·11 nm, there is such a discontinuity at an atomic number of 32, which lies between

Table 4

The cross-sections for scattering and absorption, in units of 10^{-28} m² (barns) for neutrons ($\lambda = 0.108$ nm) and X-rays (0·11 nm)

Element	Neutrons			X-rays
	Scattering, σ_s	Absorption, σ_a	Total, σ_t	Total, σ_t
H	81	0·2	81·2	0·7
Deuterium	7·6	0·0005	7·6	0·7
Li	1·1	40	41·1	4·3
Be	7·5	0·005	7·5	9·8
B	4·4	430	434·4	18
C	5·5	0·003	5·5	36
O	4·2	0·0001	4·2	114
Mg	3·7	0·04	3·7	580
Al	1·5	0·13	1·6	810
S	1·2	0·3	1·5	1,780
Fe	11·8	1·4	13·2	11,900
Co	6	21	27	13,900
Ni	18·0	2·7	20·7	14,700
Cu	8·5	2·2	10·7	17,400
As	8	2·5	10·5	3,940
Ag	6·5	36	42·5	15,700
Au	9	57	66	28,000
Pb	11·4	0·1	11·5	33,200
Bi	9·4	0·02	9·4	35,000

Question 32. *Calculate, using the data in Table* 4, *the percentage absorptions (taking into account scattering as well as true absorption) of a sheet of aluminium of thickness* 1 mm *for X-rays and neutrons of wavelength about* 0·11 nm (1·1 Å). (*Density of aluminium* = 2·7 × 10^3 kg/m³. *At. wt.* = 27.)

Ans. 99·2%, 0·9%.

copper and arsenic in the table. It is the high value of absorption coefficients of the heavy elements for X-rays which leads to the use of lead, in particular, as a screen to prevent the access of radiation to unwanted positions in laboratories where X-rays are used. At the same time this behaviour of the absorption coefficient also provides the

129

basis for radiography, the process whereby any discontinuity in density, caused for example by some foreign object lodged in a human body or by a flaw in a metal casting, is noticeable on the shadowgraph obtained when an X-ray beam traverses the object concerned. There is a similar process of neutron radiography which will detect not simply changes in mass density but variations in neutron cross-section. A study of Table 4 will show that this process will be valuable in particular cases, such as the detection of boron in steel and the detection of materials which are particularly rich in hydrogen. A classic picture which was taken by neutron radiography at the Argonne

---

Question 33. *Calculate the effective linear absorption coefficients (taking into account both scattering and true absorption) of (a) water, (b) lead for neutrons of wavelength* 0·108 nm. *The density of lead is* $11{\cdot}34 \times 10^3$ kg/m^3 *and its atomic weight is* 207.

Ans. (*a*) 555 m^{-1}, (*b*) 38 m^{-1}.

National Laboratory in the U.S.A. revealed a piece of waxed string within a 50 mm thick lead block—a quite impossible feat for X-rays! Ideally a beam of monochromatic neutrons from a nuclear reactor is used for the measurement and a very convenient arrangement is to use the beam which is designed for the diffraction studies in fig. 40. This has the advantage that the beam is well collimated, with only a small angular divergence, and largely free from the disturbing effects of fast neutrons and γ-rays, but it is not strictly necessary to use a monochromatic beam. The main problem from the practical point of view is the recording of the radiographed pattern. Success depends on the achievement of both high sensitivity and, even more important, high resolution, which will enable the fine details of the radiographed objects to be distinguished. These requirements are much more difficult to achieve with neutrons than for X-rays. Whereas X-rays can easily be detected directly with a photographic film, the direct detection of neutrons with a film is insensitive, but various indirect methods have been used successfully. In addition to a photographic film itself a thin ‘ converter ’ screen is used, from which film-sensitive particles are ejected. Early measurements used a sheet of indium foil which, in the way which we have seen in Chapter 5, absorbs neutrons with emission of γ-radiation, followed by a breakdown of the product nucleus with the emission of a β-particle. The β-particle then affects a photographic film which is placed in contact with the indium foil. The arrangement is shown in fig. 70. Further experiments have shown that a very thin foil of gadolinium makes a much more satisfactory screen. The advantage of gadolinium is that the neutron absorption cross-section is extremely high, equal to about $19\,000 \times 10^{-28}$ m^2 when λ is 0·108 nm, so that a foil of thickness 0·02 mm is a very efficient detector. Because the foil is exceedingly thin it will cause a negligible amount of blurring of the shadow pattern of the object which the neutrons produce. Consequently a film placed in contact with the gadolinium foil gives a very sharp image. The highest sensitivity is achieved by placing a foil on each side of the film, but at the expense of some loss of resolution. The

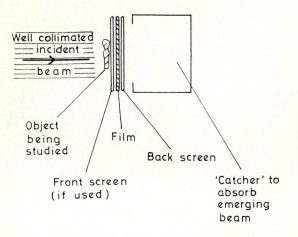

Fig. 70. Experimental arrangement for neutron radiography, employing as detector a photographic film sandwiched between detecting foils, such as gadolinium, from which electrons are ejected.

best resolution is given with a single foil. Exposures of about 5 min are usually required when a nuclear reactor is used as the neutron source, with correspondingly longer times for weaker sources.

Question 34. *Calculate the percentage absorption of a gadolinium foil of thickness 20 μm for neutrons of wavelength 0·108 nm (1·08 Å). The atomic weight is 157, the density $7·9 \times 10^3$ kg/m³ and the absorption cross-section $19,000 \times 10^{-28}$ m².*

Ans. 68%.

Figure 71 shows an interesting example of the relatively strong absorbing properties of hydrogen for neutrons. These radiographs were taken by M. R. Hawkesworth using a single gadolinium foil of thickness 0·02 mm placed behind Ilford Industrial G film. The illustration (i) shows five 9 mm revolver bullets, four of which are filled with a coarsely powdered propellant. The empty cartridge is readily distinguished in the neutron radiographs whereas no obvious distinction is apparent in the corresponding X-ray pictures (ii) in which the absorption of the metal casing is the dominating feature.

131

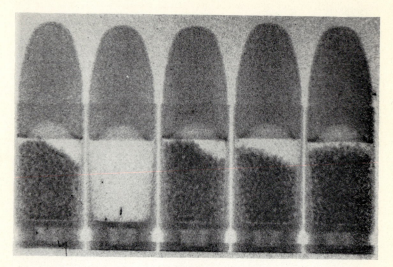

(i)

(ii)

Fig. 71. A comparison of (i) neutron and (ii) X-radiographs by M. R. Hawkesworth of a set of revolver bullets in one of which the hydrogen-containing propellant is missing (reproduced from ‘ X-Ray Focus ’ published by Ilford Ltd.).

In fact, under optimum conditions it is just possible to make a distinction with X-rays. Figure 72 is in some ways more striking, since in this case the neutron beam has passed through the lead of the bullet and a successful radiograph with X-rays in these circumstances

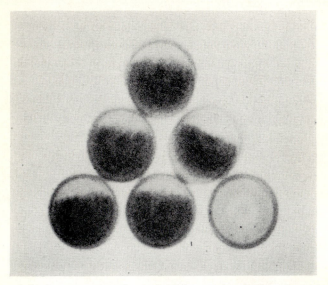

Fig. 72. A further neutron radiograph of the revolver bullets shown in fig. 71 in which the neutron beam travels axially along the bullet, including passage through the lead tip, but nevertheless is preferentially absorbed by the hydrogenous material (by courtesy of M. R. Hawkesworth).

would be completely impossible. Although these techniques have not yet been very much used, their possibilities have been demonstrated for a wide variety of materials, ranging from thin biological specimens to the fuel elements which are used in nuclear reactors. Considerable efforts are being made to improve methods of detection and to develop small neutron sources which will provide intense beams, with the aim of making the technique independent of nuclear reactors and, possibly, as widely available in industry as X-ray radiography has been for many years.

Some classical papers in neutron physics

L. W. Alvarez and F. Bloch. "A quantitative determination of the neutron moment in absolute nuclear magnetons." *Phys. Rev.*, **57**, 111–122 (1940).

R. E. Bell and L. G. Elliott. "Gamma-rays from the reaction $^1H(n, \gamma)^2D$ and the binding energy of the deuteron." *Phys. Rev.*, **74**, 1552–3 (1948).

J. Chadwick. "Possible existence of a neutron." *Nature, Lond.*, **129**, 312 (1932).

J. Chadwick. "The existence of a neutron." *Proc. R. Soc.* A, **136**, 692–708 (1932).

J. R. Dunning, G. B. Pegram, G. A. Fink, D. P. Mitchell and E. Segrè. "Velocity of slow neutrons by mechanical velocity selector." *Phys. Rev.*, **48**, 704 (1935).

E. Fermi. "Versuch einer Theorie der β-Strahlen." *Z. Phys.*, **88**, 161–177 (1934).

O. R. Frisch. "Physical evidence for the division of heavy nuclei under neutron bombardment." *Nature, Lond.*, **143**, 276 (1939).

J. M. Robson. "The radioactive decay of the neutron" *Phys. Rev.*, **83**, 349–58 (1951).

E. Rutherford. "Nuclear constitution of atoms." *Proc. R. Soc.* A, **97**, 374–400 (1920).

L. van Hove. "Correlations in space and time in systems of interacting particles." *Phys. Rev.*, **95**, 249–262 (1954).

Some constants used in the numerical questions

(In SI units)

Mass of proton	$1 \cdot 67 \times 10^{-27}$ kg
Mass of neutron	$1 \cdot 67 \times 10^{-27}$ kg
1 u (unified mass unit)	$1 \cdot 66 \times 10^{-27}$ kg
Electronic charge, e	$1 \cdot 60 \times 10^{-19}$ C
1 eV	$1 \cdot 60 \times 10^{-19}$ J
1 u	$931 \cdot 48$ MeV
Speed of light, c	$3 \cdot 00 \times 10^{8}$ m/s
Planck's constant, h	$6 \cdot 63 \times 10^{-34}$ J s
Boltzmann's constant, k	$1 \cdot 38 \times 10^{-23}$ JK^{-1}
Avogadro's number, N_A	$6 \cdot 02 \times 10^{23}$ mol^{-1}
Volume of mole of ideal gas at s.t.p.	$22 \cdot 4 \times 10^{-3}$ m^3
Degrees per radian	$57 \cdot 3$

139

THE WYKEHAM SCIENCE SERIES

for schools and universities

1 *Elementary Science of Metals* (S.B. No. 85109 010 9)
J. W. MARTIN and R. A. HULL

2 *Neutron Physics* (S.B. No. 85109 020 6)
G. E. BACON and G. R. NOAKES

3 *Essentials of Meteorology* (S.B. No. 85109 040 0)
D. H. MCINTOSH, A. S. THOM and V. T. SAUNDERS

4 *Nuclear Fusion* (S.B. No. 85109 050 8)
H. R. HULME and A. McB. COLLIEU

5 *Water Waves* (S.B. No. 85109 060 5)   N. F. BARBER and G. GHEY

6 *Gravity and the Earth* (S.B. No. 85109 070 2)
A. H. COOK and V. T. SAUNDERS

7 *Relativity and High Energy Physics* (S.B. No. 85109 080 X)
W. G. V. ROSSER and R. K. MCCULLOCH

Price per book for the Science Series **20s.—£1.00 net** *in U.K. only*

THE WYKEHAM TECHNOLOGICAL SERIES

for universities and institutes of technology

1 *Frequency Conversion* (S.B. No. 85109 030 3)
J. THOMSON, W. E. TURK and M. BEESLEY

Price per book for the Technological Series **25s.—£1.25 net** *in U.K. only*